T0304836

The House of Mirrors

Also by Erin Kelly

The Poison Tree

The Sick Rose

The Burning Air

The Ties that Bind

He Said/She Said

We Know You Know
(Hardback edition titled *Stone Mothers*)

Watch Her Fall

The Skeleton Key

With Chris Chibnall

Broadchurch

Erin Kelly

The House of Mirrors

HODDER &
STOUGHTON

First published in Great Britain in 2024 by Hodder & Stoughton
An Hachette UK company

1

A CIP catalogue record for this title is available from the British Library

Hardback ISBN 978 1 399 71196 8
Trade Paperback ISBN 978 1 399 71197 5
ebook ISBN 978 1 399 71198 2

Typeset in Sabon MT by Hewer Text UK Ltd, Edinburgh
Printed and bound in Great Britain by Clays Ltd, Elcograf S.p.A.

Hodder & Stoughton policy is to use papers that are natural, renewable
and recyclable products and made from wood grown in sustainable
forests. The logging and manufacturing processes are expected to
conform to the environmental regulations of the country of origin.

Hodder & Stoughton Ltd
Carmelite House
50 Victoria Embankment
London EC4Y 0DZ

www.hodder.co.uk

The clothes of the dead don't wear well. They fret for the person who owned them.

Barbara Vine, *The Brimstone Wedding*

For Marnie

PROLOGUE

Real life was never enough. The magic was always down the rabbit hole or on the other side of the mirror and you always chased it.

Eat me: a bitter pill of unknown provenance, dissolving on the tongue.

Drink me: don't mind if I do.

When you were seven, you accessorised your school uniform with a velvet hairband and stripy socks, stood solemnly before the hall mirror and tried to push your way through to the back-to-front world on the other side. In the storybook, the looking glass turns first to gauze and then a kind of mist. You pressed your small hands against the surface until it cracked, carving a light-ning bolt in the glass and a gash in your palm. By the time your mother arrived, the blood had already dripped on to the chess-board floor below. The porous old tiles drank it down.

The black squares hid their stains. You'd never know anything had happened. The little red stars on the white squares would fade to brown but never quite disappear, despite the vigorous application of bleach, vinegar, soda and soap. Really, they should have been changed for new ones, but nothing in that house ever was. The scarred mirror, beyond repair, never replaced, shattered every face that looked in it from that day on.

That same glass bore broken witness years later, when in that same hall more blood was spilled. Not yours this time. You watched in horrified fascination as the liquid red carpet rolled out in all directions, and you understood. The best way to hide blood is with more blood.

PART ONE

I

Karen

'The things we do for Alice,' says Rex, reversing the hired van around a corner. The tarmac under the wheels turns to cobbles. The crate on my lap, carefully packed with beads and chains, starts to clack and rattle. A peacock feather stuck in a vase nearly stabs me in the eye.

'The things we do for Alice,' I echo.

He has no idea.

It's December, dark at four o'clock. This back alley, at the Angel end of Islington, was made for horses, not motor vehicles. Currently dressed for Christmas in white lights and cut holly, Camden Passage is flagstones and wrought iron, alleyways and pubs straight out of Hogarth, antique shops and boutique galleries. Even the modern barber shops are done up to look like something from the Industrial Revolution.

A kid on an e-scooter with no lights punctures the snowglobe illusion, shooting out from the van's blind spot, forcing Rex to brake hard. Something in the back of the van shatters.

I lower the window and lean out. 'Are you trying to get yourself *killed*?'

The kid raises his eyebrows at Rex. 'Can't talk for yourself, bruv?'

I slide the window up, not wanting to get into it. The boy can't know why Rex outsources his road rage duties to his missus. He can't know that Rex does not have the luxury of losing his temper. It's safer if I funnel his anger through my lungs.

'At least this is the last drop.' Rex inches the van backwards into the space we've been illegally using as a loading bay all day and throws on the hazard lights. In the wing mirror our daughter approaches, dressed against type in an old sweatshirt and leggings that make her look a lot younger than twenty-three. Behind her, the logo she designed herself gleams gold and black on the window. It's her take on Leonardo da Vinci's *Vitruvian Man* sketch, only instead of a spreadeagled naked man it's a young woman in the kind of flowing gown Alice specialises in, arms flung out so it looks as though she's dancing. Above that, the shop's name, in writing that flows like thread through a needle: she's called it Dead Girls' Dresses.

'I still hate the name,' murmurs Rex, and of course he has good reason to. Dead girls are not an abstract concept for him.

Alice throws the van doors open and the three of us fall into place, a human chain passing the stock from the van to the shop. Lace froths in my face, ribbons trail on the floor.

'I'd better . . .' says Rex, nodding backwards at the empty van, which has miraculously escaped a parking ticket, but Alice throws her arms around our necks.

'Thank you both. So, so much,' she says. 'I won't let you down.'

A horseradish tingle starts up behind my eyes and when Rex says, 'Better take the van back,' there's a crack in his voice.

The shop still has its fresh-paint smell. 'I've made a start on it,' says Alice. 'Tried to, you know, evoke a *demi-monde*.'

She has more than made a start. This morning the space was black walls, naked brass clothes rails and a mound of charity-shop furniture under dust sheets. Now it's a . . . a . . . I want to use a word like *realm*. A jade glass chandelier glitters overhead. A stuffed swan's head hangs above a cast-iron fireplace. Two gilt mirrors face each other, a glass concertina projecting Alices into infinity. A Chinese silk fan hangs behind an old-fashioned cash register, and Venetian masks and figurines wink from a cabinet of curiosities.

'The vibe's supposed to be sort of Dickensian hovel meets Weimar Republic boudoir. What do you think?'

What I think is that Dead Girls' Dresses is like Biba's old bedroom in the house in Queenswood Lane, that it's like going back in time, that it's uncanny. What I think is that all it would take is one line of an old song and I would be a young girl in a bikini dancing in a garden again, rather than a middle-aged woman in a FatFace midi dress and orthotic inserts in my boots. What I think is that there's a hand pulling a scarf tight around my throat, making it hard to breathe. But what I say is, 'Very good. Very Instagrammable.'

She adjusts an ostrich feather in a *cloisonné* vase. 'Well, what's the point of having a bricks-and-mortar shop if you don't make it a destination?'

'There's just so much to look at, wherever you – *oh*.' My eye falls on a dressmaker's dummy, bound tight in a corset decorated with a painting of a shepherdess. Vivienne Westwood, 1990.

Alice reads my mind and rolls her eyes. 'For the last time,' she says, 'it was an *investment*.' In her third year of university, she spent her entire student loan buying this in an auction. 'It's already doubled in value,' she adds. 'It's virtually a pension.'

'Hmmm.'

I turn my attention to the gallery wall of her fashion heroes: Marilyn in her 'Happy Birthday, Mr President' sequins, Princess Diana in her off-the-shoulder revenge dress, Kate Bush in a red gown, Billy Porter at the Oscars, a full skirt twirling beneath his tuxedo.

'All the major icons.' Her big black eyes dart towards a smaller, faded picture and then hopefully towards me. 'I found it in an old *Vogue*. It's perfect for my brand.'

'Oh, *love*.' My hand flutters to my heart. She's framed one of the most famous advertisements of the 1970s, the Natura shampoo girl with her gleaming dark hair in her white dress in the meadow. It's a multi-sensory experience, that photograph: you can hear the harp music from the TV advert and smell the herbal tang of the shampoo. I had no idea, when as a child I sat in the bath and screamed as the lather stung my eyes, that one day I would marry the Natura girl's son and raise her grandchild, although I would never meet her. Sheila Capel hanged herself on the landing of the Queenswood Lane house when Rex was sixteen and Biba was twelve.

Rex's dead girl number one.

'You *must* know you can't have this on the wall.'

'I can say it's me?'

Anyone Alice's age would believe it; a bit of retro dress-up, run through a filter to give it a sun-drenched vibe. The likeness is certainly strong enough. Sheila's pale face with its huge dark eyes and strong nose is Alice's face, it is Rex's, it is Biba's. It passes down the generations like an heirloom. It bulldozes other genes out of its way. But anyone my age and older would recognise it at once, note the similarity between the girl in the painting and the girl behind the till, and the questions would begin.

'But it's a famous picture. It connects you to Dad's old name. It only takes one person to join the dots and he'll have to start all over again.'

I could remind her what it was like last time she slipped up, but we agreed not to use The Fallout as leverage. Gently, I take Sheila Capel down from the wall and set her face-down on the counter.

Alice's hands form fists. 'I'm not going to throw it away.'

'I'm not asking you to. It's a beautiful picture. You *should* own it.'

Alice capitulates with only the briefest of scowls. 'Right . . .' she dusts her palms '. . . let's hang some of these girls.' She looks at Sheila's picture, realises what she's said, and is horrified. 'Jeez. I didn't mean . . . good thing Dad didn't hear that.'

I tear the cellophane off a pack of pink velvet hangers. 'Let's go.'

The clothes are already grouped by colour and size. I was up all night double-checking the measurements of bust-darts and waistbands. When everything is in place, the shop looks less like Biba's bedroom. *Her* clothes were more likely to be found on the floor than all facing the same way on matching hangers.

My belly growls. 'Have you not eaten?' asks Alice, apparently forgetting that I've been on the move since dawn. My Fitbit tells me I've climbed fifty flights of stairs today. 'OK, I'm going to go to the coffee shop over the road, introduce myself to the neighbours, get some grub.'

She grabs a peach kimono from a railing, throws it on over the leggings and instantly looks like something from an F. Scott Fitzgerald novel. She swishes out of the door, all tassels and hair. Half a minute later, the brass bell above the door clangs, and Rex enters, holding a Morrison's carrier bag.

'Bloody hell.' He runs the fingers of his free hand through his hair. 'It looks like . . .'

'I *know*.'

Rex's dead girl number two.

He removes the Paisley scarf that Alice has draped over a standard lamp. '*She* never had any fucking sense of fire safety either.' He coughs one of those laughs that's not really a laugh and looks at the door. 'I almost expect her to . . .'

'I know what you mean. But this is Alice. This is all Alice.'

It's not, and we both know it.

Biba's ghost, never far away, has put on her best dress and slid in through cracks in windows, gaps under doors, through tightly closed eyes. She moves like mist, like poison gas.

2

Karen

I peer into Rex's carrier bag. 'Any food in there?'

'Nothing that useful, I'm afraid.' He shakes something free from the plastic. 'Honestly. What was she thinking?' Dangling from his hand is an old-fashioned rotary-dial telephone, salmon-coloured, encrusted with seashells. A curly pink wire boings into a chunky receiver. I know exactly why she wants it.

'It's like the one in *Desperately Seeking Susan*,' I say. He looks at me blankly. 'The Madonna film?' He remains unenlightened. 'Never mind. I suppose she thinks it's quaint, or more *real*, some-how. Like how she listens to music on vinyl. And she'll like the way it looks in pictures.'

'But it's terrible business sense. A landline, in this day and age! I didn't think analogue phones even *worked* any more. You can't see when you've got a missed call, you can't tell who's calling.' He picks up the receiver and frowns into the mouthpiece.

'She does all the selling on apps anyway. Don't worry about it. If it doesn't work, she can just change it.'

Rex sets the phone on the counter. 'I know, I know. I've got to stand back, not interfere. Let her make her own mistakes.'

With our money, I think. Well, the promise of our money, or the gamble of it. All we did was put our names on the shop lease, act as her guarantors. All we did was risk our house, the one *my* hard slog enabled us to buy.

'And I guess one good thing about her being an only child is that we can put all our eggs in her basket, so to speak.'

My hands go to my belly. 'Rex, don't.' It was only recently, when I crossed the age Rubicon of forty-five, that we truly gave up.

He realises as soon as he's said it. 'Sorry. Sorry. I'm an idiot. Sorry.'

'S'alright,' I say, straightening a hat on a stand to let him know that's as far as we need to take that right now. I know he's trying to find comfort in tragedy but I hate it when he tries to make a virtue of Alice being an only child, as though it hasn't been a source of heartbreak. I fell pregnant within a month of Rex's release from prison in the autumn of 2007 and showed almost immediately. But the Homecoming Baby, as we had begun to call her – I thought of all my babies as girls – was gone by Christmas. The one after that – the Snowflake Baby, because it began to snow as the line formed – stayed for five weeks. The Lanzarote Baby, conceived on our first family-of-three holiday, was outlived by my tan. The baby books track a foetus's progress by comparing it to fruits; I got to know the weeks by heart, I could recite them like a nursery rhyme. Poppy seed, apple seed, blueberry, grape, fig, lime, nectarine. None of my babies ever made it to pear but with every pregnancy my belly swelled a little more, as though each one was leaving a layer of herself behind.

Alice breezes back in, re-hangs the kimono and is a grubby kid again. There's a blob of chocolate on her upper lip but she's empty-handed.

'Did you not get us food? Coffee?' I ask her. 'Wasn't that the point of you going out?'

'Oh, crap.' She slaps her hand to her forehead. 'DeShaun in the churros shop gave me a few and then we got chatting and . . . sorry.'

My hands are still on my belly. I feel as well as hear it gurgle.

'Right, so the guys are coming round for drinks in a bit,' says Alice.

'Who're "the guys"?' I presume she means her university friends, the fashion students who came to London and never left.

'From around. The other traders. Aggie from the lighting shop's got a special thing for cleaning the chandelier. Hollie's going to burn some sage, cleanse any negative energy.'

'Hollie?' I ask, while Rex says:

'*Sage?*'

Only one of us gets our answer. 'From the kids' boutique.' Alice waves across the flagstones at the lemon-yellow shop with tiny, tasteful beige clothes strung on a washing line across its window. A stocky girl with huge glasses and pink dungarees flicks an apparently affectionate V sign in response. Alice has established a rapport in five minutes. How does she do that? We've been in our current home for five years and I've still never been inside our next-door neighbours' house.

'We'll get out of your hair,' I say. 'We should get back to Peggy anyway.'

'Stay for *one.*' She produces a bottle of sparkling wine from a carrier bag, expertly pops the cork and fills a trio of those little coupe glasses that everyone always says are supposed to be modelled on Marie Antoinette's boobs. The drink goes straight to our heads, every burst bubble a dead brain cell, a loosened muscle. Alice is full of her plans: she's got fliers, her Instagram and Etsy accounts, she's got a list of influencers and stylists she needs to befriend. (She hires out clothes to stylists and film companies as well as to ordinary women. Every now and then she sends me a video featuring some barefoot wraith twirling and chanting in one of her dresses.)

One glass becomes three while we wait for 'the guys' to turn up. When her grandfather clock strikes six, Alice leaps to her feet. 'They'll be here in a minute. I'd better change.' She disappears behind a folding screen.

'I'm a bit pissed.' Rex puts out a hand to steady himself, lands on a taxidermy weasel in a top hat, and withdraws in alarm. 'I *really* need to eat.'

'We'll go to that Turkish place on Upper Street, get a chicken shish.'

'Whaddya think?' Alice walks like a model through the shop's narrow aisle in a figure-hugging orange dress with a sheen to the fabric and a ruffle at the neck. Next to me, Rex stiffens. The light in the room changes, as though the walls got blacker and absorbed too much. 'What? What are you both looking at?'

'Biba was wearing something a lot like this on, you know, The Night Of,' blurts Rex. I reach out to silence him, the pads of my fingertips rest in the shiny craters of scar tissue on his forearm, but it's too late.

'The Night Of,' repeats Alice meaningfully, because when do you ever hear that phrase in a context other than crime?

'The night of Biba's birthday.' My mouth feels as if it's filling with sand. 'What Dad meant was, Biba was wearing something like that the night we met.'

I press his flesh, feeling through ropes of muscle the bone beneath. Finally he catches up. 'Yes that's right!' he says, in a voice that's somehow both mechanical and slurred. 'The night I met your mum.'

We are saved by the brass bell. Half a dozen young people, who appear to be dressed as clowns but what do I know, ooze into the shop, proclaim it 'sick', and other adjectives that have changed their meaning since I was young. Rex and I back out in a hail of 'nice to meet you's, and face each other in the lamplit alleyway. Pub lights glow at either end of the lane but the shops are tucked up for the night behind accordion shutters.

'I—' begins Rex.

'Not here.' I march him past the kinds of shadows that look as though they might hide pickpocketing urchins, out to relieve us of our fob watches, and when we are out of earshot I let rip.

'You fucking idiot! What were you thinking, The Night Of?'

'I should've eaten,' he says feebly. 'Wine on an empty stomach. Karen, she didn't work it out. She's all excited by the shop, new mates, she won't dwell on it.'

He traces an arc with his toe on the ground. I take his left hand in my right, rub the gold of his wedding ring.

'We can't trust her with the truth, not after The Fallout.'

'She *learned* her lesson.' His voice is a teenage whine.

'She learned it *for now*. Is it worth risking you getting recalled to prison?'

He winces. None of this is new, but every now and then we play out the script to keep each other in check.

'I'm a *twat*,' he slurs.

'No argument from me there.' But we hold hands on the way to our favourite Turkish place where the ceiling is strung with glass lanterns and a basket of warm bread is on the table before we've even sat down. I tear a chunk in two and give half to Rex. 'Soak up the booze.' He holds it in his fist like a toddler, smooshing it into his face. When he talks again it's about Alice: how good the shop is, what an eye she has for an interior, how she must get it from him.

I relax, just a little. Another near miss. If Alice starts to question the version of events she has grown up believing, then it sets her on a dark, bloodied path. Not even Rex knows what lies at the end of it. The only one who does is missing, presumed dead. If she were going to tell, she would have done so by now.

3

Alice

The first rule of Capel Club is you don't talk about Capel Club. I kept that rule for the first twenty-three years of my life and I promise you, no one was more surprised by this than I.

I have what my school reports called poor impulse control. When I was tiny, Mum signed me up for a re-creation of the famous marshmallow experiment, that willpower test when you sit a little kid in front of a marshmallow and tell them that if they leave it untouched for like two minutes they'll get *two* marshmallows as a reward. While my mum was signing the forms, I found the packet of marshmallows and ate the lot. Then there was the infamous glitter bomb incident of 2005, when Sophie's mum told us off for trying on her shoes and we sprinkled glitter into the base of the pedestal fan in her walk-in wardrobe. She's probably still finding little flecks of gold in the creases of her clothes.

I've always called it The Surge. It's a compulsion, a loss of control that you couldn't define as a bad temper because it can be a high as well as a low, a force that's as likely to see me waking up in a different country or tracking down a once-in-a-lifetime piece as it is lashing out at someone who has wronged me. It's a wave I can ride, so I can't hate it, even though I know it doesn't have my best interests at heart. The Surge is the opposite of a mother.

It was The Surge that broke my silence around Capel Club.

After The Fallout, I learned to manage it.

Mostly.

I can't remember a time when I didn't know my dad's history. The story I grew up with was that a Bad Man who sold drugs had turned up on the doorstep one night at Dad's old house in London with a gun. (I took that in my stride: I knew London by its prisons the way other children knew it by theatres and toy shops. I presumed that finding gun-toting drug dealers on one's doorstep was a daily feature of big city life.) They'd argued, and Dad had used the Bad Man's gun to kill him. Then came the tricky bit: a neighbour came to see what all the noise was about, and Dad shot him in a panic. I swear it didn't occur to me that there was any kind of contradiction in the fact that this double killer was also the kindest, gentlest human I had ever known.

After his release, they drip-fed me the remaining details. The new facts were these: Dad was not an only child. His sister's name was Bathsheba but everyone called her Biba; the Bad Man had been her boyfriend. Biba went missing not long after Dad went to prison, a car found abandoned at a suicide spot. In the space of one conversation I went from not knowing I had an aunt or my paternal grandmother's name to finding out they had both died by suicide. Not a great thing to have in your genetic make-up, is it? Let's hope it's one of those things that's passed through the women in a family. Karen Clarke is as solid as they come.

Biba's remains have never been found. The closest thing was an earring police divers found on the seabed during a search for another jumper a year or two after Dad's release. It was one of a pair that Biba never took off, and which my parents had listed as something that might identify her.

Of course, where there's no body, there's always hope. One of the newspaper reports in September 1997 described the siblings as being 'as close as lovers' which is obviously gross, but if Biba loved Dad even a tenth as much as he obviously loved – still loves – her, there's no way, if she were still alive, that she wouldn't have come back to him. I used to fantasise that maybe she'd survived the fall, washed up somewhere like a message in a bottle, and was living on a pastel ward on the other side of the world, waiting for the magic word that would unlock her past.

It was the only scenario I could picture in which her return would be a cause for celebration, and not salt in a wound that will never quite heal.

With new facts came new rules. I must never mention the name Capel to anyone, not even my best friend. If anyone ever called asking about Rex Capel or Biba Capel or any other name I didn't recognise, if anyone threatening or nosy or just *off* approached me or called the house, I should get out of the conversation and then I should tell Mum and Dad *straight away*. Mum just dumped all that in my lap and *then* she told me not to go looking for details! Like: had she *met* me?

Naturally my first instinct was to Google everything, but Mum had always watched my internet access like the absolute hawk she is. It's hard to fathom now when every Year Six child has a smartphone, but I was *fourteen* before I ever had unsupervised access to the internet. While other kids might pretend to go to the library and actually be shopping, I lied that I was shopping and went to the library, opened an incognito window, typed *Rex Capel Highgate Drug Dealer Murder 1997* into the search bar and came face-to-face with *this*:.

JUDICIARY OF ENGLAND AND WALES
REGINA v CAPEL
SENTENCING REMARKS OF THE
HON. MR JUSTICE RAMAMURTHY
WOOD GREEN CROWN COURT 9 November 1997

We are here because on the 14th of September 1997, you, Rex Capel, murdered Thomas Wheeler and caused the death of Guy Grainger. I have your confession so I am sure that what follows is an accurate description of the offences for which I am to sentence you.

On the date in question, just before 6pm, you were home alone at your home in Queenswood Lane in Highgate, a home you shared with your sister Bathsheba, known as Biba. Biba was at that time with your father, Roger Capel, in nearby Hampstead and you were surprised when her on-off boyfriend, 19-year-old Guy Grainger, paid you a visit.

Mr Grainger was known to consume and occasionally deal drugs and you did not consider him to be a good influence on your sister, with whom you had an almost paternal relationship, having left school early to care for her after the untimely death of your mother by her own hand in 1990.

You were listening to loud music when Mr Grainger arrived. You did not invite him in and you stayed in the entrance hall of your home. Your voices quickly became raised in an argument over his suitability for your sister. The situation escalated rapidly and Mr Grainger produced a handgun which he pointed at you. A tussle ensued, during which you took possession of the gun and shot Mr Grainger. The bullet entered his shoulder but the cause of his death was a broken neck as he fell.

Moments later, a neighbour, Mr Thomas Wheeler, resident at 46 Queenswood Lane, appeared on your threshold. You had a history of conflict with Mr Wheeler, whose diaries record several occasions upon which he asked you and your sister to turn down loud music or cease other antisocial behaviour and you refused to comply. In a state of shock and panic, you shot Mr Wheeler. The bullet travelled approximately four inches into his heart. He died shortly afterwards.

You called the emergency services, requesting an ambulance as well as police. You then called your father. In a conversation which lasted for under one minute you asked him to send a solicitor to the police station, which he duly did. The following morning at Highgate Magistrates' Court you indicated a guilty plea, this confirmed at the next available hearing at the Crown Court.

The major aggravating factor in the case is your history of confrontation with Mr Wheeler and that fact that during this incident he posed no threat. I have heard moving Victim Impact Statements from Greta Wheeler, his widow, and from his two teenage children. I know that you found those statements difficult to listen to. How much more difficult must they have been to write? There is nothing I can do to take away the pain that you inflicted on this family. They will have to learn to live with it, but, because of what you did, it will never end.

I had to stop reading for a bit then. I was feeling too many confusing things at once. I did not like the way the judge's words made me think about Dad.

We also heard from Guy Grainger's father. He was obviously a very well-loved son, although his associates at the time of his death were of concern.

Against that, I bear in mind that the offence was not premeditated and your reaction afterwards is not consistent with an intention to kill. You are a young man of previous good character and you are entitled to substantial credit for that. You were immediately horrified by what you had done. That you called the police so soon after the shooting also counts in your favour.

You are assessed as posing a low likelihood of reoffending and a medium risk of physical harm to the public. I am satisfied that you do not meet the criteria for dangerousness and that I should not pass a life sentence or an extended sentence upon you. You are therefore to serve two sentences of two years and twenty years, for manslaughter and murder respectively, to run concurrently, minus the time you have already served.

Take him down.

I closed the document but, while I'd been reading it, more search results had been loading in a different window. I saw newspaper headlines, grainy photographs of the victims: a kind-looking man with a bald patch and glasses and a much younger, better-looking blond man. I hit Escape and pushed myself away from the desk so hard that my chair carved lines in the carpet tiles. Knowing the details wasn't worth the risk that I might stop loving my dad.

I only read that court report one time, a decade ago, but whole sentences imprinted themselves in my memory and I've been carrying it in my head ever since. I can consult it as easily as a note in my phone. So I knew that Dad had been alone in the house when Guy Grainger and his gun came to visit. Biba had not been there. I had no reason to doubt that.

Until last night.

4
Alice

The shop-warming was a success, on the surface. I had a good feeling about my new work neighbours. But, underneath the getting-to-know you chat, all I could think of was my parents' reaction to that dress and Dad's remark and the way they had both turned to robots.

Was Biba there on the night of the murders?

And if so – why didn't anyone say anything?

The questions are still on my mind when I wake up at seven o'clock the next morning with no memory of getting home. My tongue is stuck to the roof of my mouth, I'm still in the trouble-some orange dress plus a fake fur coat, I am holding a glowstick and somehow I'm both sweaty *and* cold. My little attic flat, which was stuffed floor-to-ceiling with my stock until yesterday, seems cold and empty.

I wrap a hundred-year-old Welsh blanket, too holey to sell, over my coat. In the 'kitchen' – a cooker in an alcove, really – I boil a kettle and spoon sugar over a teabag. When I pull the curtains, the sky is white as paper and the wires above the train tracks opposite make ruled lines in the sky. Dad's words seem to write themselves like lines in an exercise book.

Biba was wearing something a lot like this on The Night Of.

Biba was wearing something a lot like this on The Night Of.

Biba was wearing something a lot like this on The Night Of.

I recall Mum digging her fingers into his arm until I thought she was going to break his skin. Whatever he nearly said, she knew to stop it.

Why would they lie?

Memories play like a slideshow.

21

Me taking the wing mirror off a neighbour's car when Dad was teaching me to drive. Dad took responsibility. Mum accidentally taking out our old neighbour's apple tree with a chainsaw, and Dad taking the blame because everyone hated him anyway by then and what was the point of both of them getting it in the neck? Me leaving my A-level art portfolio on the bus, and Dad telling my teachers it was his fault so I wouldn't get marked down. Not to mention The Fallout.

Rex Clarke protects, he absorbs – that is the essence of who he is. Of course he would have covered for his sister.

How did I not . . .

How did I not *guess*?

I plug my dead phone into the wall. When it lights up, I call Dad.

'Morning,' he says nervously. 'How's the head? I was pretty far gone last night.'

I feel an emboldening baby-Surge. How dare he use the weren't-we-pissed line of defence, as if it's a regrettable one-night stand?

'Was Biba there on the night of the murders? No one says "The Night Of" about the time they met their wife, and right afterwards, you and Mum went really weird.'

He is so quiet that I can hear Peggy's claws on the kitchen floor.

'Because if your sister *was* there, and *you* killed those guys, then you would've had a different defence. You would've said you were acting to protect her. But I don't think you wanted anyone to know she was there at all. You don't even want *me* to know. It's so blatant. It's obvious Mum knows as well. I think *you* took the blame for something *Biba* did.'

'Alice, *please*.' He sounds like an old man.

'No, because isn't it better that I think you did something kind? That you covered for your sister rather than see her go to prison?'

He takes a deep breath but then I hear a door slam and Mum's voice closing in. 'Is that Alice? Hello, sweetie!' She must have wrestled the phone off Dad. 'You're overthinking it, love. Of course Biba wasn't there. Don't upset your dad. Go and open up your beautiful shop.' She cuts the call.

Unless Dad had me on speakerphone, which I don't think he did, how could she know what I might be overthinking, unless they'd been overthinking it too?

They don't trust me. Knowing it's my fault doesn't stop it hurting.

I don't open up the shop, not immediately. I sit on my bed, watching the trains rumble past over the road, and then I pick up my iPad and input words I haven't typed for nine years into the search bar. I re-read the court document through this new lens and go on to the newspaper archives. The Highgate House of Horrors, as it came to be known, was a common headline in the summer of 1997. Roger Capel, my paternal grandfather, had been quite the minor celebrity. He took photos of the beautiful people in the sixties and seventies – rock stars and the models they married. He married two models himself and his children, from his first marriage at least, were beautiful. Throw in drugs and sex and guns and parties in a beautiful house in an affluent area that most readers could never dream of owning and it was tabloid heaven.

I've sometimes overheard my parents reminisce about 'The House' in strange, breathless tones. It's a family thing to give significant events or places capital letters, give them proper-noun status – The Surge, The Fallout – indeed, The Night Of – and The House definitely falls into that category. The pictures of the place on Queenswood Lane show somewhere that deserves a special voice and a definite article. Outside, it looks like something from a period drama. Inside – someone had sold a handful of party photos to the press – it looks like a cross between a minor royal palace and a crack den. Dirty mirrors on the walls, floors carpeted in bottles, cans and ground-out cigarettes. Everything confirms my parents' version of events. Nothing suggests that Biba had been there.

I've had this before, this sense of mission, a need that will only gather momentum if I don't satisfy it, only we aren't talking about acquiring some rare gown here, we're talking about my family, my life. I save everything to a file on my iPad and call it 'Sewing Machine Warranties', a title so boring that no one would think to click on it. And then I set up a Google alert, just in case I am right. If there's a bomb at the heart of my history, I want to be able to hear it ticking.

Six months later

5

Alice

Print maxi dress, Elsa Schiaparelli, 1970s
Slingback shoes, Dolcis, 1960s
1930s Art Nouveau lavalier necklace

@deadgirlsdresses
#outfitoftheday #ootd #vintagefashion #sustainablestyle

Clothes tell tales on their wearer. Not only can I take your measurements in a single up-and-down glance, I can read in your outfit your relationship to sex, food, dancing, power, money, and nine times out of ten I'll get your star sign right first time. I can find you a dress that will not only fit you but *suit* you better than anything new you have ever worn. Fashion is art, like a painting, like a sculpture, like architecture. More so. Not only does it have to look good on a hanger, it has to understand a human body. A well-made garment is reborn with every wearer; it breathes with your lungs and moves with your skin.

Take the woman browsing now. I can tell from her floaty cardigan and skinny jeans and the wrinkle in her nose as she scrutinises a pristine 1910s slip dress that she's going to be a hard sell.

'It's beautiful, isn't it?' I ask. 'That's Italian silk and Nottingham lace.'

'Get these in a charity shop, did you? Must be a nice mark-up for you there.'

Ah, this old chestnut. I smile sweetly. 'Actually, I source my clothes from all over the world. I got that one from a museum that was closing down. Just think: the first woman to own that dress would've been born when these streets were still full of horses and carts. She was probably just about old enough to wear it around the time of the First World War and just about young enough to wear it during the Second.'

My words may be well-worn sales patter but they're heartfelt every time. Waterfall Cardigan's nose wrinkles further. She looks like a rabbit who's been offered a rotten carrot as she fingers the price tag. 'I'm not being funny, but why spend three hundred quid on vintage when the high street does a viscose knock-off that you can throw in the washing machine and doesn't have that musty smell?'

'Fuck off to Oliver Bonas, then.' I nod towards the chain boutiques of Upper Street.

Waterfall Cardigan presses her hand to her collarbone. 'Charming!'

'You can see yourself out.'

Not the most mature encounter, but deeply satisfying.

With the shop once again to myself, I pop in my earbuds and listen to my favourite podcast. *Travesties* is hosted by Tracey and Faye, a stand-up comedian and a tabloid journalist respectively. They specialise in cold cases that contain unanswered questions. Abandoned trials, dodgy confessions, wrongful arrests. It's half criminal investigation and half comedy show and *yes I know* it's in extremely poor taste; my friends never tire of telling me. It has a solid three-star average because listeners either give it five stars for its trailblazing irreverence or one star for being offensive. They play their jingle on a child's xylophone and call their fans 'criminoids' and I am *obsessed*.

Gabe, who doesn't know the real reason I'm drawn to true crime, thinks I'm ghoulish. He says that cycling the streets of London for a living and speaking truth to power by lying across motorways in the name of climate justice bring him into close enough contact with potential violent death.

Why hasn't *there been a millennial serial killer, Faye?* asks Tracey.

The thing is, we don't have time, what with the side hustles and the housing crisis. Plus we're all tapping in on our phones with public transport, laments Faye.

And Uber: you don't want to get kicked off the app for getting blood on the back seat, amiright?

I'm here not just for the content but for tips. Six months into my 'investigation' and my Sewing Machine Warranties folder has hardly changed since the day I created it. My early zeal faded as it became apparent that I didn't really know what I was looking for. A signed confession on the internet? One of the few things I do know about Biba is that she could barely turn on a computer. That's not to say she's completely without a digital footprint. She was an actress, quite a good one apparently, and she's on YouTube, playing a nymphomaniac nun in a romp about Charles II and the Restoration court. Sister Saint-Esprit, as her character was called, can be seen raising the skirts of her habit while giving the king come-to-bed eyes. She's not credited in the video; I only found it by going to her short page on IMDb then manually sifting the clips. Most of the comments underneath were just fans thirsting after the actor who plays Charles II, but one leapt out.

I was at drama school with the girl playing the nun. WILD
PARTIES. Her brother did time for murder.

It made my palms sweat. Someone who'd known Biba! Who knew what they might be able to tell me!

I followed the comment back to an account of an actress whose posts of herself performing Shakespearean monologues had views in the low hundreds. When I messaged her, she admitted she'd never met Biba; they hadn't even been in the same year. She was just trying to entice viewers to her own page. Gain a bit of notoriety by association.

My first lead was my first dead-end and it knocked my confidence. How did a person with a degree in fashion, and no old Fleet Street chums to call on, even start? Was there a secret database? A way to access old phone records?

The brass bell jangles and I pause the podcast. *Travesties* doesn't exactly scream *spend spend spend*. It's only a postman with today's returns. It's always a nerve-racking moment, opening the bag to see if a piece has survived the rental process. I want my girls to go out dancing but I also want them back in good condition and, although they're all insured, a ruined dress feels like a death. Today is a good day. A seventies prairie dress and a late-twenties silk coat have both made it back in shop-fresh condition. I email the customers to thank them for taking such good care. It's not just customer service. I need them to know that I appreciate their appreciation of the piece.

I re-hang the dresses, mark them online as available again, and think, fuck it, I will ask the *Travesties* girls how they do their research. What, at this stage, have I got to lose? It's the work of a moment to set up a new email account (I feel as though using my work address to message about murder would be icky) and then I shoot off a message before I can change my mind.

From: number1criminoid@gmail.com
To: traceyandfaye@travesties.com

Hi there, big fan of the show. I was just wondering if there are any specific steps you take when you're investigating a case and would a normal person be able to do something similar or talk to journalists if they didn't already know them? Thanks so much.

I take a screenshot of the email and save it to Sewing Machine Warranties. Then I check my new email address every minute for twenty minutes. There is an urgency now that things are serious with Gabe. One day my bloodline might pool with his, and he needs to know about the Capel legacy. He will have to know one day; he doesn't count as 'other people'. I want the version he gets to be right first time.

6

Alice

I'm about to break for lunch when a customer walks in who unsettles me right away. I don't believe in fate or a sixth sense but I believe in pheromones and instinct and body language. Call it the lizard brain if you want: there's a level at which we know things before we know them.

This one, I can't get a read on. Her clothes are all wrong. Individually, they're quality pieces. Her deep-V top is this-season Versace. Her crystal-studded Bulgari sunglasses are last year's: you could get a second-hand car for what they cost. But the way they're put together doesn't make sense. She wears a headscarf tucked expertly at the chin but a thick dark fringe like mine pokes out the front, and I've never seen a hijab worn with so much skin on show. Her face is unlined but that could be Botox. Her skin is freckled and lightly tanned but that could be fake. Her scent unsettles me for reasons I can't put my finger on. She moves in an invisible cloud of a fragrance I know, or have known: in passing, but intimately. Rose and pepper and something else that makes me think of Indian silk. It feels like a perfume I tried on in my childhood; it has touched my skin. It's not just the scent but its density. You can tell she's got the bath oil *and* the hand lotion *and* the eau de cologne.

It'll come to me if I wait. As I said: lizard brain.

'Are you looking for anything in particular?' I ask.

Lots of women like to feel the clothes, they shop with their fingers as well as their eyes, but this one thrusts her fists into her pockets. Another thing that's off. Customers who don't like to chat scuttle into a corner, focus on the clothes. They don't engage me in one-way staring contests like this.

31

'Alice, is it?' Her voice is as uncanny as her clothes, somehow high *and* husky, like a little girl who smokes unfiltered cigarettes. Even so, it's her words, her use of my name, that shoots a cold arrow through me. I never put my name on my socials; I never even show my face, only a neck-down shot of whatever I'm modelling. 'So that's what you look like.' She inhales the air in front of me, deep and long, before bursting out with, 'I *can't,* not now.'

She is gone before I can think of a response, leaving a mist of rose and pepper and a bow-string tension behind. What the fuck was that about? It's not *impossible* to find out my name, and the world of vintage fashion has its fair share of . . . let's be generous and call them *characters*, not to mention would-be traders who think I'll share my hard-won, jealously guarded sources if only they ask nicely.

I scoot back through my CCTV. If I can get a good enough capture of her face and Google Lens it, something might turn up – an Instagram avatar or, God forbid, a journalist's byline photo – but even the clearest picture of her face is fuzzy, impressionistic.

I wish I had someone I could talk to about this. It's *hard* carrying this on my own. As a child I wanted a sibling more than anything. I would have welcomed a brother but I longed for a sister. It didn't occur to me then that the ten-year age gap meant it was already too late to share my childhood, and that gap widened with every baby that didn't stay. By the time I was in my teens this phantom sibling became another ghost, like Biba.

Gabe is my best friend but I've never had one of those female friendships all the books are about: intimate, complicated, life-long. I was raised on the idea of the Girl Squad, friendships that were as meaningful as, if not more so than, romantic relationships. Men are easy. Sex means there are rules; dating has a framework that even the most obtuse people have picked up. I can attract playmates, but whatever skill it is that takes a friendship from surface to deep, I don't have it. I mean, there was Sophie, but then there was very much *not* Sophie. Even pre-Fallout I don't think our bond was actually that deep. I mistook a shared child-hood for intimacy. I put my trust in the wrong place.

I let my eyes roam the shop, drink in the clothes and their colours, the pale blues, ivories and creams, ebonies and onyxes, blood-red, forest-green. Sometimes I wonder if these dresses aren't, on some level, company. That I have surrounded myself with the sisters I never got to have.

I've lost my appetite for true crime. Instead of resuming *Travesties* I flip through my LPs, Florence and Stevie and Kate and other singers I'd kill to have dressed, before sliding the first Bat for Lashes album from its sleeve. I open the doors wide to let the music out. Behind his vat of bubbling oil, DeShaun – who is wearing a Marni cardigan I gave him for his birthday – starts dancing. Yuki in the Japanese art gallery turns her music down to make way for mine and even Soldier Steve nods in time behind the gleaming brass of his military memorabilia.

A message from Gabe pings through.

Have you told your parents yet?

It's a needle scratch across the groove of my good mood. Did I say I only had one secret?

Better make that two.

7
Karen

'Beach.' Rex is behind me in my study, Peggy's leash in his hand.

'Let me get to the end of this chapter,' I say.

'No,' he says. 'You've got five minutes. If I don't force you out you'll be here till dinner. *Beach.*'

Rex is a barometer of other people's moods, a holder of their pain. He knows before I do when it's time for me to take a break from the desk. The book I'm working on is heavy going. Usually German-to-English translations are my favourites. I am in nerd heaven breaking down a twenty-letter compound word into exactly the right English ones or determining which of the many forms of *bitte* is intended. But this time it's personal, as they say. *Liebesbomb – Love Bomb*, as it'll be called over here – is five hundred unflinching pages about coercive control in relationships. Difficult material at the best of times, but on every page I see my daughter's boyfriend. Gabe is the best, most extraordinary, most wonderful human being the world has ever produced and he loves Alice more than any man has ever loved any woman and that right there is the problem. Forget Cupid's arrow; this is Cupid's taser. I know young love is intense but there's something about the way he swept her off her feet that unnerves me for reasons that go beyond my own experience of jumping into relationships not so much at the deep end as in the middle of the ocean.

The only reassurance is that Alice hasn't told him about Rex's conviction. At some level where her self-preservation instincts are still functioning, she knows Gabe is not to be trusted. Of course I don't want to see her with a broken heart, but I hope this relationship burns out like the rest of them, and that he's long gone before she confides in him.

'Beach!' Rex interrupts my thought spiral.

'Okay okay *okay*.' I rise from my chair and the bones in my back click like abacus beads. In the bathroom, I piss out a litre of coffee, check my reflection and wince. My hair looks like straw and I have these huge grey circles under my eyes. They weren't even there a year ago but now they gather depth and darkness by the day. I keep waiting for someone to comment. To me, it's as obvious as if I'd got a new nose or something.

'Your carriage awaits,' says Rex from behind the wheel. I once worked on a book about love languages, how we all have a preferred way of saying I love you, and it's not always with words. Some people buy gifts; others say it through touch. Rex's love language is acts of service, and that includes driving me every-where. Peggy, tail thumping on the back seat, can't believe her luck. It seems like only yesterday that the back seat of my car used to be squashed raisins and toys. Now it's dog chews and poo bags.

'No work on today?' I ask Rex.

'It's an admin day,' he says. 'I've been filing receipts.' He, like me, is self-employed. He's a project manager for homeowners having loft conversions and kitchen extensions, managing their budgets and contractors and trying to persuade them to paint everything white. He's finally out of the dip his work took after The Fallout. Sophie's father Andrew used to put a lot of work Rex's way, and that dried up overnight.

Peggy rests her chin on my shoulder while I scroll through my phone, deleting old photos. While we're idling at the level cross-ing in Melton, I show Rex a picture of a slim white gown I saw in a charity-shop window. 'D'you think Alice might like that? She sells a lot of wedding dresses.'

'You're asking the wrong person,' says Rex, gesturing at his own clothes, which, as usual, look like they've been blown on by a gale.

I send her the picture. If she wants the dress, hopefully it'll still be available this afternoon.

'Which beach?' I ask.

'I thought Sizewell.'

'Perfect.'

Sizewell is not the most popular beach on our part of the Suffolk coast – the hulking, Soviet-looking nuclear power plant puts a lot of people off – but it's *our* beach. We lived just a couple of miles inland when Rex was released, and it was where we'd walk with Alice in the evenings, watching rabbits bob across the greensward that runs between the power station and the shore. After he was 'outed', we moved further inland to Woodbridge. It's a small town – everywhere in Suffolk is a small town; even Ipswich is a village by London standards – but it's big enough and far enough away from the old place that we could walk down the street without people whispering. The one mercy of The Fallout was that the news travelled the old-fashioned way. No one has yet posted about Rex online. Word of mouth was bad enough.

The car flies past the water tower on the edge of Leiston, a landmark which is Peggy's cue to start whimpering as though scared we're going to change our minds. By the time Rex parallel-parks outside a row of fishermen's cottages – the pay-and-display is for *tourists* – Peggy is hurling herself at the window. It takes both of us to get her lead on.

'Coffee?' I gesture to the café as she pulls Rex up the boardwalk.

'And a Twix!' he shouts, then disappears behind a ridge of seagrass.

Even queuing outside the café I can feel the sea doing its thing. Sun on my skin, salt on my lungs. Rex was right. I needed this. Two blue ticks on my phone tell me Alice has seen my message. I call her, wondering which version of her will answer the phone.

'What do you think?' I ask. 'Thirty quid, it won't be there lo—'

'Why are you texting me fucking *wedding dresses*?'

Ah, it's that one. 'You're welcome. Just thought you might want me to pick it up for you?'

She sighs. 'Thanks for thinking of me, Mum, but *no*, you know I like to source my own stock.' Yes, she's told me this a thousand times, but she's all the way over in London and how else can I let her know I'm looking after her? This is *my* love language. 'It's twenty-first-century, a dress like that. I can't sell it. It was nice of you, but leave it where it is.'

Her voice is pulled tight with impatience and another quality I can't identify over the phone. *Something* is wrong.

'Everything OK with Gabe?' I regret the question even as I ask it.

'Oh, my God, *leave* it.'

Since Alice met him even her spikes have spikes. 'Because you know you can always tell me if—'

'Ivegotacustomergottagobye.' She cuts me dead.

Rex says *Liebesbomb* is clouding my judgement. It's true that when I'm mired in a book I start to see the whole world through the prism of its concept. But I know my child. There's something she's not telling me.

I carry the coffees in one of those disposable cup holders I promised Alice I'd stop using. Sustainability is kind of built into her work but she was never judgemental before she met Gabe. He spends his days on nebulous eco-warrior 'activism' that makes Alice swoon, it's just so attractive that he stands for something. He is *real*, apparently. Real! His name is Gabriel Villiers, he grew up in Windsor, he went to a posh school, but he still says 'Whagwan?' instead of 'hello'. Comparisons with Guy Grainger are uncomfortable but I can't help it.

As I crest the dune, Peggy appears from nowhere and drops a dripping, barnacled lump of wood at my feet. I bend to pick it up. As far as I can tell, Gabe's 'activism' consists of preaching to the converted in pubs and occasionally lying in a human chain across busy junctions to hold up traffic – which will surely lead to *more* emissions as drivers back up for miles. I know I can be a bit *la la la, I'm not listening* about the climate crisis but I'm not sure it's healthy to think about it constantly the way the kids seem to, and it's certainly not great to tie your whole identity to your cause. He's just such a pompous little prick. The first time we met him, a passing remark from Rex about how the Iraq war was a shame but that Tony Blair was *alright, really, compared to this lot* and we got an earful of polemic, and when I intervened Gabe said, 'Don't be a Karen, Karen,' and Alice *took his side.*

'What are we going to do about him, Peggy?' I ask. Her brown eyes hold no answer. I hurl the wood back towards the sea so forcefully that something in my shoulder goes pop. Is Alice's devotion to Gabe *my* fault? Has Rex's conviction scarred her? Was my parenting too intense or not intense enough? If she'd had a sibling, if she weren't so desperate for love, would she have let someone like him into her heart?

8

Karen

Rex is at the shoreline, eyes on the wind farm that's just visible on the horizon. Peggy scatters pebbles in her wake as she lollops towards him, a bolt of rust on the washed-out greens and beiges of seaweed and pebbles.

I hand him his paper cup. 'Here, have your half of the Twix before it melts,' I say, even though it's already liquid in its wrapper.

'Enticing.' He looks at the brown slime. 'It's gonna be even hotter tomorrow.'

'God, really?'

'What? You love it, you freak.'

When we met I was a real sun-worshipper, braising my skin in oil while Rex and Biba lurched from one shadow to another. I'd be lying if I said I wasn't loving these hot summers. I know the world is on fire but if I'm going to burn I might as well do it with joints that don't hurt and a full stock of Vitamin D. And I know we're not supposed to tan any more and every summer I say this is the last time but then I feel it melting knots out of my muscles even as it crepes the skin on my forearms and paints spots on the backs of my hands. Next year. I'll stop next year.

'I love the sun when I can lie in it. I'm supposed to be going into London to see my editor. The thought of the Tube, in this . . .'

Georgia runs an independent publishing house that specialises in translations. We've been working together since Alice was at primary school. I started by translating really boring business etiquette books and gradually she started trusting me with juicier projects, although the experience of *Liebesbomb* has made me long for the tedium of listing how many air kisses are appropriate in the Netherlands or whom to address first around a boardroom table in Japan.

'Is she still in that office in Holborn?'

'Actually no. She works from home, since Covid. I need to find out her address. Thanks for the prompt.' I thumb Georgia an email on my phone. 'She always wants to meet in person if she's offering me work.'

'Fingers crossed, then. God knows we need the money. I mean, more so than usual.'

My head turns sharply in his direction. 'How come?' I've jinxed it with my thoughts. Word is out. Someone's gone and posted a full account of his conviction on Checkatrade. I force myself to breathe in time with the slow back-and-forth of the shingle in the waves.

'I might've had to put a bit of cash into Alice's business,' he says. 'This coffee's lukewarm.'

'Never mind your coffee. We talked about this. You need to learn to say no to her.'

'It wasn't her fault, it was her energy bill,' protests Rex. 'Businesses are folding all around her. We can't let that happen.'

'Even so.' I fold my arms primly. I am aware of the hypocrisy: me having a go at him for keeping things from me. But only I know this, so I can claim the moral high ground uncontested.

Rex throws back his head to drain his cup. I know what he's going to say to the extent that I can pretty much mouth the words along with him. 'It's just. You know. I couldn't provide for Biba, but for Alice, I can.'

The notion of providing for the women in his life and protecting them has shaped everything Rex has done since he lost his mother. Arguably his efforts to secure a home for his sister began the chain of events that ended with blood on the tiles.

'It's not really providing for her if we bail her out the whole time, is it?' I keep my voice gentle but firm. 'Giving her survival skills is more important than giving her money. And it's not helping anyone if we lose the house because the business isn't viable, and we *all* end up living in her shitty flat.'

He doesn't answer. The mood has soured. Back in the car, Peggy settles on her tartan blanket and I clip her into her harness. Rex employs the experienced sulker's technique of talking to the dog while completely ignoring me.

'Who's a clever girl, then?' he asks her in a stupid baby voice.

I snap, 'Peggy, sit,' with such authority that a cockapoo on the pavement outside drops to its haunches. Before Rex can pick up much speed, he's already slowing down, halted by a set of temporary traffic lights that wasn't there on our outbound drive. Just beyond it, ROAD CLOSED signs stretch into Leiston. There are constant unexpected diversions that arrive and dissolve like mirages on this part of the coast. I think it's something to do with the third nuclear power station they've been threatening to build since I moved here.

'Oh, for God's sake,' says Rex. '*Another* diversion? We'll have to go the long way round.'

I close my eyes and let my hair fly, only understanding as the car gathers pace that he's not taking the scenic route past the ruined abbey but the main road that goes by the cottage Alice and I lived in, the one he came home to when he was released. To get there, you have to go past a cluster of homes that were a building site that winter. I saw the brochure for the development – houses built in a fake olden-days style with clapboard cladding and thatched roofs – but I have never seen them. I have not driven this way for nearly fifteen years.

'I wonder how long it'll be before we stop calling them "the new houses",' Rex says, not noticing that the bags under my eyes have darkened, that I look like death.

9

Alice

As soon as I put the phone down on Mum I regretted it, but ring-ing me up about wedding dresses right after Gabe's text? Of course I was going to flip out. I should text her before she goes into a spiral.

Sorry for being a brat.

I delete it.

It was a really nice thought I was just busy chat later.

I can't handle her now, with the pressure from Gabe. It was actually the perfect window to tell her but she gets this tone in her voice and I just *cannot*. In the end I send her a love heart emoji. Three seconds later, she sends me one back. I tap to acknowledge the love heart emoji with a heart notification, hoping that she recognises it as a full stop.

The deep pink scent of The Woman – another proper noun to add to the list – still lingers when it's time to lock up. Petals, spices, sari silk. I take a noseful, as if I can bank it. I turn on the alarm at the back of the shop, between the two huge mirrors. I punch in the code, watched as ever by my own reflection, a troupe of doppelgängers moving in perfect formation.

The walk from Angel to Drayton Park can be done with one right turn into Upper Street and then a left one on to Holloway Road but I like to take the back and side roads, where streets of three-million-quid Georgian houses abruptly give way to ungen-trified social housing estates, a pattern that repeats two or three times. I pause on Liverpool Road to admire a faded mural adver-tising Hovis bread that must be from the early twentieth century. Ghost signs, they call these. Once you've seen one, you notice them all over London. Crossing Holloway Road is a brief culture shock of noise, fried chicken shops and nail bars, then it's more terraces and maisonettes, all dwarfed by the red glass drum of the Emirates stadium.

Avalon Road started life as a row of posh houses for the emerging merchant class in the nineteenth century, and spent most of the twentieth century as a slum before all the people who couldn't afford to live in actual Islington bought them up and now it's posh again. Mostly. Our house, an end terrace, lowers the tone, and, according to our next-door neighbour Priyanka, the price of hers. I can't argue; it's a proper hovel. The lower three storeys are boarded up, riddled with asbestos after some mid-century 'renovation', and we have three poky rooms on the top floor. If you've ever seen a documentary about Dennis Nilsen, the dude who killed and cooked men in Muswell Hill, you'll have an idea. The landlord, Malcolm, charges me fifty quid a week – less than we spend on groceries – in return for not grassing him up to housing standards. In six months, he's going to gut the house and start again. I don't know how we'll afford somewhere else within walking distance of the shop.

I climb the staircase in near-total darkness. There are mirrors on every landing – nothing special or I'd have nicked them for the shop, mostly those horrible long wavy ones from IKEA – presumably there to bounce the light around, make this skinny chimney of a house seem a little brighter. The mirrors catch the thin shafts of dusty light that poke through the holes in the window grilles, reflecting the beams at sharp angles to make nets at chest level. Gabe once said he half-expected to come home one night to find Tom Cruise trying to slip through the gaps between them.

When I reach our floor, the smell of damp that pervades year-round is stronger than usual. Gabe's exiting the bathroom, a towel around his waist.

'The leak in the shower's getting worse,' he says, holding out his arms to me. 'If you peel up the lino the floor's all mushy like Weetabix.'

I breathe him in, let the toothpaste and the olive oil soap he buys for 50p from the corner shop and the cream he puts on his dry skin flush out the odours of my day.

'Dare I hope you've told them?' he asks.

I draw my nose away from his neck. 'Give me *time.*'

'How much time d'you need? The ceremony's in three weeks!'

Ceremony, not wedding. Civil partners, not husband and wife. The way we want it. To show that we stand for something. Unlike my parents, who have no beliefs. They aren't worried that the planet is dying and I don't know why. Even religion would be better than this weird moral void they live in. Making their house nice, walking Peggy, dinner and a West End show four times a year – it's perfectly pleasant, but what does it *mean*?

'Maybe we should have them over. For dinner, and a nice time, rather than a debate.'

He bristles. 'What, so I suppress my personality and my politics and everything I stand for?'

'If it's not too much trouble.'

He laughs, his blue eyes disappearing. His laugh is why I fell for him, really. He takes the work seriously but not himself.

Gabe's the first man in years I didn't meet on Tinder. It was my birthday – the day after Valentine's Day – and I got a room in Lucky Voice for karaoke for me and my friends. At least, I *meant* to. I was exhausted; it was only two months into having the shop and I was working crazy hours, frustrated by the lack of progress on my investigation, and I fucked up the booking. Instead of going home, me and the gang crashed another group's room. Gabe was there with a ragtag bunch of people from his activist group.

'You have to let us in,' I said, even though Yuki was already browsing the song menu. 'It's my birthday.'

'The more the merrier, I guess?' was his way of admitting defeat as we stormed the microphones.

All the other girls were looking at Stef, who's sexy in a silver-back-gorilla, huge-and-hairy, throw-you-over-his-shoulder sort of way, but I've never gone for the obvious ones. I liked what I saw of Gabe. *Peaky Blinders* haircut, a frayed band T-shirt, deep lines on his face and gaps of baby-soft white skin between the leathery planes of his cheeks and forehead that suggested laughter.

There was a screech of feedback as Hollie launched into an Eminem rap, followed by a moment of awkwardness, broken when he said, 'That's a *lovely* frock.' It was an original Laura Ashley, 1979, calf-length, puff sleeves and a bluebird print, and it gave me curves where there were none. '*Lovely frock*?' he repeated, clapping a hand over his forehead. 'How old am I, ninety?'

'I rescued her from landfill,' I said, and we were straight into it. Gabe was a climate missionary, part of a collective called Global Rising. He didn't just go on marches and demos, he'd occupied building sites and even spent a week down a tunnel – a proper, crapping-in-a-bucket, vigil activist. He was working as a cycle courier until he could find a way to work for the movement full-time. He'd done a few nights in the cells, something he shrugged off as an occupational hazard but it made my heart contract. I didn't know if I could love another man through prison walls. I didn't have Gabe and already I was worried about losing him. We duetted on 'Islands in the Stream' and brought the house down. I had never been surer that I would take someone home with me.

It was a mild night for February and he walked me home, even though it was in the opposite direction to his place in Stoke Newington. At my front door, I closed my eyes and waited. For quite a while. When I opened them, Gabe was pinching the skin between his eyes.

'I'm sorry, Alice. I'm actually with someone.'

You fucking *what*? 'But I thought—' I drew lines back and forth in the air between us to illustrate the pull I was feeling.

'Yeah. That's why I didn't mention her. I thought I could forget I was in a relationship but look, it turns out I'm not that guy. And I don't think you're that girl, either.'

I actually was that girl, I would have elbowed sick children out of my path for an hour on my back with him, but he was resolute.

Delphine was critical of his work with Global Rising so he knew it couldn't last, but she was also delicate, highly strung, and he didn't know how to get out of it. I went upstairs, kicked the wall, masturbated, passed out, and spent the next few weeks trying unsuccessfully to put him out of my mind.

Three weeks later, he turned up at Dead Girls' Dresses.

I was modelling a Halston one-shoulder dress I'd picked up at a car boot sale for five quid and would be able to sell for a hundred times that, although I was tempted to keep it. Fire-engine-red with a single pleat, it held its shape as though it was made yesterday, and made me look as if I was about to go dancing at Studio 54. Gabe had on his cycling gear, black, green and pink, like a big sexy licorice allsort.

'I've left her,' he said, in a moment of pure Richard Curtis rom-com.

'Because of me?'

'No, I caught her putting Diet 7Up cans straight in the landfill bin.'

'Oh.'

He laughed, his face collapsing into folds and dimples. 'Yes, of course because of you.'

For the first time ever, I flipped the shop sign to CLOSED two hours early. He put his thumb on my lower lip and said, 'I'm yours now. You can do anything you want with me.'

Oh, God, I thought, another one who wants to recreate what he's seen on Pornhub. 'Right. I'd like to do some *really vanilla stuff*,' I said.

'Thank fuck for that,' he replied.

I bit down on his thumb, and the match was struck.

While Gabe puts the world to rights on the phone, I'm in bed, watching *Cruella* with my earbuds in. The first night I spent here I thought the trains would drive me mad, rattling past at almost all hours. Now I don't even hear them, and I barely notice the way they shake the building. One of Gabe's few faults is his taste in films. He won't watch anything heartwarming or fun. He likes subtitled Japanese and Korean horror films which always seem to feature a girl in a white dress and matted hair climbing out of something – a TV screen, a well – with their elbows sticking out. I much prefer what I'm watching now, the bit where Cruella sets fire to her white cloak to reveal the slinky red dress underneath. It's second only to the scene where she turns the contents of a dustbin into a dress then makes a fabulous departure on the back of a bin lorry.

When the credits roll, Gabe and Stef are still batting the same old shit back and forth. 'That's what I'm *saying*!' Gabe's voice carries. 'We need to move away from inconveniencing people and focus on inconveniencing power.' I can't make out what Stef's saying but Gabe's response is a pained, 'But power can be *made to* care. Isn't that the *point* of the movement?'

I play back the shop's CCTV on my iPad. Who was she? The footage is grainy – I probably wouldn't be able to identify her clothes if this was all I had to go on – but I can still study her body language, weird and stiff. I don't dare play the footage of Biba on YouTube, not with Gabe in the next room, but I can run through it in my head. *Could* she be The Woman?

I wait for him to come to bed, knowing I won't sleep until he's next to me, but too proud to beg.

I'm not sure if Gabe's worked out my sleeping problem. At the moment I like to think he still believes it's him I crave, not that I just need another body – almost any body – in the bed. I slept with my mum every night until Dad's release. She taught me Spanish, and it's thanks to her that my pronunciation of French couture terms is impeccable, as well as how to lay a table and please and thank you, but she never gave me one of the most basic skills of all: the ability to sleep alone. It's put off dozens of friends over the years, my keenness to share a bed. People mistake it for an attempted seduction and they back away saying they're sorry but they just don't think of me in that way. It's never about sex; it's the need for a *presence*. I sometimes wonder if I didn't have a twin who was lost in the womb.

'Who's that?' Gabe flops down on his belly next to me, presses his flank into mine, absent-mindedly slides his hand under the waistband of my underwear.

I could say, *Oh, yeah, there's an infinitesimal chance it was my dead aunt who is possibly a murderer even though officially my dad is, didn't I mention it?* I don't of course.

'I'm not sure. This woman came in today and I got weird vibes off her anyway – like, I recognised something about her – but then she knew my *name*. You know I don't have that on my socials.'

I'm trying to play it down but I must transmit my unease; the texture of his skin on mine changes. 'Can you zoom in?'

I enlarge the picture as best I can. 'Am I mad, or does she look like she's somehow in disguise?'

He squints and says, 'Could be anyone. Did she ask you about your sources? She might be, like, trying to undercut you.' I shake my head. 'At least she's not stealing,' he says. 'Would it make you feel safer if I could see that as well? I mean there's not a lot I could do about it, if I was on the other side of the city, but . . . I dunno. Just an idea.'

Gabe's protective instincts remind me on some level of Dad; maybe that's why he feels so much like home.

'Why not?' I say. 'You need the code whatnot on the back of the camera. Come into the shop tomorrow and I'll set it up. I'm probably making a fuss over nothing.'

He moves his hand an inch lower. I close my eyes. The way Gabe makes me feel carries shame as well as pleasure. Not in the slut-shamey sense. What I mean is that I'm ashamed of how weak he can make me. I worry about it being taken away from me and how I might live without it. This is what my mother really needs to worry about. Not how much Gabe wants me, but how much I want him.

10

Karen

It's the first real scorcher of the year so naturally the train tracks on the line to London have buckled and I have to drive to my meeting with Georgia. She lives in Muswell Hill, literally a minute's drive from Queenswood Lane. The easiest way to go is via Crouch End, so I don't have to force myself into a diversion. Over the years I've added hours on to journeys to avoid the two-mile radius around Highgate station.

'Karen!' She opens the door and bends down to hook a finger in the collar of a rotund beagle. 'Come. Come. So good to see you in the flesh.'

'You look great!' I say, and mean it. Georgia must be over sixty now and I always presumed her flame-red hair was natural. But she started growing out her grey during Covid and the transformation is finally complete, a silver curtain that makes her look younger rather than older. 'Lovely place,' I add. Her house is stuck in the nineties, in the best possible way: terracotta walls, furniture made of rattan and cast-iron, lots of pottery that looks as if it's been painted by a three-year-old. In a pine kitchen, an old-fashioned kettle approaches climax on the hob. She serves Earl Grey tea and lemon drizzle cake while we whinge about Brexit and talk about dogs. Snoopy has been spitting his heart medication out and hiding it behind the sofa. She found a pile of tablets an inch high while she was vacuuming.

It's a good hour before we get to the point of our meeting.

'How would you feel about fiction?' asks Georgia. I stifle an ironic laugh: I can do fiction alright. 'Because I've just acquired a German author, two-book deal, sort of literary crimey thrillery novels. I know it's a leap but I think you'd be perfect.'

49

My body answers for me: a full-spine tingle at the thought of a new challenge, followed by an internal thud. Murder mysteries are not escapism for those who live inside them. But it's only a story, and I need the money.

'I would love it,' I say. 'How exciting, to branch out at this stage in my career.' I raise my teacup in a toast.

'I'm so pleased,' says Georgia, and then there's the kind of gear change you get on daytime television when they're about to segue from the cookery section to a tragic story. 'There's another reason, apart from your suitability for the job.' She splays her fingers on the tablecloth like a fortune-teller. 'I wanted to let you know face-to-face that, as of next year, I'm winding up.'

'You're retiring?' I squeak.

'I'm *tired*, Karen,' she says. 'It's getting harder and harder every year. I'm being squeezed in all directions by Amazon and Google Translate and now there's bloody AI on the horizon . . . Better to go out now while I still love what I do.'

'Right.' I press my fingertip into individual cake crumbs, gathering a little ball of dough as I dot my way around my plate. Georgia isn't my employer, we have no contract, she doesn't owe me anything, but she is well aware that she is my main source of income.

'I thought if I gave you some fiction, you'd have another string to your bow. And this author's only thirty, so if she likes you, hopefully she'll take you with her. And of course I'll be recommending you to all my contacts.'

Georgia didn't have to do this for me. I can feel tears pressing the back wall of my eyes. I thank her, and hug her – a first – and get back in the car, which I left facing up the hill, towards Highgate, as though it knew where I would go before I could admit it to myself. As suburbia gives way to the wildwood, the trees throw their familiar lace scarf over my windscreen. Is it my imagination, or is the green less vivid than it was back then? I don't drive as far as the house, pulling up instead at the first parking space I see. I'm nervous, as though I'm visiting an ex; in a way I suppose I am.

II

Karen

Queenswood Lane. Sheila Capel and Tom Wheeler and Guy Grainger died here but it's where I came to life. Before I lost my innocence to guilt, I lost it to experience, and it's that which draws me back. As though if I breathe in hard enough I might inhale a trace, snort a line of whatever pixie dust was in the air that summer.

The paved footpaths through the trees were unmade back then. The Capels could find their footing on moonless nights, and eventually I could too. It's fanciful, I know, but I can't help thinking that the paths had to be made good when their original custodians left.

The wood is a shallow bowl, all paths sloping to a central point. I head for the lowest point, where there is a concrete circle, once a paddling pool, its base a faded blue. Rex and Biba played there as children. As a young woman I lay in the centre of the ring, on my back, grit against my spine, and watched the stars spin above me. If I hadn't passed out I would have kissed Biba. It's been re-wilded now, fenced off and turned into a frog pond. I turn my back on the space, but not the memory, and my feet decide what happens next.

The House.

The house.

I find myself smoothing down my hair. An ivy-choked faded beauty when I lived there, today the Victorian villa gleams with the polish of Jules Capel's renovations. There are five buzzers next to the lacquered black front door. The first time I came here, for Biba's twenty-first, I spent hours looking for buzzers like that, which would show me their flat. I couldn't believe that a house this big could be all one residence, not in London, and certainly not occupied by someone my age.

It wasn't theirs to keep, though, and soon they would be expelled.

There must have been a hundred people in that house that night, crammed into what we called the Velvet Room, but only a handful I came to know by name. Nina the silversmith, with her blackened fingers and skirts full of children. Tris and Jo, the eco-warriors with their dreadlocks and army boots. Intimidatingly beautiful Rachael, the natural blonde.

Guy Grainger was at that party and Tom Wheeler too, the uninvited guest standing in the black-and-white hall in his chinos, both men unaware that they only had weeks to live, that they were standing more or less where they would die, overseen and chopped into fragments by the crazed overmantle mirror.

And of course that was the night I met Rex, walking from room to room filling a bin bag with litter. We watched the sun rise together and he said, 'I've always thought it was funny that dawn should be called daybreak. This is when the day is made: it's the beginning. It's the best part: you've got all the potential of the day to come, and you haven't wasted it yet. When it gets dark, *that* should be daybreak. When the day is broken. When it turns into night-time, that's when it all starts to go wrong.'

Rex isn't generally given to poetry or prophecy, but that speech contained both. My days that summer were his, but the nights belonged to Biba. The nights were where it went wrong, more wrong than any of us would have guessed.

I look up to the top of the house, my old room where we first kissed, an awkward boy with string-bean limbs and messy hair and a girl who didn't appreciate her loveliness, both exhausted, wrung-out after a different kind of all-nighter, one that began in a theatre and ended in a corridor at the Whittington hospital. That was the night I began to transfer my affections from her to him, a process I still sometimes wonder if I ever truly completed.

The memory makes me shiver. My eyes travel down a storey to a window once hung with lace and tie-dye, now battened with white plantation shutters. Biba's room. The first time I saw it, the unmade bed and the overspilling wardrobe, someone – I think it was Jo, or maybe Nina – said, *Don't go too far or you'll end up in Narnia*, not understanding that the wardrobe *was* Narnia.

A face appears at the window and I step backwards, off the pavement and into the road without checking for traffic, my heart banging. What the hell am I *doing?*

I couldn't tell you what route I take home, only that at some point I seem to come to and I'm on the M25 at the junction with the A12, bound for Suffolk. Even after that I'm only going through the mirror-signal-manoeuvres on autopilot. Really I'm walking through The House, the hotch-potch of rooms with its mismatched carpets and furniture from all the decades of the twentieth century. Bought with Sheila Capel's money, morally, ethically The House belonged to him and Biba. God knows Rex loved the place as if it were his name on the deeds and not Roger's. God knows he tried to take ownership.

The letters he wrote to his dad, that were never meant to be read.

That were never meant to be sent, and when they were . . .

If he hadn't—

If I hadn't—

If we hadn't—

The blast of a car horn alerts me to the sparks I'm making on the crash barrier and I am back in the present just in time. Heart racing, I pull over at the next services. I've scraped a line of pewter into the silver bodywork of the car. I get a doughnut and a coffee at Greggs and sit at the table until I'm fully in the here and now.

Life, not death, I tell myself.

Now, not then.

Alice, not Biba.

I text her.

Enjoying the sunshine?

It's disgusting. Literally I've got sweaty shins I didn't even know that was a thing.

Any plans for tonight?

Out with my uni mates.
Have fun!

My spirits soar. It's good. The more she sees of people who aren't Gabe, the better. I send her a line of yellow emojis and get back on the road. The commuter towns and industrial estates of Essex turn into the villages and churches of Suffolk, and I turn back into myself, whoever she is these days.

12

The drama corridor at Queen Charlotte's College is congested with final-year drama students. Theatre people are not known for their easygoing natures but even by their standards the air is humming with tension. You wonder what the collective noun for actors is. An ego of actors, a childhood trauma of actors, a neediness of actors.

One of the musical theatre boys is cracking his knuckles. 'This is what the last three years have been leading up to!' He's not a serious person, just another West End Wendy who'll be lucky if he ends up in cruise ship cabaret.

Never mind the last three years. Your whole life has been leading up to this moment.

The graduate shows – the casting of which is the cause of today's agitation – are make or break. You perform for the biggest agents in London and if you don't get signed on the back of that performance you become tainted. It's not like being a writer, where you can do the work alone. Actors die in a vacuum. You need an agent because you need to keep working. I mean, everyone does; but you must keep working at the rate and intensity with which you have been studying. Once you've finished your degree, only jobs will keep you in that glorious state of flow.

Acting is the safest way to get rid of The Feeling, which has been stirring lately after a couple of mercifully dormant years. The Feeling is an emotion, a state, a condition, that lacks a name. It is peculiar perhaps to you. It is a broken bottle to the heart, a cigarette stubbed out inside you and you will do anything to make it go away.

Your tutor emerges from his study, his arms laden with scripts. He announces the roles by production. First up, A Doll's House. A ripple runs through the women. You want the lead, along with every other actress here. Nora is the dream role for a showcase. No nasty surprises. Everyone knows who she is and expects you to make her your own.

They give it to fucking Rachael. Rachael who doesn't understand that the gap between her ambition and her talent is bridged only by her Barbie-doll looks. The best you can say about Rachael is that she is very good at hitting her marks and remembering her lines.

'Amazing!' You clasp your hands to your bosom. Lying is so much a part of the acting life – everything is always wonderful *– that you wonder they don't teach a module on it.*

The tutor presses a script into your hands. 'Congratulations,' he says.

Fucking . . . you've been cast as Elma in As You Desire Me. *You are a nightclub singer in post-war Germany who may or may not be who she says she is. When you studied the play people said things like 'it's a meditation on identity' or 'a tantalising intrigue' which is what you say when a play is boring or hard work.*

Rachael tries to thread her elbow through yours. 'Let's celebrate!' She senses your reluctance, and adds, 'I'm buying.'

You just want to get out of there. You read the script on the Northern Line to Highgate and in the tunnel between Kentish Town and Tufnell Park, the text prompts an internal shift. They've given you this because you're the only one in the year who has the talent to turn a metaphor into a thriller. Any old turn can play Nora.

The only problem is, they want you to sing a song in German. Not English with a German accent but German in a German accent. You can't learn foreign languages for shit.

In Queenswood Lane, cherry blossom petals are browning on the pavement but the trees are in vibrant green leaf. The front door of your house is open. Fuck's sake, Rex. This happens every summer: the wood swells and the door won't shut. It's been three years. It's not like he's got anything else to do all day. In the black-and-white hall, with its bloodstained tiles – you've given up on Rex ever doing anything about them – you dump your bag and let your script slap to the floor.

'Rex?' The walls bounce his name back at you.

You go upstairs, past the landing, where—

no point dwelling on that

—to the floor where you and Rex sleep, and push his door. His spartan room is empty. Maybe it's his signing-on day. You check the attic for signs of life. Tris and Jo are out. Down in the kitchen there is no one at the table. No food in the fridge or the oven. Nina has been cooking less and less lately. This feels ominous. Uncertainty vibrates at the exact frequency that the Feeling feeds off.

You go through the kitchen to the garden room where Nina is at her desk, working by the late sun's rays. She's wearing a kaftan with a flamingo print and a halo of honey curls.

'You must know a German,' you say.

She puts a sooty finger to her lips.

'Sorry.' You sit on the edge of the bed, taking care not to wake the sleeping children whose limbs are tangled in the blankets. The cloths are silk-route-and-spices colours, orange and purple. Nina brought them with her when she moved in; threw them over the bed and turned the garden room into a Bedouin tent.

You repeat your question, in a whisper this time. 'You must know a German. Your social circle is like the United Nations.' You show her the script. 'They want me to sing this.'

She sets down the silver wire she's twisted into a coil. 'I honestly don't think I do.'

You twizzle the tassels on the edge of the bed. Inigo snuffles in his sleep. Nina puts a hand on his head but it's you she's looking at. 'Since you're here . . .' she says in a we-need-to-talk voice that rings a bad bell inside you.

You sit in stunned silence as she tells you she's moving on. Taking the children travelling before they are absorbed by the school system. She says it's nothing personal, nothing to do with you and Rex. She says it three times, so you know it's everything to do with you and Rex.

The Feeling bubbles up: black lava in your guts. As though it has never been away, as strong as it was the day it was born, the day you came home and dumped a different bag on hallway tiles, looked up those stairs, saw—

Do you know what? It's time for a drink.

There's a bottle of aniseed-smelling spirit in the kitchen with lettering on it that you guess is Greek. No matter how fast you drink, the alcohol and The Feeling are neck-and-neck, like two raindrops on a window pane. You find a packet of Skittles in a cupboard. They're out of date but you drop them in the ouzo, where they dissolve and you can't tell. You're halfway down the bottle when Rex comes in. His eyes are red. It is a long time since he and Nina were lovers but she means as much to him as she does to you, and the children mean more.

'Where ya bin, Rexamundo?'

He mimes two fingers walking. You have no idea where he goes on these walks.

'Nina told me she's leaving,' you say.

Rex's chin takes on the texture of orange peel. 'It's like Mum all over again!'

Oh, you think. So that's why *it's hurting.*

'It's really not.'

Rex drops his head on to his folded arms and his shoulders are shaking. You should comfort him, you know you should, it's what he'd do for you but right now you're too full of The Feeling to absorb anything from Rex. You have no reserves of comfort to offer. That's Nina's job, you realise. She is where he puts his anxiety. She and the children are the focus of his nervous pacing energy, his fussing, his questions. When she goes, it's all going to be trained on you. Rex will want to know where you're going and when you'll be back and what you're drinking and if you've eaten and whether it's really a good idea to go out in that skirt. The thought makes you pull at your collar; it makes you open a window, it makes you itch.

You plus Rex equals too much and also not enough. What you've come to understand is that there should always be three of you. You haven't retained much maths but you do remember learning that the triangle is the sturdiest of shapes, the hardest to collapse.

You need a new person.

Another week goes by and you still haven't found your German. In despair you visit the Modern Languages department. It's a replica of the Theatre Studies floor: fire doors and fire extinguishers repeating to a vanishing point. You write your request on the noticeboard and when you're done a mouse behind you squeaks, 'I can help.'

First you think her pretty, then plain. She has the ostensible good looks that come from ticking boxes. Nothing's too big. Nothing's too small. She's thin without being scrawny, clear, even skin already tanned in May, girl-band highlights. Her features are all just the right size but you couldn't pick out her nose, say, or her mouth if you had to reconstruct her for a photofit.

'I can speak German?' She says it as if she's asking you to confirm it for her.

You take her to the godforsaken student bar and her eyes widen as though it's the ballroom at the Dorchester. Karen Clarke – even her name is forgettable – is odd without being particularly interesting. Clever, in a savante, *prodigy sort of way, but utterly without ambition. Four years in London but she's suburban to the core.*

To begin with you are her pupil but within hours she is yours. You put pills on her tongue and clothes on her back. You've never been able to see something pure and leave it alone. When Tris and Jo move out of the attic, you move her in. It's the room above

Rex's. He spends most of May lying on his back, staring at the ceiling.

By true summer, Karen's face has changed. She is no longer plain. You could even call her beautiful. Love did that, although you couldn't say whether it is yours or his.

You doubt she could tell you herself.

13

Alice

I wait for Mum's final sign off. There's always a you-hang-up-no-you-hang-up element to our text conversations that can only be closed by a few paragraphs of emojis. When she's exhausted herself, I acknowledge the message with a double-tap love-heart, set my phone down and look up to see Gabe in the doorway, cycling clothes tight to his frame, helmet swinging on a tanned forearm, bearing a cup that says I AM BIODEGRADABLE on it. He presses it into my hands and kisses me on the lips. I peel back the lid to inspect his offering.

'It's that matcha latte shit you like,' he says. 'Four quid. *Four quid* for something that looks like algae.'

'Algae's actually very rich in iodine,' I say, taking a sip. 'What're *you* having?'

'Builder's tea.' He raises his collapsible cup. 'A pound from the caff. How's it going with all the haunted nighties?'

'You mispronounced "high-end vintage fashion". How's *your* day going?'

'Got hands like an iguana.' He reaches for the lotion on my counter, rubs it into the rough skin on his knuckles. 'Same shit, different day. No mystery visitors this morning?'

I shake my head. 'No, but let's get this CCTV shit sorted anyway. The doodah's on the back of the thingy.'

He scans the QR code on the camera, downloads the app and I log him in on my account. He swishes through the feeds: one exterior, someone eating one of DeShaun's churros: one interior, the two of us curved in the fish-eye lens.

'There's a blind spot outside,' he says. 'You could do with another camera facing the arcade.'

'I'm still paying for this lot.'

'Something to think about. Have you got any food? I'm *starving*.' He looks at the stuffed swan as if it's a snack. Gabe has the appetite of a stoner and the metabolism of a meth addict. He has to drink vile protein shakes, gets through about six thousand calories a day, and often gets to restaurants half an hour before me so he can have a main meal before the real meal. Otherwise he snarfs down his main course in sixty seconds and he's still hungry.

'There's a packet of Hobnobs near the kettle,' I say. By the time he emerges from the stock room it's already half its size. 'I forgot to tell you,' he says through the crumbs. 'Big Nonna's moving next week.'

Big Nonna is Stef's great-grandmother, and she's going into sheltered accommodation. Older women downsizing often have a lifetime's worth of clothes to pass on. It's one of my favourite ways to source stock. Every dress has a story and I'm all ears. Clothes are so much easier to sell when they have meaning. I'm especially excited about Big Nonna's wardrobe. She was a nightclub singer back in the day, and, as her name suggests, she was no toothpick. Most vintage clothes are tiny, made in the era of corsets and malnutrition, or cut for a time when food and fabric were rationed, or women kept skinny with cigarettes and amphetamines.

'What does she want for it?'

There's a bit of a situation going on with my company credit card. I didn't read the small print and the interest rates are insane. I mean, it'll be fine, I'm sure I can sort it, they wouldn't have given me such a high limit if they didn't think I would need it and most new businesses take a year or two to turn a profit. It just means I haven't got much cash to hand.

'Nothing. She's just glad to give them a good home.'

'Oh, thank God.' I could cry with relief.

'Let me take you out to dinner to celebrate.'

'Oh, no.' I have other plans with neglected friends. Along with 'poor impulse control', another feature of my school reports was my tendency to flit from one clique to another, never settling. 'I'm out with the uni lot tonight.'

Gabe's face hardens along with his voice. 'You didn't tell me that.' He picks up a 1930s compact mirror and squeezes it so hard that a delta of veins rises on the back of his hand.

'I'm telling you now.'

He goes missing for a moment, as if he's fighting something I can't see, then just as quickly sets down the compact and puts his sex face on, a dimple big as a fingerprint appearing at the top of his right cheek. 'Come here.'

'No. You're covered in Hobnob.'

He wipes his mouth, then hooks his thumb over my lower lip. He *knows* what this does to me.

'Come on,' he says. 'A quickie on the counter.'

When his other hand creeps under my skirt, I don't stop it, although I do say, 'Not the petticoat!' Lesson one for my lovers: tearing off my clothes is not an act of passion but of desecration.

His radio interrupts us. 'Pick-up at Coal Drops Yard.'

'Aw, *man*.' He disentangles himself from me and backs out of the shop. 'Tell your parents,' he says as he unlocks his bike. 'Then it can be a double celebration.'

'I'll do it tomorrow. And I didn't say I was coming with you.'

Gabe rises from the razor of his saddle. 'I'll see you in the Alpaca at seven,' he says over his shoulder. I watch him ride away, his calf muscles pumping like hearts.

If I'm honest I *could* do with a quiet one. I text my uni group chat to cancel.

Not AGAIN, Alice.

Quelle surprise.

I feel bad, but what can I do? When they meet *their* person, they'll understand.

14
Karen

I carry the jangled energy of Queenswood Lane and my near-miss in the car almost to my front door. As always the sight of my home, its thatched roof, and its wonky walls plastered in the shade called Suffolk pink, re-sets me.

In the living room Rex is trying to read a building supplies catalogue while shoving twenty kilos of red fox Labrador off his lap. 'This dog would want to sit on my lap in *hell*.'

'You need a haircut, let the heat escape.' I tousle his hair, threaded with silver now but as thick as the summer I met him. He got his name because when he was born he had a full head of hair and three thick dark whorls coming out from every angle. A man with three crowns, his mother Sheila had said. I have to give him a name that means *king*. 'Could've been worse,' he always says. 'It could've been Roy.' I'd never tell him this, but I would miss his hair if he lost it. His father would have been around the age Rex is now when I met him and he had pretty much no hair by then. If you're going to go bald, will it happen by fifty? I search my hands for strands between my fingers and find only two, one mink-brown, the other brilliant white.

'It's too hot to cook.' I flop on the other sofa.

'I thought that,' says Rex. 'So I've booked us a table at the Gallery.'

'What's the occasion? Can we afford it?' The Gallery is proper fine dining, a cut above our usual chain restaurant or gastropub date night.

'Got a voucher from a client, so it's guilt-free. Go on. Put your glad-rags on.'

Standing in front of my wardrobe is the usual depressing experience. It desperately needs an edit. There are three different sizes of clothes here: a handful of size tens from my youth, the maternity clothes I wore when the fibroids made me look pregnant, and then about five hangers of things I actually wear. At one end, hidden in a blue suit carrier so I don't have to see it, is a dress I know I'll never throw away. It's the red dress Biba gave me on my twenty-first birthday. Like Alice, she only had to look at a garment to know who it would suit, how it would fall, who it would allow the wearer to become.

'Come on!' Rex jangles the keys downstairs.

I yank on the same black jersey dress I wear to everything and let platform sandals and loads of costume jewellery do the heavy lifting.

'You look stunning,' he says, which is bollocks, but I appreciate the gesture.

The evening is yellow and wide. Pollen dances over the kind of field in which Sheila Capel had her most famous photograph taken.

'She's in a restaurant with Gabe.' I show Rex the photo. The caption says *Date nite. Worth it just for the air-con.*

"What's he eating, a whole cow? How does that sit with the eco-warrior thing?'

'It's probably some grass-fed cow that had its own butler,' I say, before steering back to my point. 'She was supposed to be going out with her friends tonight. He's isolating her. This is stage two of the coercive process. He's swept her off her feet; now he's making sure no one else gets a look-in. You wait, any day now it'll be, *Gabe thinks we should get a joint bank account*, or *Gabe wants me to cut my hair.* Look at the body language.' I thrust my phone under Rex's nose. 'Rex, I'm serious. His hand on her shoulder like that. It's not affectionate, it's controlling. And it's her phone but he's the one taking the photo. I personally see the potential for something really dark between them.'

I watch him closely. What's he really thinking? The slightest threat to Biba and he was pacing the floor, making hysterical phone calls and she was only his sister: this is his kid.

'Well, there's always the potential for that, isn't there?'

Sometimes I think Rex is the most predictable man in the world. Other times I can't read him at all.

Lavenham is a pretty little town apparently untouched by the past five hundred years. Americans and film crews love it. So do I. In the restaurant, white tablecloths are laid in diamonds under medieval beams.

Every night echoes another one.

Another beautiful restaurant, atmospheric, torches of real fire on the walls and the three of us dressed up to the nines. It *was* just the three of us then, or so we thought. Guy was back on the scene, but Biba hadn't told us and we were too wrapped up in each other to notice.

When the waitress comes to take our orders Rex has to snap his fingers in my face to bring me back to the present.

'Try not to dwell on today.'

I feel my mouth making goldfish shapes. How the hell does he know I went to Queenswood Lane?

'Georgia's not the only publisher in the world. You're so talented. I have faith in you.'

I shake out my napkin and allow my heart rate to drop back to normal. 'I don't think talent means what it used to. AI's coming for us all.'

'It'll all come out in the wash,' he says airily.

The resentment is so permanent I almost don't notice it except in moments like these when it spikes. For a man obsessed with providing, Rex has always been provided *for*. First by his father, then by Her Majesty, and then, for a long time after his release, by me. I wash my irritation down with celeriac soup and cold Picpoul. He's boring me about some new time-management software that's going to revolutionise his working day when he sees something over my shoulder and his eyes blow wide.

'Don't look,' he says, but I don't need to. A voice I haven't heard in five years carries through the room, cutting through the chatter like a clarinet soloist rising above an orchestra.

'I'm sorry, we can't sit here. You'll have to find us another table.'
'Style it out,' I instruct Rex.
He grimaces. 'We should go.'
Grow a pair, I think, rising from my seat and turning around to face a lioness in gold lamé, the mother of Sophie, Alice's childhood best friend, architect of The Fallout. 'Hello, Dawn,' I say.

15

Karen

It was bittersweet: the last sleepover before the girls left for university; Alice to London, Sophie to Edinburgh. They were young women by then, old enough to drive, vote, drink, marry, but that evening they set up a den in the living room and had a nostalgia movie marathon, *Mean Girls* and *Legally Blonde* and *Heathers*. Rex and I turned in at around eleven o'clock and were woken an hour later by a frenzy of barking and screaming and a hammering on the door.

'The girls!' said Rex, and thudded down to the living room. I put a hand on Peggy's collar and went to the front window. Andrew Saunders' Lexus hummed on the road outside. The screams were turning into words. From Alice, *how could you* and *I'm sorry* and from Sophie *I just want to go home*. The girls had had some bust-ups before but never anything like this. Even Peggy's barking couldn't drown out the noise from outside. Any attempt Dawn had ever made at cultivating her grating, adenoidal voice was abandoned in her panic. 'Sophie! Sophie! Get out while you still can!'

I heard Sophie say frantically, 'I can't open the door!' and then, when Rex tried to calm her down, 'Get him away from me!'

I knew that the little life we had built was over. I found that I was surprised it had taken this long.

'You *promised*!' Alice screamed. 'I trusted you.'

'I'm *scared*,' cried Sophie.

'What's happening in there?' shouted Dawn outside. 'I'm calling 999!'

I shut Peggy in the bedroom and watched from the top of the stairs as Alice yanked open the door, karate-chopped Dawn's phone from her hand, then did the same to Sophie's. Andrew bolted from the car as Sophie scrambled into it. He came to stand at Dawn's side. She looked almost satisfied as she regarded the splinters of glass and silicone on the ground. 'The apple doesn't fall far from the tree, does it?' she said. 'Maybe we can add criminal damage to kidnap and fraud.'

'It was hardly fucking kidnap, Dawn,' said Alice.

'Everything alright?' Our neighbour's voice carried on the cold air.

'Did you know you were living next to a convicted murderer? Double murderer?' asked Dawn.

'What?' gasped the neighbour.

I stood next to Rex. 'You *know* he's a good man,' I appealed to Andrew. 'Have you ever heard him raise his voice? Has he ever let you down? Andrew, come on.'

But Andrew was more frightened of his wife than any man, no matter how violent his crime.

'Karen.' Dawn thrusts forward her bust now, aiming for authority but getting ship's figurehead. Andrew wobbles behind her, an egg on legs.

'We cannot sit near these people,' Dawn tells the teenage waitress who, out of her depth, summons the *maître-d'*.

'I'm so sorry, madam,' he tells Dawn. 'This is our last sitting. We can offer you a drink and snacks at the bar?'

Andrew looks longingly at our plates. 'I had my heart set on the pork belly.'

Dawn huffs. 'We'll take our custom elsewhere.' She rounds angrily on the waitress, who looks on the verge of tears now. 'I expected better of a place like this.'

The other diners are staring at us, and we leave before dessert. We drive in silence through fields that are a dull dark green under a weak moon.

'I'm sorry,' Rex says, and my heart twists for him. There's nothing to say that we haven't already said a hundred times, so I take him to bed to have sex we've had a hundred times, hoping he'll find comfort in the verse-chorus-verse familiarity of it.

At half-ten, when I'm brushing my teeth in the en-suite, one of our phones rings. I drop my toothbrush. Who calls this late unless something is very wrong?

In bed, Rex is propped on one elbow, half his face lit up, the rest a map of caves. Something's happened to Alice, I know it. I'm looking for clean underwear, yanking a T-shirt off its hanger, pulling leggings out of the laundry basket.

'When?' he asks, and then, as the other voice tickles the speakers, 'Right. Are *you* OK?'

There's concern in his voice, the tone he only ever uses to talk to family. It *is* Alice. I drank but with dinner and that was hours ago now. I'll have to stop for petrol in Saxmundham but there won't be much traffic on the A12. I struggle to put on a bra as if I've never worn one before. All the straps are in the wrong places.

'What's happened?' I mouth. Mentally I am choosing a dress to lay her out in. Rex swats me away. A dismissive gesture but one I find reassuring. If it were life-and-death he wouldn't do that. I pause my struggle with my bra.

'Well,' he says, 'good of you to let me know. Will there be . . .' His face falls. 'Of course. Yes, I understand. Well. Er, take care, I guess.'

I know what Rex's face looks like when the news is bad. I have been the one to deliver it. But his mood is one of resignation, not urgency or even horror. Alice is not in immediate danger. Still half in, half out of my bra, I sit next to him, knowing only that he needs me.

'That was Jules,' he says flatly. 'My dad died yesterday.'

I am shocked and I shouldn't be. It's hardly a surprise. Roger Capel must have been in his . . . he may technically be my father-in-law but I still have to do a bit of mental arithmetic to work it out – mid-eighties, at least.

'Oh, *Rex*. I'm so sorry. How?' I touch his neck. There's nothing, no racing heartbeat, no heat coming off him.

'A stroke. He'd had a mild one a few weeks ago, apparently, then a massive one yesterday morning. Instant. Painless.'

'Well. I suppose that's something,' I say, inanely, then his words sink in. 'Hang on. He died *yesterday* and she's only telling you *now*?'

'She said she thought she'd better tell me before they put out the press release thingy. That's me. Ever the afterthought.'

'What do you want to do? Do you – shall we get back up? Go downstairs for a drink, or . . .'

'I think I'd just really like you to hold me,' says Rex.

I curl myself around the familiar knobbles of his spine and hook an arm over his chest. I place my right hand over his heart. It seems to be beating more slowly than usual. My chin is soft in the crook of his shoulder.

'It doesn't matter,' he says. 'It doesn't *change* anything. I hadn't spoken to him since 1997; it's not like he was ever going to thaw.'

Rex had never stopped hoping for that thaw. How *can* a shunned child stop hoping for reconciliation with a parent? Now it will never come.

'Will there be a funeral or anything?'

'Jules said it was best if I gave it a miss,' he says. 'The other kids . . .'

The other kids. Roger Capel's second marriage produced three more children. Rufus, Xanthe and Oscar. The only time I saw them the boys were blond preschoolers and Xanthe was a babe in arms. They'll be in their late twenties and early thirties now.

'No, I get it. No one wants to be the spectre at the feast. All eyes on me. I'd hate it.'

'We should tell Alice,' I say.

'Why? It's not like they had a relationship. She hasn't mentioned my family since . . .' Rex grits his teeth. He's still ashamed of his drunken slip last December, but he's right: Alice, the girl least able to contain her thoughts, hasn't uttered the name *Biba* for months.

'Yes, she's too caught up with work and Gabe to care about anything else.' And thank God for that. 'But he was still her grandfather. And he was well-known. There'll be obituaries and stuff.'

'And they'll mention me,' he says. 'Christ. Churning all the details up again.'

'Honestly, Rex, she's dropped it,' I say.

He gives me a sidelong look. 'I was thinking more of the victims' families.'

'Well, yeah, that's a given,' I say, even though I hadn't thought of them at all. The Graingers and the Wheelers had melted back into anonymity after the case. 'But, Rex, Alice lives on the internet. You don't want her finding out about this on bloody Twitter or something.'

Rex nods. 'You're right. Can we tell her in the morning, though? I just want to absorb the fact that I'm an orphan.'

With the word, the years peel away. *We're orphans, me and Rex.* It was one of the first things Biba said to me. It wasn't real – only her mother was dead – but Roger's abandonment made her feel like an orphan, which she deemed grounds to justify the lie. Now it is finally true.

16

Alice

1960s Mary Quant minidress
1980s jelly sandals

@deadgirlsdresses
#outfitoftheday #ootd #vintagefashion #sustainablestyle

I wake up after one of those midsummer nights where it feels as if the sun never set, to find a lime-green Post-it stuck to my forehead upon which Gabe has written TELL YOUR PARENTS. He made me swear on my Vivienne Westwood corset that I'd do it today. There's a similar note on the landing mirror, another on the bathroom mirror, and when I flip the toilet seat I'm instructed to tell my parents again.

I ball the Post-its in my fist and shout, 'Alright, then!' into the empty flat. 'I will.'

I wake up my phone for the day and ignore my gazillion emails and WhatsApps and Google alerts and call Mum before I have a chance to chicken out.

'Is Dad with you?' I ask, opening the fridge in the hope of a beautiful cold can of fat Coke and finding only another Post-it stuck to a carton of oat milk.

'Hmm?' She seems distracted, like I've interrupted her at work, even though it's only seven-thirty. 'Why?'

'Is he, though?'

'No, he's gone to walk Peggy before it gets too hot. Listen, I—'

The words burst out of me like shot from a cannon. 'I'm getting married!'

The quiet on the other end is so complete I have to take the phone away from my ear, check the call is still connected. I watch ten digital seconds pulse by before breaking the silence. 'Well, technically it's a civil partnership. We feel that marriage is very patriarchal and we want to show that—'

'But you've only known him, what . . . a few months?'

'When you know, you know. Dad says he loved you when he first set eyes on you.'

'You're very young,' she says feebly.

'You and Dad were younger than me when you got together. Nanna and Grandad had you when they were my age.'

The phone buzzes against my ear as a bunch more notifications land. Mum inhales noisily. 'Are you pregnant?'

'What *era* are you living in? I'm civil-parterning Gabe because I love him.' Now I'm saying it to someone other than Gabe, *civil-partnering* does seem like a bit of a mouthful. Say what you like about the patriarchy, at least *marrying* trips off the tongue.

Mum presses on. 'So you've told Gabe about Dad's conviction?'

'There's no right answer to this, is there? If I say I have, you'll have a go at me for spilling the family secret. And if I say I haven't, you'll say, *Oh Alice, how can you marry someone you can't trust with something so important?*'

I can hear her swallow. I have a long history of shouting her down but it's not often I get the better of Karen Clarke using logic, or her own twisted brand of it. I savour the moment.

'I know what I'm doing,' I say. 'Can I not just have your blessing?'

'Of course you've got my blessing.' She's gone from vague to hyper-focused, but the tired note in her voice that's been there from the moment she picked up is increasing. 'Listen, I promise I'm not trying to change the subject but I've got some bad news. Your grandfather passed away a couple of days ago.'

My legs go from under me. '*Grandad?*' I have a sudden memory of him teaching me to ride a bike, going fishing in rock pools, ferrying me to swimming lessons, drama club, ballet. Doing that stupid thing where he pretended he'd got my nose but it was really his thumb.

'Jesus, Alice, no! God, Sorry. No, not Grandad. I wouldn't have been so calm, would I? *Dad*'s dad. Roger Capel.' She snarls his name. Even after all these years she's still furious that he didn't want to know me. 'Anyway, given his high profile there might be obituaries of him and so on and they're bound to bring up the, you know, and that means . . . I'm so sorry you're in this position, Alice, but there's a very tiny chance that journalists might come crawling out of the woodwork.'

'There was someone here yesterday,' I say. 'She knew my name.'

Mum's voice sits up straight. 'What did you say to her?'

'Well, nothing. She just asked who I was and then left.'

'What time?'

'Hang on.' I find the screenshot and check the CCTV time-stamp. '10.03.'

The sound Mum makes has me picturing her blowing her cheeks out. 'He was already dead by then. It could've been a reporter.'

I almost correct Mum, tell her that if Roger's death had been in the news I'd have had an alert, but I check myself in time.

'Some of them seem to know things even before they happen. What *exactly* did she say?'

'She said, *Alice, is it, so that's what you look like*, and then, *I can't, not now*. Like she was chickening out of something.' Repeating it to Mum, recalling The Woman's words, it's clear she wasn't a dealer after my trade secrets. This was personal. Some memories change their meanings when you say them out loud. 'Does that sound like a reporter to you?'

'No. The ones I encountered were vultures,' she says. 'It's possible she was just confirming your identity. Which means there's a House of Horrors article on the way. *Fuck.*'

'It might not be that.'

'What else could it be? The timing's hardly a coincidence.'

I pull the telephone wire so tight that the tip of my finger goes purple. I focus on that, rather than the sacrilege I'm about to utter.

'I don't want to be dramatic, but I thought it might be Biba,' I say. 'I mean there *still* isn't a body so there's always a chance—'

'Trust me, love, I know how tempting it is.' Mum's using the special voice she puts on on the rare occasions when she talks about Biba: like a school psychologist, or an especially patronising teacher. It is, I think, designed to soothe herself as much as me. 'But we left no stone unturned. And – Biba hated Roger Capel. If she were still alive, she wouldn't have come back for him. She'd have come back for Rex.'

The Biba-shaped genie in my head is sucked back into her lamp; it's a relief to see her go.

'If anyone else gets in touch, you know the drill. Deny, deny, deny.' There's a triple beep on Mum's end of the line as the dishwasher cycle comes to an end.

'I remember it well. How's well,' I say. 'How'd Dad taken it?'

'It's thrown up all his other losses, you know, but he'll be OK. As he says, it doesn't really change anything.'

'Can I talk to him? When he gets back?'

'I don't know how long he'll be. He's gone for one of his yomps.'

'Oof.' Dad's epic solo walks are legendary. I used to presume it was a reaction to all those years circling a prison yard but Mum says he's always done it.

'I tell you what, we'll come up to see you later in the week, shall we? I'll cook.'

I glance at my iCal. 'We're already going to Wimbledon next week.'

'But that's just a girls' day out. I meant both of us. It'll be good for Dad. Nothing like a wedding to take your mind off a tragedy.'

'Civil partnership.'

'You know what I mean.'

She won't stop until I concede. 'So long as you promise not to try to talk me and Gabe out of it.'

'Hand on heart,' she says, but I can hear her unloading the dishwasher, and that's a two-handed job.

The call ends, but my phone keeps buzzing, the Roger Capel alerts I set up in the winter finally spitting out gold coins. I scrub through my mounting notifications so fast things blur but certain words leap out of me. *House of Horrors, The Curse of the Capels, Rex, Sheila, suicide, tragedy, Jules, Wheeler, Grainger* and the odd, less prurient reference to his work. *Groundbreaking, pioneering, working-class royalty, Swinging Sixties, boomer, Carnaby Street.*

I put my own name into a search engine along with Roger Capel's. There are no results. I am one quarter this man and there is nothing to link us. If The Woman was a journalist she must have found out through some source I don't know about. How do they do it? *How?*

I make a pint of orange squash and read as many Roger Capel puff pieces as I can stomach. The events of 1997 are mentioned, of course, but not dwelt upon. I expect it'll take a while before the long reads come in. Sick and angry, I text the man who more than filled the space Capel left blank.

Hiya, Grandad. You and Nanna OK in the heat?

I realise as I hit send that my mother is probably on the phone to her mother right now, breaking the awful news. Grandad is typing. He's more addicted to his smartphone than any teenager I know.

The trick is to stay indoors between 10 and 2.

Eminently sensible, I write back.

I'm in a Wetherspoons that used to be a hat factory. Did you know the carpet in every Wetherspoons is different? Custom designs depending on local history or what the building used to be.

He sends me a picture of his feet in Skechers and an extremely busy carpet that could be anything. I send him a thumbs-up.

Your mother says wedding bells are in the air. Your bloke hasn't got you in trouble, has he?

No, I write back. *We're not in trouble.*

In the shower I turn my face to the ceiling, where black dahlias of mould bloom. I imagine deadly spores are floating invisibly, lacing the air with slow-acting poison, and keep my shower as short as possible. I dress for work and I'm already halfway down the dark staircase when a hammering on the door makes me jump. The tread gives way. You've got to hand it to this house, it really wants to kill someone. 'Not today,' I tell it.

The delivery woman's face has gone the same tomato red as her Royal Mail polo shirt.

'Signed for,' she says, swaying a little.

'Shit,' I blurt, 'are you OK?'

'I've felt better,' she says.

'Here.' I offer her the water that's in my bag. 'It's clean. I can go up and refill it.'

She looks as if she might cry. 'That is so nice of you. I don't suppose I could get thirty seconds in the shade while I drink it?'

'Sure.'

I usher her into the gloomy entrance hall, watching her eyes adjust to the dark. There's not much to see, just a row of hooks groaning with winter coats and hoodies and a bunch of shoes on the floor. The entryway mirror is too thick with dust to wink even in this blazing sunlight. 'D'you not get spooked out living here?' she asks.

I shrug, wipe a porthole in the glass. 'You get used to it.'

She returns my water bottle. 'Thank you. Oh! Almost forgot your post. Can you sign?'

She hands me a thin envelope and her digital device. I scratch my name with the stylus and close the door, hoping she doesn't have long left on her round. I go back upstairs to rinse and refill my bottle and read the letter in the light. It's one page long, on stiff cream paper. The letterhead tells me it's from a firm of solicitors called Crawford Southern.

Dear Ms Clarke,

    I write to inform you that you are a beneficiary of the late Roger Capel's will. The executors are currently working through probate but they have instructed me to let you know. The exact amount is to be determined while the liabilities are offset against assets. We shall be in touch in due course.

    Yours sincerely,

    Maya Gopal

    Partner, Crawford Southern

What the shit? I call the number at the bottom of the page and get straight through to Maya Gopal. I introduce myself, then say, 'Are you sure you got this right?'

I repeat my details, and give her my date of birth and confirm my address, as well as my parents' house in Suffolk and the last two flats I lived in.

'It's definitely you, Miss Clarke. I'm sorry for your loss. Were you very close?'

17

Alice

Black Paisley Droopy & Browns floor-length dress with thigh split
Bottle-green Afghan coat embroidered with purple butterfly motif
Tan knee-high boots with suede tassels

@deadgirlsdresses
#outfitoftheday #ootd #vintagefashion #sustainablestyle

Maybe a month after I'd opened the shop, when Dad had run his mouth off, I had taken things as far as I could with searching, i.e. a court document, some newspaper reports and a liar on YouTube. The not knowing was driving me insane and so, one blustery January morning, I found myself in Keats Grove on the edge of Hampstead Heath. The most recent photo I had of Roger Capel was a couple of years out of date. He was bald and thick-set, with the even white teeth of someone with serious money. I kept his face in mind as I buzzed the gate of a mansion that looked like it had been carved from a block of vanilla ice cream. No one answered. Anticlimax was followed by shock as I turned to leave and all but ran into my quarry, carrying a copy of *The Times* and a takeout coffee the size of a small bucket. We both yelped.

'Roger Capel?' I said, nervously. 'I'm—'

'Jesus Christ, love, I think I can work out who you are.' His nose looked like one of those purple potatoes you get in Waitrose, that Mum used to put in salads when we were hosting Sophie's parents for lunch in the garden in pre-Fallout times. 'What do you want?'

'To talk to you,' I said.

His surprise had already mellowed to resignation. 'I'm surprised it's taken you so long.' He pointed a key at the gates and they slid slowly apart.

I followed him through glossy wine-red double front doors into a marble-floored entrance hall and from there to a kitchen. Everything was pale and shiny like in a five-star spa hotel. It wasn't just the fittings that were undomestic, it was the dimensions. The place was *vast*. Rooms and ceilings all seemed twice as wide and high as they needed to be. I'd always assumed that rich people liked big houses because they were flexing. I had never understood the effect space could have in its own right. Something inside me wanted, but did not dare, to expand to fill it. No wonder my dad had been so sad to lose the big house in Queenswood Lane.

'What do you do for a living that means you're at a loose end on a Thursday morning?' he asked, ushering me towards the breakfast bar.

'I run a vintage clothes shop.' I hopped on to a high stool covered in cowhide.

'That explains the outfit.' His laughter seemed affectionate at the time, although maybe I was just desperate to think that. 'Can I get you anything?'

'Um, just a glass of water would be great.'

'Still or sparkling?'

'Sparkling would be lovely if you've got it.'

It came from a tap by a double sink. He set it before me then folded his arms. 'Fire away.'

I went in too hard. What I should have said was, *I want to get to know you*, or, *I'm interested in your work*, or, *I want to build bridges*. Instead I just went, 'I want to know about the night of the murder.'

He did a double-take. 'I haven't spoken publicly about that, ever.'

'I'm hardly the public. I'm your granddaughter.' He winced at the reminder and I recognised with dismay the first stirrings of The Surge. 'I'll just come out with it. I think Biba was there on the

81

night of the murders and I think she might have done it and my dad took the rap. The official version is that she was here with you, but I don't buy it.'

Roger Capel shook his head. I was losing him. 'Sheila's bloody kids . . .'

'Your kids too.' I told The Surge to subside. It didn't quite manage that, but it did stop moving. It hovered obediently behind my breastbone, unsure what to do with this unprecedented plateau. 'They're your kids too,' I repeated, trying to channel Mum: calm, controlled. 'Don't you miss them?'

Roger looked at his lap. My water fizzed angrily in its glass.

'I just don't get how you could cut yourself off like that,' I said. 'My parents spent money they didn't have trying to find Biba before getting the Presumption of Death certificate. You never even reported her missing. But I'm offering you the chance to make it good. Tell me what happened that night. Do this one thing for them.'

'For them?' He raised his eyebrows.

'OK, for me. As your granddaughter. Give me something.'

I saw him wrestling with something internal. I didn't know him well enough to name it. After what seemed like a whole minute, he rolled his eyes. He *rolled his fucking eyes*. The Surge wanted out. If we'd been in a horror film, that was the point at which my telekinesis would've kicked in and objects would've started flying across the room.

'Look, it is what it is, love. I'm knocking on a bit. I'd quite like to see out my days without all that muck being raked up again.'

Muck. That was my dad he was talking about. His *son*. I'd never felt The Surge this strongly without acting on it before. Stay where you are, I willed it.

Roger sighed. 'My family have suffered enough.'

The obvious comeback was *Which family?* but I kept it together. I'd come here to find out more about Biba and The Night Of, and although the thrill of mastering The Surge was giddy, I didn't want to tempt it.

'Just tell me and I'll go. Was Biba here that night, or was she at the Queenswood Lane place? I'm not going tell anyone; it's not like I *want* to see you done for perjury. I just need to know for my own sanity.'

Roger's darkening face told me there was a gap between my intention and his interpretation. 'Now we see your true colours,' he said, looking almost satisfied. 'You must have come here with a figure in mind. How much do you want?'

Of course. He thought I'd come to grab a slice of the Capel cake. It was so far from what I wanted that begging for money hadn't occurred to me. I would've laughed if I hadn't worried that The Surge would escape through the gap.

I punched my heart. 'I grew up without needing a penny from you and I'm not going to start asking now.'

'Impressive,' he said. 'Did you rehearse this? I know a little actress when I see one.'

I looked at this sneering, smug, vulgar old man and felt sick at the thought of his blood in my veins. I understood as it broke free that The Surge hadn't been plateauing but crouching, gathering strength. 'Actually, I do have a suggestion,' I said, rising from my seat, letting it go with an almost orgasmic relief as I threw ice-cold, sparkling water in my grandfather's face. 'Why don't you roll up your money and shove it up your fat old arse?'

18

Alice

1930s day dress, rose-pink poplin
1990s platform sandals from Dolcis

@deadgirlsdresses
#outfitoftheday #ootd #vintagefashion #sustainablestyle

Sundays are the busiest days in Camden Passage. The tourists roll in, and the niche stalls in Pierrepoint Arcade open up. This funny little souk must be the last undeveloped piece of real estate in a mile-wide radius. Traders lay out rare books like toppled dominoes, arrange antique maps in modern frames. On days like today, it's easy to imagine the Passage in its sixties heyday, before the chain shops began their pincer movement on the indies. Half-close your eyes and you can see Sheila Capel shopping here, picking up a dress in a boutique, choosing a picture for the wall of The House.

I'm always glad of the increased takings but never more so than today. With my focus on enticing customers over my threshold, there won't be time to think about the letter from Roger Capel's solicitors. I dare to hope that some parcelled-off corner of my mind is quietly processing it, and that by the end of the day I'll know how to feel.

Soldier Steve borrows one of my dressmakers' dummies to display a Beefeater uniform he's somehow acquired. 'Is that even legal?' I ask him, as I expand the dummy's chest as wide as it'll go. 'Isn't it, like, property of the Crown or something?'

'Off with your head,' he replies with a grin.

Hollie is sweeping dog mess off the front step. 'Third fucking time this fucking week,' she says. 'What kind of cunt lets their dog shit on a fucking doorstep?' Behind her, a baby mannequin in a dress embroidered with lambs rides an oatmeal-coloured felt rocking horse.

'Your language is a bit off-brand for your wares, you know.'

'You should hear how my customers talk to their kids.' Hollie wipes her brow, then looks at the sky. 'I think we might have passed the sweet spot between *nice and sunny let's go to the shops* and *too hot let's stay in.*'

'Maybe we'll get *more* footfall,' I say. 'The plus side of being in a shadowy alleyway?'

She doesn't sound convinced. 'I'm gonna put a sign in my window saying I've got air-con. People will stay longer and browse if they're comfortable. It might even entice them in.'

'I'm jealous,' I say. 'Gabe doesn't approve of air-conditioning.'

She narrows her eyes. 'Gabe isn't the one who has to work in a sweatbox all day.'

I'm grateful when my shop phone rings and I don't have to get into defending Gabe's principles. It's bad enough that my mum's always picking at him without it ruining things at work, too. I pick up the seashell receiver and trill, 'Dead Girls' Dresses!'

'Alice.' She makes it statement, not a question. I recognise the voice instantly. I can picture her clothes down to the individual crystals on her sunglasses, even if her features are misty, even if I can't quite conjure her smell.

'Is that you?' I ask, not sure what I mean.

'I need to talk to you,' The Woman says.

'Who *are* you?' I ask, but voices in the shop drown out her reply.

'Incoming!' says the bundle of sequins with two wiry legs poking out underneath it.

'Special delivery from Big Nonna!' says the mound of taffeta with thick, hairy legs. 'Where d'you want it, Gabe?'

'Stock room, mate,' says Gabe in his special Man of the People voice. 'Door at the back, behind the stuffed swan.'

'Hang on,' I say to the caller, but she's gone.

Erin Kelly

If it hadn't been for the boys' voices, I'm sure she would've told me her name. I doodle my thoughts on a pad. Journalist? Vintage fanatic? *Stalker?* If *Travesties* has taught me anything, it's that the world is full of *them*. Jesus! A new, horrible thought occurs. What if it's one of the victims' families, out for revenge? I scribble everything out, drop the paper in the bin and join the boys in the stock room.

'What do you reckon?' asks Stef. From the clothes mountain I can see a handful of labels that make my heart sing, shiny fabric in Quality Street colours: amber, magenta, mint-green, electric blue. There are puffed shoulders, low necklines, short skirts, sequins and lace in sizes that are all too rare.

'Thank you.' I reach up to hug Stef, astonished as ever by the size of him. He shrinks, as much as a six-foot-five lump of muscle can. I don't think he's used to platonic friendships with women and it's taken him a while to learn that I'm off limits.

I drop to my knees. Tulle and satin billow around me. I let my hands explore a Pierre Cardin cocktail dress in mint-green, a bolero stitched with bronze embroidery, a headband with beaded fringing. 'These are incredible. How can I thank her?'

'Honestly, she's just happy they're not getting binned,' says Stef.

'I'd love to go and say hello, take her some flowers.'

'She'd love that. I'll set it up.' He wipes his sweaty forehead, then assumes his resting state, which is rapid successive left swipes on Tinder, before remembering something and raising his head from the screen. 'Did anything come of that complaint?'

Gabe, who's been drinking from the tap, takes his head out of the sink, chin dripping. 'He rang the desk but as he's not a client they didn't care.'

'What complaint?' I ask.

Gabe rolls his eyes. 'Some prick in a suit had a go at me in Aldgate. Driving into his underground car park in his gas-guzzler, nearly knocked me off my bike and when I called him out on it he said he'd make sure his firm didn't use us ever again, made a note that he was gonna ring the company.'

I get hot, defensive, ready to push the prick in a suit off the top of his skyscraper. The Surge is always happy to step in on behalf of the people I love. 'Fuckers! Don't they know you're a real person? That you've probably got a better degree than them?'

Gabe's mood switchblades. 'So it'd be OK if I was just unqualified? You think my degree gives me more humanity than someone who's not educated?'

Gabe's militancy, so attractive when I'm not its target, is terrifying when it turns on me. I feel small and stupid. Even The Surge slinks back into its cave.

'Or an immigrant?' chips in Stef. They are a unit, two abreast, ganging up on me. I was only trying to sympathise.

'I didn't mean . . .'

Gabe picks up on the hiccup in my voice. 'Nah, sorry. I'm taking it out on you. I think I've probably got low blood sugar.'

I give him one of the protein bars I've decided to keep in the stock room for exactly this eventuality.

'Sorry,' he says, back to himself again as soon as he's eaten.

The boys stay behind, help me divide Big Nonna's clothes by size and colour. I'll ask Hollie to model these for the website. It's early evening when we finish, and hotter than ever.

'Want a lift home?' asks Stef, nodding at his trailer.

I consider for a moment, anticipate the breeze in my hair. I mean, how different can this be from taking a rickshaw home from a club? A fuckton more terrifying, I quickly find out. I fear for my life as the restaurants of Upper Street rush by in a blur.

'Bro, I found something new for the next potato banquet,' Stef shouts over the rush-hour traffic.

'I'm listening,' yells Gabe. The potato banquet is an occasional but significant event where the boys try to consume as many different potato-based foods as they can fit on a plate. Rosti, gnocchi, French fries, wedges, Alphabites: nothing is off limits except for, for some reason, boiled potatoes.

'*Pierogi*,' Stef replies. 'It's a Polish dumpling. They do them at the Polski Sklep near me.'

I scream as a motorbike slices between the boys, its engine rattling, blasting warm fumes in my face.

'We must add it to the *smorgasbord*!' says Gabe, unfazed by the near-miss.

'That's what I'm *sayin'*.'

I envy the boys their traditions, their in-jokes, their easy back-and-forth. Another argument against a trad white wedding is that Gabe would want Stef to be best man and I'd have to come up with a fucking bridesmaid. It's not only budget and the will to break with tradition that makes me want a low-key ceremony, it's the exposure of the loneliness. For the first time in ages I miss Sophie. I could easily fill a marquee with dozens of guests; it's having *one* that is the problem. Everyone I know would be surprised – suspicious, even – to be invited to a small wedding.

As we cross Holloway Road, Stef branches off to where he lives, still with his parents, in Southgate (every soldier makes their sacrifice for the cause; Stef still living at home, to free up time and money, is his). Gabe bends to help me out of the trailer and the boys part with a complicated series of fist-bumps and back-slaps, like two little girls playing a clapping game.

'Do you think the heat will affect the asbestos?' I ask, as I turn the key. 'Like, melt it? Release the spores, or whatever the dangerous stuff is?'

'Isn't the *point* of asbestos that it's heatproof?' he replies.

'Unhelpful.' This is exactly the sort of thing Dad would know – it's the kind of thing he has to deal with at work – but I've told my parents the lower rooms are off limits owing to water damage. If they find out what's *really* in these walls, they'll probably kidnap me and take me back to Suffolk.

We have a lazy evening, beer and Deliveroo, rickety French windows thrown wide to get a breeze from the living room at the front of the house to the bedroom at the back. Gabe's not sulking, exactly, but detached. Not instigating conversation and he's barely touched me.

'What's on your mind?' I ask, when we're getting ready for bed.

'The reason it took you so long to tell your parents. I keep thinking about what you said earlier. It's not because I'm "only" a cycle courier, is it? Because I had enough shit off my dad.'

I'm mortified. I *know* Gabe's parents don't approve of his life choices, I *know* that hurts him. I can't believe I've been so insensitive. 'No! Oh, God, no. *Gabe.* I couldn't be more proud of you. It's why I love you.'

'Days like today, even I'm like, what am I *doing* with my life? Getting honked at and abused all day long.'

An idea arrives fully formed, so obvious I can't believe I haven't thought of it before. 'What if you come and work with me?'

He pouts. 'I'll never carry off a negligee with my hips.'

'I'm serious. I'm hiring out as many dresses as I'm selling. The post office are constantly on strike. Most of my deliveries are in London. I could offer same-day delivery service. I'd rather my girls were safe with you than have Evri yeeting them over a garden wall. You could set your hours, have more time for GR.'

'Seize the means of production,' he ponders.

'We'd be together pretty much the whole time.'

I mean it as an incentive; only when the words are out do I realise they might put him off. But he hooks an arm around my waist and says, 'Good. It's best when it's just the two of us.'

19

You had hoped that Karen and Rex would have turned their beams on each other by now, but if anything she's even more intense than him. She seems to want to be you and have you. It's flattering, but it's also like having two Rexes trotting around the house after you. Where are you going? Can I come with you? What are we doing today? Acting is your only escape so thank God for the graduate show.

The theatre is a squat concrete block near Lisson Grove. Pre-show, Karen and Rex hover like nervous parents. But the dependable spotlight melts them away. You give the performance of your life and the agent you wanted signs you on the spot. The Feeling turns on its heel and runs away into the night.

Backstage, you bump into someone you recognise but can't place. Levi's-advert handsome, army trousers and a Prodigy T-shirt. You place your finger in the centre of the 'o' and push gently.

'I was at your twenty-first,' he says. 'My name's Guy.'

Of course! Friend of a friend of a friend. A small-time dealer. Owns a mobile phone. You look him up and down. A bag of pills bulges from a pocket halfway down his thigh. What better way to prolong the elation?

'Want to come back to ours?' you ask.

Rex drives Karen's little yellow car back to Highgate. You and Guy sit in the back, giggling, with your hands down each other's trousers. In the Velvet Room, Guy sprinkles leaves and rolls paper and chops powder into lines with unexpected grace. Rex, at his most morose, throws Guy's generosity back in his face. Karen, radiating acid-green jealousy, has worked out you're going *somewhere she can't come. When at last they go to bed – alas, not together – there is no one to tell you to stop.*

Down your neck, up your nose, into your lungs.

The night expands and contracts.

A pounding heat transfers itself from his body to yours and back again.

You regain consciousness at the Whittington hospital twelve hours later, sticky between the legs and with an IV in your arm.

Oops.

It's really not the big deal Rex and Karen are making it out to be. Nobody died! Still, to calm Rex down – if his stress levels climb any higher he'll end up in A&E himself – you promise not to see Guy again. You go to bed with a heavy heart. Rex is going to be harder to shake off than ever now. He'll monitor you day and night, force you to keep your word.

Overnight, a miracle.

The next morning, the air on the landing between Rex's room and yours smells of fresh sex, and from that moment no one is looking at you. You can see into their bubble but they can't see beyond it. More than once, while they're huffing away in Rex's bedroom, you have Guy in yours.

They haven't got a clue.

By July, you've fallen into a rhythm of two or three castings a week. There are so many girls fresh out of drama school, so much competition. No work yet, but each audition is an education and the prep gets you out of your head, keeps The Feeling at arm's length. You've got call-backs for half a dozen roles and casting directors are already requesting you by name.

Occasionally Rachael will be in the corridor, mouthing the same lines as you. It beggars belief that she is being considered for serious roles. She tells you that model agents are beating a path to her door. You encourage her to go for it. One less pretty girl on the circuit.

One empty day, you go downstairs at one o'clock. Karen and Rex are already out. You must have just missed them. The kettle is warm to the touch. You refill it. You cobble together a cigarette from two ends in the ashtray and take your coffee to the back of the house. The garden through the windows is lush as a rainforest. On the bureau in the Velvet Room are a few sheets of A4 covered with Rex's writing.

Dear Dad,

I've been thinking about the house. What I'd really like is to make all the repairs and redecorate and then let out the rooms, probably to actors and artists who need digs in London. It sounds like I'm asking for a handout but if you think about it you would really be giving me independence.

Oh, Rex. This must be the hundredth such letter you've come across. He's been writing them since your mother died. Teenage Rex, puny in his school uniform, would take himself off to Highgate library, researching the idea of inheritance and property and trusts and estates. He'd write screeds to your father imploring him to sign the house over to the two of you. He never sends the letters. It's like a psychological thing that he does for comfort. Your brother, who never loses his temper, sets his howl down on paper, dusts himself off, and gets on with the washing up.

Which is just as well. You know your father. The more Rex begs, the more he'll dig his heels in. It's better to stay where you are and say nothing. It's almost as though your father hates to be reminded of your existence.

You pick the letter up, only to find another beneath it. The words slope down and to the right. You picture Rex with a ball-point in one hand and a drink in the other.

Roger – you don't deserve to be called Dad even though you like getting women pregnant – you selfish cunt, you cruel greedy bastard. When are you going to do the decent thing? This house is ours. It was Mum's before it was yours. Don't you have enough already?

You roll all the pages into a scroll and touch the tip of your cigarette to the paper until it smoulders, then throw the burning pages in the grate, watching, smoking, until only blackened scraps remain.

Rex will keep writing these letters and you'll keep destroying them. You shudder to think what would happen if your father ever laid eyes on one.

20

Karen

'*Qualcosa da bere, signora?*'

I order a carafe of house white and wonder when waiters stopped calling me *signorina*. I crack another breadstick in half and shove it in my face. I'm waiting for my mother at the Italian restaurant just off Bloomsbury Square where we have lunch once every six weeks or so. A mile west is Biba's and my *alma mater*, Queen Charlotte's College. Closer by is my mother's present seat of education, Birkbeck. Linda Clarke left school in 1973 with four CSEs and spent her life looking after me and my dad until, around the day he took early retirement, they both realised that the longevity of their marriage was largely due to them spending ten hours a day apart, and Mum announced she was going to sit her English literature GCSE at evening school. More GCSEs and a handful of A-levels followed and now there's no stopping her. She's got her favourite desk at the British Library and everything. She's such an eager beaver, a keen bean, she's spent this morning there. I was incredibly studious before I met the Capels and even *I* never went to a library on a Sunday.

'*Prego.*'

The waiter half-fills my glass. The wine tastes like vinegar but has the desired effect of slowing down my thoughts. Rex has barely spoken since he got the news about Roger. I was reluctant to leave him this morning but he was insistent on needing a bit of alone time. He even suggested I stay in London, given that Alice and I have tickets for Wimbledon on Tuesday, but I can't let him stew for that long. I can't help picturing him . . . I mean I *know* he wouldn't, not with his history, he wouldn't do that to Alice, but

94

I'd rather shuttle back and forth to Woodbridge than take the chance.

I text him a warning him to keep his cap on and his head down when he takes Peggy out. It shows as undelivered.

I Google his name for the tenth time today. Nothing new, thank Christ. If the Sunday tabloids were going to do a Curse of the Capels piece it would've run today. Glass in hand, I do my daily sweep of Alice's socials. On DeadGirlsDresses there's a story showing wilting traders braving the sun. Nothing on her private Instagram since yesterday. She logged on to WhatsApp at around eight this morning. I'm not sure when I made it part of my routine to search Gabe's name after checking up on Alice. It wasn't a conscious decision, but it's a habit. He deliberately keeps his online presence light, but if he does raise his head above the parapet I want to know about it.

Ten minutes later, Mum opens the restaurant door with her hip, her arms performatively full of ring binders.

'*Tua sorella aspetta*,' says the waiter, flourishing her towards my table. I tell him in Italian that his flattery is wasted on Mum as I air-kiss her across the table.

'I've had one of those mornings where you look up and you're surprised to be in present-day London!' she says, setting her books down on the spare seat.

'Are you still doing, what was it, women in Shakespeare?'

She tuts. 'That was last term. This term it's Jewish coming of age in the Second World War.'

Sometimes I find it hard to believe this is the same Mum who raised me. Until ten years ago she got all of her culture from whatever author was plugging a book on *Loose Women*.

'Is Alice not joining us?'

'Sundays are her busiest day. She doesn't finish till late.'

Mum shakes her head. 'All that education just to be a shop girl.'

'Mum, she's not exactly stacking shelves. She's incredibly skilled; she's like a museum curator.' A thorn of guilt pricks me as

I hear myself. I'm quicker to show pride in Alice when defending her to my mother than I am to her when she's in the same room as me.

I tell Mum about my new foray into fiction.

'I love a bit of Scandi noir,' she says. 'I actually only read thrillers in translation.'

'How come?' I ask as the waiter slides plates on to the table.

'More intellectual,' she says, then thanks the waiter in Spanish. *There's* the woman who raised me. My heart swells with complicated love.

'So, this wedding.' She twirls her fork in her linguini carbonara, sending flecks of claggy yellow sauce everywhere.

'Not allowed to call it a wedding,' I correct her. 'Civil partnership, to overthrow the patriarchy.'

I aim for flippant but fall short. I've fooled my mum a lot over the years, but she can still see through me better than anyone else.

'You think she's making a mistake.'

My throat tightens without warning. I can only nod.

'I know it's hard.' Mum puts her hand over mine and squeezes. As though my hand has a direct connection to my tear ducts, my eyes dispense two fat drops. 'But look at me and your dad and Rex. You'd never have thought we'd come to be so fond of him.'

The first time my parents had met Rex they'd loved him. So well-spoken! Such lovely manners, and he was obviously madly in love with me. The connection was instant – which meant his arrest hurt them in their own right. While he was in prison they could pretend he didn't exist. I don't think they really believed I'd have him back. It was seeing him with Alice that had finally begun the thaw. That, and the fact that he'd project-managed their whole extension for free.

'I guess,' I say weakly, but of course it's completely different. Rex made one bad decision in the heat of a horrific moment. Not to lessen the impact of what he did, but we're talking about sixty seconds of madness bracketed on either side by twenty-odd years of goodness. Gabe, on the other hand, is a consistently egregious bastard who's too clever to give himself away like that.

'And she's going to do what she wants whether you like it or not. She gets that from her mother.'

'Yes,' I say weakly. She speaks more truth than she knows. I screw up my face, determined not to have a nervous breakdown over my aubergine parmigiana. Mum notices and puts a sympathetic hand on the tiller of the conversation.

'So, the big day. What's the dress code? You know where you are with a church but city weddings have always thrown me. Is it a nice dress and a fascinator? She doesn't expect us all to turn up looking like something out of *Bridgerton*, does she?'

I laugh. 'Wear what you want. I think it's fair to say all eyes will be on Alice. Have you booked a hotel room?'

'Travelodge, like you said. How many guests are they having?'

'Immediate family only, so from our side it's me, Rex, you, Dad. Gabe's one of five, so . . .'

'*Five*,' she says in wonderment. 'How anyone goes through childbirth more than once is beyond me – oh, love. I didn't think.'

'It's OK.' I pick up my napkin. I needed to blow my nose anyway.

After we've eaten I walk Mum to Euston, through private garden squares shaded by flaking plane trees. 'I'd love a flat in one of these buildings,' she says, gesturing to a creamy Regency block. 'Little pied-à-terre. Start my own Bloomsbury set with my Birkbeck crowd. Literary salons. You could borrow it, have your publishing friends over.'

'That's the dream,' I say flatly. I don't have any publishing friends. I don't have *any* real friends. I wear my secrets like a bloodstained dress. I radiate something that tells people not to come too close. I'm happy that Mum's found her people but it's depressing that her life has expanded while mine, small to begin with, can only shrink. I have always lived in tiny units: me, Mum and Dad. Me and three housemates. Me, Biba and Rex. Me and Alice; me, Alice and Rex, and now me and Rex again.

Lack of intimacy outside my family is the price I pay for safety. It is worth it.

When reach the ticket barrier, my shoulders loosen in anticipatory relief.

'I suppose the next time I see you will be at the wedding!' says Mum.

'Not a wedding,' I correct her.

'Not a wedding.' She nods to herself, internalising the concept. 'How long will it take you to get to Liverpool Street?'

'About fifteen minutes,' I tell her.

Which would be true, if that were where I was going.

21

Karen

I never asked for a key to Alice's flat. I think that's important. She gave it to me of her own volition, long before Gabe moved in, which means that in a way she has given me her tacit permission to enter whenever I want. My current chapter of *Liebesbomb* has a case study of a woman whose husband was so obsessed with order that he would beat her for not having the jars facing the right way. A wave of Coca-Cola cans arranged just so, with the stripe forming a continuous, contiguous ribbon. Alice's *shop* may be ordered but that's because it has to be. Her domestic standards are much lower. If the flat is tidy beyond recognition, it will be a sign that he has imposed his way of doing things on to her. It's a flag. I'm looking for the things that she isn't ready to tell me. Wouldn't any mother do the same?

Avalon Road always looks like half a street to me; those uniform terraces seem to demand an identical facing row, not bushes full of litter and graffitied fences. Today, however, I appreciate the train line: no opposite neighbours means no curtain-twitchers to watch as I let myself in. The front door closes behind me with a click so soft I have to double-check it's caught. I've got a thing about doors. The door to the house in Queenswood Lane used to bounce where the wood had swelled and the frame didn't fit any more. Anyone could have come in, and anyone did. Rex said he would fix it. If he had, then The Night Of would have gone very differently.

The air is thick and soupy with a sickening fungal smell. The torch on my phone finds splinters sticking out of stairs. God, I hate her living in this place. As I reach the top floor my smart-watch flashes a warning about my heart rate and I pause before entering her flat, trying to regulate my breath and the part of my mind that's feeding me one worst-case scenario after another. As I crest the top landing, light floods in from all sides, giving me the disorientating feeling of leaving a cinema in the middle of the day.

After the excesses of my imagination the flat is almost an anti-climax. It's quite tidy but not anally so. Gabe has stacked his books in front of Alice's *Vogues* and Brontë novels and her collection of *Alice In Wonderland*s and *Through The Looking Glass*es (she was still getting them as birthday presents well into her teens). I bend to the side, read the spines. There's a row of classic left-wing texts, all in the blue covers of second-hand Pelican books, the pretentious goon, plus current titles on climate activism, anti-fascism, allyship. I basically agree with most of the books' messages but that doesn't stop me wanting to sweep them to the floor. On top of the *Vogues* lies a handful of orange flyers advertising a Global Rising meeting in Holborn tomorrow night. I put one in my pocket. A magnetic letter 'g', like the ones I taught Alice to spell with, holds a photo-booth strip to the fridge. They're snogging, and the underside of Gabe's tongue is a mottled map of veins. The bed is loosely made – I itch to straighten the duvet but even I have limits – and I'm strangely heartened to see a pair of Alice's dirty knickers, gusset-side-up, on the rug. A controlling man would not let his woman get away with that. Women have been beaten for less. Closer examination tells me that at least she's not pregnant. That's the oldest trap of them all.

I let myself out of the flat, confident that no one has seen me. As I approach the barrier at Drayton Park station, something else compels me to turn around, retrace my steps along Avalon Road and let myself back in. I put Alice's knickers into the laundry basket, just in case Gabe hasn't seen them yet. You can't be too careful.

22

Alice

*Ankle-length Edwardian mourning dress with high neck and
   satin sash*

@deadgirlsdresses
#outfitoftheday #ootd #vintagefashion #sustainablestyle

Mondays are my weekends. I have the house to myself and I don't
do anything, not even respond to online orders. It's three o'clock
and so far today I've done nothing but read, re-read, fold and
unfold the letter from Maya at Crawford Southern.

Of course the only thing I really wanted from Roger Capel –
the truth about The Night Of – he has taken to his grave. Still, a
girl can dream. A couple of grand, maybe? Ten? A *hundred*? I
could pay off my credit card and we'd still have enough for a
deposit on a little flat. Or it could just be a framed photo of my
dad when he was a baby. And do you know what? I would love
that.

According to the internet, the executor of a will is usually the
spouse. I dress respectfully in black, check my reflection in the
mirror at the top of the stairs and judge it just the right side of
cosplay. I pick up an orchid in a Tesco Extra en route to the
Hampstead house. The clematis that was bare twine on my last
visit is in full bloom: bees flit from one flower to the next, almost
obscuring the sound of the buzzer.

'Hello, is that Mrs Capel?' I ask, when it's finally answered.

'Can you stand in front of the lens?' asks a fuzzy voice. I step to
the right.

'My name's Alice Clarke.'

'God,' she says, and then, '*God*. We really should do this through Crawford Southern.'

'I'm here now,' I say.

It takes a long time for the gates to slide open. Jules Capel, the second model Roger married, the one who outlived him, is slumped against an ivory pillar as though it's the only thing holding her up. She wears taupe linen culottes and a box-fresh white T-shirt and her hair is pulled back into a ponytail. Even in grief she looks like a glossy magazine advert. She is ageing the way women want to, the way skincare ads promise we all can, except the only way to look like Jules does aged sixty is to have looked like she did when she was twenty. In the neutral interior of her house, in her colourless clothes, she almost disappears.

'I brought you this.' I hand her the Tesco orchid. 'To say sorry for your loss.'

She sets it on the breakfast bar, next to a bunch of lilies that must have cost a hundred quid. Her wedding ring is loose. 'That was nice of you. I suppose you're here about the will?'

I'm grateful to her for dispensing with the small-talk. 'Yeah. I don't get it. We only met once and he threw me out.'

She aims for a smile but doesn't quite make it. 'Yes, he said. He liked your spark. That's why he included you.'

'Really?'

'When you have money, everyone seems to want some. And you refused to take a penny.'

I'm glad Roger saw integrity through The Surge, but it's bitter-sweet. He could've been someone I connected with. Grief for something I've never had is familiar to me. 'So – am I OK to ask what it is?'

'The solicitors' letter would have said that it's going to take a while for the assets to be weighed up. And I'm supposed to go through them, so . . .' She trails off, looks me up and down, as if only now taking in my clothes. 'I'm right in thinking you run a vintage clothes shop, aren't I?' I nod. I'm surprised to find how much it matters that he told her this. 'It's not as if anyone's going to contest *this*. Come with me.'

She leads me into a huge walk-in double garage that's bigger than my flat. It's lined with storage units. From the back of one, she retrieves what look at first glance like a dozen plastic children's mattresses.

'I had two boys and a girl,' she says, and I wonder what that has to do with anything. 'The boys' wives aren't interested, they like shiny new things, and Xanthe, bless her, got her father's build. But I think these would find a happy home with you.'

A close look reveals that these are not mattresses at all but vacuum-packed clothes: tens, dozens, hundreds of garments compressed into a fraction of the space they would normally take up. My heart starts to pound against my breast.

'Biba had a thing for clothes, and an eye. And her mother before that. Some of this stuff was probably Sheila's, come to think of it.'

The thought of holding one of my grandmother's dresses makes me feel weak with longing.

'Don't get too excited,' warns Jules. 'Biba didn't look after her clothes. But there might be *something* in there you can use.'

This is better than any money. This is a gift from a man who I thought didn't know or care but who had, it turns out, *seen* me. In the few moments we spent together, he understood what I wanted. A connection to my family history, through the thing that I love so much I made it my living.

I order an Uber people-carrier to take it all back to the shop and tell Jules I'll be out of her hair in ten minutes. In the excitement, I have almost forgotten why I came here in the first place. This could well be the last time we see each other – she's passed my inheritance on and she doesn't seem keen to envelop me in the bosom of the family, so I decide to ask the question that her husband never answered.

'There's no nice way to say this so I'm just going to come out with it. Was Biba *really* here on the night my dad is supposed to have murdered two people, or was she actually at the place in Queenswood Lane? I know Roger said she was here, but could he have lied?'

Jules rubs her arms as though she's cold, even though there's sweat on her upper lip. 'I was in the country with the children.'

'But you must have spoken about it?'

'No.'

Either Jules is lying or Roger deliberately kept her ignorant of the truth. Whatever it is, she's not giving me an inch. 'Why don't we put these in the street?' As she lugs the bags across the floor and then the gravel her triceps stand out. She's stronger than me, two bags in each hand. I wonder what her regime is. Hot yoga? Reformer Pilates? I wait until the last one's in place before I ask another question.

'It's not like he can get into trouble for it *now*, is it?'

I've crossed a line. 'For Christ's sake, Alice, I haven't even *buried* him yet.'

'I'm sorry.' I glance down at my phone. The little toy car is on Heath Street, two minutes away. 'Can I just ask you one last thing?'

She massages her forehead. It crumples like a piece of paper that's been used to wrap things a hundred times. 'Go on.'

'Do you think Biba was capable of murder? Given the choice between Rex killing someone and Biba killing someone, who would you say had done it?'

Her face has been hollowing throughout our conversation, like a time-lapse of someone losing weight. Now her cheeks looks as though they might implode. 'If you need to be in touch again I think we should do it you should do it through the solicitors. Ah, look, there's your car.'

The Uber driver kisses goodbye to five stars by leaving the engine running while we heave the bags into the boot. Leather, satin, lace, straps and chains, prints and pleats. A Westwood orb glints on a button. A Bus Stop label peeps over a square neckline. I want to be alone with these clothes the way I want to be in bed with Gabe.

As the last bag goes in, Jules mumbles something in a voice so low I have to ask her to repeat herself.

'I said, she wasn't cunning. Biba, I mean. She would never have planned to hurt anyone. She just had no . . . it's hard to explain. She had no sense beyond the moment. She had no real sense of the world, or time, or people existing beyond herself.'

23

Alice

It's seven by the time I get back to Dead Girls' Dresses. Gabe is at a Global Rising thing and the evening is mine to unbox the ultimate dresses from the ultimate dead girl. I turn off the CCTV, not just because I still haven't told Gabe about the Capels – and anyway what could he deduce from a feed of me shaking out clothes, he sees me do that all the time? – but because this feels ceremonial, clandestine, deeply private. I place my dressing screen across the shop door so I can't be seen. I bend the edges to make a little booth.

When I break the seal on the first bag the vacuum is punctured and the clothes inside expand to fill it, like breath in a lung. I tear at the aperture and a chorus line of women tumbles out. A twenties flapper, a thirties siren, a forties pin-up, a fifties bombshell, a sixties flower child. Each of these bags is like Mary Poppins' carpet bag: the clothes just keep coming and coming and coming and every item is a thread across time, stitching me to my lost aunt. Dresses, tops, skirts, jeans, costume jewellery, headbands, shoes . . . I'm torn between wanting to linger over each one and wanting to see what's next. Around half the clothes are nineties high-street classics that don't fit my brand but which I can sell anonymously on eBay: Miss Selfridge, Topshop, Kookai, Morgan, Ravel.

But the rest are *treasure*.

I shake out a diaphanous peach gown, chiffon and marabou, a seventies dinner-party piece from a suburbia of my mother's childhood, which evokes pampas grass in the front garden and shagpile rugs. It's one of dozens of highly covetable labels from boutiques that might have dressed Sheila Capel – Ossie Clark,

Phool, Droopy & Browns, Missoni, Anokhi. Their floor-grazing hems with nipped waists and angel sleeves make them Dead Girls' Dresses heartland pieces. There are inevitably a couple of Biba items, the iconic black-and-gold label faded and curling in a lace blouse, a floral cotton skirt, a yellow linen suit I've seen go for seven hundred quid at auction. I try not to think about the ethics of selling a murderess's clothes, if that's what Biba really is.

This collection confirms my aunt's death more than her years of silence, more than any abandoned car or any washed-up jewel. If you owned a wardrobe like this, only death could part you from it.

Most will need to go to the theatrical dry cleaners, which will mean an initial outlay of thousands, but the mending I can do myself. A floor-length Diane von Furstenberg has enough in the hem for me to cover the hole at the waistband. An antique white lace dress – I'm guessing Edwardian, if not older – has a yellowed armpit that I reckon I can get rid of with a bit of bicarb and vodka. There's a single laundry bag of vaguely ethnic-looking stuff that was meant for a far larger woman: ponchos and muumuus. Either Biba wore things baggy or – and I prefer this – sometimes she saw a piece and just loved it so much that she had to own it, even if she would never wear it. I picture her belting this pink flamingo-print kaftan around her waist, wrapping herself up like a sweet.

Some pieces are unsalvageable. One green cheesecloth garment falls so utterly to pieces in my hands that I can't even tell what it used to be. The clothes tell stories of parties, of someone who took great care getting ready and then became increasingly hedonistic as the night wore on. Someone who never saved anything for best because the clothes *were* the occasion. Every now and then that tips into a wanton carelessness. There's an oyster-pink Jean Paul Gaultier conical bustier from the 1987 runway collection that I should be able to sell for thousands but there's a cigarette burn in its dead centre. Who would be so careless with such a work of art, with a *museum* piece? The woman was a fucking monster.

An orange dress stops me in my tracks, the one whose twin I already own, the one Dad let slip that Biba was wearing on The Night Of. I hold the dress up, thinking of her as a witness. What did you see? I want to ask her. What do you know? Are you *evidence*? I know from *Travesties* that gunshot residue is a kind of powder that dusts the hands of whoever fired the gun. It can last for up to twelve hours, but I doubt it would stay for twenty years. I wrap the orange dress in tissue and set her aside, even so.

There are handbags full of costume jewellery and loads of silver pieces that seem to be from the same maker. Bangles and chunky chains, rings set with orange and turquoise stones, very nineties. The logo stamped beside the hallmark is sort of rune, or perhaps a Roman numeral. It's hard to make out through the tarnish. I've seen one of these before, on a dulled twist of silver and green amber that Mum keeps in a pouch in her jewellery box, the earring that confirmed Biba's plunge into the sea. Who made this jewellery? Why is there so much of it? What could it mean?

I bin half a dozen compacts of dried-out make-up and a lip gloss covered in fluff. A clubbing magazine called *Mixmag* has a bunch of Polaroids tucked inside. They are faded, darkness encroaching on the colour, but the stories they tell are undimmed. There's one of Mum and Biba wearing bra tops and billowing trousers, each with a pill on their tongue. Karen Clarke, I think, you dark horse.

Another square captures Guy Grainger giving Biba a piggy-back through the woods behind The House. She's got her head thrown back and she's laughing. He's wearing an Orbital T-shirt. He looks far younger than nineteen, and brimming with life. Finally here's Dad reading *House Beautiful* magazine at the kitchen table, surrounded by collapsing shelves and piles of washing-up. He can't have been any older than I am now but his careworn expression paints middle age on to his features. The final Polaroid takes my breath away. It's Mum, more beautiful than I've ever seen her. She's got a black ribbon choker around her neck and her hair is piled high. She looks like a Moulin Rouge can-can girl. I know the red dress she's wearing. It's always in her wardrobe. I once caught her crying with it on her lap. She said she was sad she didn't fit into it any more. I offered to let the seams out but she wouldn't let me touch it.

I put the pictures under the counter and turn to an anomalous item, an old book of aerial photography that falls open on the picture of a cliff. Cannabis buds are pressed flat in the creases. They've lost their scent but I'd know their shape anywhere. I read the caption, then recoil. Beachy Head. This is where she went. This is where she died. If the clothes have brought Biba back to life for me, then this image seems to kill her all over again.

The last piece in the last bag is a wedding dress. Ivory satin, buttons covered in the same material, one missing. With its leg-of-mutton sleeves and high neck, at first glance it looks authentically Edwardian, but the care label and the deep V-cut back suggest it's 1980s. The hem is black and stiff with old dirt but worst-case scenario I can lose an inch and wear flats so it still sits right. Some clothes carry the weight of everyone who wore them. In my hands this gown is more dense than its material suggests and it resists yielding to my touch. Its rustle is more paper than cloth. Some clothes invite superstition. I wonder about the woman who wore this dress on her wedding day, whether her husband carried her billowing over the threshold, the state of their marriage now. Is it blessed or poisoned? Did it shape, in the subtlest way, the fate of its last owner? I will know when I try it on. It will tell me.

Behind the dressing screen, I fight my way into the dress. It feels like that stage in changing a duvet cover where you've lost all sense of what's up and what's down. This dress was designed for someone with a bridesmaid, a best friend or sister to guide and align. At last it's on, in conversation with my body. It makes instant, perfect sense. Even filthy and creased, with missing buttons, it could have been made for me.

I slide between two mirrors, examine myself from every angle. The usual girls stretch away into a vanishing point. I like to think that this time one of them, one so far away that I can't quite make out her features, is not me but my missing aunt. Perhaps farther back still, in an image no bigger than a music-box ballerina, my grandmother twirls in bridal white.

This dress has history. This is the one. This is the dress I will wear when I promise my life to Gabe.

24

Karen

The orange Global Rising flyer I took from Alice's flat doubles up as a fan. I wave it under my chin in a pub a few doors down from the meeting room where the Global Rising event is being held. The Princess Louise is a beautiful space, a proper Victorian gin palace with little booths like a row of confessionals set against a long mahogany bar. In my little cubicle, between two panes of frosted and cut glass, I could not feel more obvious if I were wearing a trenchcoat and peering through eye holes cut into a newspaper. I'm not going incognito because I'm afraid of confrontation – a big part of me would relish a showdown with Gabe – but because the whole point of this exercise is to observe him when he thinks that I am not there. I need to know what he's like outside his relationship with Alice. I must stay one step ahead. I've held secrets for so long – for over half my life – that knowing more than other people has become my default state. If I don't know, I'm not safe. If I'm not safe, no one is.

Rex thinks I'm giving a talk at a language school.

I follow a woman about my mum's age, the words I INCITE THIS MEETING TO REBELLION stretched over an enormous bosom, up a black-painted staircase and slink into the back row, next to an Asian man in his twenties with face tattoos and a man-bun. On stage, Gabe and Stef are talking out of earshot, nodding performatively, to a cluster of secondary school-age children. The meeting is more mixed than the caucus of Gabe clones I was expecting: it's the muddle of ages, classes and colours that you'd see in a Tube carriage.

At 8pm on the dot Gabe taps a microphone and it is immediately apparent that this is not a meeting, this is a . . . lecture? A performance?

'Thanks for showing up. New faces, welcome. I'm gonna start by recapping our mission statement. We demand that the government immediately halts all oil and gas licences, and we know that waving placards isn't working. People will hate you for joining us. People hate to be inconvenienced. But is two hours in traffic really more inconvenient than your home flooding three times a year? Than your children dying from foul air?'

The room has that strange positive charge that occurs where humans gather with joint intent. The easy laughter of the wedding-reception speech, the nervous pride of a primary school nativity.

'Old faces—' he continues.

'That'll be me!' cackles the older lady in the slogan T-shirt.

'You've got more energy than the rest of us put together, Anne,' Gabe grins, then regains his focus, pacing the stage as if he's giving a TedX talk. Does Gabe's ability to work a crowd mean he thrives on attention, or control in every aspect of his life? 'You'll have noticed that Kev's missing. He got eight weeks after the M11 lie-in, but get this: he's gone down for contempt of court. Why? *Because he told the jury his motivation was climate crisis.* Westminster are literally criminalising our *intent* as well as our action. This is dark, dark shit. Amer's doing the appeal pro bono . . .' A hand in the front row waves, and there's a smattering of applause. The man next to me nods so vigorously my chair shakes.

The longer Gabe speaks, the weaker grow my doubts. He is mesmeric. His eyes shine, his body language is open, forward-facing. Even his accent changes, climbing the social ladder in a way Dawn can only dream of. Sincerity strips a speaker of affectation. You can think about what you're saying or how you're saying it but very few people can do both for any length of time. It's why my mum can never maintain her telephone voice for the duration of a conversation. As Gabe punches his arm, it is hard to escape the idea that he was put on this earth to save it. 'But Kev won't be the only one. This is *systemic*. It's already beyond what Amer can do in his evenings and weekends. We're going to need serious dollar to fund a serious defence. To that end, Stef's gonna be collecting for the legal fund at the end of the meeting.'

To his right, Stef jiggles a red bucket full of change. 'Obviously we're grateful for online donations and obviously you can always give via the GoFundMe, but obviously we want to keep cash in circulation.' He sways when he's talking; unlike Gabe, he wasn't schooled in public speaking. 'Use it or lose it, right? We'll be providing receipts on request so you know we haven't run off with it.' There's a ripple of laughter, and Stef beams.

If *only* I could catch Gabe out in an act of hypocrisy. What would that do to Alice? It's been ages since the last Surge but isn't a dormant volcano the most dangerous kind? The women of the Capel line don't take betrayal, in any form, at all well. Biba finding out that Guy Grainger wasn't who he pretended to be was the beginning of the end for them. Not that I want Gabe to end the way Guy did, Jesus, no. I just want him . . . disappeared, harmlessly, with no distress to Alice. Is this what they call magical thinking?

'Back to you, mate.' Stef stands with his hands clasped, as if he's Gabe's security guard. I'm appalled to find myself attracted to him. He's young enough to be my son, for goodness' sake. It's the size of him, the shoulders, the hairy legs, so virile compared to Rex. It's probably evolutionary; I'm sure I've read that after enough time in a relationship you start to crave the opposite of what you're used to. Or maybe I'm ovulating, dropping another useless husk of an egg.

'Custody is an inevitability now, not a risk,' he says, and I'm thankful that Alice, so far, shows no interest in protesting. 'We need to update our go-bags. Pack like you're not coming home for a week. Contact lenses, meds. That's on top of the essentials, which are, to recap, saline solution to rinse the eyes in case of tear gas. Shatter-resistant goggles, a respirator mask, water, a first-aid kit . . .'

'Amer's number!' comes a voice from the audience, to more laughter. As the boys run through a demonstration of how to wear and operate a bodycam, it hits me how serious Gabe is. How serious *this* is. Climate change is real and the government don't care and someone's got to take one for the team and isn't this about the greatest thing a person can do with their lives right now? This means more to him than anything. Even Alice. What would happen if he had to choose?

He finishes by telling the assembly that he can't reveal the details but that they should keep the first weekend of September free. 'And those of us with privilege – colour, youth, money, whatever – let's own it, let's work with it. Let's get this shit *sorted*.'

Afterwards, Anne stuffs a bunch of twenties into Stef's bucket. It's so easy for these boys. They know the power of a young man's smile to charm the birds from the trees, the gold from an old woman's pocket.

'You sure you can afford this, babe?' he asks her.

'You can't take it with you.' She touches him on the chest, her fingers playing a chord on his heart, holding it for a bar too long. 'I'm on a final salary pension. It's you youngsters I feel bad for. You try to keep yourself out of prison, OK? We need a bit of muscle on the outside.'

Anne's a fucking mug.

I sidle out of the pew, head down, mind whirring. What would Gabe's being jailed do to Alice? Would it get her away from his influence? Or would she follow our example and strengthen her commitment?

At the top of the stairs, there's a fire door which someone has propped open with a brick. If I stand there, I'm out of sight of the stage but I can hear every word. There's a good hour before the last train out of London, so I linger a moment. The hot air feels loaded with particles of what might be the awful truth. It was inconvenient before; now it's fucking terrifying.

Eventually the last of the hangers-on have gone, and it's just Stef and Gabe in the room. I press myself against the wall, straining to hear their words, both longing for and dreading a moment when they drop their guard and reveal their true, venal selves. Instead, all I hear is the jingle of coins being decanted into money bags.

'I'll deposit it first thing,' says Stef. 'Send everyone a screenshot.'

'She always comes up trumps,' says Gabe.

'She's a darlin',' replies Stef. 'Got no kids, you know. Big fuck-off house up Canonbury that she bought for about five quid back in the day. I reckon she's in the one per cent.'

'Money like that, I feel like it'd be clean, you get me?' replies Gabe. I don't know if it's the linguist in me being hyper-attuned to accents but this isn't the nice RP meet-the-parents voice he uses with us, and I bet he's got another one he saves just for Alice. I know we all do this to some degree but in Gabe it feels calculated, guileful. 'Not just because Anne's one of us,' he continues. 'But, like, the equity in her house, I know there's shitloads of it but it's *passive*. Anne didn't make that money. It'd be taking from the system, really. Christ, the lawyers we could hire with money like that.'

I hear some back-slapping and shuffling and suddenly they're on the other side of the door, so close I can smell their hair and feel their body heat. Stef sticks his head out of the opening and looks up at the sky. If he turns his head a degree to the left we'll be eye to eye. It's one thing to be spotted in the audience, another to be caught sweating on a fire escape.

'Fuckin' 'ell,' Stef retracts his head. 'It's still *boiling*. It's like midday.'

'Pint?' suggests Gabe.

Stef follows him down the stairs. '*Pint*.'

25

Alice

Four hours have passed in a blink. I'm still sorting through clothes – and wearing the wedding dress – at eleven pm. I'm about to get changed and book an Uber when there's a hammering on the shop door. My skin prickles under the satin. It's got to be The Woman, I think. Or a journalist. Or a Grainger or a Wheeler coming to take an eye for an eye. Or—

'Alice!' Gabe shouts. In my relief that it's him, I forget what I'm wearing. As I slide back the bolts I see myself reflected in the back of the door, white dress, big black eyes. All glass becomes a mirror at night. The bad luck of the bridegroom seeing the dress before the ceremony seems to have landed early. There's lager on Gabe's breath and a fury in his eyes I've never seen before. It can't be about the dress; he hasn't even registered it. 'Are you on your own?' he snarls.

'Why wouldn't I be?'

'You turned the CCTV off.'

'I was trying on dresses and I didn't want you to see. I know it's a bit tragic, but . . .'

My voice falters. Gabe's usual laughter lines have become deep, angry grooves. 'Have you been truthful with me, Alice?'

My cheeks burn hot as my extremities turn cold. What has he found? Did I leave my iPad lying around? Even if I did, what would possess him to open a folder called Sewing Machine Warranties?

'I can't believe I put a *ring* on your finger.'

I glance down at my bare hand. Gabe's voice rises.

'It's a metaphor, fuck's sake. I left a relationship for you, Alice, I thought you were solid.'

'I *am.*' I glance at my phone for the first time in hours to see seven missed calls from him. Shitty shit *shit.* Is it The Woman? Has a journalist found him, somehow, and told him about my family? I pull at the neckline of my dress, which seems to be shrinking, trapping me inside it forever.

'Let me see your phone.'

So he's on to me. A seam of relief runs through my despair. I always knew I'd have to betray my parents, share our story eventually. This is not how I wanted to tell him, but being uncovered sort of gets me off the hook – with *them* at least. I watch him slide through my apps, holding my breath when the Dropbox icon appears – then choking on shock as he slides right by it. What is he looking for if not that?

'You've hidden it,' he accuses, after another fruitless minute on my phone. 'Deleted it. When Stef was on to you.'

'Hidden what?' I'm really confused now. 'What's anything got to do with *Stef*?'

Gabe folds his arms and nods to himself, his mouth twisted in bitter satisfaction. 'Yeah, right. So you haven't reactivated your Tinder account?'

This is so far from what I was expecting that I start to laugh. '*Obviously* not.'

Gabe's expression shuts my laughter down. 'So why's Stef just got matched with you?'

This is starting to feel like a bad trip. 'He *hasn't.* Show me what you think he saw.' I tug harder at the dress and hear something rip.

He hasn't got a screenshot; he has to get Stef to send him one. The message whooshes through and the profile he shows me – *Alice, London* – is of a girl with long dark hair in profile, who could be anyone. Gabe looks even more indignant. 'You've obviously changed the picture.'

'I fucking *what?*' Deep inside, I feel the first bubble in a pan that could come to the boil in seconds.

'Prove it's not you, then.'

'*Prove* it? Isn't my word good enough for you?'

'Alice, I *saw* your picture.'

I've never seen Gabe cry but he looks on the verge of it now. His sincerity is unmistakable, as is his hurt. He really thinks I did this. He really thinks I'm *capable* of this. The Surge hasn't been this strong since I threw water in Roger Capel's face. It won then because I tried to hold its head underwater. If I give it voice, maybe it will stop me physically lashing out.

'OK, but also, fuck you.' I show him my camera reel, a photo every few minutes throughout the night, time and location stamps locking me here.

He runs his hand over his chin, dry skin rasping over day's-end stubble. 'I don't understand.'

A horrible thought forms. 'Could Stef have been fucking with you?' I mean, I *do* take up a lot of Gabe's time.

Gabe shakes his head. 'Stef would never.'

The Surge inches forward. Where is his 'Alice would never'? Where was that conviction when it came to *my* integrity?

'But I mean, no, it was live, on the app, you couldn't fake it. It was you, Alice. I mean, it obviously wasn't, but it was?'

We stare each other down, both of us cresting the sick adrenaline high of our first big argument. When it looks like he's going to break eye contact, I duck and weave like a boxer to maintain it. He's not getting away from me that easily.

'I don't understand.'

'It's called *making a mistake*,' I say. 'A really fucking big one.'

The Surge and I wait for an apology that doesn't come. 'Well.' He shakes his head in bewilderment that seems genuine. 'Just – don't turn off your CCTV again, alright? If someone *is* up to something, we want you safe.' He pulls me close. I fight the urge to melt into his arms. 'No more lies?' he asks. I rip myself away. *More* lies suggests I was lying to start with. Before I can protest, he goes on, 'No more secrets?'

Ah. *Secrets* are another matter. The Surge recedes abruptly. I'm not guilty of the thing he's accusing me of, but that doesn't mean I'm innocent.

'I've just got a handful of things to deal with.' I peel away from him. 'I'm at Wimbledon with Mum all day tomorrow. I'll have a migraine if I know there's stock all over the floor.'

He watches me change into a slip dress. 'This is all from one house clearance? How much did you pay for it?'

'A freebie.' It's not exactly a lie.

He whistles. 'Result. What can I do to expedite the process?'

I toss him an old bag whose clasp is stuck. 'Can you open this?'

He flexes a bicep. It's a lambskin quilted bag with a padded chain and needle scars from where a Gucci insignia, two interlocking Gs, would once have been. In perfect condition these can go for up to five thousand but if I can source a spare charm on eBay I could sell it as 'restored' for a few hundred. Gabe picks up my Victorian letter-opener. 'Try not to destroy the whole thing,' I say, but he's levered it open already.

'Sick! It's got random old photos in it.'

Oh, crap.

I watch helplessly as Gabe arranges maybe a dozen photographs taken in The House on the Turkish rug. He splays them in a fan like someone arranging playing cards in bridge, only instead of King Queen Jack it's Rex Biba Guy. 'What the hell?'

The date's printed in the corner in fuzzy, orange, digital-clock numbers: 2 April 1997. I see a very beautiful girl with white-blonde hair, and a fat woman in a zigzag-print poncho that I am pretty sure is behind me in the dry-cleaning pile. She has thick loops and ropes of silver wherever you can put jewellery. I know that if I could zoom in they would have the runic logo on them. I see a very dark-skinned Black man in some kind of African dress, and a white couple working the crusty look: dreadlocks, army boots, stripy jumpers unravelling at the sleeves. There are, in short, half a dozen people here who might be able to tell me more about what kind of person Biba was, her relationship with Guy, and they might have their own theories about what happened on The Night Of. But of course they're not the ones Gabe is interested in.

'Who's this with Rex?'

If the door were open, I would walk through it. Take a walk around the block to get my thoughts in order, or perhaps keep putting one foot in front of the other until I found myself outside my parents' pink house in Suffolk.

'My dad is a good man in all the ways that matter, OK?'

I retrieve Sheila Capel's framed picture from its drawer and set it on the floor between us. She is both exhibit and witness as I tell Gabe everything. He stares at the bag in his lap, doing and undoing the clasp as I tell him about growing up with my dad in prison, life when it was just Mum and me, how Sophie broke my heart and pushed Dad's business to the brink, and how hard it is for me to trust and how much it hurts that they don't trust me even though they shouldn't but I've changed, I've grown; and then to prove that I trust Gabe I tell him about Dad's slip of the tongue, and my suspicion that the sentence he served should have been Biba's. At that point he drops the bag and regards it with disgust, as if it's stained with crime-scene blood. I tell him about Roger Capel dying and leaving me these dresses, and my desperate hope that they somehow hold the key to the past. I open up the Sewing Machine Warranties and give him a moment with it, disappearing behind the screen and fighting my way out of the white dress. When I emerge, he's cross-legged on the floor, head bowed over the screen.

'I just can't believe you've been keeping something this big from me.'

That's it, then. It's over. I close my eyes. It's bad enough that I'm going to remember his next words for the rest of my life. I don't want to be able to replay the expression on his face while he says them.

'You've carried all this on your own since you were a child,' I hear him say, and my eyes flicker open to see his own brimming with tears. 'Fuck. What a *mess*. Makes my family look positively functional. My God, Alice. You poor baby. I honestly think you must be one of the strongest people I've ever known.'

Hang on, what? 'You're not going to leave me?'

He looks at me the way he did the day he turned up on my doorstep with his bike and his rucksack. 'I've never wanted to look after you more. This is a big deal for you, isn't it? Telling me this?' I nod my head. 'Honestly, Alice, I'm *honoured*. And was that her dress?'

I touch my collarbone where my skin still burns from the friction of ripping it off. 'Yes. It was only a thought. I know it's silly.'

'You looked beautiful in it,' he says, which is not the same as giving it his blessing.

We take our time on the walk home through the midnight streets. Gabe asks me questions, repeats names and dates as though he's studying for a test, interrogating my ideas, wanting to know all the details.

'So if you found out,' he says carefully, 'that Biba *was* at Queenswood Lane the night Grainger and Wheeler were murdered, that still wouldn't prove she'd pulled the trigger.'

'It would for me.' I need so much for him to understand this. 'I can't think of any other reason for my parents to lie about it other than that she did it, Dad took the blame, and they don't want me to find out because they're worried I'll shoot my mouth off.'

'But if she's dead, what's the problem? She's only dangerous if she comes back.'

'My dad would go back to prison. I wouldn't do anything with the information. I just need to know. I need to fill the hole. I hate unanswered questions. I hate loose endings.'

'This is why you're obsessed with those true crime podcasts, you little ghoul,' he says, but there's no judgement in it.

'The correct term is criminoid,' I reply.

He kisses me on top of my head. '*Ghoul*,' he repeats, fondly.

Despite the heavy subject matter there's a lightness that's been absent until now. Is this intimacy? I feel as though we've lived a year of our relationship in one night. He is the Tracey to my Faye, my partner in crime. This is what it feels like when there's nothing left to hold back. I can't believe I worried that sharing my secrets would send him away from me. Instead, it has set me free.

26

Karen

'*How* much for a Pimms?' Alice's voice is shrill with indignation. 'Are they taking the *piss*?'

Alice is dressed for Wimbledon in the 1920s in a a drop-waist white dress with a pleated skirt. All that's missing is a wooden tennis racquet in its little square press. She's dressed me too, an old St Michael dress, a floral shirtwaister that even my mum would have baulked at in the eighties and which at first I refused to wear because I thought it would make me look like a sofa but Alice said *trust me* and she was right.

We stand elbow-to-elbow at the bar. I'm so tense it feels like someone's got my head in a hydraulic press. A day at a big tournament usually means a few hours out of my head, my focus reduced to the trajectory of a little yellow ball. The game – watching it and playing it – was my life before I met Biba. I even did a stint as a ball girl at Queen's. When I was caught in her whirlwind I became ashamed of it. Tennis seemed like such a good girl's hobby, pure and almost childish. Then, after everything settled, I fell back in love with it as something I used to do, untainted by the Capels.

Today, however, it's not working its magic. Not only has Rex retreated into a private, thorny grief, Gabe knows about 1997. This is a gift for someone like him. And if there's two of them on the case, that doubles the chances of them uncovering something that's been buried for a reason.

'It's my treat,' I say, flexing my credit card.

'In that case let's have champagne,' she says. 'You get more alcohol for your money and I can't be arsed picking mint out of my teeth all day long.'

I ignore the insinuation that a day at the tennis with me is something that must be drunk through, and pay for a bottle. No arguments today, I tell myself. I'm brittle enough as it is. No pressure, just enjoy Alice, be with her, treat her. Be the indulgent parent for once.

'Just to circle back to telling Gabe about Dad. He knows not to, you know, spread it around?'

'I *said*, didn't I?'

'And any more funny visits?'

She swirls her champagne in her flute. 'No. A phone call, but they never rang back.'

The Tannoy calls us to number two court. We take our seats in sun I've rarely felt in this country. I can smell Alice's hair, so like Biba's. They're the only two women I've known who wear their natural scent like high-end perfume. I hoik up my skirt to get some sun on my legs. Next to me, Alice extends a forearm that glistens with zinc.

'Some of us can't sit in the sun without literally cracking like a vampire. Why did I have to get Dad's shitty genes? You'd think evolution would've somehow bred out the kind of skin that burns in thirty seconds, especially with no ozone layer and climate change, but no. You don't know you're fucking *born*, Mum.'

An elderly woman in the row in front turns around. 'You're not on the football terraces now, young lady.'

Alice opens her mouth to retort but I put a warning hand on her arm.

When there's a break in play, we head for the bar. I have a lemonade, Alice another half-bottle of champagne. 'By the way,' she says, 'if all goes well, Gabe's going to come and work with me. I'm getting more and more rentals and I need a full-time courier.'

An alarm goes *ding ding ding* inside me. 'And whose idea was that?'

'Mine,' she says.

But of course. An accomplished controller will find a way to make his victim think it was really their idea. This is textbook coercion. Find a reason to be with Alice all day every day so she never gets a moment to herself. Yesterday I was working on the 'murder path', the timeline of escalating violence that made *Liebesbomb* such a hit in Germany. I plot Gabe's actions against bullet points in my head. Early relationship behaviours: love-bombing and early commitment to isolation and then inevitably to gaslighting. Armed, now, with the leverage of Rex's history. I want to march her away from Wimbledon, drive her down to Suffolk and lock her in her bedroom at home. But all the literature for families and friends of victims says support, support, support. Make sure that, when it all goes wrong, she knows she has a haven in me.

The things we do for Alice.

27

Alice

1920s rayon tennis dress with box pleats
1920s mary-jane shoes with low heel and button fastening

@deadgirlsdresses
#outfitoftheday #ootd #vintagefashion #sustainablestyle

While I've been getting skin cancer on Centre Court at Wimbledon, Gabe's been at his laptop. There's a bowl of Greek salad in the middle of the table and, bizarrely, a stack of bagels, which he appears to be eating dry and possibly swallowing whole.

'I didn't have time to make hot food.' He drops crumbs from his lips. 'Busy doing this.'

He's gone into Sewing Machine Warranties and added a time-line of the Capel case. Everything from Sheila and Roger's marriage to Roger's death is laid out in Excel. 'What do you think, my dear Watson?' He puts a pen in his mouth like it's a pipe.

'*I'm* Sherlock Holmes. *You're* Watson. Has it led to a breakthrough?'

'Not yet,' he admits, bringing up a scan of the group photo from The House. 'I did a reverse-image search just in case there's a duplicate copy online somewhere – long shot, I know. Nada. But I posit—'

'*Posit?*' I spray tap water across the screen.

'Gross.' He wipes it clean. 'Yes. I *posit* that these guys are the key, to Biba's missing months, at least. If you get chucked out of your house, you're likely to live with someone you've lived with before.'

'What makes you think they lived there?'

126

'Look.' He clicks on another picture. 'This woman with all the silver jewellery, that's got to be her bedroom because her clothes are hanging up behind her. And this one of them all around the dinner table. That guy with the dreads is taking out the rubbish. You don't do that in someone else's house. You might wash up but you wouldn't do the bins.' He zooms in on the man, scrutinises his face. 'I feel like I've seen him before. It'll come to me.' He gets a whole bagel into his mouth in one go. 'Roger Capel had a few quid, didn't he?' he asks when he's swallowed.

I raise my eyebrows.

'I looked up his limited company online. They've got assets in the millions.'

'I didn't know you could do that.'

'S'easy. I do it all the time when I name and shame firms. And he never gave you a penny. He could've paid your uni tuition fees, at least. Thirty grand would've been nothing to him.'

'It is what it is,' I say, even though it stings. 'And some of those clothes could fetch good money. Do you think I'd have to pay inheritance tax on it, or capital gains?' Even as I ask, I know I'm being ambitious. In spite of the influx of free stock, Dead Girls' Dresses will be lucky to make a profit, let alone hit the tax threshold. 'Anyway, it was the thoughtfulness, not the money.'

I get up to rinse the dishes, steering the same plate round and round under the running tap.

'You never think about asking the family for a lump sum?' asks Gabe.

The plate stops still in my hands. I couldn't be more shocked if he'd spat in my face. 'I thought you didn't believe in inheritance. I thought property was theft.'

He colours a little. 'Yeah, I don't really mean it. But, you know, capitalism wouldn't be so successful if it weren't seductive. I mean, if The Woman *was* Biba, it's probably the idea of an inheritance that's basically bought her back from the dead.'

The Surge moves too fast for me to catch it. 'If she could do that – if she could let my dad think she was dead, then come back for money . . . fucking hell! I'd kill her myself!' I know I'm shouting but it's only when Gabe looks at my hands in alarm that I realise I've snapped a thick dinner plate in two. I didn't feel myself doing it.

'Then let's hope it *wasn't* her.' Gabe gently takes the cracked half-moons from my hands and sets them aside. 'Not just because of what she brings out in you.' He takes my right hand, which appears to have frozen into a claw, and straightens my fingers one by one. 'But because of what she might do *to* you.'

'What do you mean?' I offer him my hooked left hand.

'Well . . .' he works his fingers into the tendons of my palm '. . . she seems like the type who'd fight to the death. If you're right about her being back, let alone about what you call The Night Of, then Biba's got one hell of a self-preservation instinct. She may be your aunt, but this woman's *dangerous*.'

28

The summer of 1997 is coming to an end. You are no longer students but graduates; you are expected to be working actors. You have filmed your first TV role. Small, but a start. You knew you would love the work but not how much you would love being on set. It is a wonderful no man's land where intimacy is instant and ends just as quickly. You lay yourself bare and then you move on.

And it keeps you out of the house.

In the house, it has all gone wrong.

Moving Guy in was a mistake. His gangster credentials don't stand up to scrutiny. The flat that he led you to believe was little more than a squat turns out to be his parents' four-bed apartment off Ladbroke Grove. You wouldn't have judged him for it: don't you, too, live in your childhood home? It's the inauthenticity you can't stand.

The more you push him away, the more desperate he becomes to please you. Presents. Declarations of love. Mix tapes. More drugs. A computer you have no interest in. Hours of earnest cunnilingus (you use the time to run lines in your head). He boasts that he knows people with guns, which would be more convincing if his mother weren't constantly calling asking if he's eating enough vegetables.

When none of this works, he offers to acts as an intermediary between you and your father. He honestly seems to think he can talk Roger into signing over the house when you and Rex have failed.

Rex is all for throwing Guy out, but you anticipate protracted attempts to win you back – you have a ghastly premonition of

Boyz II Men blasting from a boom box in a shopping trolley outside the house – and you can't handle the distraction. You've got a callback for another TV show that needs all your energy. You'll ask Guy to leave on the other side of it.

It is September. Any day now, the woods will turn gold and die.

It is a Sunday evening and you are listening to music in the garden when your father bangs on the door. It wasn't closed properly (of course it wasn't) so he lets himself in. You find him in the black and white hall, staring at the wonky paintings and stains on the walls. It's the first time he's been back since the day he left, revving his engine to drown out your cries.

'What the hell is this? What the bloody hell is this?'

He's got one of Rex's letters. He's holding it at arm's length, pinching the paper so hard that his fingertips have turned white.

Rex has never sent any of those letters. Why would he start now?

'I want the lot of you out.'

Expulsion. Something in your heart aches and eases at the same time. Now it's happening, you no longer have to worry about it happening.

When the engine of your father's expensive car is out of earshot, Guy holds out his hands and says, 'I did it for you.'

Guy sent it. Of course he fucking did. Rex should never have left that letter lying around. Between them they have fucked everything up. All your organs contract to make way for The Feeling. The Feeling is making a noise; a vat of it clanks and bubbles and goes siss-siss-siss.

Guy's ever-present mobile phone starts up one of its arcade-game beeping sessions. Rex goes to silence it, but when his hand emerges from Guy's pocket he is holding a gun.

Guy swings for Rex. When his fist connects with Rex's chin there's a sound like rotten fruit splitting. A voice is shouting stop it stop it stop it. It might be you. The Feeling has changed its state of matter, it is liquid nitrogen, hissing out of you, so loud you lose all sense of what's happening and who is where and then—

Bang bang.

The Feeling is shocked into silence, broken only by the crack of Guy's neck as he is thrown backwards into the stairs and then a choking sound, a dry retching that isn't coming from you or Rex. You turn as one to see the neighbour framed in the doorway, frozen mid-complaint.

Bang bang bang.

Tom Wheeler drops as if his feet have been kicked out from under him.

Rex looks down at the gun, then up at you. His bloodied face mirrors the horror on your own.

Wheeler bleeds out. The black and white squares are washed red. The stain you made when you were a child disappears. It was that easy all along.

Rex tells you to go and you do. You leave the house you grew up in and dart through the woods where you played with your brother as children. The woods have your back. Tree roots recede to smooth your path. The branches are arms ushering you through. You know what will be happening at home. The scenes play out, disjointed but clear, like the first cut of a film.

Rex will be by the telephone, calling your father, and the message will be something along the lines of Just go along with whatever I say and leave Biba out of it. *While he's talking his thumb will slide across Karen's phone number that you drew on the wall with eyeliner. It will be like she never existed.*

You have no idea if your father will go along with Rex's plan. Not after what he's read tonight. He wants a life where you don't drag him into the headlines. If he does take you in it won't be out of love for you. It will be for the new wife and children's sake.

When you are at the far edge of the trees, you can hear the sirens on Queenswood Lane. You look down to find that you took your script, the one that you were learning. You can't remember picking it up. It was like the part of you that needs to work was acting on autopilot, even as the blood sprayed and the bodies dropped.

You have just about enough distance to realise that that's not normal.

29

Karen

Rex calls the hotel lift. Peggy sniffs excitedly at remembered corners of worn carpet. The Finsbury Park Travelodge is no one's idea of luxury but dogs are welcome and it's five minutes from Alice's flat and infinitely preferable to her ancient sofa, which always feels slightly tacky to the touch.

'Good girl,' he praises Peggy absent-mindedly. He's still blind-sided by Roger's death but he's coming back, one word at a time. The past few days' monosyllables have expanded into whole – if short – sentences. The corridors are hot but the rooms are bliss-fully cold. Rex unpacks, replicating the layout of his sock drawer at home: pairs balled in a certain way, toes facing the same direction.

'It's the funeral tomorrow,' he mutters, sliding a shirt on to a hanger.

'Oh, Rex. Are you thinking of going?'

'No.' The cords in his neck pull tight. 'But I feel like I should do something to mark it.'

'Like what?' We never had any kind of ceremony after we made Biba's death official. It didn't feel like my place to suggest it then, and it doesn't now.

'I don't know,' he admits. 'There's this ball of . . .' He strikes his clavicle. 'It's like there's something stuck here, like when you've half-swallowed a pill but it dissolves in your windpipe and it makes everything taste bitter for the rest of the day.' It's the most he's said since he learned of Roger's death: it appears to have exhausted him. 'I'm gonna take Peggy for a walk in the park.'

'I've got to go to Waitrose, pick up dinner,' I say, even though he didn't invite me. 'I'll see you at Alice's.'

Our faces are still damp with sweat but our kiss is dry. How's he going to make conversation with Alice and Gabe tonight if he can barely talk to me?

In the supermarket, I fill a shopping trolley then lug two jute bags to Drayton Park, underboobs sweating and thighs chafing. I rattle Alice's letterbox but get no answer. A plume of steam from the vent tells me she's in the shower, so I let myself in. The empty house throbs with whatever she's listening to, a radio show or a podcast, bass up so loud that the words are distorted until I reach the top floor. I climb uneven stairs, moving through shafts of crazy light.

What's on the menu today, Tracey? The nasal, Estuarine voice is no lovelier for being played through speakers. Oh, God. I hate this bloody podcast. Two screeching millennials milking true crime for laughs and calling it satire.

For your delectation, Faye, comes the buzzy reply, *I am serving up William Burke and William Hare, a pair of nineteenth-century serial killers who sold their victims' corpses to medical schools for dissection.*

What I see in the top landing mirror – red, glistening face, straw hair – makes me want to throw a blanket over the bastard thing.

Burke and Hare – I know these guys. Like, running around London looking for people who were about to die of natural causes?

'Alice, it's me!' I call, but the water's running and she can't hear me. I identify the source of the noise, a very long, very thin sound bar, but can't work out how to turn it off.

At first, yeah. And then when they realised they were on to a winner their specimens, if you will, started to die of less natural causes. Burke was so good at killing people without being detected that he had a murder method named after him.

It's the serial killer equivalent of having a university department named after you, or an airport. Fuck that. This is the true accolade.

In the shower, Alice laughs.

Yes, Faye, 'Burking' is the art of strangling someone without those telltale petechial haemorrhages appearing. Petechial haemorrhages are those burst veins in your eyeballs when you've been strangled.

The sound bar vibrates in my hands as I turn it over to look for the off-switch.

Lacy eyeballs: what a tell, what a look, what a VIBE. So, tell me how one might Burke, should one wish to murder undetectably.

This is *horrible.* Who listens to this for *fun?* What's *wrong* with Alice? I've tried so hard to parent the Capel out of her, so what is this? Nature overcoming nurture? Or is it something more external, a fascination borne of growing up with a convicted murderer for a father?

It's a twist on your bog-standard strangulation. So there's a specific position. Your victim lies supine, you're astride their neck with your thighs pressing against their shoulders.

Like a sort of Kama Sutra position but with murder?

Exactly like that. The point of cutting off the blood supply at the shoulder is that way no blood gets to the arteries, so they can't burst and give away the method of death.

It's a dying art. See what I did there? Dying art?

Faye, I'm embarrassed for you.

Abruptly, the noise dies. Alice is wrapped in a towel, phone in hand. 'You're supposed to *knock*,' she says, taking the sound bar from my hands and setting it back on its shelf. 'Your key is for *emergencies*.'

'I *did* knock,' I say. 'Repeatedly. You couldn't hear me over the murder show. The ice-cream was melting.'

'It still is, by the looks of things.' She nods at the carrier bag that's oozing beige slime on to the kitchen floor. While she dresses, I attempt to slide the tub of salted caramel into her freezer compartment, which is bunged up with two inches of ice, a letterbox of storage available. I get a knife and chisel out room for the ice-cream. Ice chips melt as soon as they hit the floor. I bend down to mop them up with a cloth (Gabe doesn't approve of paper towels). Alice is behind me, dressed in a stiff mini dress that makes her look like a lampshade.

'Death isn't something that should be served up as light entertainment, Alice.' The sentence hangs unfinished: *you of all people should know that.* 'It affects real people.'

I swipe the dirty cloth in a figure eight on the floor.

'Christ, I know that, Mum.' 'I wouldn't play it in front of anyone who'd been a victim. Or their families.' I hold her gaze, until she catches on. 'You mean the people who kill?' she says. 'I would never play it in front of Dad. Give me a bit of credit.' Clearly sensing the mood for a gear change, she bounces on her tiptoes, her lifelong expression of excitement. 'Here, I've got a dress for the ceremony. Shall I try it on for you before Gabe gets back? Keep an eye out for him, yeah?'

From the bedroom there's the sound of rustling and grunting. Gingerly, I stick my head through the French windows that give on to a Juliet balcony, a ledge really, not quite big enough to stand on. A little row of terracotta pots are filled with dried-out mud and yellow stalks. Avalon Road is deserted except for a neighbour pressure-washing immaculate steps. A rainbow glistens in the spray. The front 'garden' is a mess of wheelie bins, wild buddleia and unidentifiable smashed masonry.

'Is the coast clear?'

I do a last left-right-left with my neck. 'Yup.'

'I can't do it all the way up on my own but you'll get the idea.'

A puffball silhouette, the dress blazes white as she steps into the light and my insides contract violently. This dress's resemblance to the one Biba wore on her twenty-first birthday is uncanny, right down to the dirty hem. I spent a long time staring at that dress while she slept on the floor beside me in the debris of the party. I try to collect my thoughts, but they're rolling all over the floor like marbles, multiple versions of the question *what the fuck fuck fuck fuck fuck.* The party dress had eighteen buttons, with the seventeenth missing. Alice twirls slowly and it's not her back I see but Biba's, her spine a row of pearls that rolled as she danced.

'Can you do it up for me? I know it's a bit scrappy but I can get a new button and cover it with material from the seams so it matches.'

My fingers don't belong to me as I slide buttons into satin loops, counting them as I go, knowing long before I get to the missing one that it will be the seventeenth.

'Alice.' My voice is shaking. 'Where did you get this dress?'

30

Karen

Alice wears an expression I haven't seen since she was little. On the eve of her seventh birthday she broke into the fridge and ate the cake I'd spent all day making. She denied it and denied it until she threw up flecks of Victoria sponge and tiny white pellets of sugar that had begun the day as silver balls. After the telling off I gave her then, I saw what I'm seeing now: the relief that she could abandon the lie.

'I inherited it from Roger Capel.'

The puncture is dull but deep: a slow spearing in my side.

'But you never knew him,' I say.

'Yeah, no, that's actually not true?' she says. The spear twists, dislodging things that settled years ago. 'That night you and Dad helped me set up the shop . . .' Now that her mouth has been unstoppered, it's all coming out; she's so desperate to explain that she's forming words on the in-breath.

Idiots.

We've been *idiots*.

This is Alice: stolen marshmallows and glitter bombs and smashing phones out of people's hands and following a corset to Paris. All the lies we've told, and the easiest people to fool were ourselves all along.

'We found this in one of Biba's old bags.' The photo she hands me sends me falling down the rabbit hole. I can smell their incense, taste Nina's hit-and-miss cooking, the farty smell of Jo's magic mushroom tea and the smoke from Biba's roll-ups, the spunky ammonia reek of the privet that lined the garden and hid the hole in the fence, the one that led directly into the woods. Biba is wearing the silver earrings, the lone twin of which is now in my bedroom at home sea-smoothed and dull, Nina's hallmark almost worn away. I keep it in my jewellery box, in its own compartment, in a little pouch whose ribbons I tie in a way that lets me know when Rex has taken it out to hold, to remember, to wonder and maybe to regret.

'Well?' Alice breaks my reverie.

I shake my head. 'They had a lot of parties, house guests who came and went.'

She points to Tris. 'Gabe says this bloke's familiar.'

'I don't know them.' My voice comes out in a croak. All those years of *Friday Film Night*, popcorn and duvets on the sofa just so she'd never alight on BBC2 and the television show that he and Jo hosted. I close my eyes. Even if Gabe works out who Tris is, he and Jo and Rachael had left The House before everything kicked off. Arouna was around long enough to know more, but he died a few years ago.

'Not even this one?' Alice points to Nina.

A bow of sweat springs from my upper lip. I wipe it away with my forearm. 'Why d'you ask?' Biba was in touch with Nina after Rex was sent down. If anyone living knows the full story, it'll be her. A few candid words from Nina could see me cast out not just from Alice's life but Rex's too.

Alice taps Nina's head. 'I reckon she's the one who gave Biba her earring. You know, *the* earring.'

The spear in my side twists another notch. 'You know about that?'

She puts her hands on her hips; white satin rustles. 'Well, yeah. Why else would you keep one shitty earring? You don't even wear silver.'

'What were you going through my jewellery box for?'

'What little girl *doesn't*?'

If I deny knowing Nina outright, it could trip me up later. I pretend to examine the photo. 'She does look familiar, actually. Let me have a think. Just going to nip to the loo.'

In the bathroom – that mould does not look good; I must get

Rex to look at that – I bring up a Facebook page I've checked in on every few months since I got an account. Nina Vitor Silverworks is a business page and not a very well-run one – the response time is given as one to two weeks – but it's the only trace she has left on the web. I've never made contact before, but now is the emergency. It's time to break the glass.

> Hi Nina. It's Karen, Rex's wife. Has it really been twenty-five years since we last saw each other? I hope all's good with you and the kids – they must be adults now! Slightly delicate situation here, with Alice fixating on the past and possibly attracting attention that we understandably don't want. If she gets in touch please don't respond – and please let me know about it. You're probably the only other person who understands how fragile Rex is, and what opening up old wounds might to do him.
> Thanks so much, and all my best,
> Karen

Thanks so much, and all my best, the way I'd sign an email to an author or an editor. I hit send and hope I haven't just added more gunpowder to the bomb. Alice is still scrutinising the old photograph.

'Maybe Dad knows who she is.'

Dad knows her alright. Dad knew Nina the way Gabe knows Alice. I have to shut this down now.

'Alice, I need you to stop digging,' I say. 'Biba's not coming back. The only possible consequence will be that you alert some journalist to a story that doesn't even exist and they make every-one's lives a misery.'

Alice's bottom lip is sliding out. I could shake her.

'I said *drop this*. Suicide runs in the Capel blood. You'd never forgive yourself if your dad went the same way.'

Her pupils splash wide.

It is a cheap threat, and unfounded – Rex would never take his own life, not as long as he has us to look after – and I hate myself for it. But, like every sacrifice I've ever made, it's for Alice's good as well as Rex's. It's for our family.

'I'm serious. Stop.' Better for her to believe that this is the bottom layer of the story. Better for her not to guess at what might lie beneath. 'In fact, take that dress off. If he sees you like that . . . it's going to be tense enough without this in the mix.'

'Are you saying we don't tell Dad about Biba's clothes?'

Uttering lies is easy; maintaining them is hard. I don't have it in me to withhold anything else from Rex in the long-term.

'No. I'm saying I'll tell him later, when it's just the two of us.' I feel sick with disloyalty at the thought of Gabe knowing more than him about the Capel situation even for one evening. But tonight, this attempt to bond with Gabe, to celebrate his union with Alice, is a pretence anyway. 'Will you explain to Gabe? Ask him not to say anything?'

My display of trust in him brightens her face a little. She fires off a text, then slides the dress off her shoulders, lets it fall to a grubby puddle at her feet so she's standing in mismatched underwear. 'Maybe it's cursed after all,' she says gathering it in her arms.

'What?'

'Nothing.'

While she's changing, I get to work in the 'kitchen'. Her cooker is the kind with curly metal hotplates and a grill at eye-level, the sort of thing that was old-fashioned when I was a child. How does she *live* like this? I cook her spaghetti *alle vongole*, throwing in chilli and garlic and white wine with half a kilo of Waitrose's finest clams. My thoughts calm as the sauce comes together. Alice appears beside me in a red tea-dress, takes a teaspoon from a drawer and tries the sauce.

'That's fucking lush,' she says, a gloss of orange oil on her lips. I resist the urge to dab her chin. I miss physically looking after her. Feeding her is as close as I'm allowed to get now.

31

Karen

Noises climb the stairs. A clatter of claws and paws, the clack of a dog collar being unhooked from its lead, bottles clanking in a bag and two male voices in murmured conversation.

'Look who I found in the street!' announces Gabe.

Alice doesn't know who to hug first, her dog or her dad. Peggy makes the decision, all but knocking Alice flying. They roll around on the sofa for a bit while the rest of us look on indulgently. Rex is sweating, a Rorschach print between his shoulderblades. Gabe offers him a beer and the four of us stand awkwardly in the living room.

'We agreed to keep it neutral,' says Gabe. 'No talking about politics.'

Rex tilts his bottle and sings, 'We don't talk about Tony, no, no, no,' in a way that makes me suspect that Peggy's walk went via at least one pub. I raise a weak smile. I would happily debate the Iraq war, I would go up against Jeremy Paxman on live TV rather than risk the conversation turning to Biba and the past.

Gabe turns to me and gives me an our-little-secret wink that makes my gorge rise. One evening, I think. I can let the little prick enjoy his power trip for one evening.

The things we do for Alice.

Peggy pops her head out of the window and noses at the dead plants on the ledge.

'That's not a great idea,' says Rex, but Gabe's already on the case.

'Come on, Pegster.' He has one hand on her collar, and with the other he pulls down the window. Flakes of paint drift and settle on the carpet.

I put the pasta on, have one cheeky glass of wine, then another. By the time I come back to the table with four plates of steaming spaghetti, I'm almost relaxed.

True to his word, Gabe avoids politics. He talks instead about his family, making us laugh with stories about his dysfunctional parents. His dad is on something like his sixth marriage and his mother's addicted to plastic surgery. In the silence that follows the laughter, the void of our own family histories looms.

'That reminds me. It's Grandad's birthday next month.'

Alice lowers her head to the table theatrically. 'He's such a pain in the arse to buy for,' she tells Gabe. 'He doesn't want anything. He just likes the History Channel and going to the pub.'

'Has he got a membership to the National Trust, or English Heritage?' suggests Gabe.

'Oh, that's entry-level stuff. He's *way* beyond that.'

'I was thinking of one of those ancestry tests,' says Rex. 'Bloke I've been working with, he thought he was a hundred per cent Sephardic Jewish and it turned out there was all sorts in there. Indian, Armenian, Italian. The whole family were! Can you imagine?'

I feel my cheeks darken. 'I'm not sure that'd be the case with my folks. As far as we know there've been Clarkes sitting on the same hillside for millennia, waiting for it to turn into Leighton Buzzard.'

'You never know,' Rex says to me. 'You might find a dash of Viking or something.'

'You've got that sort of Swedish, blue-eyed, blonde look about you,' Gabe fixes me with a hard stare. 'Although Alice hasn't.'

It's almost as if he knows. He couldn't. My paranoia is infecting everything.

'Or maybe there's a bit of Celt or something?' Rex wonders.

I smile indulgently but inside I'm screaming *would you just fucking drop it all of you.*

'Grandad would *love* to find out he's got a bit of Celtic blood,' says Alice. 'He's watched every episode of *Outlander.*

And you get your colouring from Nanna, Mum, and you know how she loves her Nordic police books. What if she was from Sweden? Why don't we all get done? We could make a family tree?'

Gabe looks very slowly from Alice to Rex to me and a rat-scuttle of fear runs up the back of my neck. There's no way Gabe could have worked out in one evening what Rex still doesn't know a lifetime later, but there's a level of intrigue in his gaze, a level of intent, that goes beyond casual interest in a family dynamic. It's as though there is a fissure in the box that keeps my secrets and they're all swarming out at once. Gabe points his fork in the air, as if he's about to make a huge statement. I reach for my glass but it's empty. My blood is on fire for more wine. Before I can think of a way to intercept him, he's off.

'Commercial DNA tests are the devil's work. It's all Big Pharma wanting to own your soul.'

This is so far from what I was expecting that shock cancels out my relief.

'Gabe, you promised,' groans Alice.

'No, hear me out – this isn't politics. This is beyond that: we're in human rights territory here. There is literally nothing more individual than your personal genome. People don't understand the privacy implications of this shit.'

'How so?' asks Rex. The adrenaline flooding my veins is subsiding from gush to trickle.

'So officially law enforcement can't pressurise these companies to share your DNA, but the way our rights are being eroded, how long before the small print changes? The only way to stay safe is to opt out completely. You think they're just going to sit on this information?'

Gabe makes unblinking eye contact with each of us in turn. Am I imagining a smirk when he hooks his gaze on me? Is he taunting me, letting me know that he could very easily be making a different speech?

'People talk about Orwell's *Nineteen Eighty-Four* but they're smarter than that. They don't force it on you, they sell it to you. They make you want it, they make you buy into it, because, if it's your choice, how could it be wrong that Elon Musk now owns your genome, or whatever? How can you back out?'

'Blimey,' says Rex mildly. 'Maybe we should be thinking more along the lines of a jigsaw for John's birthday.'

'Another bottle?' I don't wait for the answer.

Later, when the sun has set over the railway line and the temperature has dropped from Hell to Purgatory, Rex goes round the flat checking the batteries in the smoke and carbon monoxide alarms, Alice takes Peggy out for a wee, and Gabe washes the dishes. When I bring the last plate to him in the kitchen, I stagger a little and he catches me by the waist, then holds up his palms the way young men do when they want a medal for not groping. I hold on to the worktop to stay upright. Gabe fills a glass from the tap and watches me drink it.

'Thanks for a really lovely evening, Karen. It's been great getting to know you both a little better.' His voice has changed now it's just the two of us. He's dropped the softness he uses with Alice. Which, if either, is the real him? 'I hope you didn't think I was too over-the-top earlier.' He sets a glass in the draining rack. 'With the DNA thing.'

'I couldn't agree more. It would be *disastrous*.' What have I just said? How did he get that out of me? 'I mean . . . you know . . . Big Pharma. All that.'

I'm not even convincing myself. Truth leaks out of my every pore. I've been so busy thinking about the secret we were all keeping from Rex, I took my eye off my own. I see something grind behind Gabe's eyes. He's banking my every word.

No. He *can't* know. I take a tea towel and dry the glass, holding it up to the light to check for smears. It trembles in my hand.

'Also,' he says, 'I didn't want to bring it up in front of Rex . . . But I want you to know, learning about his history doesn't change my feelings for Alice. And I would never betray a confidence.' He pauses meaningfully. Is this it? Is this how it comes out, next to a badly plumbed sink in a shitty flat near the Holloway Road?

'Nor would I tell her anything that would upset her.'

He puts a hand on my shoulder and lightly squeezes it, a reassurance that he makes feel like a threat.

32

While Rex is in the headlines, Karen has done a vanishing act, wiped herself out of your lives as surely as Rex smeared her number from your kitchen wall. Without needing to be briefed, she's come to the same conclusion as you and Rex. It's cleanest and safest to break contact completely. It's for everyone's protection. When a life is that little, it must be easy to return to it.

Over the next few months, the air around you thickens with smoke from burning bridges. Your father and Jules take you in, only to throw you out. Arouna lets you sleep on his boat for five nights before shunting you off to a shitty sublet in Gospel Oak where the walls are made of paper, there are needles in the stairwell, the bed is a dirty mattress on the floor, and the electricity keeps cutting out because you forget to top up the meter. You sit there watching daytime TV and smoking. Even The Feeling doesn't want to know you. It's been replaced by a vast static nothing.

By the time you work out why your clothes don't fit you any more, it's too late to do anything about it. You watch old films and wait for someone to rescue you.

At the end of January, she comes. Her highlights have grown out and her tan is long gone. Her eyes, when they take in your new shape and size, are fog lamps in the dingy hallway.

That night, the two of you sleep curled like two prawns. She puts her hand on your belly. When the baby kicks, she seems to feel it more than you do. She seemed so entranced by your old life that it's surprising how easily she is willing to be absorbed into this new one.

One morning, a couple of weeks into her stay, you're watching BBC Breakfast News when every appliance in the flat powers down.

'Karen . . .' You make your eyes as big as they will go, then flick them down to your belly. She heaves herself off the sagging sofa, wraps a scarf around her neck, takes a crisp purple twenty from her purse and goes out to put money on the card.

You are bored enough to read one of the baby magazines she has been leaving out for you. You have got as far as the editor's letter when your waters break.

'And how's Mum doing?'

It's good that the overstretched midwives call all their patients 'Mum' and 'Baby'. That way, you don't need to worry about answering to the name you borrowed for the occasion without asking, like it was a party dress. You took Karen's purse because you needed money for the taxi. In it were her driving licence – the paper bit with no photo – her NHS card, her bank card. By the time you got to the maternity ward, you were beyond language and they had to go through your things to find out who you were. It's not your fault they allocated you her name.

'Bit tired.' You cannot believe you survived childbirth. You cannot believe how many ordinary, boring women have gone through this. Why isn't everyone talking about the horror of it all the time? The midwife tells you you're lucky you didn't tear and you are incredulous because you feel like a house with no floor. Slices of chopped liver exit your body at irregular intervals.

'We're ready to discharge you. Is Daddy coming to get you and Baby?'

The laugh you stifle is hollow and rotten. No. Daddy can't do a lot where he is. His face forms in front of you then, as it sometimes does. Not his face as it was in life, but in death. His spun-gold hair flattened and matted with blood that spread out into a mane, a headdress, a peacock's tail, a cape, a red carpet, the kind you will never now walk.

The baby is a yellowy-peach colour with purple fingers and toes. It's too early to say if his bronze skin tone or your silver one has won out. All humans are alloys. Perhaps she'll be white gold, something less pure but stronger, more resistant.

'Not Daddy, no,' you say. 'A friend.'

Motherhood is a headlong fall through a trapdoor into hell.

The baby screams all night. Its shit smells like sugar and looks like mustard. You have big sore tits that go square when the baby needs feeding. Karen buys books on breastfeeding — a bluestocking to the last, she thinks she can study her way out of this — but you refuse, even when your skin threatens to burst and your T-shirts reek of cheese. She gets bottles, sterilising fluid, powder. She runs, greasy-haired, in a triangle between Boots and this flat and the launderette. You drink wine by the box and smoke on the balcony.

Babies make you live from minute to minute. You don't discuss the future and you still haven't discussed your shared past. When eventually you broach the events of that night, you tell her that Rex broke your heart. If he hadn't let Guy know about the letters, if he hadn't left them all over the house, none of it would've happened.

Karen starts to tremble. 'Rex didn't tell Guy about the letters,' she says, her voice dying a little more with every word. 'I did.'

The mouse has betrayed you. The mouse is a rat.

How could you have doubted your brother? He's the only one you can trust. He always has been. You light a cigarette and suck until the insides of your cheeks touch.

The Feeling has evolved again: this time, it's the sensation of plates of steel slamming from the sky to make walls around you, one-two-three-four. No one can see these walls but you. You are on your own in there. Karen and the baby are on the outside.

Rex will take his secrets to the grave, only now there are new secrets and you don't know if Karen can handle them. If she has betrayed you once, what's to stop her going to the police?

You would rather die.

The Feeling is getting stronger and you're getting weaker and now there is only one thing you can do that will beat it.

Once the decision is made, you feel lighter.

Karen wanted your life? Well, she can have the wreckage of it. See how she likes that.

33
Karen

We lost three babies in a row, hitting the threshold for NHS care, but Rex insisted we go private.

'We're already ten years behind because of me,' he said. 'I'm not spending another twelve months on some shitty waiting list.' With recurrent miscarriages the problem was almost always with the mother but he felt so guilty – 'I couldn't bear for another thing to be my fault' – that he got tested too.

My parents took Alice to Regent's Park Zoo while we went to a hospital in St John's Wood in London. We were playing at being rich people, just as we had all those summers ago when we lived in a big house that didn't belong to us. I had the ridiculous feeling that we'd see someone from the Capels' old life there. One of Biba's acting friends, perhaps, or someone Rex had been to school with.

In the clinic, Rex's swimmers went under the microscope while I ran a whole gamut of tests. They took my blood. I had external scans, the ultrasound handset smothered in KY jelly cold on my skin. Internal scans, KY jelly on a probe, a cool violation inside me. We got our results a week later. That's what you really pay for with private healthcare. It's not the lilies in reception or the Molton Brown toiletries in the en-suite, it's time. You spend less time in limbo.

Above the doctor's shoulder was a poster saying that domestic violence often began in pregnancy and that staff at the centre were trained to help. Rex was fine: wonderfully motile sperm apparently. But when it was my turn they slid a folder of images across the desk. A cross-section of my uterus, cruelly similar to a pre-natal scan, only instead of a foetus there were big black bubbles in the empty space. Fibroids, aggressive lumps of muscle that crowd life out and make it impossible for a baby to take. I could *get* pregnant, as we knew, but there was nowhere for the baby to go.

Rex took my hand. 'How long has she had them?'

The doctor shook her head. 'Impossible to say.'

'We had Alice without even trying,' he said. 'If I'd—'

He couldn't go on. I knew he was thinking that if he'd got out sooner, Alice could've had a sibling.

His voice was close to breaking. 'Can't they be removed?'

'There is a procedure,' said the doctor gently. 'But Karen also has such bad internal scarring that I'm doubtful – do you need to get some air, Mr Clarke?'

His Adam's apple was bulging dangerously. When he nodded, it looked like it hurt.

'Could you get me a coffee, maybe?' I asked him gently. 'There's a Costa in the lobby. And then come back and we can talk through our options?'

When the door had closed behind him, the doctor looked at me evenly.

'Is there anything you want to tell me in confidence, Karen?'

My eyes went to the domestic violence poster. I thought that was what she was driving at. He was Rex Clarke on the paperwork but you never knew who might remember a news report from 1997, who would be familiar with the Highgate House of Horrors.

'Rex has never raised his hand to me,' I said, 'if that's what you're getting at.'

Her eyebrows quirked; that had thrown her. 'Actually, no.' She made a see-saw of her pen, tapping each end on her notepad. 'Karen, the cervix of a woman who has given birth, parous, to give her the medical term, is uneven and wide in appearance. The cervix of a woman who has never given birth stays round as a ring. Which do you think yours resembles?'

We cannot know what we do not know. How many criminals has that tripped up? It was my name on the birth certificate and

Alice had Rex's face, but the truth had been written – or unwritten – in my body all along. The pen in her hand teetered on the fulcrum of her fingers. The silence stretched to breaking point but I didn't drop eye contact. My on-the-hoof reasoning was that fertility doctors must see paternity issues the whole time, but this? If not unprecedented, then so vanishingly rare that there could be no protocol. I had to catch the silence before it got too wide.

'I must be a miracle of medical science, then,' I said.

I can only assume she decided that the money we were paying her was worth her discretion. She dropped her eyes to her notes. 'Yes,' she said. 'You must.'

34

Alice

Blue silk day dress, circa 1910
Yellow Birkenstocks

@deadgirlsdresses
#outfitoftheday #ootd #vintagefashion #sustainablestyle

The morning after my parents' visit, the flat still stinks like a Neopolitan kitchen, garlic and fish. Dad doesn't text me his usual invitation to breakfast of rubbery scrambled eggs and oily mushrooms at the Finsbury Park Travelodge, which feels ominous.

Did you tell him about the dresses, I text Mum.

Yes, this morning over breakfast. He's pretty cut up about it.

Is he angry that I went to see Roger?

I don't think it's that. You know what he's like. He'll open up when he's ready. Driving home now chat later.

I watched the dots ripple until a car emoji, dog emoji and a house emoji land. I close the conversation with a pulsating pink love heart.

'Fuck!' Gabe yells from the bedroom. I panic, thinking the floorboards or ceiling must have finally given way. I run to check on him; he rushes into the living room. We collide, me in the T-shirt I slept in, Gabe in his underpants and socks.

'I've worked out where I recognised that couple from the photos. The ones with dreadlocks.' He thrusts his phone under my nose. It shows the BBC website, archived notes on a TV programme about self-sufficiency. 'Do you remember this? I was only about five but I was well into it. It was one of the things that turned me on to the movement. He's called

Tristan Lewis and she's Jo Vine. They must have a website . . .
yes!'

He follows a link, and a picture appears of the couple in a
hostile landscape. The dreadlocks are gone – all Tristan's hair has
gone – and their faces are weathered, but it's definitely them.

'Gabriel Villiers, you're a genius.'

'*This* is why you should've told me sooner.'

He sends me the link to their contact page. I click the email
address and start to type.

Dear Tristan and Jo. My name is Alice Clarke. I believe you knew
my parents Rex Clarke (formerly Rex Capel) and Karen Clarke,
and my aunt Biba Capel, in Highgate in 1997. I am looking to
talk to people who knew them and would greatly appreciate you
getting in touch with me. Yours sincerely, Alice Clarke

I leave my personal phone number and the shop landline. My
finger wavers over the send button. 'Should I say what it's about?'

'I'm sure they'll work it out.'

Gabe walks me to work, wheeling his bike between us. We arrive
to find that Hollie's phantom doorstep-shitter has struck again.
The whole passage smells of bleach and she's taped signs to lamp-
posts warning dog owners that she's watching them.

'I hope you don't mind,' she says, 'but I turned your camera to
my shop. Whoever's behind this dirty protest gets up *early*.'

'I do mind, actually,' I say, my eyes watering from the chemical
fumes. 'That CCTV's a condition of my insurance. If someone
sets fire to my shop or breaks into it and there's no footage, I'm
not covered.'

My key is poised over the lock when she rolls her eyes. 'No
one's going to burn down your shop.'

I take my key and come at her with it, stabbing the air in front
of her. 'Fuck's *sake*, Hollie! Get your own.'

Gabe gently lowers my arm. Both he and Hollie look shaken.

It's a relief to get into my shop, the soothing smell of candle-wax and old clothes.

'You alright?' asks Gabe.

'Fine,' I snap, to cover how much I hate that he saw me like that. That Surge wasn't really directed at Hollie. It was a release of last night's tension, guilt about hurting Dad. Hollie was just . . . in the way.

While I fire up the card reader, Gabe squats to pick up the junk mail on the doorstep. A pile of takeout flyers, a window cleaner's card. He sifts through them like a card sharp, then says, 'Oh, hello,' in a tone that intrigues me. 'What d'you reckon this is?'

He passes me a page torn from a reporter's notebook, the rings making rough lace at the top, the bottom half an unpicked hem. Someone's written with a ballpoint:

Alice,
   I'm sorry if I freaked you out before. Hopefully we can talk in person soon.

The handwriting is uneven, as if it was done in a hurry on a soft surface. I picture The Woman balancing a single leaf of paper on her thigh.

'The Woman?' I suggest. 'I mean, it *must* be to do with Roger Capel.'

'Or a reporter?' Gabe strokes his chin like an ancient philosopher. 'They can't want to talk to you *that* badly or they'd have left a number.'

'They're not asking me to contact them, though, are they? They're just saying they hope we can talk in person soon.'

'So is that an apology, or a threat, or what?' wonders Gabe.

'Either way it's a mind game I could do without. I should hold on to this.'

I put the note in the safe, with The Night Of dress. Gabe's frowning over the CCTV app on his phone.

'Can you see who it was?'

He shakes his head. 'It was pointing at Hollie's shop all night.'
I rest my chin on his shoulder so I can see what he's seeing. He
brings up a still of a dachshund taking a crap on Hollie's doorstep
at 5am. 'That's one mystery solved, at least. Are you going to give
her the satisfaction?'

'No.' I delete the footage, relishing my own pettiness.

'We need eyes on the shop twenty-four-seven if we're going to
get to the bottom of this.'

While Gabe's outside, retraining the camera on my doorway
and trying to lock it into place, I get a notification that someone's
selling the Gucci charm I need to restore the fateful handbag. The
starting bid for the logo is three hundred and to my horror I don't
have it. The outlay of getting Biba's clothes dry-cleaned has
cleaned me out. I call Gabe in, show him the picture and bat my
eyelashes at him. 'Can I put it on your credit card?'

'Sure.' He hands it over. 'Use it whenever you want.'

I bid successfully for the charm. I like to think it came from the
very same bag and that I'm reuniting the two components.

He's outside, one leg hooked over his bike, the other toe on the
ground, giving me an excellent goodbye snog on the doorstep,
when my phone goes. It's an area code I don't recognise.

'Alice Clarke? Joanna Vine.'

'That was quick.' I flap my hand at Gabe, who intuits what's
happening. He's off his bike and looking for a notepad in seconds.
I put the phone on speaker.

'Thanks so much for calling.' My voice sounds girlish and
breathy compared to her clipped, brisk tones.

'I'm presuming you didn't get in touch because you've developed a sudden interest in the self-sufficient lifestyle?' Jo says wryly.
'If it's about the murders, I can't give you anything. We stayed
there for a few weeks but we'd gone off-grid long before those
poor men died. I lost touch with everyone from the house.
Deliberately, if you must know. There was a weird energy gathering there that summer. I'm sorry to say this about someone who
passed before his time but I didn't connect with Guy at all. Very

spiritually immature.' I can hear hen clucking in the background and a sound that reminds me of maracas being shaken. I picture chicken feed in a metal pail.

'Do you remember my mum? Karen?'

'We broke bread together a couple of times, yeah.'

'And can I just check – you've never spoken to a journalist?'

'Never been approached by anyone till you. But I wouldn't. We didn't want to be associated with it then and we don't now. We've kept our names away from it so far and I'd like to keep it that way.'

I can tell by her tone that we're coming to the end of our conversation. I play the only card in my hand. 'I have a photo of a bunch of you in the house. If I send it to you, can you let me know who the others are?' Even as I talk I'm sending the photo to the email address I used before. I hear the sound it makes as it lands in her inbox. Gabe gives me a thumbs-up. There's a level of blackmail implicit in the picture. Jo doesn't want to be associated with Queenswood Lane; we're showing her that we've got the receipts.

'Woah,' breathes Jo. 'This takes me back. OK, the mixed-race girl, she's called Nina something. She made silver jewellery.'

Nina, writes Gabe beside me. Maybe the name will jog Mum's memory.

'The Black guy was her on-off boyfriend, until she got together with Rex.' I do a double take. This is dad's ex girlfriend? I baulk at the idea of my parents being with anyone but each other. Beside me, Gabe is writing all of this down. I hear Jo click her fingers. 'Arouna, that was his name. Uh, the girl with the peroxide hair . . . I honestly don't remember her name. She was one of Biba's actress friends.'

'And you all lived there?'

'People drifted through that house, you didn't exactly put your name down for council tax . . . you could fill a Tube carriage with people who crashed there over the course of a season.'

'But it's from that summer. Do you know where the others went next?'

'Nina was planning to take her kids travelling; she was an unschooler before it went mainstream.' The curled lip in Jo's voice makes her sound like a teenager describing how their favourite band were so much better before they started playing arenas. 'We literally only found out about the case by coincidence three years later. We were in the Smoke for the day, thought we'd ring on the buzzer for old times' sake, and the opposite neighbour filled us in. We couldn't believe our ears.'

I seize on this. 'What, because you never thought my dad was capable of murder?'

'It's a bit of a moral grey area, isn't it, whether some deaths are even murder at all?'

'Is it?' I don't follow her but I notice that Gabe is nodding.

'I have perhaps a different view of things, living as I do,' says Jo. 'Close to nature, red in tooth and claw. But I can't speak for a situation I wasn't present at.' We end the call with a sense of anticlimax.

There are lots of women called Nina Silver cluttering up the internet but a few pages into Google I come across a Nina Vitor Silverworks on Facebook, her profile picture a brooch that looks like a model of an atom. From the tallboy behind the counter I retrieve a chunky plaited ring from the bits of mismatched of silver. The hallmark, I now see, is NV, the two letters wound together.

'It's a match,' I say. I send her the same message I sent to Jo. From there I find her personal page and go through her friends list. Arouna's dead, and there's no sign of the Barbie doll.

'Remind me where Biba went to drama school?' says Gabe. 'I'll have a look through their intake for the blonde girl. If she's still acting she's bound to be easy to find. She'll have a website or an agent or something.'

'Queen Charlotte's,' I say. 'Same as Mum.'

It doesn't take him long. 'Rachael with an extra A,' he says. 'Rachael Veitch.'

We spend an hour chasing Rachael-with-an-extra-A. Veitch down a series of dead ends. Talent agents that have closed, theatre companies that have disbanded. She's not on Spotlight with the other working actors. Gabe has the brainwave of contacting Equity, who say her subscription lapsed years ago. His radio crackles, and he can't put off going to work any longer.

I put the ring in my palm and close my fingers around it, like a medium trying to contact a loved one who's crossed to the other side.

35
Alice

1950s prom dress in yellow organza
Buffalo platform trainers, circa 1990

@deadgirlsdresses
#outfitoftheday #ootd #vintagefashion #sustainablestyle

We're in a pub called the Magdala not far from Roger Capel's house, or Jules's house as it is now. I push my untouched plate towards Gabe and he harpoons a sausage with his fork.

'There are bullet holes on the outside of this pub that are left over from when Ruth Ellis – who was the last woman in Britain to be—' I make a stop sign with my hand and he says the words 'executed for murder' in a small voice.

'Gabriel Villiers, are you mansplaining true crime to me?'

He laughs. 'Guilty as charged.'

'Sorry to disappoint you, but it's fake news. A pub landlady got her brother to drill the holes in to attract tourists.'

Gabe wrinkles his nose. 'What kind of person wants to tour a murder scene?'

'Me. Right, let's do this. You can eat the sausages as we go.'

On the heath, smoke wafts from ill-advised barbecues and drifts over high garden walls. 'You know half of these are empty,' Gabe gestures to the gazillion-pound houses. 'Oligarchs using bricks and mortar instead of bank accounts. You think about the families going without, who that money could feed. All the activism it could fund, if they'd left you a tenth of what those children stand to get.'

As we turn into Keats Grove, he kicks a stone along with his toe. It ricochets off the hubcab of a shiny black Lexus.

'*Good,*' he says, and then, looking up and down the street, 'Oh, shit.'

Gleaming cars are double-parked outside the Capel mansion. Its gates are open and men in black suits sweat while women in black dresses and high heels struggle with the gravel path. I recognise a handful of them: half a dozen septuagenarian rock stars with their model wives, a Radio 2 DJ, someone who used to be in *Hollyoaks*, even one of the influencers who buys my clothes. Jules is talking to an elderly couple, both her hands in theirs. Her funeral dress looks like an Armani. She is its ideal wearer; it drapes from her broad, bony shoulders exactly as the designer intended.

'Fuck,' I say. 'I had no idea.' The yellow dress that seemed so bright and cheerful this morning is suddenly, horrifically, inappropriate. My face, more so.

'The one time you *don't* look like a Victorian widow walking behind her husband's funeral cortège . . .' says Gabe, then checks himself. 'Let's go. This doesn't feel right.'

'Agreed.'

But before we can, Jules spots me. She picks her way towards me on unsteady legs.

'You again,' she says in a savage whisper. 'I thought I told you. *Through the solicitors.*'

'Sorry – alright,' I say, and then to Gabe, 'Why's she acting like she's been the subject of a harassment campaign?' Before he can answer, a blond man in his early thirties, the image of Roger Capel – Rufus – takes Jules's right arm, and a sturdy girl who must be Xanthe takes her left.

'My cousins,' I tell Gabe. We've never met but they clearly recognise me. They look at each other, unsure what to do. Gabe swoops to the rescue.

'Sorry for the bad timing, mate,' he says to Rufus. It's a very different 'mate' from the one he uses with Stef. 'Another time, maybe. Sorry for your loss.'

'Not a problem, mate.' Rufus, clearly relieved, mirrors Gabe's tone. 'All the best.' He and Xanthe steer their mother into the house.

A white-haired couple are staring at me and nudging their friends. Heads begin to turn. 'She's the image of Sheila,' says an old woman with a wind-tunnel facelift.

'Let's bounce,' says Gabe.

My legs keep me upright until we've rounded the corner but once we're out of sight all my limbs turn to noodles. His hands are under my arms; he's the only thing keeping me upright.

'They're only a few years older than me . . .' I can't get the rest of the words out. I can't tell Gabe that I'm crying because in another life Rufus and Xanthe and their brother Oscar could have been my playmates; we could've had in-jokes and secrets and sneaky cigarettes and the kind of holidays people write books about. I can't tell him that I'm not just grieving a grandfather I never knew but a family who didn't want to know me. I can't tell him that my childhood seems even lonelier from this vantage than it did at the time.

I don't have to.

'I know, baby.' He lets me soak his shoulder with my tears. He strokes my hair. 'I know.'

36

Alice

1930s negligee in emerald satin, worn as dress
It's too hot for shoes!

@deadgirlsdresses
#outfitoftheday #ootd #vintagefashion #sustainablestyle

The climate emergency has a new metric: my takings. I haven't made a sale in two days. There's not much call for high-necked, long-sleeved gowns when the mercury's hitting thirty-nine. The churros shop is closed after the fridge broke down. Soldier Steve fainted from heat exhaustion yesterday and is on a drip in hospital. In non-apocalypse-related news, Hollie is being an absolute clattering *dick* about my CCTV camera, having moved it again during the night. Nina Vitor has not read my message. Jo Vine doesn't want to know. Rachael-with-an-extra-A Veitch has vanished off the face of the earth. The *Travesties* girls ignored my email asking for help. Mum says Dad's mood has plunged even further. It's fair to say I've had better weeks.

At eleven o'clock the seashell phone rings. It's a mark of how tense I am that I yelp in fright, and need to take a beat before lifting the receiver. 'Dead Girls' Dresses?'

'I'm looking to talk to Roger Capel's granddaughter.'

Mum's voice butts in, clear as though she were listening on an extension. *Don't engage. Deny, deny, deny.*

I hang up with such force that a scallop falls off the telephone receiver.

I text Gabe. *She called again.*
In person????

No, on the phone.

I'll pick you up at six. Love you.

I take a long coffee break during which I have my eyebrows and moustache threaded. I return to the shop with pink skin above my eyes and on my upper lip, hoping it's gone down by six: Gabe has no idea how hairy his girlfriend really is.

I dust the shelves, buff a marcasite brooch that's looking a bit dull and think about changing the window display. My bad energy is showing in my face: every time I engage with a customer I lose a sale instead of closing it. When my phone trills again, I'm more ready for a fight than to sell clothes.

'Hi, hello, hey,' says the voice. It's a bad line, like the caller's under a flight path, so it's hard to make out the timbre of her voice. 'This is a bit – are you Rex Capel's daughter?'

'Who *are* you?' I ask The Woman. 'What do you want with me?'

There's another burst of distortion on the line. 'This is a conversation that should really be had face to face. I can come to your shop.'

'Fuck off! Just fuck off and leave me alone!'

I crash the receiver into its cradle. This time a cockleshell falls off. I put it next to the scallop and rummage in the tallboy for Superglue. Biba wouldn't have asked for Rex's daughter or Roger's granddaughter. That's journalist-speak. Why are they after me? I didn't ask for any of this. I turn off the lights, pull the shutters across the window and sit behind the counter with my back to the wood, knees pulled up to my chest, waiting for Gabe.

He isn't here at six.

At seven, my bottom is numb from sitting. I call him three times. He does not pick up.

When he does arrive, at close to eight, he doesn't apologise or explain. Instead of joining me on the floor, he sits down on the damask chaise longue so heavily that a little cloud of dust puffs out of the upholstery.

'I am well aware I sound like a broken record, Alice, but is there anything *new* you're not telling me?'

He is so convincingly angry that I wonder for a moment if there is. Have I spent some money he doesn't know about? I wrote Big Nonna a thank-you card. I put out the recycling. Have I discovered anything, or taken a phone call and forgotten to tell him? No. I'm as sure as I can be. No.

'No?'

He clamps his lips together for a beat. 'So you're not having secret meetings at Crawford Southern?'

'Who?' In the few seconds it takes me to remember that that's the name of Jules Capel's solicitor, the trench between his eyebrows deepens. 'I was here all day, you know that.' I laugh nervously, but Gabe is further from smiling than I've ever seen him.

'I happened to be delivering there when you walked out, and when I called you, you walked off. You flinched when I called your name,' he says. 'You turned around, you looked straight through me, and then you couldn't get out of there fast enough.'

The Surge is readying itself under the surface bewilderment. It knows that we've been here before.

'And you *weren't* here all day, so don't lie to me. I checked on the CCTV and the shop was empty. The shutter was locked.'

Fuck! I'd forgotten. The Surge knows when we're busted. It switches from fight to flight, retreats into its shell. 'No, I went out for . . .' Even in the glare of his rage I can't bring myself to tell him I was having my moustache ripped out, so I answer, 'I went to get coffee.'

Bad move. The lie is obvious. My tongue is abrasive against my teeth.

'I don't know what you want me to say. I didn't go to any solicitor. You saw someone else. It's bloody Tinder all over again.'

His eyes throw blunt daggers my way. 'Don't try to gaslight me.'

'*Me*, gaslight *you*?' I could choke on the irony. 'My mum said you'd start doing this and she was right.'

Now he does laugh, but it's harsh and spiteful and his eyes are cold. 'Good old Karen. She's never liked me.'

The way he curls his voice sarcastically around Mum's name gives The Surge permission to let rip. 'No, she hasn't! And is it any wonder when you do shit like this?'

'Shit like what? I *saw* you, Alice! You're lying to my face!'

'I'm not lying! I've told you everything! I've given you my fuck-ing soul on a plate!' I am engorged with The Surge. I am a tick, fat with blood, full to bursting. '*How can we be together if you don't trust me?*' I hear myself scream.

The dresses on their rails seem to flinch. Gabe's cheeks are shaking, his skin mottled. 'You know what?' He doesn't let any tears go, just a slick of drool. 'Maybe we shouldn't be.'

He slams the door behind him, then pulls the shutter so hard it bounces off the window frame. The space where my love used to be has bared teeth. It has talons and spurs.

37

Karen

Driving against the traffic and over the speed limit, I reach London in under 90 minutes. At the end of Camden Passage, I honk the horn so loud that a stringy blonde woman dragging a dachshund behind her on a sparkly gold lead tells me to fuck off. Alice appears between two tall buildings and the sight of her sends my heart into my throat. She is a wraith on the cobbles, a knock-kneed child in a slip and Birkenstocks. She carries nothing but a spare dress over her arm and her phone.

'Thanks, Mum.' She throws her arms around my neck the way she did when she was little. I can't enjoy the closeness, born as it is of her grief. One day she will realise what a narrow escape she has had, that she was lucky to get out of the relationship before it was formalised, but for today she is broken, and all she needs is her mum to put her back together.

'You can stay as long as you like,' I say as she clicks her seatbelt. 'Get some space, get some air. Take Peggy out. Just let yourself *be* for a bit.'

'Thanks.'

Once we're out of London, the road has its own rhythm. Stripes of tangerine light slide repeatedly over Alice's face, picking out its hollows and turning her tears into sequins. Every now and then she takes a great big gulp of air, the way she used to after a tantrum. It's a good while before I dare to ask, 'So, what, he said he'd seen you at Roger Capel's solicitors?'

She presses her forehead to the window and delivers her reply to the glass. 'Yeah.' A flower of condensation blooms around the word.

'I mean, that's a pattern now, isn't it, love? Believe me, I don't enjoy saying this. One false accusation is weird but, you know, it's forgivable. Two is just – it's not good, Alice.'

She turns on me so sharply that a bone clicks in her neck. 'You think I don't know that?'

I concentrate on keeping my face expressionless. He has shown her who he is and she has seen it. What will it cost her? What will it cost us? I still don't know if Gabe is on to the secret of Alice's parentage, but he knows about Rex and that's more than enough.

'I'm just sorry it turned out that way for you, love.' I give her until the end of the song to respond and when she doesn't I ask, 'Has anything else weird happened? Any more phone calls, visits, things like that?'

She chews the inside of her cheek while she decides whether to reply. Eventually, she says, 'Someone left a note in the shop.'

Oh, fucking fucking hell. Who is doing this? What do they *know*? 'Oh, yeah?' I say breezily.

When we hit a red light, she shows me a photo on her phone. A scrawl on a scrap.

Alice,

I'm sorry if I freaked you out before. Hopefully we can talk in person soon.

'D'you recognise this writing?'

I examine it. 'It could be anyone's.'

'Could it be Biba's?'

For fuck's *sake*. I shut Alice down hard. 'She's *dead*.' A fleck of my spittle lands on her eyelashes. 'Please don't start this up in front of your dad.' I try not to let my panic spill into my tone. 'Are you worried that – do you think – Gabe won't tell anyone about '97, will he?'

'Look, I know I fucked up, alright?' she screeches at glass-shattering volume. 'You don't need to remind me. It's punishment enough. I'm sorry, OK? I'm sorry!' She takes another of those juddering in-breaths, then says, 'He won't say anything, alright? He's a shit boyfriend, Mum, but he's a good person.'

As if the two are separate things.

The light turns green. I stall the car twice.

Do you know what? I wouldn't be surprised if Gabe wrote the note and planted it himself. This isn't how I thought he would weaponise his knowledge about Rex, but it fits. Mind games, designed to bewilder. It's an escalation. She's on the next stepping stone of the homicide path: separation. Women are most in danger when they leave. And Alice has handed him a weapon that could take us all out.

38

On its last day, your life replays itself to you as a series of clothes: versions of you parade as though on a catwalk. The Alice in Wonderland outfit, your school uniform, the white dress you wore on your twenty-first, the dress you wore to become a cabaret singer with a perfect German accent. And now, the end is near, and you face your final curtain in slubby sweatpants and a cheap acrylic jumper with a lacy collar.

It's three o'clock in the morning and London is as deeply asleep as it ever gets. Karen and the baby are flat on their backs, mouths open. You are wide awake as your fingers explore her handbag. She's hidden her bank cards and money – rude – but she's left the keys to her car.

You scrawl a note that, if she has any kind of cunning, she will destroy.

You leave behind your daughter's name.

Her yellow car is like something from a fucking museum, with its crunchy gears and its AM radio. Still, the wheels go round and there's enough petrol in the tank to get you where you're going.

This is how it has to be. There is nothing to come back from. The child is a millstone. Rex might as well be dead. Karen knows everything. She has the power to put you away for life. You thought she was a harbour; she is a dangerous current.

You've known for years how you'd do it. Suicide is folk wisdom, passed down the maternal line. One afternoon in the Velvet Room, Guy had a picture-book open at a photo of a clifftop. You were high as a kite and feeling dramatic and you said that if you wanted to die that was where you'd do it. You said you'd put on a beautiful dress, so the skirt would billow like a parachute on the *way down. You had just the outfit: a mille-feuille skirt that Karen said made you look like a Degas ballerina. You wonder if Jules gave it, along with the rest of your wardrobe, to charity, or threw it straight in the bin. You hope the former. You like the idea of all your clothes being given a second chance by someone who hasn't fucked up their entire life.*

Karen keeps a road atlas on the passenger seat. You work out your route with the interior light on, the book balanced on your knees. The road is a grey ribbon unspooling before you. Service stations leap out and spring back. You do not stop.

You reach the edge of the world at dawn. The rain that has been falling all night has thinned to drizzle. The clifftop light is cold, as though someone's placed a blue filter on the rising sun. You leave the keys in the ignition and step out into an empty car park. The edge is calling your name. The Feeling is shooting cannons of black glitter through your veins because it knows it's won.

Heart thrumming, you raise your arms as though to dive. Your earring catches on your collar: the effort of disentangling it rips the lace from the neckline. You stand with your earring in one hand and a cheap lace rag in the other and prepare to take flight.

It doesn't matter what you're wearing. The water, you have read, undresses its dead.

39
Alice

Phool Indian cotton smock midi dress in block print, 1970s
Espadrille wedge sandals, 1980s

@deadgirlsdresses
#outfitoftheday #ootd #vintagefashion #sustainablestyle

I wake spooning Peggy in my old bedroom. There's a moment of oblivion, the mingling scents of a good dog, honeysuckle at the window and my mum's lavender Bold 2-in-1 on the sheets, before the pain of losing Gabe folds my body in half. Peggy shifts obligingly to accommodate me. 'Thanks, Pegs,' I murmur into her shoulderblades. It's a few blessed degrees cooler here than it is in London and the only sounds are Peggy's snuffling breath and leaves rustling at the window. I reach for my phone before remembering I surrendered it to Mum last night with strict instructions to keep it hidden from me and turned off. If Gabe still isn't calling, I don't want to know. It's ironic: when I was a kid she'd confiscate all my electronics at nine o'clock, muttering about sleep hygiene. We must have had the same argument every evening for about four years.

'Knock, knock,' says a soft voice outside the door.

I prop myself on my elbows. 'Come in.'

Dad hands me a cup of tea in my ancient *Friends* mug. Sophie and I would drink Nescafé from it and pretend we were in Central Perk. We had no idea about coffee and we'd tip in four heaped tablespoons and half a pint of semi-skimmed, then get the shakes and not be able to sleep until dawn.

'Thanks, Dad.'

He puts his hand on my shoulder as if he's doing reiki, as if he's trying to transfer something from him to me, but all he says is, 'I'm making eggs.'

Mum is at the kitchen table, pushing away a slice of granary toast with one bite taken out of it. The bags under her eyes are darker than ever today. I could tell her how to hide them but I don't think she's noticed them. I suppose you stop caring about what you look like after a certain age.

'Phone's in the bread bin, if you need it,' she says, nodding backwards at the kitchen counter. The hitherto innocent bread bin begins to emit a radioactive charge.

'I wish I didn't need to turn it on for work.'

'Can I help?' asks Mum. 'Can't you log into your work accounts on my computer or something, and let me keep an eye on things? Just respond to messages, tell them you'll send them when you get back. Then you won't be tempted.'

'Could you?'

She shrugs. 'How hard can it be?'

'I've seen you try to work a printer.'

That gets a smile.

Dad sets my breakfast in front of me. Boiled eggs and soldiers, the strips of toast fanning out from the eggcup in a sunburst. The pure childish comfort of it sets me off again. He takes one hand: she takes the other. Eggs and tea and a kitchen table and the only two people I can trust with my heart.

After breakfast, Mum goes into her study to work on her depressing book, and me and Dad drive down to Sizewell beach with Peggy.

'Do you need anything, love?' He has a way of making it sound as though he'll lend me a hundred quid when really I know what he's saying is that he'd gladly sell an organ for me.

'Don't worry about me.'

'It's my *job*.'

The sun bounces off the golfball roof of the power station. The tide is high and there must be fifty people in the sea. We kick off our shoes and tread an excruciating two metres across the pebbles to the water's edge, plunging our bare feet in and digging our toes into the sand. Peggy dances excited circles around us.

Here, on the beach, out of signal, out of contact, all my suspicions are beginning to feel unfounded.

Peggy starts to doggy-paddle and on impulse I follow, stepping from a shelf of shingle and letting myself fall forward.

'Alice! You're fully dressed.' Dad shakes his head indulgently, then the next thing I know he's in there with me. Two humans and a dog bobbing about in the North Sea with a bunch of strangers.

Dad lies on his back, his shirt stuck to his chest, and closes his eyes. 'When I came home, the first thing you wanted to do was go swimming. Do you remember?'

'I do! I have extremely fond memories of you throwing me in the pool at Leiston Leisure Centre. You said you could do a handstand underwater but you'd forgotten how,' I remind him. I don't add that when the lifeguard blew his whistle in warning Dad cowered like he was in trouble with a prison warder. As a child, I'd thought only of his separation from us, that not being able to come to my school assemblies was punishment enough. That moment in the pool was the first time I'd begun to understand that the prison experience held myriad grim experiences that had nothing to do with missing me.

'I hadn't been in the water for so long,' he says, eyes still closed. 'It was *religious*. The experience of immersion. You can understand why they use water for baptisms.' He seems to remember that he's supposed to be cheering me up. The next thing I know, his feet are sticking up out of the gritty water. 'Still got it,' he says, when he surfaces.

Dad's flashes of playfulness are rare and bittersweet. I was nine when he came home, and the years of silliness were almost behind me. When he lets himself go like this I get a glimpse of the fun dad I could have had, instead of the uptight, earnest mum who delegated all the physical mucking around to Grandad.

After we're done, we lie in starfish shapes on our backs and let our clothes dry. Peggy shakes herself off and I wish I could do the same. For a mostly pebbled beach, Sizewell deposits an impressive amount of sand in my ears and hair. Dad picks up a skein of seaweed and starts popping the little pouches like a kid playing with bubble wrap.

'It wasn't anything to do with me, was it?' he asks. 'Your split with Gabe? I wonder if all the press, around my dad, and stuff . . .'

'Not really.' I say, although it kind of was. It was Roger Capel's lawyers Gabe accused me of seeing. But no: the Tinder argument had nothing to do with the Capels. That was inexplicable, spiteful, *weird*. 'I'm so sorry I told him.'

'It's done now.' Dad doesn't hide his disappointment but he doesn't weaponise it either. 'What I will say for Gabe is that he didn't strike me as petty. I guess we'll find out, won't we?'

I'm properly crying now, the kind of gloopy tears that hurt on the way out. It's guilt and shame but I can't deny there's an element of frustration, too. I've lost him. And any chance he was ever going to open up to me about *the night of* is gone forever.

When we get back, Mum's on the sofa, entranced by the DuoLingo app.

'Why are *you* on *that*?' I ask her.

'I'm dipping a toe into Estonian.'

'What, for *fun*?' I did not inherit Mum's gift for languages. She tried to give me a head start with the whole Spanish-speaking thing but language-learning at school was a chore.

'It's her version of going for a walk,' explains Dad. 'It's how she sorts her head out.' He puts a hand on her shoulder and gazes down at her with the dumb, puppy-dog awe that never seems to lessen. She shuts down the app, to the disapproval of the DuoLingo owl.

'It's just nice to kick back and relax with something outside the Indo-European language family,' she sighs.

'What now?' I ask.

'Estonian's *Uralic*. It's got fourteen different noun cases!' I'm none the wiser but I recognise her energy. She's in the zone, doing what she was made for. Not for the first time I glimpse the life she could have had. Karen Clarke in her power suit on a private jet, an interpreter between two rival heads of state, her sensitive choice of words averting World War III. If she resents my arrival shrinking her life, she's never let it show. That's Karen Clarke for you. A model of self-control.

That evening we settle in front of the telly with fizzy rosé and an episode of *Who Do You Think You Are*, which Peggy watches with her paws on her chin.

'Nothing will ever be as good as the one where Danny Dyer found out he was descended from Edward III,' says Dad.

'A classic of the genre,' I agree.

Mum tops up my glass. 'You didn't follow up on that stupid DNA idea for Grandad, did you?'

'No,' I say. 'I got him a book about narrative carpets in Wetherspoons pubs.'

'He'll love that,' says Dad.

'I think Gabe was right about handing over your DNA to a company,' says Mum. 'Nothing good can come of it.' There's a tension in her voice. Even now we've broken up, it costs her to take his side in anything.

40

Alice

Comfort cloys, slowly at first and then quickly. After over forty-eight hours of *Grand Designs* and nursery food I'm getting itchy, reverting to the worst of my teenage self. I leave a wet towel on the floor and decline to join Mum, Dad and Peggy on their afternoon walk. Too spoilt to cook, I go to the bread bin looking for carbs, presuming Mum will have taken my phone out with her, but when I lift the lid it's there on top of the sourdough crumpets. She has left it behind, in an act of trust. She shouldn't have, because my resolve not to turn it on lasts for all of three seconds.

There are so many red dots on my screen, it takes a moment to process them. There's a glut of Google alerts – the coverage that Dad mentioned – a message from DeShaun saying most of the shops are closed, another one from Hollie saying she hopes I don't mind but she moved the camera again and it's OK because she caught the phantom doorstep shitter, and thank God, thank *God*, there are some from Gabe. The first was sent three days ago, five minutes after I turned my phone off. It has been crouching, waiting for its second grey tick, all that time.

Alice please come home. I'm losing my mind here. I must have been mistaken, it's just that I love you so much that I see you everywhere I go. I want to be with you and that's all there is to it.

I haven't slept more than an hour since you went. I called in sick to work, I can't eat. I never knew how physical heartbreak was.

The bed still smells of you.

If I've lost you I'll spend the rest of my life winning you back. Please. My love. Come home to me.

The words slide down like wine. *I love you so much that I see you everywhere I go.* He's a victim of his own devotion. Gabe was wrong and he's sorry. Isn't that what adult relationships are all about? Not bailing at the first big row but working through it? The fragments of my heart reassemble into something bigger, stronger, redder than it was before the fracture. I text him. *I'm taking the next train.*

I leave my parents a note saying there's an emergency at the shop and I'll call them tomorrow. They won't buy it for a moment but I have to say *something.* Once on the train, I put my phone on focus mode, blocking everyone except Gabe. The bleached fields and empty towns can't rush past my window fast enough. After Chelmsford, I'm the only person in my carriage, and at Liverpool Street the air is hot and dry as a kiln, the station deserted. Gabe is waiting for me at the barrier, a bunch of fat pink peonies in his arms.

'I've missed you so much,' he says. Our kiss is a bit stagey, a bit *Brief Encounter.* I'm into it. 'Let's go to bed forever. I'm never letting you out of my sight again.'

We drag our boiling, horny corpses through Finsbury Circus to Moorgate station. The streets are pandemic-level deserted. Gabe buys ice-cold, full-sugar Cokes at a little shop – one-time-use packaging *and* a Big Food corporation, this really is a celebration – and we roll the cans on our necks before pulling the tabs.

'Your parents must hate me,' he says, as we descend the escalator.

I think about the inevitable mounting communications from Mum in my phone. 'They'll come round,' I say.

'Did you get any further with the Biba thing?'

I shake my head. 'I wasn't in the mood.'

Zone 3 is no cooler than Zone 1. The trees that line the railway have gone yellow in the three days that I've been away. Their leaves crackle like tinder. If one of them burst into flames I wouldn't be surprised. This is the fucking apocalypse. I glance up at Gabe.

'I *know*,' he says, grimacing, and, as terrifying as the world is, there's comfort in knowing he feels the terror with me. We turn on to Avalon Road and a voice in my head says, clear as a bell, *There she is.*

Which is an odd thing to think about a stranger hammering on your front door.

Not a stranger. She's a song I sang in childhood, a bed I slept in years ago.

'You know her?' asks Gabe.

Yes, I want to say, although I couldn't tell him her name.

He clutches at my hand. 'It's not The Woman, is it?'

Is it? No headscarf this time, denim shorts and a crochet vest instead of a playsuit, but similar glittery bug sunglasses and long dark hair with a fringe cut blunt. I take off my own sunglasses and wipe the lenses, but all I do is smear eyelash grease and sunblock on them, making it even harder to see the details. 'I couldn't say.'

I sniff the air, as though I could pick up that provoking scent of hers from across the road, but all I can smell is something sharp and male coming off Gabe, a tomcat spray. He takes a photo of her and zooms in, then compares this fuzzy picture to the one he grabbed from my CCTV feed. 'I'm pretty sure it's not her,' he says.

'Fuck,' I say. 'What if she's a journalist? What if she's found out that I've got Biba's clothes? What if she's gonna out my dad?'

'Then I'll find a way to get rid of her.'

Gabe and I play Grandmother's Footsteps, inching closer as she drops to a squat and calls my name through the letterbox. When no answer comes, she slumps against the door, cross-legged on the top step, and pushes up her sunglasses, hand under her fringe shielding her face so she can see the screen of her phone. She hasn't seen us.

Gabe swallows audibly. 'You don't think it's . . .'

'She's *dead*.' It sounds more convincing on the outside than it feels on the inside. There is a swarm of bees in my chest cavity, hope and anger and fear.

'Only one way to find out.' He leaves me at the bottom of the steps and climbs them, hand outstretched. 'Can I help you?'

She lifts her head, and takes her hand from her eyes, causing Gabe to yelp, 'Jesus *Christ!*'

He moves to one side, and I let out a 'What the *fuck?*'

I climb the steps until I'm standing opposite the woman with my face. I touch her cheeks with my fingertips, just as she touches mine, and she says, 'I know, right?'

PART TWO

41

Your arms are raised above your head, your fingers an imperfect point. In your left hand, you hold a silver earring. In your right hand, a scrap of synthetic lace. The water of the English Channel churns grey and green below you. Gulls divebomb unseen prey.

It is not your past but your future that you see. A list of all your nevers.

You will never act again.

You will never dance again.

You will never artfully wipe away tears during an acceptance speech.

You will never reach for a beautiful boy in the dark again.

You will never ask Rex to forgive you.

You will never see Karen again. (Where did she come from?)

You tilt your upper body forward but your feet won't move. You are straining at an invisible leash.

You will never jump.

You imagine your mother's arms outstretched to receive you. You stare at the water looking for a sign of her. After she died you used to lie on your back in the old paddling pool in the centre of the woods and see pictures in the clouds and sometimes they would suggest the point of her chin or the hollow of her eye. But the sea moves too quickly, and your mind superimposes images, and all you see of your mother is her legs.

Where is The Feeling when you need it?

The sun shoulders its way through the mizzle then gives up.

'Fuck!'

You throw the earring and the lace in the sea. The silver plummets. The fabric floats.

185

Why can't you jump?

If only you could climb into a storybook. If only a little white rabbit with a gold fob watch would offer you a way out. If only you could lose yourself in a character, disappear.

You will never jump.

You can't do it.

You step away from the edge, then shut yourself in the yellow car and scream until you taste blood. You flail with your fists and kick with your feet, bursting the glove compartment open to reveal

– oh, hello –

a manila window envelope bulging with paper and card. Karen's driving license, her credit card. She knew you went poking into every corner, scavenging for coins and cigarettes. And here's your passport, stashed away in case you try to do a geographical. She had the idea before you did. It must be that on some level, this is what she wanted.

Guy once told you that there's no real secret to obtaining illegal things. You just ask the worst person you know, and if you only know good people then you find out who's selling drugs and you ask them.

You consult Karen's road atlas, running your finger along England's southern edge. Ports are supposed to be full of criminals, aren't they? One thumbed ride and two journeys hiding in train toilets, a Dover station photo booth, all the money you have left in the world and some fluttered eyelashes later, you have a British passport bearing Karen Clarke's name and your face. The guy who created it is a fucking artist.

That evening, your sweatpants are round your ankles and your jumper bunched around your neck on the surprisingly roomy front seat of the cab of an articulated lorry bound for Lisbon. If the man on top of you can tell your recent medical history, he doesn't say anything. As he pumps away inside you, you calculate from the names and dates inked on his forearm that Jade must be seven, Cody must be five and Rocco is just coming up to his third birthday.

Technically speaking, legally speaking, your passage across the Channel is people-smuggling, but no one looks for people being trafficked out of the UK. You're pretty much mates by the time he drops you in Spain, near the Portuguese border. You feel bad for helping yourself to the roll of pesetas you found tucked behind the passenger sun visor. You hope that wasn't meant for Rocco's birthday present.

You stand on the southbound autopista *and stick out your thumb. Twelve hours later you leave Biba Capel on the shore of Southern Spain. The records, if anyone is checking them, will show that Karen Clarke booked a one-day boat trip to Africa. The boat carves a white V in the dark blue Mediterranean sea, powering you forward to the only person left who might take you in.*

You befriend a French-Moroccan couple on the ferry who are driving from the port of Casablanca to Marrakesh and thank fuck for that because without their help Morocco would have defeated you. The signs that aren't in Arabic are in French which is no good to you. Where's Karen when you need her? On the three-hour drive the couple give you a crash course in Moroccan culture so by the time you arrive you know that the noise in your ears is a muezzin sounding the evening call to prayer from some unseen minaret.

The neighbourhood has a run-down charm. Shops display olives and spices in conical piles outside their windows. Red dust adheres to the sunscreen on your skin. Only your hair, hidden under the scarf, is clean. You look so different that when you finally find the apartment, set in a vaguely Art Deco block a mile outside the riyadh, it takes her a few blinks to recognise you. When she does, she drags her blackened hand across her brow. 'Give me strength,' she says, as though you're her teenage child and you're late home from a club. She doesn't actually ask you to come in. She jingles when she walks. You remember how constant that sound was in your house for years, how much you missed the music of her bangles when she left.

The children are playing Gameboys on the familiar bedding. Inigo greets you with the nonchalance of a kid who sees adults come and go all the time, but Gaia doesn't know who you are. The dart of pain surprises you.

Nina makes tea with her back to you. Rose petals in a silver pot.

'How's he coping?' she asks, which is how you know that she knows, knows what the rest of the world does, anyway. 'You are the only person he would have killed for,' she says, and it could be a compliment but it sounds more like she's blaming you.

The Feeling begins its internal tugging. You thought you would come here and she would calm you down, stop the spiralling, but there is none of the old warmth. It is abruptly, awfully clear that Nina is not your mother; she's only six years older than you, she's not even your big sister, she's Rex's ex. You cannot forge a family; only blood contains enough iron for that.

She serves the tea in little coloured glasses. The sugar hurts your teeth.

'I can't be in London without him,' you hear yourself say, and that's the first time you know the truth.

'You can stay for a week,' she says. 'I literally crossed a continent to get away from this shit.'

'Thank you,' you say, but she doesn't return your hug, she just tolerates it.

Later you have showered, leaving a russet puddle in the shower tray. You smell like rosewater. You change into the shorts and top you bought in Spain, then you stand at the window and stretch, like a cat, in the winter sun. Too late, you realise that your midriff is exposed. Nina has seen the loose belly with its violent purple streaks on the underside and of course she knows what it means.

'B. You have to go back,' she says. 'You can't run away from this.'

*   *   *

One week turns into two. What's Nina gonna do about it, really? She lived rent-free in your house for, what, three years? You make yourself indispensable by getting a job. You can contribute to the rent, which is more than she ever did.

There's a backpacker bar in an alleyway just outside the souk. A bright blue door through a keyhole archway. Pool, table football, a few double rooms and the rest dorms with bunk beds. A lemon garden on the roof with views over the medina, where a cat with huge ears sleeps on an empty rice sack. It hates you on sight.

The owner photocopies your Karen Clarke passport and adds it to his filing cabinet, but he pays you cash in hand. So there you are, the great hope of your year at drama school, changing sheets and fishing used condoms out of toilets and serving drinks and hoping against hope that no one you know has decided to go backpacking.

Weeks become months. Nina has accepted you. The rooftop cat still hisses at you.

One night, the last of the matches is a dead one you must've put back in absent-mindedly. Beer in one hand, a throat-scouring Moroccan cigarette on your lip, you ask a bloke smoking on the balcony if he has a light. He turns to you from behind a flame.

He has golden hair and skin to match and you think you might be about to throw up.

It is as though Guy has been brought back to life. You remember him not how you last saw him but as he was at his best. Inches away from you on the pillow, blowing smoke into your mouth. He was always wreathed in sweet smoke, as though he were a ghost long before he died.

'Thanks,' you say. You lean in, inhale, close your eyes.

Freddie is Danish. He speaks with an English accent but uses Americanisms. Gotten, faucet, I guess.

In the dark your body no longer betrays your secret. You hold on tight and milk him dry. It's not that there's reluctance on his part but you are always the one to initiate sex, you realise. It is desire but also necromancy. Atonement? You picture the blood being reabsorbed into Guy's head. The tiles on the black and white floor being cleared of their stain. Out, damned spot.

When you call him Guy he doesn't flinch. He thinks that 'guy' is something you say, like 'man'. 'Hey, guy!' he says, when he wants someone's attention.

The lemon garden cat lets Freddie feed her scraps of chicken and carry her like a baby. You are jealous.

If there's an empty room, you spend the night together. You go through his things while he sleeps: memorise the address on the flyleaf of his passport. Frederik Christian Hambro of Dragør is twenty-four, an age that Guy never reached. He has traveller's cheques but also carries cash, which you know he is careless with because he hasn't noticed you skimming off the top.

He cries in the night. 'I'm so fucked up,' he says. 'This isn't what I want. This isn't me.'

But he is what you want. He is what you need.

There are arguments. He finds the credit card that you have borrowed from Nina, just in case. 'That's not your name,' he says.

A month in, he says he's moving on. He wasn't supposed to stay this long in Marrakesh. As it is, he's got to skip Granada and Gibraltar entirely if he wants to complete his itinerary.

You scream. 'You can't go again!'

He looks at you like you're nuts. 'What do you mean, again?'

You are crying, covered in snot. Even in your hysteria you know it's not really him you miss. It was hardly even him you were sleeping with.

'I don't like drama,' he says, which is quite the statement given the things he says in his sleep.

The next morning he is gone. The cat spits like it's your fault.

The thing about not having regular periods is that you don't know how many you've missed until it's too late. The thing about your body having changed shape already is that it's easy to mistake loose skin filling out again as the 'snapping back' people talk about. Fuck . . . this is not fair. Where are the other symptoms? Where are the sore tits and the puking women get in films?

When Nina works out what's going on she tries to get you to go back to London but most airlines won't let you fly and there's no way you're doing that road trip in this condition.

'What the fuck is wrong with you?' Nina asks, over and over. 'People are supposed to learn from their mistakes, not make them all over again. I could've helped you sort it out. I mean, it's not as if you even enjoyed it last time.'

The child comes in three hours, smooth as a fish. Nina rocks back on her heels, wipes bloodied hands on her apron, looks up from between your knees. She grabs your breast and shoves your nipple to the roof of the infant's mouth. 'You at least owe her this,' she says. You don't know what to do but the child does. Her mouth docks on your breast. The feeling that floods you is like nothing you've ever known. It is chemical, it is better than anything you could put on your tongue. It fans out through you. It is so pure, so blissful, that it's almost painful. It is the opposite of The Feeling and yet akin to it, for it demands to be let in.

'You're in the pink cloud,' Nina says indulgently. 'You're lucky; it's the opposite of the baby blues. It's a natural high. There's nothing to beat it.'

Even in the fuzz of the pink cloud you have enough clarity to recognise this as a kind of mania, but if this is motherhood then you'll take it. You are full of good intentions, full of hope. You might even be full of love. The child tips her head back, a bubble of milk on her upper lip. You cannot believe you wasted your baby's name on the first one. This child deserves it. This is the one.

'I'm going to call her Alice,' you tell Nina.

She rolls her eyes.

Outside, the breeze bowls red dust along the streets.

Forty-eight hours in, almost to the minute, the pink cloud turns into a rolling indigo thunderhead. Your arms are the first things to go. The effort of lifting them to brush your hair, let alone picking up the child, is unthinkable. Even The Feeling would be better than this. At least The Feeling plays chase, and dares you to outrun it. This has turned your muscles to mercury, heavy metal running a river under your skin. Nina holds the baby to your breast. Within three days she is spoon-feeding you and taking you to the toilet, her hands in your armpits, your heels dragging along the floor. Gaia, not long out of nappies herself, learns to change a baby, Inigo to mix formula that comes in tins covered with Arabic writing and a picture of a blonde, blue-eyed baby.

'B, I didn't sign up for this,' she says. 'You need help. Like, clinical help. We need to do something official.'

Nina never does anything official so this must be bad. She writes home. You see her address the envelopes to Londres, Royaume-Uni. One to Rex Capel, HMP Pentonville, another to Roger Capel. She and Inigo go to the postbox on their way to collect Gaia from a friend's house. You watch them through the window; Inigo tiptoes to drop the envelope into the rictus grin of a yellow letterbox shaped like an old-fashioned parking meter.

Two live wires of panic touch inside you.

You are suddenly, violently reanimated. You get out of your bed for the first time in ten days. You pack what you can. You strap the baby to your chest with a length of fabric, the way Nina taught you. You wind Nina's silver around your neck and wrists. If she didn't mean for you to take it she wouldn't have left it out for you. She knows what you're like.

You spark a cigarette on the way down the stairs, then throw the butt into the yellow postbox without grinding it out. When it starts belching grey smoke, you walk on.

You are visited by an angel at the airport. In the departure lounge a woman in her fifties sees you crying and offers to hold the baby while you get some sleep. She's desperate for grandchildren, she says, but her own children show no signs of providing any. She inhales the baby's head. 'God, I miss this smell.' You sleep for five beautiful, numb hours. At the end of the journey, she thanks you.

You break down and ask if you can come and live with her. Please. 'We can raise the baby together,' you say. It's only when the woman tries to break free from your embrace that you realise you're holding her. 'You'll hurt the child!' she says, sliding her arms inside yours and breaking the ring. 'Oh, darling. I don't think you're very well.'

She has baggage to reclaim; you don't. As she waits at the carousel, you see her looking towards the police officers on patrol, weighing up whether to report you. You wait until she's heaving a Samsonite case off the belt and tuck yourself into a crowd heading for passport control. At the taxi rank, the baby starts to cry again.

'Oh, fuck OFF,' you say.

Dragør turns out to be a little fishing village just outside Copenhagen. Mustard-coloured houses have red roofs that don't perch on top of the houses like in England; they reach as far as the ground-floor windows, giving the appearance of brows pulled down over eyes. This place disapproves of you.

There is salt in the air; you taste it when you lick your lips. In a little bar on the edge of town, the barmaid boils water for you to mix into formula and sterilises your bottles for you in the glass-washer. You say you're looking for Freddie Hambro. You met backpacking and he said to look you up if you were ever in Denmark. She tells you they were at school together and describes the house where 'they' live, a one-storey place on the edge of town.

You don't like the sound of that 'they'.

Freddie's place is beyond the harbour, an unpretty area where you can't imagine many tourists go, more industrial than residential. Lights from giant cranes spangle the sea. Through the window you see Freddie drying up a mug and placing it on a rack. Behind him someone comes up: a handsome Black guy. They kiss, deeply.

Ah.

You wonder if they were together when he was travelling, if this was the stuff he was trying to get his head around. This is what Freddie meant when he said, 'This is not me.' You get that now. You are relieved. It was nothing personal.

You are trying to work out what to say when the baby starts screeching, so loudly that the door opens. Freddie is horrified to see you.

'Karen,' he says weakly.

'Hello, Daddy!' you say, doing a kind of 'ta-daaaah' with your hands. You think it's funny. You get the giggles. No one else is laughing.

'You should have told me.'

You really hope he's not going to be dramatic about this. 'I'm telling you now.'

'This is the girl from Morocco?' asks the Black guy.

'Kofi, I swear to God, I had no idea . . .' says Freddie, then switches to Danish, a speech that goes on for so long it's actually quite rude. After a rapid-fire conversation you can't understand a word of, Kofi shakes his head, then turns to you. 'I suppose you'd better come in.'

Kofi's from Bristol, of all places, he tells you as he makes some of the strongest coffee you've ever tasted. You show them the birth certificate, Freddie's name on it, the Arabic and English words. Kofi sniffs the air. 'Yeah, she needs changing,' you say. Freddie looks horrified.

Kofi rolls his eyes. 'Give her to me. I've got six nieces and nephews; I can do this blindfolded. Have you got a nappy?'

'It's the last one.'

You drag a little square from your bag. A cigarette has unrolled itself in transit, leaving flecks of brown tobacco in the folds of the nappy.

'I would've supported you,' says Freddie, then turns to Kofi. 'We will support you?'

There's another exchange in hurdy-gurdy gibberish as Kofi takes the baby from you. He switches to English and uses a stupid baby voice to talk to her. 'Hello hello hello,' he says, 'hello hello hello,' before resuming his debate with Freddie.

He shakes the tobacco out of the nappy, wipes her up, doesn't even baulk at the shit. Three minutes in and he's more of a parent than you'll ever be.

'We'll support you,' says Freddie again, eventually. 'We want to be part of Alice's life. Talking of money, did you have fun with my credit card?'

'Yes, thanks,' you say.

'Look, this is the start of a lifelong relationship here so let's not get nasty,' says Kofi. 'Let's sleep on it. I'll make the sofabed up for you. And then in the morning we can talk. Come to an arrangement. Money. Visitation. We'll do it all properly. Formally.'

You need cigarettes and nappies, in that order. Freddie drives you to the twenty-four-hour supermarket on the ring road. You barely speak. He stands bewildered in front of the baby aisle. You're not much more clued-up than he is.

'I'm just going to get some fags,' you say, tilting your head at the tobacco kiosk.

You light up outside. The smoke rides a magic carpet into your lungs. You see a sign for the airport and here comes The Feeling. It yanks you about like the puppet you are. It raises your arm, and then it sticks out your thumb.

42

Liss

The name on her passport is Alice Boateng Hambro but she has always been known as Liss. She has tattoos on the middle three fingers of each hand. Her names for the two most important men in the world spelled out in Morse. Dot dot dash dot, dot dash, dot dash dot for Far on the left hand. Dash dot dot, dot dash, dash dot dot for Dad on the right. Liss's *far* is a fisherman and her dad teaches guitar. She could spear-fish and play 'Jolene' on a full-size acoustic by the time she was nine. There is no *mor* or mum. Well – of course there *was,* Liss wasn't grown in a petri dish – but the surrogate who carried her, a British woman called Karen Clarke, died when Liss was a baby. Liss has tried looking her up but there are tens of thousands of Karen Clarkes and she had no living relatives. Liss doesn't want for family. There are cousins, dozens of them, blonde ones here and Black ones in Bristol, who've given her accent a trace of West Country, a slow drizzle of Somerset honey on her short Danish vowels. Liss doesn't tan; her eyes are large and hooded, her nose beaky. The children in her class had snub noses, almond eyes, golden skin. She would feel ungrateful to use the word *lonely,* but something has always been missing. Perhaps all motherless children feel that way.

Liss took drama at school and she works in theatre but she's not a performer. In the blistering June of 2022, her work has been a refuge in more ways than one. The usual Danish summer's endless light carries an excess of heat with it too this year, a new record high every day, and while poor Far has been slowly turning to leather on deck, sailing a little farther away every day as the halibut shoals desert the boiling shallows, Liss has spent most of it behind a dark stage, arranging and carrying and mending and sewing and stapling until her fingertips are sore and her back screams for mercy. It's an Ibsen play done in period, and Liss has used dark wood and original nineteenth-century furniture. Even the soot on the windows is authentic, Liss holding a burning torch under the glass until the sweat stung her eyes. People talk about losing yourself in work but it's here, where she's telling stories with spaces, with pictures and light, that Liss finds herself.

Now, on the eve of the first night, a summer of unemployment beckons, retail work or waitressing until the next project turns up. Folding jumpers in H&M or steaming lattes in Starbucks while firing off CVs to directors.

'Hey, Liss!' She looks up to see lighting designer Hugo, dressed in a Billie Eilish T-shirt and a pink sequinned skirt split to the thigh. 'You got a long-lost family you haven't told us about?'

On his phone there's an obituary of some British dude she's never heard of, a baby-boomer photographer called Roger Capel. So what? Then she sees the picture of his first wife and her belly pitches. The resemblance is so uncanny that Liss finds herself wondering when she dressed up in a white dress and had her photo taken in a meadow: which production, which party, which festival? Words leap out from the text. *Highgate rock stars Queenswood models London party actress gun murder.*

Murder?

'WhatsApp it to me?' she says to Hugo, as casually as she can manage.

The report hits her phone and the sensation of falling intensifies.

Roger Capel, society photographer, working-class. Sheila Capel, model, suicide. Jules Capel, model-turned-author. Rex Capel, guilty plea, life sentence. Same face, re-sexed. Two deaths on his hands. Shot a father-of-two in the *back*. Biba Capel – so like her mother, so like Liss – a once-promising actress, missing presumed. Guy Grainger, off the rails, middle-class family. Tom Wheeler, devoted father, loving husband. There's no mention of a

Karen or anyone called Clarke. She finds herself hoping that it's just a coincidence. Like, who would want to be related to *this* lot?

Liss doesn't go home to her flatshare but takes the tram out to her parents' place. Container ships glide by on the horizon. In the harbour, trawlers like the one Far captains unload shoals of silver fish on to ice. She hears her home before she sees it; the windows are open and Kofi is teaching: something classical and Spanish being picked over again and again by little fingers.

She lets herself in and helps herself to a thick slice of bread, which she dips in butter from the dish. Kofi's student leaves as Freddie comes through the door. He acknowledges Liss but doesn't hug her on his way to the shower, where he rids himself of his sheen of herring guts and bilgewater. In three minutes he's back and smelling like lemons in shorts and a Bristol Rovers T-shirt, his wet hair in little spikes.

'Good day on the water, man?' says Dad, handing Far a beer and kissing his cheek.

'Not bad, guy,' says Far. His English is almost perfect but this is a funny little idiosyncrasy that neither Liss nor Dad have the heart to correct. Far wraps Liss in a hug. 'What's the occasion, baby?'

'You might want to sit down,' she replies.

Historically, this formation – her parents on the sofa, Liss opposite – has meant that they are telling her off. Today, she's the one leading the inquisition. She slides her phone towards them.

'What does it mean?'

Far reaches for his reading glasses. He and Dad bend to read the screen, their foreheads touching. Dad finishes first. He palms his eyes.

'Can you send me a copy of that?' he asks Liss. She nods, swooshes the link. Her parents' phones chime in unison.

'Well?' asks Liss. The bread from earlier threatens to make a reappearance.

Far raises his hand. 'Just . . . let me read to the end, I'm as confused as you are.'

'I fucking doubt it,' says Liss, but as she watches them she understands that he might be telling the truth.

Dad speaks first. 'We always said if you asked we'd tell you the truth, but according to this we didn't know it ourselves. It's definitely her, isn't it?'

'I'm sure,' says Far. 'It's the jewellery. She was always covered in silver, and that beetle necklace? She had it on the first time she came here.'

'So she was using another name?' asks Dad.

'Looks like it,' replies Far. 'Not Karen Clarke but Biba Capel.' He makes a face like the name is bad medicine. '*Biba.*'

'Hang on,' says Liss, as the penny drops with a clang. 'Is *this* my birth mother?'

The axis of her world appears to have been balanced on a pinhead this whole time. One sudden move and the whole thing could topple.

'I don't remember this case,' says Dad, 'But the name Roger Capel feels vaguely familiar, in a swinging sixties sort of way. And the woman in a field, the shampoo advert, I feel like I might have seen that before?'

Far is staring out of the window. Liss knows that look. He wants to be on the water. 'Karen, Biba, whatever her name was . . .' He switches to Danish, a sure sign of stress. 'She wasn't a surrogate. I had a fling with her when I was travelling in Morocco in my early twenties. I didn't even know she was pregnant, and then she turned up with you one day . . .' He tells Liss how Karen – he's still calling her that – vanished into the night. How they tried very hard to find her at first and then less hard because they didn't want to give Liss up.

'So my whole existence is based on a lie? Cool, cool.'

'Liss,' warns Dad. 'This isn't easy for any of us.'

Kofi opens the sideboard and retrieves the little metal box they've always kept their passports in. Inside is Liss's birth certificate, her original birth certificate with Arabic writing on it and a bunch of letters on very thin blue paper which have been folded over and over until they're almost cuboid, as though someone was trying to disprove the theory that no piece of paper can ever be folded more than seven times. Undisciplined handwriting crests its creases.

i am your mother they don't need you blood is thicker than water
alice and alice and my baby girls rex and your uncle. back to
london back to the woods and all live together in the house again
all four of us

'All four of who?' asks Liss. 'Which woods?' Her parents shake their heads. They have no more idea than she does.

i have engaged a lawyer it is that simple i am going back to
england
they will tell you terrible things about me but you have a right to
know your mother
nothing but death will keep me from trying to get you

Fucking hell, thinks Liss.

i have a right to see my daughter i am going to get the best
lawyers on the planet do you hear me she is my flesh and blood

'Do you remember when you were eight and someone tried to take you away from school?' asks Dad. 'I had to come and get you in the middle of the day?'

Of course Liss remembers it. She was the talk of the school for weeks. The attention was brilliant. 'That was *her*?'

'Yup. She abandoned you, then turned up eight years later as if nothing had happened. We *kept saying*, go through the legal channels, get some kind of shared custody. She kept saying she wanted you, she tried to take you, but she never did want to do it properly. Maybe this is why. If it was someone else's name on your birth certificate, she couldn't prove you were her kid. She told us . . . she said that if she couldn't have you, she was going to, you know . . . the bridge.' Kofi jerks his thumb in the general direction of the Øresundsbroen, the bridge that links Denmark to Sweden, notorious for jumpers.

'She killed herself?'

Far uncaps another beer. 'We presume so. For about a year afterwards we'd go to the mortuary, identify the Jane Does in case they were her. But you know. The sea doesn't care about tying up loose ends.'

Liss has her phone in her hand, scrolling up and down between pictures of Biba Capel and Sheila, familiar but strange faces.

'So my birth mother probably took her own life, as did her mother before her. And my uncle, he's a fucking *murderer*. This shit clearly runs in the family! I deserved to know.'

Liss's parents look at each other, alarmed. 'You've never thought about doing anything silly, have you?' asks Far.

Liss scoffs. *Silly* is riding a bike with no hands or sliding down the banisters. To take your own life, to leave behind a child, suggests a desperation, a depth of misery Liss is grateful is beyond her imagination.

Dad takes the reins. 'And actually, knowing that Karen, I mean Biba, was troubled, I've always kept a close eye on the nature versus nurture debate and I honestly think—'

'God!' Liss is opening her mouth to say something about her upbringing she can never take back when Far interrupts Dad. '*Kofi*. If she'd taken Liss from school that day, she might have taken her home to her brother. That *monster*.'

The thought seems to knock the words out of all of them. For a few moments, they listen to each other breathing, to the music of the harbour, clashing masts and squawking gulls. As Liss processes the answers to all the questions she hadn't even known to ask, another takes shape. She unfolds herself, stands up, walks once around the sofa while the words line up in her head. 'So if her name was Bathsheba Capel, who was Karen Clarke?' Liss has summoned an indistinct image of a medium woman. Medium blonde, medium thin, medium tanned.

Far stretches his arms above his head. 'Stolen ID,' he says. 'Biba always had other people's credit cards on her; she took cash from me. I had no idea she came from money.'

'Maybe she didn't want to use her family name,' suggests Dad.

Liss feels a sudden surge of protectiveness towards Biba Capel, as though she is a daughter, someone she could've looked after, impossible as that is.

They talk in circles for another half-hour, and eventually Freddie starts dinner. He's cooking Liss's childhood favourite, *fiskefrikadeller*, fried patties with halibut and cream and onions, but tonight the smell turns her stomach. All three of them move the food around on their plates and talk about anything but the only thing that matters. Yes, Liss can get them tickets for *A Doll's House*. Yes, she's sending out her CV. Yes, she's OK for money. Kofi doggedly tries to keep it upbeat. His cousin Ike's baby smiled for the first time today. The student he was just teaching is a real talent, that once-in-a-generation guitarist you dream about mentoring. Liss can't finish her meal. She pushes her plate away and goes back to her phone, re-reading the details about the surviving Capels.

'I've got three first cousins I don't even know.'

Far's head snaps up from his plate. 'You're not thinking of getting in touch with them?'

'You've got dozens of cousins you do know, and who love you, and who aren't related to multiple psychopaths,' says Dad.

'But these people are *blood*.'

Liss says it unthinkingly. She's never thrown their lack of biology in Dad's face, never, which is maybe why she's never seen his face crumple the way it does now.

'Just gonna get some air.' He leaves the front door open behind him.

Far glares at her. 'That was shitty,' he says, and follows Dad.

That was shitty? They're lucky Liss isn't smashing the place up! She's not the one who's been lying for twenty-odd years. Her fingers are flying over her phone. Rex Capel – not that she wants to get to know *him* – seems to have vanished off the face of the earth, but surely Rufus, Xanthe and Oscar will be thrilled to know about her. Maybe they can fill the hole inside. Maybe they can tell her who she really is.

43

On Ibiza, if you are a pretty girl, or even just a thin one, jobs are easy to come by. You arrive pre-season so accommodation is cheap, and the few bars already open on the north coast are desperate for staff. It has a similar vibe to a film set: the carousel of interesting new people, the fast-track intimacies of the night. You give just enough of yourself to the other person to make a connection that burns bright then burns out.

Relationships must be temporary because of the awful permanence of what you have done.

You wake up every afternoon and head to Cala Benirrás where the hippy drummers salute the sunset. You eat breakfast as the low sun turns the sea to liquid gold. Sometimes the clouds are pink and that makes you think about how Nina described those first few days after the birth. The soft rose bliss of the child at your breast wasn't worth what followed. Hormones can't be trusted but chemicals can. You have simply decided to manufacture that pink cloud for yourself, to stay high for as long as you can. Out of reach of The Feeling. Stratospheric.

Every night that you do not die is a miracle.

Entire weekends pass without food or sleep. There's a spa on the island that will hook you up to a vitamin drip to put back what the weekend took out of you. You have a regular Monday morning appointment.

As the summer comes, you are astonished to find that you do tan, or rather the freckles join up to give the impression of it. The sun fades your hair auburn at the ends and you thread it with feathers, beads and cotton wraps. You get scouted to help plan and host private parties, the notorious invite-only bacchanals that pick up where the clubs leave off. You work with a couple, Ruben and Debbie, and move into their finca with its swimming-pool courtyard and ten bedrooms, all of which have seen more action than most brothels.

They take your Karen Clarke passport off you in return for your silence. No matter. You have an insurance policy of your own. It's incredible what girls carry in their tiny silver rucksacks, figuring their valuables are safer on their backs than in a hotel safe. Cash, credit cards, jewellery, drugs. The component parts of enough identities to be a different woman every day for a month.

Karen's parties become legendary. People on the island talk a lot about self-actualisation, the highest state of psychological and spiritual development. Acting will always be your vocation but as you select guest lists, talk set-lists with ten-grand-a-night DJs, decorate huge villas with sprays of flowers and bowls of cocaine, you experience the high of potential fulfilled. One night, as you stand smoking in the corner of another tedious orgy, you remember that your old tutor at Queen Charlotte's urged you all to get out there, live, harvest sensations and experiences. It makes you laugh. Your life experiences are something Kate Winslet would fucking kill for.

You don't think in terms of days or ages but some hidden part of you must be ticking boxes on a calendar because the day you find yourself banging on a surgery door, begging the doctor to fit you with a coil, turns out to be the younger Alice's birthday.

Rex is two years into his prison sentence.

Your daughters are one and two years old.

On your second Ibiza spring you take your Vespa out to the hills. Your hair, feathers and strings, flies behind you as you lean into a bend on the road and almost crash into a convoy of trailers that make the road impassable. You take in the equipment, the cables, the dolly grip, the lights, the fold-out chairs of a film crew and the pang for what you have lost bends you double.

The Feeling stirs, shakes the leaves off its back.

The blow is lessened when you realise it's just an advert, the kind of casting you all used to dread when you were at drama school. You could earn more in a day than you could in three months of theatre but there was the danger that you would always be the shampoo girl or whatever. This one's for hairspray. No white cotton dresses in dandelion fields here. Instead, a dozen models are dressed in space-age silver bikinis and shimmery body paint, their hair in flicks, dancing on a low wall, the sea in the background. You watch them for a moment, trying to work out what the message is. Aliens can have good hair on holiday?

After ten minutes they break for water and you wheel your scooter past the trailers. Food truck, wardrobe, make-up. You're almost off the set when you hear your name.

Not Karen but, 'Biba fucking Capel! Aren't you supposed to be dead?'

The alien's white-blonde flicks are held in place with tiny bulldog clips but you know those green eyes. You've seen them across dance floors, rehearsal rooms, stages, across your kitchen table in Queenswood Lane. You and Rachael shared clothes, nights, ideas, work, and one memorable night in 1996 you shared a Canadian student called Daryl. You think she was the one who sold photos to the press in the aftermath, and gave that icky quote to the tabloids about you and Rex being close as lovers. Eh. We've all done things we wish we hadn't.

'Not dead,' you shrug. 'Just lying low.'

'That crazy shit with your brother! We absolutely have to catch up. We're staying in Ibiza Town tonight. Come and help me drink my per diem *and tell me everything.'*

The last private party of the season has a pagan theme and the climax is going to be a giant wicker man that you float in the pool and set fire to just before sunrise. The guy who rigged it up has worked on Hollywood movies. No expense spared for Ruben and Debbie. You have sourced two hundred of the best, floatiest pills on the island. They are the Moët & Chandon of MDMA, with a corresponding mark-up.

The raid happens just after three when the dancing and the music and the fucking are reaching a climax. The policia *pull the power on the sound system as a beat's about to kick in and at first people whoop in anticipation of the drop, not understanding that the music at the* finca *has stopped for the night, perhaps for good. Then the officers swarm and people start screaming, pulling on clothes, throwing little bags of powder into the pool. You back away through a hole in the hedge that only someone who lives there would know about and watch as Ruben and Debbie leave in police cars and officers remove bag after bag of evidence. Your fake passport will be among the things on its way to a strongbox in the Comisaria de la Policia. That's the end of Karen.*

You hide in the cypresses until dawn. Wherever you are in the world, the woods will always have you.

A woman walking in espadrille wedges, a bikini and glitter eyeshadow at 10am doesn't warrant a second glance on Ibiza. You go to the hippy stallholder who looks after your safe deposit box and take possession everything you own. You open it with the key on your charm bracelet. Most of the credit cards will be cancelled by now but all you need to do is find somewhere that still uses the old-fashioned carbon swipe payment and you'll be golden. There's a bit of cash and a British passport in the name of Bathsheba Elizabeth Capel. It was issued in 1997. Your twenty-year-old eyes are at once black and bright.

'Hello, you,' you say to her, and you're overcome with grief for the life that girl might have had. The roles she might have played, the love affairs she might have had, the clothes she might have worn as the flashbulbs popped.

There's an internet cafe a few doors down. You order a pot of coffee and ask the surfer boy at the next table if he can teach you how to use a computer.

44

Liss

Liss wakes up in the Cadbury's-purple bedroom in the Premier Inn in King's Cross. Her first night in London was not pleasant. She'd idly fired up Tinder only for some angry, hairy man to call her a slag. Shaken, she'd gone back to her room, only to be woken in the small hours by the thuds and screeches of a hen party. Now, over congealed breakfast eggs, she fields anxious texts from Kofi, begging her to come home and at least talk this through properly before she makes contact with anyone in the Capel family.

An hour later she surfaces at Belsize Park Tube. She buys a copy of *The Stage* and reads it over a coffee at Prêt. There are a couple of jobs that appeal. She looks up London rents and concludes that she could work here if she lived in a boxroom in Zone 6. Copenhagen's not cheap, but this city! How do normal, not-rich Londoners survive? The people who live round here, in five-bed mansions in period-drama streets, aren't freelance production designers, that's for sure.

The Capel house buzzes like it's surrounded by an electric fence. Maybe it is. Liss's finger is shaking as she presses the doorbell on the outer wall. She positions herself in front of the camera, sees herself reflected in the fish-eye lens, all eyes and shoulders. It takes an eternity for Jules Capel to answer.

'Hi,' she says. 'My name's Alice—' and that's as far as she gets.

'Anything to do with your grandfather has to go through Maya at the solicitors. *Please.*'

The line cuts dead. Liss's reflection swims before her. The name *Alice* was enough to put her in context for Jules. *Your grandfather.* The Capels know she exists. Maybe always have done.

They know who she is and they don't want her. They must think she's after money. And this isn't even the murderous branch of the family. These are supposed to be the good guys.

Liss lets the tears fall for as long as they need to, then cracks her knuckles. She didn't come all this way to fly home without answers.

There are a surprising number of London solicitors called Maya. It takes Liss the rest of the afternoon and all the next day to determine that Maya Gopal at Crawford Southern is handling Roger Capel's estate. When she calls, she is informed that Ms Gopal only takes calls from existing clients. Every email address variation Liss tries bounces back.

When she turns up at the skyscraper near St Paul's the following morning, she can't get past the reception desk where people in headsets sit six abreast behind glass. Close to breaking point, she queues for a bus back to King's Cross when a man's voice shouts, 'Alice!' She turns around, the way you do when someone calls your name, before she remembers that she is in London, far from everyone she knows.

Or not quite everyone, because back at the Premier Inn, her favourite cousin, Noelle, is drumming her fingers in the lobby.

'Oh thank God,' says Noelle. 'Uncle Kofi thinks you've been kidnapped by some homicidal uncle. Come here.' She draws Liss into a hug.

'None of them want anything to do with me,' says Liss, through hot tears.

'Then they're stupid as well as dangerous,' says Noelle. 'I'm under strict instructions to take you home to Bristol. My mum'll kill me if I go home empty-handed. She's been cooking since this morning.'

The thought of Auntie Effua's fried okra makes Liss drool. And it is so nice, after the last two days, to be wanted.

On the train out of Paddington they split a tube of Pringles and Liss gives Noelle a fuller account of her time in London, including her encounter with Jules Capel's doorbell. 'I felt like shit on some-one's shoe.'

Noelle shakes her head. 'That's not how you treat family,' she agrees. 'Do you want to know them that badly?'

'I have to try,' she says. 'My mother's gone from some cloudy person called Karen Clarke to someone with a face.'

Noelle holds a Pringle halfway to her mouth. 'You know you tried looking up Karen Clarke before . . .'

Liss shakes her head. 'Needle in a haystack.'

'Hear me out. Have you combined her name with Biba Capel, Rex Capel, Roger Capel . . . ?'

Liss sees her own stupid, stupid face reflected in the lenses of Noelle's glasses.

'Liss. Mate. You *dipshit*.' Noelle attacks her phone. It takes her a minute to find that there are twenty-one men called Rex Clarke in the UK and one of them lives with a Karen Clarke in Woodbridge, Suffolk. The exact address is asterisked out.

'Fuck,' breathes Liss.

'Right?' says Noelle.

Liss's own search is thwarted by patchy train WiFi but she eventually finds, a few pages into Google, that Karen Clarke and Rex Clarke and someone called Alice Clarke are the joint leaseholders of a shop in Islington, *Dead Girls' Dresses*. Next thing she knows she's looking at the shop's Instagram page, square after square of incredible clothes modelled by someone who doesn't show her face but is clearly around Liss's own age. Is this Alice Clarke? Is Alice one of those family names that gets passed through the generations? If Karen and Rex are the parents, Liss is looking at a first cousin.

'Call her,' urges Noelle. Liss shakes her head. Noelle disappears for a moment and returns with three mini bottles of Jacob's Creek.

'*Call* her,' Noelle repeats, when Liss has emptied her plastic glass. 'Put it on speaker.'

The conversation starts with Liss saying 'Hi, hello, hey,' just as another train thunders past in the opposite direction. Liss fucks it up, just blurting the name Capel and not even waiting for a proper response before she invites herself to the shop. Alice Clarke screams, 'Fuck off and leave me alone!' and the line goes dead.

Noelle clicks her tongue. 'She didn't give you a chance to explain who you were,' she says. 'Email? DM?'

Liss shakes her head. Too cold, too detached. She found out about the Capels' existence on a screen. She wants her own introductions to be personal.

'I'll try again tomorrow.'

That evening at Auntie Efua's kitchen table as her plate gets refilled and new babies are passed around, Liss wonders what the hell she's doing chasing her birth family with its madness and murder when she already has people who've known her her whole life, never loved her any less for being adopted. White privilege rears its guilty head; she would rather die than share these feelings with Dad's family in case they think it's their Blackness she's rejecting. It's not just about connecting with someone who looks a bit like her. *Blood*. That's what it comes down to. It exerts a pull; it's a tide.

The next day, she calls Dead Girls' Dresses ten times but no one picks up.

'She's blocked me,' says Liss.

'You don't know that,' says Noelle. 'Loads of shops are shut because of the heatwave.'

She nods at the TV news where the ticker tape headline screams of a risk-to-life weather warning. Liss feels the climate anxiety rise in her but she stuffs it down the way she always does. If you let yourself start screaming about what's happening to the planet you'd never stop.

'If only I knew where she lived,' says Liss. They've tried searching on 192.com but North London is full of Alice Clarkes and anyway if she's related to the Capels she's probably opted out of the directory. In desperation, Liss pays ninety quid to an online tracing service. She gives them everything she has on Rex and Karen and Alice Clarke. Everything except for the reason.

Liss returns to London to find that Noelle was right. The whole city has shuttered itself against the punishing sun. All the shops in Camden Passage are dark behind metal grilles. Liss peers through the iron lattice on the window of Dead Girls' Dresses and sees a wonderland of clothes. It's like being backstage at a theatre. Who *is* Alice Clarke? She calls the shop phone again, presuming it will divert to voicemail or a mobile, but it rings out. Liss writes a note and shoves it under the door, hoping it doesn't get lost in the junk mail.

The next day – 'only' thirty-eight degrees – the miracle finally happens. The tracing service has come good. Alice Clarke has been been a few kilometres away this whole time.

The house on Avalon Road does not encourage Liss. The windows on the bottom storeys are boarded up with perforated steel, the garden full of fly-tipped furniture and sprouting purple weeds. Maybe Alice Clarke is on holiday or maybe no one lives here at all. She sits on the step and lets her head drop to her hands and curses Hugo for showing her Roger Capel's obituary. She was fine before all this kicked off. She starts looking up flights to Copenhagen on her phone, her hand a sunshield at her forehead. Muffled voices across the street draw her attention. A young couple are holding hands, backlit by the sun.

The guy is there but he isn't real. The only real people in the world are Liss herself and the girl climbing the stairs, reaching upwards, saying, 'What the fuck?'

Liss looks into her own eyes and wonders how you can recognise someone you've never seen in your life before; how it can feel so much like coming home.

PART THREE

45

Alice

'I know, right?'

The girl opposite me is not Biba. Nor is she The Woman. She is a mirror with a question mark scrawled on it in lipstick. I size her up like she's a customer. My face, my build, but scaled up slightly. She's maybe an inch bigger all around. More meat on her bones; bigger, better tits. Did Dad unwittingly get someone pregnant before he was put away? It's not out of the question. I mean, he and Mum were only together like four months before she got pregnant with me. But if she's looking for Dad, why did she come to me, why not—

'I'm Liss,' she says. 'I think I'm your cousin?'

'My cousin?' But she can't be. Both my parents are – effectively – only children.

'Bathsheba Capel – Biba – was my birth mother?'

I clutch the air to my right, feeling for Gabe. The collision of our hands prompts him to speak.

'Liss, hi,' he says. 'I'm Gabe, Alice's partner.' He looks from me to her and back again. 'What, how, can I just—' I've never seen him lost for words before. 'How old are you?'

'Twenty-three.'

A year younger than me. Gabe and I watch each other do the mental maths. She must have been born in 1999, but . . . but . . .

'But Biba killed herself in 1998,' I say.

'Yeah, no, I'm sorry to tell you this but she can't have done?'

Gabe coughs awkwardly. 'I don't want to be rude, but have you got anything to prove when you were born?'

I would never have though to ask that. Liss pauses for a second

– I imagine her slow-blinking behind those sunglasses – before snapping back to life. 'No, it's a lot, you should want to check. Here.' She shakes two EU passports out of her bag, a lion and unicorn for Britain and three lions on a shield for Denmark. The birth date on both: late January 1999. She is almost exactly one year younger than me. A million tiny holes form in my bones.

'She was alive at least until 2007. She came to see my dads in Denmark and tried to kidnap me from school.' There's only one of her but it feels like several people are talking at me at once. School. Kidnap. Dads. *Denmark?* Liss doesn't sound Danish, she sounds like she's from the West Country. 2007. I was nine in 2007. It was the year my dad came home from prison. I feel like the Red Queen trying to believe six impossible things before breakfast.

'I'm not being funny,' says Liss, 'but this is a weird chat to have on the doorstep.' She looks at the boarded-up windows. 'Is this, like – you live in this?'

'Um. Yeah. Ah . . .' says Gabe, then seems to shake himself awake. 'What am I saying? Come in.'

He opens the door and, with two showgirl kicks, adds his Birkenstocks to the shoe mountain under the coat hooks. In the dark I make a *what the fuck* face he probably can't see. We file upstairs in silence. Liss chops at the dusty beams of light like she's trying to break them, trigger an alarm. She too must be letting questions stack up with every step.

'You left a note in my shop,' I say on the first landing.

'You got that?' She sounds surprised. 'You didn't get in touch.' I finally pick up the Danish in her accent: a little puff behind the vowels.

'You didn't leave a number for me to reach you on.'

She slaps her forehead. 'Oh, my God, that is *so* me. What a dickhead. My brain's melting. But still. You get why I needed to see you in person. You can't just blurt something like this out. Although, that's exactly what I did just now, isn't it? Well done, Liss.'

'And that was you on the phone as well.' I try to remember the caller's voice but all I can recall is her words: *I need to see you face to face.* It all tracks. God. If I'd known who I was talking to! 'I thought you were a reporter,' I explain.'

All three of us are slightly out of breath by the time we reach the flat and the backs of my knees are slippery with sweat. I throw open the French window with such force that the pane cracks. The three of us flinch in unison.

'Cup of tea?' offers Gabe.

'Omigod *please*,' says Liss. She slides her sunglasses on to her head to reveal unplucked brows bleached white.

Caffeine is the last thing I want. 'Haven't we got anything stronger?'

Gabe checks the fridge, then shakes his head. 'We're all out. I'll go and get something in a bit.'

'Or now?'

He drops teabags into mugs. 'In a *bit*.'

Gentle, but firm. He doesn't want to leave me alone with her.

Liss has tattoos on her fingers, lines and dots. She wears no make-up except for eyeliner. Instead of the usual cat's-eye across the lashline, she's drawn a dot under the centre of each eye and a line at the corner.

'It's stage make-up,' she answers, as if I voiced the question. 'Even this weather can't shift it.'

I wonder if she's an actress like her mother, my aunt. Again, she senses the question before I can ask it. 'Set designer. Freelance. Your shop is incredible by the way, I'm obsessed with it. You've got such an eye for staging.'

Gabe comes back with the mugs and cracks a flat laugh. Only then do I realise we're sitting the same way, legs pretzelled up, hands resting on knees, leaning forward into each other's faces. His presence somehow shifts the mood, makes things formal.

'Where do we even start?' I ask them both.

'I guess the obvious one is whether Biba Capel is alive,' says Gabe.

'We presume not,' says Liss quietly. That word *presume*, all but worthless. She's not coming here with answers, only questions of her own. 'She was never found, but these letters are like the last trace of her?' She shows us blurred snaps on her phone.

i have engaged a lawyer. it is that simple. i am going back to england
they will tell you terrible things about me but you have a right to know your mother
nothing but death will keep me from trying to get you

'It's not conclusive,' says Gabe.
I shake my head. 'It's more than we had before.'
I can't translate the sudden urgency in his gaze. Is he saying, tell her what you suspect, or *don't* tell her what you suspect? Both seem like the right thing to do. Both seem like the worst thing I could do.
'So I'm the first one in the family you've made contact with?' I remember with a pang that the Capels don't want to know me. If they've embraced *her*, I will cry.
Liss blows mournfully on her tea. 'Jules Capel wouldn't even talk to me over the intercom. Just said I had to go to the solicitor. Not that they were any fucking help.'
Gabe lets out a groan so deep it's a vibration a good while before it's a sound. 'That was you outside the Crawford Southern offices the other day.'
'Yeah?' Liss is curious rather than guarded.
'I thought you were Alice. I called out. I thought she was ignoring me.'
'I heard you! I just figured it was someone else.' She's laughing at the mistake; my mouth swills with an aftertaste of our bitter argument.
Gabe hasn't finished. 'I'm sorry if this is a weird question, but were you on Tinder in King's Cross like a week ago?'
Liss flushes prettily. 'Until some creep on the app called me a slag.'

'Stef,' I say darkly.

'Alice, I owe you the *mother* of all apologies,' says Gabe, and then, to Liss, 'And my friend owes one to *you*.'

His fervour betrays him. It's only now, eyes on Liss, hearing it from her mouth, that he believes me. My word wasn't enough. I try to let that go, but when he takes my hand it has formed a fist, and my fingers won't let his in.

46
Alice

Gabe reasserts himself by clearing his throat and opening his laptop. 'There's a lot to keep track of here. So why don't you two compare stories and I'll take notes?' He types like a court stenographer while Liss and I talk over each other in tumbling sentences that run on. Several times, Gabe has to make us stop and repeat ourselves. I've never had a conversation like it; it feels as though I'm talking to myself.

Just as I'm about to broach the subject of our shared names, Liss says, 'Weird that we're both called Alice. What's all that about?'

It should be unnerving, the way she can see inside my head, but I only feel comfort.

'Biba was obsessed with *Alice in Wonderland* when she was tiny,' I explain. 'Tried to climb through a mirror in The House at one point, apparently, nearly severed an artery. Mum calling me Alice was a way of acknowledging Biba, keeping her memory alive, without saddling me with a ridiculous name that people would associate with her. It guess it makes sense that Biba would call her own daughter Alice too.'

'So we're both named after a spoiled brat out of her head on magic mushrooms in a book written by a Victorian paedophile,' grins Liss.

I snort. 'Beautifully put.' I nod to my bookshelf where a city-scape of Lewis Carroll books peeks from behind Gabe's blue Pelicans.

'You collect them?' she asks.

I shake my head. 'Never bought a copy in my life. People keep giving them to me. I know they mean well—'

'But it hasn't occurred to them that you might already have like a hundred of the fuckers already by now?' We grin at each other for a moment – another shared experience – then her face clouds. She uses her fingernail to scrape at a tannin stain on the rim of the mug, her expression and voice growing grave. 'Until, like, last week, I thought my dads had just chosen my name cause they liked the way it sounded. It's like every hour some new aspect of my life gets rewritten. It's a lot.'

'Oh, Liss. At least you're not going through it on your own.'

'Neither of us are.'

We go back to showing each other the pieces of our jigsaws, finding that some tessellate perfectly while others are clearly from completely different puzzles. Gabe's typed notes become erratic as he struggles to keep up. I don't mean to say it; I just hear it coming out. 'The thing is, I don't think my dad actually killed those men. I think Biba did it and he covered for her.'

Gabe's hands freeze over the keys. I don't know what my face is doing but it probably looks a lot like Liss's, damp wide eyes and a round mouth.

'Alice, what the *fuck*?' hisses Gabe. Liss might not understand the significance but she feels the frost in the room.

'Uh, where's your toilet?' she asks.

Gabe gestures towards the landing, watches Liss go with a muscle twitching in his cheek.

'It just came out,' I say when she closes the door behind her. 'She's *family*.'

'That's the problem.' He speaks softly, like the words pain him. 'What if Biba *sent* Liss? We've only got *her* word that she's even dead. They could be stitching you up. Them and the gay dads.'

Betrayal is a bruise that only fades on the surface. The lightest touch of it brings stormclouds to the skin and tears to the eyes. 'Why would they do that?'

'Money.' His voice drips with pity for me. 'Capel's estate.'

'If The Woman was Biba, she definitely wasn't poor.' It's only in articulating the observation that I realise its potential significance. Biba faking her own death is affront enough. The idea of her living *well* during her absence sharpens my teeth. 'She was wearing about three grand's worth of clothes.'

'In my experience, people with money are the best ones at getting more,' says Gabe. 'Look at my dad.'

I do a backbend, check the bathroom door is still shut. 'But Biba's legally dead. She can't inherit anything.'

'A daughter might be entitled to something,' suggests Gabe.

I don't accept the idea. I disbelieve him in the same way I desire him: at a level deep and pure and true. There's no way he'll understand how I *know* Liss is after something human, not material gain. I can't grasp it myself.

We hear the bathroom lock tumble and jump guiltily apart.

'Well, I've done it now,' I say. 'In for a penny, in for a pound.'

'Exactly,' says Gabe, under his breath, but when I take Liss through the contents of Sewing Machine Warranties and our meticulously plotted timeline he doesn't stop me.

'What are you thinking?' Liss chews the skin around her fingernail. 'Do we go looking for her and ask if she did it, or what?'

I swear I feel her pain, a pang between the ribs as it really sinks in that she only found out about Biba a few days ago, and in that time she's gone from dead to alive to missing to murderer.

'*God*, no!' Gabe sloshes tea in an arc from his mug. 'This woman is possibly a double murderer, she's manipulative, she abandons babies with virtual strangers, steals identities and fakes suicides. If she's not in the ground already she's the last person you want in your lives.'

'I deserve to know if the woman who gave birth to me is a killer. And we might even get to bring her to justice?'

I stop that in its tracks. 'Not without exposing Dad as a perjurer. He'd go straight back inside. Nothing's worth that.' I drop my face into my hands. 'Oh, *Dad*. This is gonna kill him.'

'Does he have to know?' Liss picks the cuticle on her left thumb, not looking at me.

I don't understand what she's getting at. 'How can he find out about *you* without finding out about *her*?'

'That's what I'm saying. You don't have to tell Rex about me. If it's going to fuck him up. I can go back to Denmark whenever. I never have to meet him.' Tears balance on the lower rims of her eyelids. 'I mean, you don't have to stay in touch with me, if you think it's going to be awkward.'

All I've ever wanted is for someone to experience my life from the inside. I'll never get closer than this. She'll never find anyone she can discuss this with as freely as she can with me, let alone anyone who's as invested in it all as I am.

'I won't let you,' I say, and she lets the tears go.

'Well, good, because this is far too wild for me to process on my own.'

'I'll tell my parents about you,' I decide. 'I'll do it now. Secrets are like vampires.'

'What?' Gabe doesn't get it.

Liss explains. 'The older they are, the more power they have.'

Gabe's lip curls at one side, like someone's pulling at it with a fish hook. Is he *jealous*? He slams closed his laptop. 'I'm gonna go over the road, get some booze in. Any preference, Liss? What do Danes drink?'

'Anything wet,' she says, raising an imaginary glass to him. His footsteps fade on the stairs. Liss puts her knuckles on the window sill and watches him head for the corner shop.

'You've got him well trained,' she says. 'Right, I'm going to call my dads, tell them I've found you and so far you don't appear to be a murderer.'

'You poor trusting soul.' I do a stabby-stabby mime and Liss laughs.

'And I'm going to let my mum and dad know about you. Fucking *hell*.' The air in my flat suddenly tastes metallic, corrosive. How am I going to find the words for this? 'Just be prepared for the fact that it might take them a while to want to meet you.' I daren't consider the possibility that they might *never* want to.

'I'm not presuming anything.' Liss heads for the back of the house. 'I'll give you a bit of space.'

Alone, I stand my phone on its short edge, stalling for time. I *should* call Dad. It's his family, not Mum's. But he's still reeling from Roger's death. I slide my thumb up and down my short list of favourites. Mum's the coper in the family. It's cowardly of me, but I'll let *her* break it to Dad. She always knows what to say.

I video call her and she picks up straight away. 'Hello, sweetie!' She's in the living room, a book on the arm of the sofa, green light filtering through the ivy at the window.

'Hi,' I say, thinking about The Night Of, understanding that this is how it must feel to have your finger on a trigger.

47

Karen

I let the telephone fall from my hand.

I swear, I *promise*, I think of Rex first. Years ago, in a prison visiting room, I told him that all the evidence suggested that Biba was dead. I thought that was bad. This is going to be worse, more so for coming while the silt churned up by Roger's death is still swirling inside him.

But what it means for me runs a tight second.

A text from Alice comes through. A selfie of her and the new addition to our family, another baby Biba, a ticking time bomb in human form. It's not the resemblance that's eerie so much as the expression. It's the same smile twice. Not cousins. Half-sisters, although they don't know it, nor can they ever. When one truth bursts free, countless others tumble in its wake.

Rex left with Peggy a good two hours ago; it's been a long walk even by his standards. They could be back any minute.

In the kitchen I pour myself a glass of wine, drain it, pour another, and pick up my phone. I shrink but don't close the tab giving details of tomorrow's Global Rising meeting, then open a new private search and give myself a crash course in sibling DNA. According to Google, half-siblings and first cousins show identical profiles, so if they do a paternity-style test to find out their relationship to each other, I'm safe. If they ever load profiles on to a database all hell will break loose but as far as I can see that's a different test, and hopefully Gabe's speech about the evils of genetic harvesting means that will never happen.

That blow I can protect Rex from, but I must deliver the other.

'Ro-ro-ro-*ro*!' Peggy bursts through the back door, all muddy paws and feed-me eyes. Rex is close behind her, as close to rosy-cheeked as he ever gets.

'Ow!' I say, as her claws dig into my bare thighs. I slide a shaking hand into her treat jar and toss a strip of rawhide knotted in the shape of a bone on to the floor. Rex thrusts his wrist under my nose. 'Eighteen thousand steps,' he says, then he sees my expression and the colour drains away. 'What is it?'

'There's been a development.'

'Gabe?'

Interesting, that that's the first place his thoughts went. I almost wish he were right. That would be hard, but it would be *clean*.

'It's more to do with Biba.'

'Biba?' He holds on to the kitchen table to sit down, lowering himself into his chair like an old man. Over a background scrunch of Peggy's jaws, I relay the story Alice told me. I choose my words far more carefully than she did. I set them down one by one, deliberate as tiles in a mosaic. With every revelation a little more musculature seems to disappear from Rex's face, so that when I'm done his skin appears to hang loose on the scaffold of his skull.

'But the earring they found.' He puts his hand to his own ear.

'I know. The only thing I can think of is that it was part of the false trail. She probably meant it to be found years earlier. It's only 'cos we put it in her misper report that they traced it back to us at all.'

'And she was last seen . . .'

'In 2007,' I say. 'In Denmark. Liss's parents say she was presenting with suicidal ideation.' The effort of trying to stay calm and detached has got me talking like a psychology textbook.

'Ten years?' Rex roars. He raises his voice so rarely, it feels like there's another man in the house. 'She was out there for at least ten *years*. Doing what? Living where?'

'I'm so sorry, love.' I pour him a glass of wine. He pushes it away. Two spots of high colour return to his cheeks.

'She let me believe she was *dead*. She could've got a message to

me, or you, or even my dad. Like, *I can't come home but I'm fine.*
You won't see me again, but I'm alright. Instead she let me picture
her fucking rotting in the *sea.* I used to think about it all the time;
I'd picture her clothes in rags, and her face all bloated up. Fish
eating her eyes.'

Jesus. This is the first I've heard of *this.*

'Was it that she didn't trust me, after everything I did for her?
What could've been more loyal than that?'

I am the only person in the world he can say that to who understands exactly what that means, who knows exactly what secrets
he kept, the magnitude of secrets he is capable of keeping.

'How could she? After the way we lost our mum. How *could*
she?' He says it over and over, as though if he clocks up enough
repetitions he will finally exhaust the words and in doing so
come to terms with their meaning. Just when I think he's never
going to stop, he interrupts himself mid-sentence. 'The selfish,
stupid, selfish little bitch. If she walked in now, I'd kill her
myself.'

I clap my hand over my mouth as though I'd uttered the words.
He pushes away from the table.

'I'm going for a walk.'

The sun is a half-circle dipping behind the field. 'But you've just
been for one. It'll be dark in a minute.'

'So fucking what? Come on, Pegs.'

For the first time since she was a puppy, the sight of her lead
doesn't have Peggy turning circles on the floor. She rests her chin
on her paws and looks pleadingly at me.

'Fine,' says Rex. 'I'll go on my own.'

The kitchen door slams. The plates on the dresser rattle. One
falls off and smashes on the floor. Who is this man? It's Rex, of
course: this is the dark side of his moon. This is what happens
when a love, a loyalty stretched so thin you could put your fingers
through it finally snaps.

I take the wine Rex didn't want to the sofa, and Peggy lays her
head on my lap. 'Does he talk to you, Pegs?' I ask her. 'What does

he tell you?' She wags her tail. 'You wouldn't tell on him even if you knew. You're such a good girl.'

It only hits me then that he didn't ask about Liss. The shock of Biba's deception, the scale of her betrayal, has knocked everything else out of his head.

I look up Liss Hambro online. Her Instagram is mostly professional. Her parents only feature when they visit productions she's designed. I zoom in to examine them. Her English dad looks the most approachable of the two. He smiles when the camera's on him, whereas the blond one – who looks as if he was made in the same factory as Guy Grainger – keeps his arms folded. I'm probably deluding myself that such things can be gleaned from social media, but they look solid. They look as though they've given her a nice life, full of love, although there's nothing either of them can do about her blood.

48

Alice

Gabe makes his signature cocktail: gimlets with gin, prosecco and lime. He runs a fistful of mint leaves under the kitchen tap.

'Honestly, I have no idea how they've taken it,' I tell Liss. 'I think we need to go there to make it real Make you less a thing that Biba did, more a person. Once they see you – once they see *us* . . .'

Liss nods. 'I'm up for that.'

'I've got a meeting tomorrow, then I'm working and the day after that we're seeing Grandpa Villiers,' says Gabe, handing Liss a drink and filling her in. 'He can't make it to the civil partnership, so we're going to have lunch in his care home. It's been planned for ages.'

'Aw, that's sweet,' says Liss. 'Well. Here's to long-lost family.' She takes a sip and crosses her eyes. 'God, that's delicious. A bit too easy to drink, if you know what I mean. I'd better pace myself.'

Two hours later and me and Liss are searching our phones for club nights and Gabe's calling Stef to come round with some mandy. I drag Liss into my bedroom to get ready. She looks through my wardrobe and pulls out one of the Biba pieces that didn't fit my brand, a bright blue Pam Hogg bandage dress.

'If only I'd known about you when I took all Biba's clothes. I should never have sold them, I should've let you choose the ones you wanted. I'll go through the books tomorrow, work out how much I've made on them and transfer it to you.'

'I wouldn't take a penny of it.' Liss pops up through the dress like a meerkat. 'You've had a relationship with Biba, with the idea of her I mean, your whole life. I'm still getting my head around the fact that she even existed. I mean there's loads to unpick but it's never going to be part of my childhood, is it? These clothes are part of your history.' She rearranges her boobs inside the dress so they sit high and round, suspended in Lycra.

'What do you think?' I ask Gabe, over-enunciating to counter-act the booze.

He looks Liss up and down. 'I haven't seen that blue dress before,' he says.

'It's ceroooolean,' I correct, quoting Meryl Streep in *The Devil Wears Prada*. Liss takes over, reciting the next few lines of the iconic monologue, and, when she stumbles, I complete the speech. Gabe's face retreats further and further into his neck, as if his body's too polite to run but his head's making a bid for freedom.

'Well,' he says at the end of our performance, 'that's not weird *at all*.'

A hammering on the door tells us that Stef is here with the drugs. Before Gabe goes downstairs, I say, 'Just tell him Liss is a cousin I'd lost touch with, yeah?'

Gabe hasn't told Stef any of my background. That's inner circle only.

'He won't think anything of it,' says Gabe. 'He's got something like seventeen first cousins.'

Stef fills the doorway, a bag of crystals dangling from his meaty hand, which stays swinging even after he stops in his tracks. He looks from Liss to me and back again. 'That is some mad shit.' Sweat has turned his full-body fuzz into tight curls. 'Nice to meet you, babe.'

I can tell by Liss's face that the word *babe* has landed like pigeon shit on a pavement.

'Haven't you forgotten something?' Gabe folds his arms like a disappointed headmaster.

'God, yeah. I'm sorry about having a go at you on Tinder,' says Stef. 'Lost it for a second there. But in fairness, babe, I was stick-ing up for a mate.'

The second *babe* has Liss spoiling for a fight. It's thrilling and also alarming to witness The Surge from the outside. Me plus me is going to be a lot.

Stef lines his mandy up on the back of a key, ready to snort. Gabe and I rub the bitter crystals into our gums. Liss dips a finger and presses powder on to her tongue.

'How d'you square your activism with this?' she asks.

'Say again?'

'Your climate warrior status. My dad's a fisherman; street drugs do a lot of harm to aquatic life. You think the people who cook this shit in labs are disposing of the chemical waste safely? They're pouring it straight into rivers.'

Stef gawps, a caught fish himself. 'I don't see you saying no.'

She shrugs. 'I'm not the one setting myself up as the saviour of the world.'

The silence that follows feels like the moment in a Western movie when a stranger walks into the saloon bar. The regulars stop chewing their tobacco and the barmaid quits polishing her tankards.

'You can't call Stef a hypocrite!' says Gabe. 'He literally – he would give his *life* for the movement.'

In all the time I've known the boys, I've never seen anyone challenge either of them like this. I feel unsteady, as if the floor underneath me is dissolving. Which, knowing this house, it might be.

'Well, look, there's no need to make a big thing of it,' says Gabe. 'Tonight's about getting loved up. Let's reset the vibes before the mandy kicks in, shall we?'

'All is forgiven.' Liss salutes Stef but there's an edge in it. When Gabe's eyes become two popped corks and Liss's jaw starts to tic, I decide to turn this into a real party. Me, Gabe and Stef send an invitation to every group chat in our phones, and between eleven and midnight every pub in north London seems to empty out into our tiny flat. I always think of The Surge as something to be suppressed, controlled. I'd forgotten that it's not always a whirlpool; sometimes it's a wave, and, if you let yourself ride it, wonderful things happen.

I couldn't tell you whose idea it was to open up the asbestos rooms or where the screwdriver came from but somehow the doors are off their hinges, the soundbar is on the landing and a huge empty room on the floor beneath is filled with music and beautiful souls, each aboard their own private whirligig, spiralling by the light of a hundred tiny candles. The mirrors on the landing reflect each shivering point of light that flickers in looking-glass land. The night rises up through the bass in the floor and into my veins. Gabe's idea of dancing is throwing his hands around out of time like a kid playing on a VR headset. On the landing, Stef and one of the Global Rising boys, Kostas, *look* deep in conversation but they're actually each delivering an earnest monologue, neither listening to the other. Two girls I've never met slide down the stairs on a giant reproduction of the *Mona Lisa* I had no idea was in the house.

'Which is typical of end-stage capitalism,' says Stef, while Kostas glances at the blur of bare limbs, hair and Renaissance art and says, 'Of course the thing about the real *Mona Lisa* is that it's *tiny.*'

Me and Liss are a human disco ball, sparkling, spinning. The party revolves around us. It is the kind of night legends are made of.

The last thing I remember is Gabe standing over our bed, saying, 'I guess I'll take the sofa, then,' my cousin next to me on top of the duvet, and, as the sun rises over the railway line, the sound of Liss scuffing her feet together as we both drift into twitchy, trippy sleep.

At nine, the opening of my eyes and lips is accompanied by sound effects: cracking, sucking noises as the gunk of the night is pulled apart.

'I'm dead,' says Liss on the pillow beside me.

It takes a few seconds for her face to come fully into focus. When it does, I'm impressed.

'Your eyeliner is immaculate, even in death.'

'Told you.'

'Do *I* look dead?'

She considers the wreckage of me. 'Not *dead*. Maybe like you've spent the night in a Thai prison?'

'I need some paracetamol,' I say. 'And a tea with about nine sugars in it.'

On the sofa, Gabe lies face down, head buried in his armpit. I try to identify what's wrong in the flat. The light is different: not warmer, but somehow bigger. I fill the kettle and flip it to boil, trying to identify the change in the atmosphere before remembering with horror that we opened up the floor below last night. We creep down the stairs. That's what's wrong with the light. It's being thrown around the house by a dozen starved mirrors. The landing reeks of cigarettes and spilled wine. The doors are neatly laid against the landing wall. The brass knobs are on the floor, innards of their locks spilling around them.

In the huge front bedroom, Stef is starfished on his back, on top of Gabe's sleeping bag, wearing nothing but underwear that leaves little to the imagination. 'Tempted?' I ask Liss. She shakes her head.

After pints of sugary tea, the boys re-hang the doors while Liss and I embark on a fruitless search for Stef's clothes. Eventually, he cycles back to his parents' place wearing his underwear and a giant Just Stop Oil T-shirt that I sometimes use as a nightie. Only when Liss is in the shower do Gabe and I have a moment to ourselves.

'Sorry about the bed,' I tell him. 'I was off my face. Fucking brilliant party, though.'

Gabe trails a finger from the crease of my elbow to the palm of my hand and back again. 'Just remember what I said yesterday. Don't get carried away. It's all a bit *intense*.'

'Well, of course it's a bit intense. This is not a normal way to get to know someone, finding out you've got a cousin and that your dead aunt's alive all in one go. Not to mention my family history. *And* she lives in another country. What'm I supposed to do? See her for an hour once a day? Go on a series of coffee dates?'

His eyes flit left to right, as though he's choosing his words from a selection of options and he's working out which combination is the least likely to make me explode. 'I just don't want her to take advantage of you.'

'In what way? What could she be *after*? I'm not exactly a Kardashian, Gabe. She wouldn't even take the money from Biba's clothes.'

I don't like the satisfaction in Gabe's nod; as if I've walked right into his trap. 'Yeah, she got that in pretty quick. Almost as though she wanted you to know upfront that she wasn't on the take.'

'You can be a right cynical fucker sometimes,' I say.

'I'm just looking out for you, that's all.' He kisses me, then rises to palm the debris of the living room table for his keys and phone.

'You going out?' I say in surprise.

'I'm visiting Kevin in prison,' he says. 'I'm already late.'

I watch him go from the window. When I turn round, there's Liss, dressed but with water in fat domes on her shoulders. 'I couldn't help but hear that,' she says. 'I meant what I said. I don't want anything. No dresses, no profits, nothing. Except you.'

My cheeks burn with shame. 'He's just trying to look out for me.'

'Well, you could be a serial killer and I could be a scammer, so I think that makes us even,' she says, but her smile flickers. 'Look, I'll go back to my hotel now. I don't want to crowd you and Gabe. I can tell he doesn't want to share you.'

'Nonsense,' I say. '*Mi casa, tu casa*. We'll go and get your stuff from the hotel now.'

'And then what?' she asks. 'Do we look for Biba? Do we get to the bottom of what happened that night?'

I consider Gabe's warning. Biba's dangerous, Liss is an unknown, my mother has begged me not to do this and the truth could kill my father. There's only one answer I could possibly give her. 'Yes.'

49

Karen

Following someone is surprisingly easy. People are generally looking at their phones or in shop windows or focused on their
companion, as Gabe and Stef are now, deep in conversation and
forcing the other pedestrians on High Holborn to flow around
them like water bypassing a rock. An advantage of surveillance at
forty-six is the invisibility cloak of middle age. No one looks
twice at me in my black leggings and Primark hoodie as I slink
into the ornate hideout of the Princess Louise.

I'm lucky: the glass-partitioned booth the boys tuck themselves into is next to an empty one. I take my seat and order a
glass of white by pointing. My adrenaline is coursing but the
content of their conversation would challenge the most dedi-
cated eavesdropper. Apart from an interlude of gossip about
some students who threw tomato soup at a painting, it's all
about legal aid and transport police and how someone called
Hamza *calls* himself a Leninist but if you actually listen to the
bloke he's fully a centrist and my thoughts keep wandering
home. Rex is so consumed by his quiet rage that he hasn't ques-
tioned why I'm travelling to London for 'work' again. Yesterday
evening he drank whisky until he threw up. He has never done
that before.

Only a persistent rising plinky sound from one the boys' phones
is anchoring me to the moment.

'You ever think you might be addicted?' Gabe asks Stef. 'You
don't even look at them properly before you swipe left.' I think
this is a reference to Tinder. Alice says Stef's never off the app.

Stef laughs. 'I can't get that Liss out my head, man.'

'Why would you want to get involved with something that

messy when you've got pussy coming out your ears?' This is definitely not Gabe's meet-the-parents voice.

'They look like *twins*.' I think Stef is rubbing his thighs. 'Can
you get them to lez it up?'

Ugh.

'They're cousins.'

'That's even *hotter*.'

'You're a rancid horndog,' says Gabe, with real affection. 'Also,
I think she might hate you.'

'The heart wants what the heart wants.' They clink glasses.
'Seriously though, man, isn't Liss a bit of a spanner in the works?'

Works? What works? Gabe sighs. My focus is so intense, even
my sense of smell is heightened, the hoppy aroma of his breath
finding its way to my nose.

'Potentially, yeah,' he says. 'More so if they insist on playing
detectives with Alice's family history. It's got to increase the
chances of her finding out.'

Fucking stupid imprecise English pronouns. If we all spoke,
say, Slovenian, I'd know exactly which 'her' he was referring to.

'Yeah,' agrees Stef. 'It's fucked up that you know something
that big about her and she doesn't.'

I can't help my gasp or its volume. Thank Christ for the
barmaid, pulling a pint from a spluttering tap, covering my noise.
What could he mean but the truth about Alice's parentage? I can't
make out what the boys say next. By the time she's filled the glass
with foul, yeasty foam, I only catch the last word of their conversation: 'inevitable'.

The plink – which I presume is Tinder – sounds again, three
times in succession. 'Hang on, this looks promising,' says Stef. He
shows the phone to Gabe. 'Gonna go for it before someone beats
me to it. See you tomorrow, yeah?'

I see a blur of movement as they perform their elaborate hand-
shake sequence. When Stef passes my stool he looks right at me.
I go clammy all over, but before I can even think the words *how
will I talk my way out of this*, he's gone. He wasn't looking at me

but through me. He didn't see me at the last meeting and even if he did, he wouldn't have registered an invisible woman.

Gabe stays on the other side of the clouded glass, slowly ekeing out his pint. I imagine the fog dissolving, the expression on his face if he knew who was listening. Whose shame would be greater? Mine for stalking, or his for conspiring?

I throw my hood over my head and leave the pub before I can find out.

How does he know? More to the point, how will he use it?

50

Karen

Liss wants to come down to Suffolk, Alice has texted. *She was a bit dubious about Dad at first but I've told her everything, she knows he's cool.*

Alice hasn't specified what 'everything' means, but I'm presuming she's circled back to her pet theory about Biba. I tap the edge of my phone on the kitchen counter. Thus far, she's shared it with Gabe and Liss. I don't trust him and I've never met her. I wish I could sit invisibly in the corner of their living room while they talk. I could glean their intentions then: the ones they say out loud and the hidden agendas that show in a slide of the eyes, a hand that covers the mouth. Not knowing is torture. Not knowing makes it impossible for me to keep Rex safe from knowledge that could send him over the edge – if he hasn't tipped already.

I'm excited to meet her! I text back, with a string of twin-girl emojis.

Will it be OK with Dad how's he dealing with the whole Biba thing?

I text her the emoji of walking man, next to a dog.

Again? His feet are gonna fall off.

I respond with a smiley that belies my anxiety. When he left at ten o'clock this morning, he tried to sneak out without Peggy. 'I'm worried I've reached even *her* threshold for w-a-l-k-i-e-s,' he said. I handed him her lead. If Peggy was with him he wouldn't do 'anything stupid' as the euphemism goes.

Booking train tickets now, writes Alice.

By four, I've been pacing the kitchen rug for so long that I'm starting to get little static electricity shocks. I lean on the sink, looking out of the back window to the meadows beyond. It's an

Armageddon sky, deep hot blue. The wheat sways like the pelt of a great golden retriever. Rex and Peggy will appear first as black specks, fleas in fur, before coming into focus. By six, there's still nothing and no one in sight. They have been gone for eight hours. I could be the only person on Earth.

It's closing in on seven o'clock when at last he calls, a drag in his voice. 'Can you come and get us?' He names a pub a ten-minute drive away.

Anger punches its way through my relief. 'Have you been drinking all day?'

'Only just got here. But Peggy can't go on.'

'What d'you mean?' I say, but he's ended the call.

'Fuck's sake,' I say, and reach for my car keys.

The beer garden is busy, people in colourful clothes carrying drinks, leaning across each other to reach for nachos, but Rex has cleared a moat of space around him. He looks like an escaped convict who's staggered in from the marshes and settled down under an Adnams parasol. Peggy's asleep in his arms like a giant baby, pink tongue lolling, dirt matted on her legs.

'Hey.' I sit next to him on the bench. He doesn't smell great. His grey T-shirt is stiff with dried sweat. His left foot is black and sticky. 'What happened?' I bend to examine his boot. There's a tangle of fresh seaweed in his shoelaces and traces of sand in the stitching. 'Did you walk to the *sea*?' I'm pulling up the map in my mind: our house is six miles inland. Orford must be four hours on foot, lumpy terrain of hardened clay and heather.

'I carried Pegs the last couple of miles or so.'

Peggy weighs about sixteen kilos. I can barely get her out of the bath, let alone carry her along country roads.

'Have you cut yourself?' I wipe old blood from his shin with my thumb. There's fresh blood underneath. I can't work out where it's coming from.

'Blister. It popped about an hour ago.'

I look up at his face. 'You kept going on *bleeding feet*? Why didn't you call me?'

'No, it's all good,' he says. 'It's all good.'

It is clearly not all good. I don't feel as though his rage has subsided: more that he's run out of fuel for it.

'Can you walk?' I ask, and he shakes his head. I have to back the car into the beer garden so that he can stagger the few yards to the open door.

On the way home, I steal sidelong glances, trying to read his profile. Whenever he catches me, he repeats the phrase, 'It's all good,' like a malfunctioning cyborg.

I run him a hot bath and put Dead Sea salt and coal tar soap in it. I close the toilet seat and sit beside the tub. 'Do you need a hand?'

'It's all good.' He winces as he lowers himself in. The water clouds with blood and dirt and something yellow. He slides under the water and closes his eyes. Tiny bubbles cluster around his hairline and on his eyebrows but nothing leaves his mouth or nose. I hold my own breath for as long as I can. When my lungs start to ache, I pull him up by the shoulders. 'Rex, stop it!' I shout. 'You're scaring me!'

'Fuck's sake, Karen, get *off* me.' He's breathing heavily. His wet eyelashes form jagged spokes around black eyes. 'It's all good.'

An hour later, when I think he must have gone up to bed without me, Rex joins me on the sofa with a giant bar of Tony's Chocolonely. He smells of sandalwood and his own hair and Savlon. I look up nervously. If he says *it's all good* one more time I think I'm going to have a nervous breakdown. Cleaned-up and calmed-down, he looks like a different person from the man I dragged into the car earlier. Better than I've seen him since before we got the news about Roger.

'Peace offering.' He breaks the chocolate unevenly in half, gives the bigger chunk to me. 'Sorry for shouting at you just now. I feel a bit better.'

'You look more like yourself,' I say, and then, tentatively, because the trigger words might start him ranting again, 'What did you mean when you kept saying it was all good?'

'It *is*, though!' My heart sinks. The manic edge is back. I almost expect to see sparks fly from his ears. 'I think I've finally worked something out. Or *walked* it out. I always said this is how I process things, and this was big so it took a lot of steps.'

'Go on.' My pulse spreads to my hands and feet, making the bulbs of my toes and my fingertips throb.

'The news about Biba was the best thing I could've heard.'

'*What?*' If I wasn't sitting down my legs would go from under me.

'Knowing she was alive has made her dead to me. Properly, I mean. How could anyone, even her, be so cruel? If my dad hadn't died, Liss wouldn't have found out about us, she wouldn't have got in touch with Alice, and on some level I'd still be that mug waiting for her to come back to me. I honestly wouldn't want her now if she did. I'd say she can go to hell, but she's probably there already.'

My insides wheel up and over. All those years I wanted him to let go, to move on, and now he's done it there's no comfort, only terror. If he can turn on Biba after a lifetime of servile adoration, what would happen if *my* truth ever came to light?

51

Alice

1940s tea dress
1940s low-heeled sandals

@deadgirlsdresses
#outfitoftheday #ootd #vintagefashion #sustainablestyle

The train rattles west out of Paddington towards Gabe's grand-father's care home in the Berkshire countryside. Gabe can't leave his phone alone, checking the shop's CCTV obsessively.

'Can you *not*.'

'I just think you don't know her well enough to entrust her with this.' He's repeated a variation on this theme every few minutes since we set off. Anxious to make up for the sales I lost during the heatwave (and, OK, a couple of days lost to hangovers – we've been *out* out every night since she got here), I've given Liss the keys to Dead Girls' Dresses.

I tilt his screen my way. She's unpacked a bunch of returns, and is currently hanging a red Ossie Clark up to steam.

'If she's planning to rob me blind, at least she's making sure the stock's in good condition first.' His refusal to smile raises my hackles. 'Swear to God if you check that one more time I'll lock you out of the app.'

He turns his head sharply. 'You can do that?'

'With one tap.'

The train glides towards Heathrow Airport, past acres of glint-ing car parks, billboards advertising fast fashion made by children in southeast Asia, lorries backed up on the M4 and low-flying aircraft belching aviation fuel. It should be enough to have the whole carriage screaming but everyone around us is playing with their phones or drinking water from single-use plastic bottles as if we're not putting our collective hands around the earth's neck and choking the life out of it. I breathe in for four, hold it for two, out for four more until the landscape greens a little, and I can allow myself a few minutes of the denial I need to keep me sane. A muscle in Gabe's neck flexes repeatedly, as though he's chewing on thoughts he can't voice. Is this about me? Is it the comedown? Is it Villiers family stuff?

I don't know if the tears I'm holding back are sad or angry ones.

Grandpa V's care home is in the shadow of Windsor Castle. We meet him in the morning room where half-finished jigsaws lie on occasional tables. Grandpa uses a wheelchair that looks like it costs more than most cars, wears a cravat, and talks like someone from a black and white film. He kisses my hand in a way that makes me want to curtsy.

'Aren't you an exquisite creature?'

He ushers us to a table laid with silver cruets and a bowl of sugar lumps with little tweezers. 'Pull out the lady's chair,' he orders Gabe, shaking his head in despair at his grandson's lack of chivalry. When he talks about 'the wedding', Gabe doesn't correct him. This is a side to Gabe I rarely see. I know his ability to strad-dle worlds is what makes him such an asset to the movement: that he can not only command a mob but also speak in court with the confidence of a barrister. Neither of us say much, aware that, while we have no shortage of people to listen to us, an audience is a rare treat for Grandpa. His parting words, as we sign out of the visitors' book, are to Gabe. 'Don't make a pig's ear of this,' he says. 'Learn from your father's mistakes.'

On the way home, Gabe's in a different kind of bad mood, one that's easier for me to bear because it's not directed at me.

'There's only one good way to get old, and that's with money,' he says. The word *money* leads me to unwelcome thoughts of my credit card statement, the exponential growth of the numbers every time I check it. 'What's going to happen to *our* generation? Grandpa V, our parents at a push, they're the last ones who won't have to face the consequences. We won't have million-pound houses to exchange for luxury retirement. God help us if we're still living in Asbestos Towers in our old age. If we even make it to old age. By the time we're sixty the oceans are just going to be, like, evaporated salt pits full of dead bees. And no one *gives* a shit. What's the fucking *point?*'

My hands and feet go cold. Passionate, angry Gabe, even sulky Gabe, is preferable to this resigned, pessimistic Gabe. If the fight can go out of someone like him, what hope is there for the rest of us? I squeeze his hand and offer, 'But at least we'll be living in a desert with each other.' It barely registers. He's gone somewhere I can't reach him. Heathrow looms on the horizon. Gabe slumps away from me, leans his forehead against the train window, his eyes sliding over the big, bad boiling world.

I read a text from Mum. 'She's in London, she wants to meet for coffee.'

'Not like Karen, to spring a surprise visit on you,' he says. I can't tell if he's being sarcastic. I can't be arsed to make a thing of it.

'I'd better get back to Liss, though,' I say. 'Do you want to come? Maybe you could count the money in the till? Go through her pockets, check she hasn't stolen my millions?'

'Very funny.'

He spends the rest of the journey texting and ignoring me. When we go our separate ways at Paddington, it's a relief. I put my earbuds in and listen to the latest *Travesties*, Tracey and Faye riffing on the O.J. Simpson trial. It doesn't raise a smile; in fact, I have to turn it off. Whatever comfort I once found in crime has gone.

52
Alice

The escalator at Angel Tube, my Grandad must have informed me a hundred times, is the longest in the London Underground. Today it's a stairway to heaven, delivering me from the sweltering Hades of the Northern Line on to the relative cool of Upper Street.

Maybe it's because I'm staring at my feet that I notice the pavement at the same time. Someone's drawn my Dead Girls' Dresses logo in chalk, two metres wide, but instead of a flowing gown the girl is dressed in a pinafore and stripy socks.

'The fuck?' Reflexively I turn to Gabe, before I remember he went home without me. I follow a chalk path towards Camden Passage, treading on sketches of playing cards, grinning cats, fob watches and teacups. Sky-blue arrows lead towards the passage, with the words *This way to the Mad Hatter's Tea Party* in cursive writing.

The passage is heaving with shoppers. The trestle from my stock room is covered with curtains and scraps, cake stands and tiny sandwiches. DeShaun is in a top hat, serving what looks like wine from a teapot with a picture of the Queen Mother on it, Steve is flipping playing cards from one hand to the other in an arc like a Vegas croupier, and Hollie is wearing a pair of pound-shop bunny ears and looking a little dazed. Liss is in the centre of it all, dressed as Lewis Carroll's Alice. She's haggling with a well-known influencer over a dress I picked up in a French château sale years ago. It's late 1930s, backless, made from a watery green silk that makes me want to cry when I touch it. I almost don't want to sell it, and the influencer certainly doesn't want to pay, insisting that, 'A place on my grid is worth high five figures.'

I'm about to intervene – the influencer isn't exaggerating her status – when Liss puts her hands on her hips. 'And the dress is worth five hundred pounds.'

She makes the sale. I clap my hands over my mouth. The tears that spill since Liss arrived seem to come from a different chamber of my heart.

When at last Liss notices me, she gives a Cheshire-cat grin I can't help but return. My cheeks form runnels to send the tears away.

'Is this OK?' Liss asks, taking my hands. 'It's just a few set-dressing tricks, then I went through all your followers and invited them and said bring a friend.'

By the time we pack the party away, Dead Girls' Dresses has made over twelve thousand pounds. DeShaun, Hollie and Steve have taken double what they'd expect to thanks to the increased footfall. I text Gabe a screenshot of our takings. *I think we can trust her don't you?*

The thumbs-up he fires back is hardly the slice of humble pie I was after.

Liss and I fold the trestle table flat and slide it into the stock room. I snap a rubber band over fifteen hundred pounds of beautiful cash and enter the code to open the safe.

'I wonder how much the person who traced you would charge to do a proper search for Biba, or people who knew her.'

I look at the money. I haven't seen profits like those in a long time. 'My parents did all that before they had her declared dead,' I say.

'Yeah, but that was before you knew about me. About Denmark in 2007.'

'Good point.' It's only money. We can make it back. The safe door pops open to reveal the orange dress along with the note Liss left in the shop, legible even in shadow.

Alice
    I'm sorry if I freaked you out before. Hopefully we can talk in person soon.

I pick it up, feeling on the edge of something unsettling, although it takes me a few beats to work out what. This writing is spikier than the delicate cursive Liss uses, and the ink is smudged to the right, suggesting a left-handed writer. Liss is right-handed.

'Liss.' It's an effort to face her: a slow rotation. Once again my body knows what's happening before I do. It wants to delay the moment for me. 'Is this the note you left me?'

She leans over the counter. 'Nope.' She's already walking towards the door, dropping to her haunches in front of the silk rug I use as a doormat. 'That's not my writing, and mine was a proper letter, in an envelope. I shoved it under the door?'

She pulls up the corner of the rug, to reveal a lavender envelope, dusty and creased.

She sets the letter on the counter. My name with a little curlicue underneath it. I place my palm over the letter, feel the grit on the paper, close my eyes while I try to work out the timeline of its delivery.

I slice into it with the mother-of-pearl dagger I use as a letter opener.

Dear Alice,

Forgive the old-fashioned letter but you strike me as someone who likes old-fashioned ways. I've been trying to reach you for a while and email just doesn't feel right. We've never met but we need to. I have a connection to you, to do with your family history and mine. Just fifteen minutes of your time would be life-changing. I'm in London, staying at the Premier Inn in King's Cross.

Best wishes,
Liss Hambro

Underneath, she's written her email address and phone number. 'I *didn't* forget,' she says. 'Good to know I'm not going mad. You just got the wrong message. Who'd've thought to check if there was another note?'

Me, I think. I've read enough Victorian novels to know that letters misplaced under doormats can ruin lives.

'When did you post this?'

Liss frowns. 'The day before we met. Peak heatwave, when all the shops were shut. I just assumed – you said, did I leave a note – I just thought you must've gone home via the shop, picked it up.'

I consult my internal calendar, name the date.

'I didn't even know about Dead Girls' Dresses then,' says Liss.

'I should've noticed. I should've *checked*. It should've been the first thing I checked.' If no one were watching, I'd slap my own face. The Surge is not above turning in on itself.

'No because we had so much else to share, that night,' says Liss. 'We weren't going to get into admin when we were having a life-changing meeting, were we?'

But it's *all* in the detail, this search. If we get to the truth about Biba, I'm coming to understand, it won't be some big dramatic confession. The clue will be a crumpled train ticket in a pocket, some digital breadcrumb on an archived website, a spectral image caught on camera.

'Fucking Hollie!' I slam my fist on the counter. 'If she didn't keep mucking about with my CCTV, we'd have a record of you leaving your note, and of whoever left this.'

A sudden realisation rocks me on my feet.

'Liss, how many times did you call the shop?'

She looks at the seashell phone. 'Loads of times, but I only got through once. If you remember you told me to—'

'I had two other calls that aren't accounted for.'

'If this wasn't me . . .' begins Liss, then trails off.

We don't need to say her name. We see her every time we look in the mirror. We feel her in the seams of her clothes.

53
Karen

It occurs to me, as I browse a stiff menu card, that in the past fortnight I've spent more time in London than in Suffolk. Today is unusual in that it's pure pleasure, albeit disguised as business if Georgia's accountants ask. She's treating me – as one of her favourite contributors – to lunch at a high-ceilinged restaurant in St Pancras station.

'Thought I'd milk my expense account while I've still got one,' she says, raising a fishbowl glass of sparkling water. 'I should've done it more often.'

It's such a relief to step outside of my family for a couple of hours. I want to stay out, make the most of the city, but where can I go? Queenswood Lane doesn't appeal and, even if it did, the sweatbox of the Northern Line might kill me before I got there. I watch a gang of girls with huge rucksacks queuing for the Paris train and I experience a pang of longing to take a leaf out of Biba's book, do a runner, go to the Eurostar ticket desk and tell the person behind the glass to choose my destination. I stand still, the crowds flowing around me, until it passes. Biba's disappearance means I can only afford small spontaneities. I text Alice to see if she wants coffee.

Alas no we've been visiting Grandpa V & gotta get back to DGD xoxo

Circle Line it is, then. I'm at the foot of the escalator, about to touch in, when I get a message from a number that's not in my contacts.

Karen, Gabe here. Alice is busy with work, but can I take you out for a coffee or a glass of wine? I'd like to connect.

Something in my chest contracts painfully and my inner monologue says *busted*. So much for my invisible surveillance.

'Are you going through or what?'

'Sorry.' I step aside to let the woman behind me through the barrier. The phone glows its ultimatum. My instinct is to say no, or at least ignore him. Nothing good is going to happen. This is a showdown. I think again about bolting for the continent, the impulse no longer a fantasy. But. He's alone and so am I. When else will we get a chance to speak without an audience? Not this side of the 'wedding'.

I can be at the flat in half an hour.

I don't let myself into the flat this time; I ring the bell and remain on the steps. While I wait for Gabe to let me in, I regard with dismay their front garden, where an old mattress rots behind a bank of wheelie bins. For a pair of eco-warriors they're not bothered about their immediate environment. Although on closer examination the mattress appears to be home to multiple strains of wildlife: silverfish run in pewter chains on its underside, mouse droppings collect in the stitching.

I recoil, ring the bell again. There's a bunch of post jammed in the letterbox. It's easier to pull the letters out and re-post them one by one, although I tear a padded envelope in my haste. I'm about to shove it through and hope for the best when the letterhead catches my attention. G for Generitas DNA testing. I see test tubes and labels in boxes. Panic shoots acid up my throat.

'Coming!' Gabe calls from inside the house. I shake out the contents, try to read the letter before Gabe opens the door. The text blurs but I don't have time to find my reading glasses. Odd words leap out:

percentage
saliva
mitochondrial
siblings
maternity
DNA
discreet

paternity
ancestry

He knows. The sneaky bastard knows, and he's going to use it to drive a wedge between Alice and me.

His thudding footsteps draw closer. I stuff the torn envelope and its contents into my bag a split second before the door swings inwards. Gabe's wearing a red shirt with the sleeves rolled up and the collar popped, and a pair of grey marl draw-string shorts.

'Sorry.' He leans to kiss my cheek. My recoil is nothing personal and everything to do with the material clamped under my arm. He notices and pulls back, doesn't remark, continues with his usual charm. 'Had to change out of my meet-the-grandparents clothes. Let's go round the corner, shall we? It's hot as hell up there. After you.' He gestures down the short flight of steps and I have no choice but to descend. To my ear the rustle of paper is deafening and gives away the envelope bulging with little plastic test tubes, and paperwork with Gabe's name on it. We walk in uneasy step to a pub.

'How was your grandfather?' I ask.

Gabe smiles ruefully. 'He's a man of his time, if you know what I mean,' he says. 'Of course he was captivated by our Alice.'

Our Alice. I don't think so!

He starts burbling on about how his grandparents were married for fifty years and if I'm worried that his own parents' relation-ship didn't set a good example then I needn't be because he's had that model, it just came from a different generation that's all, and he's so caught up in his own psychological insights that he's not really looking at me, so when we pass a litter-picker pushing her cart along the pavement I sleight-of-hand the letter into it. The relief I feel is, I know, only temporary. He'll only think it got lost in the post for so long before he requests a replacement. All I've done is delay the inevitable.

When we arrive at the pub, he opens the door for me – ever the knight – and gestures to a table. 'What's your poison, Karen?'

You are, you manipulative little shit. 'Dry white,' I say. 'Thank you.'

I wish I were of the generation of women who were prescribed Valium by the bottle. My heart rate is so high that my smartwatch flashes a notification that I'm in the fat-burning zone.

'So,' he says, after taking an inch off his beer. 'I just wanted to reassure you that I've got my eye on things with Liss.'

I find myself willing him to just *say* that he knows they're sisters. My body can't take much more of this.

'Look, Karen.' He tips his glass from one side to the other, watching beige foam slide down its inside walls. 'I really didn't want to do this. I thought long and hard about prejudicing you against a family member you haven't even met. But I feel like – you need to know. She's not a great influence on Alice, for a start.'

'Go on,' is all I can trust myself to say. This wasn't on my bingo card but it makes perfect sense. Of course Gabe doesn't want Liss around. She's one more person to dilute his share of Alice.

'I think I've seen Alice drink more in the past few days than in the entire time I've known her.'

I can't help looking at his beer. 'It's Lucky Saint,' he says, 'AF,' then flicks his eyes to my glass in a way that makes me feel ashamed of the very much alcoholic wine that *he* bought *me*.

'You should've seen her when she was doing her A-levels,' I say, remembering Suffolk Constabulary bringing her home in a bikini and a feathered headdress at three o'clock in the morning, a few hours after she'd gone up to bed in pink pyjamas. Or the time she and Sophie had a champagne 'brunch' on Sizewell beach that ended with a fishing boat being liberated from its trailer and the coastguard being scrambled. I can just about smile at the memories now, but Gabe's face is stern.

'I'm not happy even if you take the partying out of the equation,' he says. 'Liss came out of nowhere, just as a rich man died.'

My mind is click-click-clicking with the effort of understanding the turn things are taking. 'You think she's out for money?'

'If she's working with Biba, yeah.'

The clicks in my head speed up, become a whirr. 'With *Biba*?'

He steeples his fingers, an academic setting out his thesis. 'Liss *says* Biba was in Denmark in 2007 and she *says* she's probably dead now but she can't prove either of those things. And when she phones home, she speaks Danish. Why would she do that, if she didn't have anything to hide?'

'Gonna have to stop you there,' I say, remembering how Biba and I met, her resistance to foreign words. 'Even if Biba has been hiding out in Denmark this whole time, there's no way she'd be able to converse in Danish. She'd make everyone around her speak English.'

'Right,' he says. I can see that I've convinced him.

'Honestly, put the idea of some big return or conspiracy out of your mind.' And then, my heart fluttering at my own daring, I add, 'And encourage the girls to drop it too.'

'With you on that,' he says.

I study his face for cracks in his conviction but he is unreadable, this boy. I don't know what he believes and what's part of his game. The now-or-never nature of the moment reasserts itself.

'Anything else you want to check in about?' I ask. 'While you've got me to yourself?'

It's a dare and we both know it. Gabe takes an exaggeratedly slow sip of his beer. 'I think we're good,' he says, eventually.

Of course he wouldn't ask me about the girls without witnesses. He's not going to throw his grenade now. This was just about showing me a forefinger hooked in the pin.

'Well, I'd better get my train.'

When I stand, Gabe doesn't rise, but his fingers encircle my wrist. He has the rough skin of a much older man but the blue eyes of a baby boy, looking up and into my face. 'You know I love your daughter very much, Karen.'

That's what all abusers say. The most dangerous ones even believe it.

54
Alice

It took three days and nine hundred pounds for the tracing service to tell us what we already knew. There's been no trace of Biba since 2007, and even then we only have Liss's parents' report to go on.

'Maybe we should give up,' I tell Liss, as we shut the shop for the day.

'I'm sorry,' she says. 'I wish there was a way to have met *you* without finding out about *her.*' She rubs her fists into bloodshot eyes. 'Early night tonight.'

'Salad and water for dinner,' I agree. 'Up early for a bit of yoga.'

When we lock up, we find that Hollie's left a bottle of cava on the doorstep with a note apologising for abusing my CCTV. 'It's a *sign*,' says Liss. 'The universe doesn't *want* us to have an early night.'

I shrug. 'Can't argue with the universe.'

It's midnight when we stagger back to Drayton Park but the lights in our apartment are on and we can hear Gabe and Stef laughing from the street. The living room is strewn with Chinese takeaway foil containers. The boys are wearing some kind of cross-body harnesses over their T-shirts. Gabe turns to me, half-blinding me with a beam of light emanating from the centre of his chest. There's a black circle underneath.

'Did I interrupt a private moment?' I ask. 'You look like sex Daleks.'

He laughs, taps his chest and the light goes out. 'Bodycams,' he says. 'For the Parliament Square event. You film on a phone, the feds can just knock it out of your hand. These transmit via

Bluetooth for all your police-brutality live-streaming needs.' He nods to a pile of cardboard boxes. 'There's ten grand's worth of kit there.'

'How d'you afford all these?' I ask.

'Fundraising,' says Stef. 'Although technically this lot was donated by Anne. One of our favourite wealth redistributors.'

Liss emerges from the kitchen with two forks. She hands me one and attacks the remnants of a noodle dish with hers. I pick up a foil container and squint into an inch of rice, can't identify the dish but eat it anyway.

'When is this event, exactly?'

Gabe names a date a week after our partnership.

'Good.' My tongue finds a slice of mangetout. 'I don't want you turning up to the ceremony with a black eye. Or, worse, having to do it in prison, like I'm a serial killer's penpal.'

'Too right,' says Liss, wiping sauce from her chin with the back of her hand. 'I doubt they'll let you have visitors either.'

The look Stef gives Gabe could rot a field of crops. 'Hang on, what? *She's* going to your wedding?'

'It's a civil—' I begin, but Stef cuts me off.

'You said it was *immediate* family only.' He's on his feet, suddenly taller and wider, somehow even *hairier* than usual. 'If *she* can come, why can't I? You hardly *know* her. Just 'cos you look like twins, that doesn't make her immediate family. Me and Gabe have been tight for nearly a decade.'

Gabe's face is screwed tight, like he's braced for an impact. His eyes, barely visible, send a distress flare my way.

'Of course you can come, Stef,' I say. 'We were going to ask you anyway.'

Stef's shoulders drop a notch. Gabe claps him on the back. 'She beat me to it, that's all.'

I see the moment Stef decides to believe Gabe: he resumes a normal human size. A fragile peace descends on the room, which we fill with talk about the restaurant we've chosen for drinks and dinner after the ceremony and how exactly we're going to keep

Gabe's warring parents apart all day. Gabe and I communicate in stolen glances: *Thanks for that*, he says. *A truce at last*, I telegraph back. *I'll thank you in bed*, he replies, jerking his head backwards towards the bedroom, with a smile. While Liss and I discuss future window displays, the boys review the downloaded footage from their bodycams, trying to figure out how the zoom feature can be operated hands-free.

'Takeout is always so salty,' says Liss.

'*You're* salty,' mutters Stef under his breath as she fills a stolen pub pint glass with tap water.

She doesn't hear him but on the way back she glances over Stef's shoulder at his phone and the whole room seems to crackle with sudden violent energy.

'What the fuck is *this*?'

Stef colours. 'I was just—'

'He was filming my tits!' she shrieks, twisting his hand so I can see the screen, filled with footage of Liss's glistening cleavage. 'All that time I thought we were having a civil conversation and you were filming my tits like some creepy upskirter on a train!'

I've been told my voice carries when I raise it. Is that what people mean? They must be able to hear it streets away. Horrible as it is, a thrill runs through me. I've never dared to speak to Stef so freely. Liss grabs the phone from Stef's hands, stands in the open French windows and threatens to drop it into the garden below. He's on his feet, and then so's Gabe, making a human barrier between them.

'What do you think you're doing, you mad bitch?'

'Deleting your mucky little film, you Neanderthal hypocrite.'

A clatter of bottles and a bang from the street below shocks us all into silence. Liss leans over the railings.

'What the hell's going on up there?'

It's Priyanka from next door. She always takes her recycling out last thing at night. I try to picture Liss from Priyanka's viewpoint, dramatically backlit on the balcony, glass in hand.

'What's got into you?' asks Priyanka. 'You've been a dream neighbour for a year, last weekend you had some kind of *rave* and now a domestic in the middle of the night?'

'Sorry,' says Liss. 'It's just that he's a *total fucking prick*.' She directs these last words – which emerge with such force I know she'll have a sore throat tomorrow – over her shoulder at Stef.

'For goodness' *sake*,' says Priyanka. 'My kids are awake, thanks to you two, and I don't want them hearing language like that.'

Gabe comes up behind Liss. 'Sorry, Priyanka,' he says weakly. He slams the window closed so forcefully that another crack appears in the glass.

'Just another fuckboy.' Liss is swaying on her feet. 'I don't know how you put up with him, Alice.'

Stef erupts. '*I'm* not the one forcing Gabe out of his own bed!'

Gabe flashes a nervous glance my way.

'I'm family.' Liss punches herself in the chest. '*Family*.'

Even I know that's not fair. Stef is more of a brother to Gabe than his actual brothers. 'Liss, shut up,' I order. 'You don't know what you're talking about.' I'm angry but kind of excited. I've never known what it's like to fall out with a friend and know that it isn't the end of the friendship. This must be what it feels like to argue with a sister.

'Family!' cries Liss, as if she hasn't heard me.

Stef looks close to tears. 'Thanks a lot, bruh,' he says to Gabe. 'Thanks a fuckin' lot.' There's a moment of unintentional comedy as he disentangles himself from the bodycam harness, before pounding down the stairs and slamming the door behind him so hard that all the windows shake.

'Have we got any more drink in?' asks Liss.

'I think we'd better call it a night,' says Gabe with impressive mildness. 'You can have the sofa.'

'Oh, my God,' she says. 'I've already *got* two dads, I don't *need* another one.' She lies on her back and Gabe throws a sheet over

257

her. It silences her instantly, like throwing a cover over a parrot's cage. Within seconds she's asleep.

Gabe threads his fingers through mine and says, 'Well, that was horrible.'

It's only when we're lying on our backs that I realise Stef was right. That this is the first time since Liss's arrival that we've shared a bed; in my excitement I've let her oust him.

'I'm sorry,' I say. 'It's a weird dynamic but it *will* settle down. We're all getting to know each other. Liss has just found out her mum isn't who she thought. She's got even more to work through than me, in some ways.'

Gabe's not convinced. 'She's been here a few days and she's come between me and Stef, the asbestos rooms are open and now Priyanka thinks we're a bunch of ASBOs. It's like whatsisname, Tom Wheeler, from Queenswood Lane, all over again.'

'I hardly think *this* is going to escalate like *that*.' I say, but, as his breathing slows beside me, Jo Vine's words echo in my mind. Aren't we all capable of killing? And who's to even say what's murder and what isn't?

The following morning, I wait on the front step for Gabe to finish his call with Amer and for Liss to come back from Londis with some Anadin Extra. I'm sitting with my chin resting on my hand just in case my fucking head falls off my neck when Priyanka leaves her house, hair swishing, baby on her hip.

'Morning.' I've brushed my teeth twice but I can still taste stale booze on my breath.

'Oh, hi,' she says. Even her kid looks as if it's had a blow-dry. It's wearing the kind of funky, ungendered clothes that Hollie sells. Priyanka straps the baby into its car seat, then approaches me, hesitation in her tread and her voice.

'I know we don't know each other well, but I have to say something. That got pretty full-on last night. I thought you were going to come to blows. I'm not being funny but if I hear anything like it again, I'm going to have to call the police. I couldn't bear having anything on my conscience. I hope you understand.'

I'm too hungover to explain who Liss and Stef are but I can't let Priyanka carry the idea that I'm in danger. 'God, no. Honestly, I get it, but don't worry. Gabe would never lift a finger.'

Priyanka looks to our upstairs window, to her baby, back to me. 'It's him I was worried about.'

55

Karen

We wait nervously on the platform for the train from London. Rex is pacing squeakily in Crocs, the only shoes he can wear while his blisters heal.

'Liss is a person in her own right,' he keeps repeating, as though revising minutes before an exam. 'None of this is her fault.'

He hasn't noticed the sudden change in me. My shorts hang loose on my hips. I have lost two kilos in the past week. I'm wearing so much concealer on my eyebags that it's started flaking off in chunks, like paint from an old fresco. I've hardly slept. Gabe can't have got hold of a new DNA test yet, it's not until he has the results that he can pull that nasty little rabbit out of his hat, but his suspicion is almost as powerful. I spent two hours this morning going around the house with a lint roller, lifting every bit of hair from every surface in case one of them was Rex's and Gabe decided to pocket it.

The gates of the level crossing descend and the London train glides towards us on shimmering tracks. It's a moment so dramatic, so loaded, it feels as though the train should be wreathed in clouds of steam. It halts, the doors beep-beep-beep open and Gabe steps on to the platform, an Alice at each elbow. Two sets of *Clockwork Orange* eyelashes flap under identical blunt fringes. A boy and two girls: Gabe, Alice, Liss. Rex, Biba, Karen. It's impossible not to impose our past on their present.

People who know Rex's history can be weird when they first meet him. They often circle him for a few days, physically hold back. There is no such hesitation in Liss's body language – she throws her arms wide and calls him, 'Uncle Rex!'

Her enthusiasm suggests she's staked her flag in Camp Biba Did It.

'Oh, my goodness,' says Rex. 'Oh, Liss. It's – this is all a bit overwhelming.' He goes to wipe his eyes on his sleeve but he's in a T-shirt so he just ends up smearing his forearm with tears.

There's a moment where Rex and Gabe grapple for the honour of carrying the girls' bags, dispelled by Alice saying, 'Get over yourselves,' and hoisting her own rucksack on to her shoulders.

'It's just a ten-minute walk,' says Rex. The five of us walk in shifting formation from the station to our home, five abreast when the pavements are wide enough, in a crocodile when they narrow. Gabe raises a complicit eyebrow at me, as though we're having an affair or something, making me want to puke.

'How long are you here for, Liss?' Rex flattens himself against a pub so a mum with a buggy can get by.

'I've persuaded her to stay for the big day,' says Alice.

'Yeah, I'm between contracts at work, so there's no rush,' Liss says.

'Oh, that'll be nice,' says Rex. 'Gabe, you'd better hope you don't marry the wrong one by mistake.'

Gabe's grunted laugh has a bitter edge to it.

'Here we are,' says Rex.

'Oh, my God, your house is *adorable*.'

At the sound of our voices, Peggy barrels through the dog flap, on to the lawn, then turns a confused circle before running from Alice to Liss and back again.

'Maybe we even smell the same?' wonders Alice.

We put Alice and Gabe in her old room and Liss in the space in the eaves. Dinner is already prepped – it's too hot for anything but salad – and we eat in the garden, under the awning. I'm grateful for a glass of creamy white to take the edge off my nerves. Gabe sips; the girls guzzle, throwing their arms wide, talking with their mouths full, interrupting each other.

'And there was this guy in *full leather* . . .'

'She just cut her plait off! Just like that!'

'And the manager was like, I will *pay* you to leave . . .'

They appear to have banked more memories in the past week than I have with any friend since – well, since Biba. I know what it feels like, to fall for a friend like that. I know how quickly a life can change.

'It's mad, isn't it?' says Alice when she catches me staring. 'We're basically the same person.'

Something is tugging at my heart. The word I need for it doesn't exist in any language I speak. Is it an only child's longing for a sibling? The best I can do is that it's a blend of nostalgia and envy. I tune back into the anecdote I'd previously zoned out of as Liss's voice rises to a screech. 'And we *still* don't know whose bra it was!'

Alice can barely speak through tears of laughter.

'I'm going to wet myself!' wheezes Liss, slamming the table. The more they look at each other, the more they laugh. It's infectious, as laughter always is, but there's the unsettling feeling that the girls are the only ones really in on the joke.

The way they are with each other doesn't *remind* me of my friendship with Biba, it shines a harsh, unforgiving light on it. It's a meeting of equals. There is no dominant, influencing force. Liss is making Alice more Alice-like and I dare say Alice is doing the same for Liss. Or are they both becoming someone else? Biba and I had a rapport but I was the lover and she the beloved. She absorbed me into her world but never set a toe in mine. Watching these girls together, I can't avoid the truth: I blew up my life for a *crush*. Blue sky green ivy white powder black gun red blood and it was nothing more than a teenage infatuation I was already too old for. I grip the rim of the chair so no one can see my hands shaking. Beside me, Rex is laughing, as loose as I am rigid.

'It's like having Biba back, Karen.' His usually measured voice is giddy, almost manic.

'This morning you were virtually making voodoo dolls of her.'

He swats my words away. 'Not the side of her I've learned about in the last few days. It's like having the *best version* of her back again. It's like . . . someone's invented *time travel*.'

I wonder with a shudder if Rex might be losing his foothold on reality.

My appetite is still non-existent but that's not a problem when Gabe's at the table. The boy can *eat*. I find it hard to equate the speed he consumes with his lithe frame and impeccable table manners. The food runs out but the wine keeps coming, although I switch to sparkling elderflower. I need to be attuned to every word, every gesture.

'How's work, Rex?' Gabe uses a man-to-man voice, a part of his repertoire I haven't yet had the privilege of seeing.

'Not bad, not bad,' says Rex. 'Got a possible extension up at the New Houses.'

Bile rinses my mouth. Do I look green? I *feel* green.

'Why would anyone want to alter a new-build?' asks Gabe.

'They're not really new,' says Rex. 'They must be fifteen years old. But that's the countryside for you. Anything that hasn't been there for a century is new.'

Gabe isn't listening to him. He's looking intently at my face.

'More water, Karen?' he asks. 'You're looking a bit . . .'

Knew it.

'Look at that, we're all out of ice.' I push my chair back and retreat to the kitchen. Gabe watches me through the open door as I pop ice cubes from their silicone trays. It's as if he can see into my *mind*. He's loving it, the sociopath. If I call him out, he can bring down my world and he knows it. It's a long minute before he turns his face back to Alice. When I rejoin the table I move my seat so he can't look directly at me. Gabe shifts his so that he can. I give in, allow the move. Better stalemate than checkmate.

Alice puts her hand into the ice box, takes out a cube and crunches it. Liss does the same.

'Are your dads coming for the w-ivil partnership?' asks Rex.

'Wivil partnership!' scream Alice and Liss in unison. 'Oh, my God, we've *got* to start calling it that.'

Gabe's lips thin.

'We thought about inviting Freddie and Kofi.' Alice talks about

263

them as though they're old mates. 'Obviously we want to get to know each other.'

'But then we were like, would it be too much to meet everyone at once?' says Liss, spitting ice chips. 'Far – that's my Danish dad, my biological dad – he can be a bit withdrawn; it's his idea of hell?'

'And Gabe's entire family's gonna be there, and they're *a lot*,' says Alice. Gabe's eyebrows flicker almost imperceptibly.

'Then you've got the day itself, which has to be about Alice and Gabe, I mean it's gonna be weird enough that I'm there?' says Liss.

It's the quietest I've ever known Gabe to be.

'Also a bit rude really when we want to make a fuss of them?'

'Do they know about me?' Rex drags the elephant into the centre of the room by its trunk. Everyone around the table falls silent. The birdsong is so loud it sounds fake.

'What are you doing?' I mouth. The old Rex – by which I mean the Rex of last week, who lived with a sad but stable acceptance of Biba's death – would never have rocked the boat like this.

Liss looks to Alice for guidance; I can't interpret the head-shake Alice gives her, but she can. Rex swallows audibly. When, at last, she responds, her voice is stripped of her earlier confidence. 'You couldn't *not* know about your conviction,' she says hesitantly, 'in the context of how I discovered you.'

A hot dry flush fans out across my chest and climbs my neck. I will Rex – who is starting to look out of his depth, wishing he'd never said anything – to stay quiet. I wish I had a glass of red wine to hand, just so I could knock it over someone and create a diversion. When I realise Gabe is gearing up to speak, the heat spreads further, parches my cheeks and prickles my scalp.

'Don't worry about it, Rex,' he says. 'I reckon when Liss's dads meet you they'll realise the truth.' There's an element of showmanship in the next pause he leaves. You're enjoying this, you little shit, I think, as my skin broadcasts its red alert. 'Which is that you're obviously a brilliant human, who'd do anything for his family.' He raises his beer bottle in Rex's direction, and the girls copy him.

It has worked. Rex seems satisfied, the girls relieved. I remain on scarlet hypervigilance. What just happened? What's Gabe's game?

When flies start to crawl on our plates, Gabe and Rex clear the table, but only Rex returns.

'He's in the loo,' says Rex, when I raise my eyebrows.

The main bathroom in our cottage is downstairs. I can see from the garden that the door is open.

'The en-suite.' His sheepish face tells me all I need to know. Rex spent the morning hiding his beloved Zoflora and Cillit Bang and replacing them with eco-friendly cleaning products to impress Gabe. He wants Gabe to notice the Ecover toilet cleaner and the Faith in Nature soap. He won't, of course, because he'll be too busy trying to get DNA from our toothbrushes.

I sprint upstairs but it's too late: I hear the flush, and find him outside my bedroom door, wiping his hands on his shorts. As we pass awkwardly on the landing I frisk him with my eyes, looking for the outline of a test tube or swab in his pockets.

I go straight for the bathroom cabinet. Both our toothbrushes are dry to the touch. Suspiciously so? Have the bristles just been rubbed over with a cotton bud? In the bedroom, there are no stray hairs on the pillows as you'd expect to find. If he's got even one strand from each of our heads, it's all over. I could find a cotton bud, but hair? I survey the room in dismay, noticing that something else is wrong, or missing, or has been moved. The room looks marginally different, like a familiar image reversed in a mirror. I turn a slow circle, playing a memory game with myself, but I can't think what it could be.

56

Karen

When the kids leave the following afternoon I'm no closer to identifying the anomaly in our bedroom, and a cursory fingertip search of Gabe's bags yielded nothing. Rex, still on a high, doesn't notice how tense I am. He strips their beds and puts linen in the tub. 'It's perfect drying weather!' he says, in a tone that suggests we've just won the lottery. 'I'm just so happy for Alice, finding a cousin and a best friend rolled into one!'

His new smile seems to contain twice the usual number of teeth. Rex's sister, his beloved sister, is dead. Where is his *grief*? Is this it? Or is it gathering strength, in a low crouch behind his anger at her betrayal and the happy shock of Liss. His new mood feels like a balloon I must keep batting upwards, never letting it touch the floor.

After supper, we re-make the beds. When we're flipping the mattress in Alice's room, something dislodges from between the slats.

'Well, well, well.' Rex bends to pick up a tiny origami envelope, magazine paper folded to the size of a USB stick. 'It's been a while since I saw one of *these*.'

When I first met Rex I thought him puritanical about drugs, although I quickly learned that he had to be. Biba didn't have an off-switch. I unfold the wrap, splay it out on the tallboy. 'It's white, at least,' I say. 'Heroin's brown. Coke?'

'Alice thinks cocaine's a wanker's drug.' Rex makes a face like he's trying not to sneeze. 'It's probably MDMA. Why don't they take it in pills, like we used to? Powder's so messy.'

'Easier to share?'

We unfurl a clean duvet cover, turn it inside out, line up the corners with the duvet and shake it down in one practised, fluid movement.

'Did you know MDMA was first developed for use in marriage counselling?' says Rex, smoothing the bed.

'Every day's a school day.' I fluff a pillow and throw it to him.

'It's to do with the rush of dopamine, or serotonin, or whatever it is. That loved-up feeling, it brought couples' guards down, enabled open communication without judgement. The fact that you can dance all night was actually a side-effect.' He inspects the wrap again. 'Eyeballing this, I'd say there's a good gram left. What d'you reckon? Shall we?'

'Rex!' I couldn't be more shocked if he levitated. I look at the scattered crystals, then back up at him. 'Are you serious?'

And suddenly he is: he's looking at me with a focus, an intent, that I haven't seen in a long time. Big brown Beanie Boo eyes in a sharp-edged face. He takes my hand. 'It might bring you back to me.'

'*Back* to you? You're the one that's been walking till your feet bleed. *I* haven't gone *anywhere*,' I say automatically, but he's right. Our closeness masks a distance. Maybe it's only in the last few days, with his great Letting Go, that he's been able to feel it too. This new Rex is dangerous. Anything might happen.

He licks his finger, dabs it in powder, and offers it to me. The bitterness jolts me back to the summer we met, evoking only the good nights.

'Nothing's happening,' I say after half an hour.

Thirty seconds after that, I feel as though I've been dropped into my body from a great height, and I'm really wearing my skin for the first time in years and years and years.

One hour and two Portishead albums later and we're reliving the early days of our relationship on top of our John Lewis duvet cover, every inch of my skin burning with a pinprick, feverish intensity.

'There you are.' Rex looks into my eyes, runs his thumbs over my cheekbones. '*There* you are.'

Tell him. The drug is a voice in my head. *Tell him everything you've been holding back. Look how much he loves you. He'll forgive you anything. Wait till you're done,* answers my body. *Stay in this moment.* I understand with a perfect clarity that before we fall asleep I'm going to tell Rex every secret I've ever kept and I'll tell him why. *Of course he'll understand,* says the drug. *It'll only bring you closer together: look at the connection you share, nothing can undermine this.*

It is light by the time we finish. *Now,* says the voice, *now,* but it's less insistent than it was, less convincing, and then Rex is asleep, one arm pinning me to the bed. A merciless sunbeam picks out flecks of white in his eyebrows and the stubble on his jaw. I lie on my back, wide eyes on the ceiling, the aftershocks of the night's rushes fanning through me. Outside, the sun sails across the sky, shrinking and stretching the shadows. I'm pinned to the bed as if by centrifugal force.

If you tell him, he'll leave you. Look how he's turned against Biba's memory. If he can feel that way about her, he'll drop you like a stone.

That wonderful sense of openness has mutated into defence-lessness. The drug has turned on me, as it always does. What was I thinking? Why did I even want my barriers down? They're all that's been keeping me safe from myself. Truth serums are not the stuff of marriage guidance counselling, they are the stuff of espionage dramas. The voice has dropped an octave. *If anyone ever finds out you'll lose everything you love. Look at you, trying to recapture your youth, convince yourself you've got a bohemian side. You're pathetic, parochial, try-hard, transparent. You played at being the cool girl and look where it got you.*

I stare at the ceiling, knowing – remembering, now, too late – that the punishment of morning is inevitable. I curl into the foetal position and put my hands over my ears.

You evil piece of shit, you fraud of a wife, you counterfeit mother, growls the voice. *You nasty lying bitch.* A slice of light idles across the wall. I track it in real time across the foot of my bed, my dressing table, my jewellery box, which is not how I left it—

oh

oh

oh no

The catch that I always leave at a slant is horizontal. I force myself up and out of bed, turn it with numb fingers and feel in the velvet squares for the pouch containing Biba's earring. It has gone. I've solved the mystery of my bedroom but another, more terrible one has taken its place. What could Gabe possibly want with Biba's earring?

He knows. The voice has gained a menacing, up-all-night rasp. *Gabe knows who Alice is. He knows what you are.*

57

Alice

Alice
Floor-length scarlet kaftan with angel sleeves and deep V neck
Hand-embroidered with Greek key design and mirror inserts
Greek, probably 1960s

Liss
Jet-beaded lace cape, Granny Takes a Trip, 1960s
Lime-green bri-nylon bikini top, 1950s
Purple crushed velvet flares, Miss Selfridge, 1990s
@deadgirlsdresses
#outfitoftheday #ootd #vintagefashion #sustainablestyle

As stag and hen dos go, we're not having the most raucous of wedding eves. Gabe and Stef are at a GR meeting in south London and me and Liss are at Dead Girls' Dresses. As I re-hem a white petticoat, the fabric glides under my fingers and emerges in a cascade of white ruffles. Being at one with my sewing machine can be a sensual pleasure as much as a source of artistic satisfaction.

Liss is re-dressing the shop window. She doesn't think I do enough to advertise the fact that I can customise my pieces, so she's building a display around my old-fashioned (but useless) Singer sewing machine, and mirror-writing *Alteration Service Available* on the glass.

We're both wearing Biba Capel's cast-offs. Actually it's possible that Liss's cape and bikini top once belonged to our grandmother. She fills them out in a way I could only ever dream of. Supporting the notion that Liss and I are essentially two halves of the same person, it turns out that, while my favourite items from my aunt's dressing-up box don't do much for Liss, the ones that look awful on me could have been made for her.

'Done,' she says eventually, crawling arse-first out of the window.

'Hang on.' I get to the end of the hem, then say, 'Let's see how it looks from the street.'

We stand side by side on the pavement and for a moment I'm lost for words. The antique Singer on its wooden table is centre-stage but she's suspended dresses on wires so they look as though they're dancing. Yellow dressmaker's tape measures defy gravity, seemingly suspended in mid-air. They twist and wind through the garments, here and there cinching waists, or spanning shoulders, suggesting that this one-of-a-kind dress could be made to fit you perfectly.

'I put them in wallpaper paste to make them stiff,' she explains.

'You're a genius. Please let me pay you for this.'

She flaps her hand at me. 'I'm living in your flat and eating your food.'

A lightbulb goes on in my head: I know just the thing. I unhook the photograph of Princess Diana that hides the safe, punch in the code, and retrieve the earring I purloined from my mother's jewellery box when we were in Suffolk.

'Here.' I drop it into Liss's palm. 'This was Biba's. She was wearing it when she jumped. Or didn't jump. They found it on the beach, years after she went. But it was definitely hers. It was hand-made by Nina Vitor. You should have something of hers. I've got a soldering iron somewhere; we could bend it here, make it into a pendant.'

Liss holds it up to the light. Green amber, like globules of liquid shot through with silver zigzags. 'I love it.' She fingers the plain silver chain around her neck. 'It can go on here. God! I can't believe Karen let you have it.'

I don't lie exactly: just offer a different truth from the one she's after. 'She doesn't look at it from one year to the next.'

Liss examines the hallmark, and the NV logo. 'Don't suppose Nina got back to you either?'

I check my phone, the message I left her on Facebook. It's wild to think that when I wrote it I didn't know about Liss. So much was about to change.

'Still showing as unread,' I say. A sudden, bone-deep exhaustion overtakes me. There are only so many dead ends a maze can contain.

58

Alice

Square-necked Edwardian dress, white lace and cotton lawn
2010s Kurt Geiger thong sandals

@deadgirlsdresses
#outfitoftheday #ootd #vintagefashion #sustainablestyle

'*Yes*!' Gabe – Hawaiian shirt, blue suit trousers – bounds to the top deck of the 43 bus. 'The front seat's free!' He extends a hand and pulls me up to join him. It's not the most conventional way to travel to one's wedding, but then this isn't a wedding. We take our place at the front of the bus, rest our feet on the plastic ledge and chug down Holloway Road.

Gabe plays air-bongos on his lap. 'Are you *nervous*?' I ask him, even though I can feel my own heart pounding.

'Not about you,' he says. 'I just hope my parents can keep it civil. To your folks, as well as each other. Dad's just never happier than when he's finding fault, or lording it over someone.' He stretches his arms overhead. 'There's gonna be a lot of conflicting values around that table later.'

'The Thatcherites, the Blairites and the Corbynistas,' I say. 'Your warring parents. And Stef and Liss. What could *possibly* go wrong?'

We meet our guests in the King's Head, diagonally opposite Islington town hall. Peals of canned laughter guide us to our table, and our arrival is met with a collective sigh of relief. On the Clarke side there's me, obviously, my parents, my grandparents John and Linda, and Liss (who looks incredible in a Bruce Oldfield bodycon dress that would be indecent were it not finished with what I *think*

– the label has been removed – is a sixties Chloé pink and turquoise silk cape). The Villiers clan have us outnumbered. Jonny and Harriet sit at opposite ends of the table. Also present are Stef, of course, and Gabe's brothers Nathaniel and Marcus and their wives, and his sister Ursula. Gabe is instantly absorbed into the scrum of his siblings. The other sister, Saskia, six months pregnant, is in Surrey with her feet in a paddling pool and, Ursula informs the group in a carrying voice, 'an ice pack under each tit'.

Mum and Liss rise from their seats and approach me in a pincer movement, each bearing a mimosa. I accept them both. Dad's looking chiselled and, dare I say, distinguished next to Jonny, whose clothes are better-cut but whose veined, blotchy face makes him look permanently on the verge of some catastrophic health event.

'I hear you're driving an electric,' says Jonny to Dad. 'Give me a good old-fashioned internal combustion engine any day.'

Dad doesn't rise to the bait. He's as calm as Mum is wired. Every time I look at Mum she smiles manically. She's trying incredibly hard to look happy for me, which should make me glad but it actually makes me want to cry. I know she's making the effort out of love, but the harder she tries, the more I'm reminded that she thinks I'm doing the wrong thing. I don't know what else I can do but be happy.

We cross the road to the town hall five minutes before the ceremony. By some terrible accident, Jonny and Harriet find themselves next to each other on the zebra crossing. He chucks her under the chin. 'Time for another facelift, darling.'

'You're paying for it,' she says, rubbing invisible coins between her fingers.

'Children, please,' says Ursula wearily. 'This is Gabriel's day.'

I fall into step with Grandad, who's giving Liss one of his London history lectures. 'Did you know,' he says, 'Upper Street used to be known as the Devil's Mile on account of all the prostitution and crime. And now look at it! It's all fancy bistro this and artisan bakery that. Linda wouldn't let me go to the Wetherspoons, she wanted us to go to some poncy pub with black walls and I got charged *six quid* for a pint.'

We clatter across marble floors to meet our registrar, passing another wedding party on their way out, the groom in morning dress and the bride in full meringue, a bunch of red roses in her hand. For a bright white second I wish we'd gone the traditional route, rather than booking the most modest room, small and plain with none of the wood panelling of the grander suites. We're not having speeches or readings and our vows come in at under a minute. The thinking was that it's a bit like doing Shakespeare on a plain stage: the unfussy space lets the words and their meaning expand.

My doubts melt away once we're facing each other. Our way *is* pure, it *is* true. There's no performance, no looking at our guests, only each other. He winks at me before saying, 'I, Gabriel, choose you, Alice, above all others to share my life. I promise to honour this pledge as long as I shall live.' I repeat my version, holding his gaze, knowing and loving that those faded-blue-jean eyes will remain true while the lids above them sag and the creases around them deepen.

Our only concession to a traditional wedding moment is a kiss to seal the deal. Gabe slides his hand around the back of my neck and pulls me close, my ear to his lips. 'I'm going to call you my wife,' he whispers, and my insides are molten. 'Not my partner, my wife. I want to call you something no other man will ever get to.'

'I love you,' I tell him, tears threatening again. 'I love you so, so much.'

Jonny is on hand to burst the bubble. 'All the pomp and circumstance of a McDonald's drive-through,' he grumbles.

'That's the spirit,' snipes Harriet.

'Ignore them.' Dad materialises at my side. 'I've never seen you look happier.'

'Or more beautiful,' says Mum, but without her usual authority.

More drinks on the rooftop terrace dissolve most of the tension, and by the time we sit down to eat the evening's flowing as I wanted it to. People stand up, switch seats, stretch their legs. It's the perfect weather for mezze. The food that keeps coming on platters is spicy but light, easy to pick at. We are rewarded by a sunset so beautiful it's almost vulgar, Aperol orange and Calpol pink over the spire of the Union Chapel.

At ten o'clock, two people-carriers arrive. One carries seven inebriated members of the Villiers family to Buckinghamshire and the other is headed for my father's beloved Finsbury Park Travelodge (where Liss has booked a room too) and then to the worst flat in Drayton Park. En route, Grandad persuades us to come to the hotel bar for a nightcap.

'Wow,' I say, as we enter. 'Dad, I can see what you love about the place.'

Its harsh strip lighting and wipe-clean seating gives it all the charm and character of an airport gate. Gabe turns a slow, appreciative circle. 'We weren't going to have a honeymoon, but now I've seen *this* place . . .'

Dad pretends to be offended, but nothing can puncture his mood. Even Mum laughs and, even though I think it's a bit against her will, it's real and natural. She'll come round to him. She can see how much I love him.

Grandad orders a round, drinks precisely one sip of Guinness then falls asleep on a slippery chair, leaving Nanna to put him to bed. Me, Mum, Dad, Stef, Liss and Gabe stay up, until Stef unexpectedly swipes right on Tinder and hops on a Tube to Walthamstow.

'I think you're finally off the hook,' I say to Liss.

'Freedom!' She throws her arms wide; her cape spreads and she looks like a rare butterfly, albeit one on a pleather pouffe in a budget hotel.

With Stef out of the way, everyone relaxes another notch. Even Mum seems to be loose enough to find Gabe funny. These are the people, I think, looking around. My parents, my husband, my cousin who is also my best friend. Even if I never love anyone else, these four would be enough.

Gabe and I return to our neighbourhood on foot. Rounding the corner to Avalon Road, we're hit by a faint smell of cigarette smoke and a strong one of weed. Two different households loudly pit Drake against Taylor Swift. I check Priyanka's window to see if she twitches her curtain for other neighbours as well as us, but all the squares are dark.

Gabe carries me over the threshold, our faces locked together. 'I don't think I can wait to get you upstairs,' he says. 'I want to throw you down and have you now.'

I peel myself away from him. 'I am *not* consummating my marriage on that disgusting carpet in a pile of old umbrellas and Crocs.'

'Reasonable,' he says, but he keeps his hands on me all the way up the stairs. In the flat, I fling the French windows wide. Behind me, Gabe disentangles the veil from my hair and slides his hands under my dress, exploring the skin my clothes have printed with creases and lines. When he tears it I don't even mind. We have sweaty, drunken, delirious sex in our newly marital bed and lie panting in the rags of my wedding dress.

'I love you,' he says. 'My beautiful wife.'

'I love you too,' I say. 'My handsome husband.'

My skin is hot and tacky, so I take a sixty-second shower. 'Leave it running,' says Gabe, sliding past me as I exit the cubicle. 'I've got to wash the ick of my family off me.'

I dress in a white boy-vest and a pair of Gabe's boxer shorts. Already wanting to reminisce about the day, I get the digital itch and feel for my phone. But it's not within reach, like it usually is. It's not in my handbag. Gabe's started to sing, the first verse of a Meatloaf song that goes on for about ten minutes. His singing makes his dancing look good. I do what Dad always tells me to and picture the last place I saw the lost object. The mental image is clear as a photo. I left my phone next to Liss's, face-down on the table in the sodding Travelodge.

In the bathroom, Gabe's using the showerhead as a micro-phone, glugging the words, upping the performance when he sees me. 'Baby, baby, *baby*!' I wait for a natural break in the lyrics before making my request.

'I left my phone in the hotel. Can I use yours to call it?'

'Sure.'

I hold his phone to his face to unlock it, then find my own number in Favourites. 'Awwww,' I say, when I notice he's already programmed me in as WIFE. He blows me a soapy kiss through the shower screen.

Liss picks up so fast I don't hear the ring. 'There you are.' I take the phone into the living room, the better to hear her. 'Me and Karen are still up. Shall I put it through your letterbox?'

'What, now? God, would you?'

'I've got three espresso martinis to burn off.'

'You're an *angel*.'

'See you in a bit.'

I look at Gabe's photos of today, deleting the unflattering ones, then checking the deleted items album to make sure they're defin-itely gone. My attention snags on an album called ALICE CLARKE. I laugh to myself at his use of such a formal title for the place where he keeps my nudes, although there are two hundred items in this file and I haven't sent that many.

The alarm bell sounds at a frequency I'm not yet ready to hear.

I open the album, then freeze.

The pictures are not of me.

59
Alice

I stare into a patchwork quilt of screenshots taken from Facebook, from Tinder, from Instagram, from LinkedIn. Old women, young women, thin ones, fat ones, white ones, black ones, all called Alice Clarke. Most of them are dated around six months ago, just before we met.

The alarm bell becomes audible, a deep bass note in my belly. He's got a shot of the electoral roll, he's got shots of lists he's made on his notes app. The name of my shop leaps out at me, the way my name would if called across a street.

Dead Girls' Dresses vintage clothes – climate-friendly business tick
Drinks in King's Head
Constant stream of friends
Personal Insta set to private?
All posts head cut off – why no face?
Lucky Voice 15 Feb 7pm
The karaoke bar where we met.
The night we met.
The alarm bell rises to a deafening clamour.
The *what* is horribly clear. The *why* is going to break my heart.
Stef, I think. There's nothing he doesn't discuss with Stef. They talk on Discord, not WhatsApp. The boys' last communication was a couple of hours ago. *Sorry to bail on the party,* Stef has written. *Alice looked beautiful and you looked well loved up. Really happy for you mate.*
No worries bro, hope the girl was worth it.
Stef has sent a panting tongue emoji in response.
I don't use Discord so it takes me a moment to work out how to scroll back. I rewind through videos, attachments, voice memos

about meetings and shopping links to bodycam equipment. The seasons rewind from summer to spring to winter. It's February when I find my name. Gabe texted Stef the morning after we met at Lucky Voice.

She's one of us, mate. Can't see her going on any marches in those frilly dresses but she vibes with the movement.

What about Del? Stef has replied.

Not committed enough.

Do what ya gotta do.

I rewind into January, before I knew Gabe, and screech to a halt when I see a picture of me talking to DeShaun outside the shop. I'm wearing an Afghan coat with a huge fur collar and big hoop earrings. That was the day I *booked* Lucky Voice. Gabe's captioned the photo: *Got eyeballs on Miss Alice Clarke.* I remember now, sitting at DeShaun's pavement table, making loud plans on the phone: shall we go here, shall we go here? I probably would've repeated it because I was stressed about taking responsibility for the booking and I wouldn't have wanted a mix-up. Anyone could have overheard me. I wouldn't have paid any attention to a cycle courier in a helmet at another table. The cancellation of our booking that saw us all pile in with Gabe and his friends was not an accident. *He* must have cancelled it, to engineer a meeting with me.

I have become the alarm bell, my whole body reverberating.

The preceding messages are about lawyers and activists. My eyes hurt with the effort of reading too much tiny text too fast. A few weeks before that, I find what must be the first mention of me.

I was delivering at Crawford Southern today, Gabe wrote.

Them cunts.

Yeah they kept me waiting like an hour.

Billable hours my arse when it comes to the working man.

Word. But I heard them talking about a case, they said, With an inheritance like this Alice Clarke's going to be a very eligible young woman.

I'm yanked out of the moment by a rare flash of doubt in my own judgement. Did I overlook something in Biba's clothes? Have I let a museum piece go for fifty quid?

Client's called Roger Capel and his net worth is eight figures. Can't hurt to check it out, can it?

$$$$$$$, Stef had sent. *Go for it mate.*

'What are you doing?' I didn't notice the water cut out but Gabe's in front of me, climbing into his underpants even though his body's still wet, shower gel suds sliding down his shins. 'Give me my phone.' His smile is fixed and his voice even but his outstretched hand is trembling.

'Why were you looking up women called Alice Clarke?'

'What are you on about?' He tilts his head and wrinkles his nose, like I'm being adorably ditzy. 'Give me the phone.'

'You knew who I was before we met. You set it up.'

'How much have you had to drink?'

'You stalked me. You *targeted* me. Why?'

He clicks his tongue on the roof of his mouth. 'Give me my phone and come back to bed. It's been a long day.'

A muscle under his left eye has gone into spasm. It tugs rhythmically at the dimple in his cheek.

'It's the Capels.' The words don't want to be words, they want to be a scream. I have to make an unnatural effort to enunciate. 'It's got to be: everything comes back to them. You're with me because of them.'

His mask slips momentarily, a full-face twitch betraying his panic. If I'd blinked a second earlier I'd have missed it.

'All that time I was trying to hide my history from you and not only did you know all along, they were the reason you were with me. You gaslighting *fuck*.'

'Not this again.' He's like a bad actor trying to embody the word *patient*. 'Alice, baby, we cleared all that up.'

I look at the phone but it's locked itself again and when I hold it up to Gabe's face he shows the camera his palm, and in the next breath he lunges for it, uses the body I have clung to so often against me. He tries to prise my fingers away from the phone and when that doesn't work he squeezes my hand so hard my bones crack.

I do not surrender my grip. I need all the strength The Surge can give me, and let it have free rein for the first time in years. It can't believe its luck.

'I love you, you stupid bitch,' he spits into the mouth he's been kissing all day. 'Calm down. Just let go of the phone.'

His soapy forearm barricades my lips, muffling my voice as I try to scream *get off me get off me get off me*. After what seems like a full minute of this uneven wrestling match, I stop trying to punch my way out of his arms and duck, dropping to a crouch on the floor, sliding under, not out, using my hands to push myself free, and then what's left of The Surge dribbles out in the lightest of shoves, just to underline the message. Gabe goes from girding himself against my weight to floundering in mid-air. His arms windmill twice, then he grabs at the curtains for support. He misses by a millimetre and the movement ends in a broadside stagger to the French windows. He stays there for a while, centring himself, reclaiming his balance on the balcony. My hands, the hands whose push put him there, go weak, confronted with their own power. Fuck. That was close. Relief escapes me in a breathless laugh; Gabe mirrors me with a nervous smile. A flicker of something passes between us. Forgiveness, understanding; there might even be an edge of laughter in it. All I know in the moment is that the near-miss has brought clarity. Whatever he's done, we can work it out.

I hold out my hands to him. 'Baby,' I say.

The balcony comes away from the wall slowly, so slowly I see the individual railings detach from the stone, and then so quickly it's as if it was never there at all. There's no balcony, no Gabe. The gunshot crack of falling stone masks the sound of his body hitting the ground.

60

Alice

#ootd
Vest
Gabe's boxers

I drag myself back into the middle of the living room, limbs spidering like one of Gabe's horror-film girls, until my spine is against the wall. I stay there, eyes on the window, scared to blink, as though the power of my gaze could summon him, pull him back, have him climb through the broken frame. I hold my position until I hear voices outside and only then do I blink, only then do I move. It seems that I plunge to the ground floor without once making contact with a single floorboard, only a hand on the banister anchoring me to the house.

Mum and Liss are outside. Liss's hands are over her face but the words, 'Oh, no,' spill repeatedly through her fingers. There's a bar of broken stone directly under the window, shards of terracotta, a square bracket of iron railings and a bare foot sticking out from behind a gnarled buddleia and the bank of wheelie bins.

Mum's face is hollow. 'I'm so sorry, darling.'

That *sorry* is not the apology kind of sorry, it's the sympathy kind. Mum's face twists with the effort of forcing the next words out. I can tell that if she could swallow them, absorb the news, carry it herself and never tell me, she would. 'Gabe's dead.'

The words are matchsticks under my fingernails.

I replay the terrible choreography of our last dance. My palms burn where they made contact with his chest. I was only trying to get safe, I was only trying to get free. Did I hesitate a beat too long before extending my hand to him? If I'd reached out a second earlier, could I have pulled him back in? Someone turns off their music: Drake surrenders to Taylor Swift.

'A neighbour's calling an ambulance,' says Mum, jerking her head towards Priyanka's house. 'But it's only going to be a formality.'

'How do you know? You're not a doctor!'

'Alice, I'm so sorry.' The arms she holds out for a hug are only barriers.

'I need to see him,' I say. I step over a jagged hunk of what was once my windowsill, flatten dandelions that sprout through the cracks, kick aside an empty can of Red Stripe to stand where Gabe's beautiful body lies broken in a diamond of light from the window above. There's no spreading puddle of blood the way there is on TV but glass beads have replaced his eyes. They point unseeing up at the blue-whale belly of the night sky. The lines in his face have vanished. He looks his age, only the sum of his lived years, for the first time. When I touch him he's still warm – of course he's still warm; five minutes ago we were fighting and five minutes before that we were fucking – but a grotesque rubbery texture is already setting in.

I angle my face towards my mother's. 'It was an accident, Mummy.' The *Mummy* surprises us both. Her features are in shadow but she's still managing to emanate a sense of calm and control. I know this feeling: this is safe, this is home; this is Karen Clarke keeping it together because she has to.

'We saw him fall,' says Liss, taking my other hand.

'People are going to think I pushed him!' I cry. 'Priyanka, the other night, she thought I was gonna hurt Gabe in a row.'

'When me and Stef were arguing?' Liss's eyes glitter. 'They wouldn't connect that to this.'

'But what if they *do*?' My voice is dangerously close to becoming a wail.

'No one's going to accuse you of anything.' Mum is as calm as I am shrill. 'Because I'm going to make it all go away.' She has ascended to some new plane of authority. Her voice is lower than usual, her shoulders look broader. 'Liss, take your wrap off and get in the house.' Liss blinks uncomprehendingly. '*Now.*'

Liss obeys, unshrugging her cape and holding it out to Mum, who drapes it over my shoulders while gently guiding Liss into the hallway. 'OK, the other day there was a black hoodie on the coat-hook. Is it still there?'

I know that hoodie; I've picked it off the floor and re-hung it on its hook a million times. It's Gabe's. It's a plain black one he wears on marches. It zips right up to the eyes so he can't show up on videos. Mum intones her instructions like a hypnotist.

'Liss, I need you to put this on, go out the back door, cut through the back alley and go straight back to your hotel room. You and Alice look similar enough from a distance. All people are going to see, all a security camera will show, what that kid round the corner just saw, is me and a girl in a pink and blue cape walking from Finsbury Park to Avalon Road. Alice, your phone puts *you* in the hotel. *You* were seen arriving moments *before* Gabe fell.'

I am stunned. Who *does* that? Who comes up with a cover story on the spot, while the authorities are on their way and a body is cooling on concrete? There's a corner of my brain not over-whelmed by horror that acknowledges that my mother's mind is magnificent. It is fucking terrifying what love can do.

Liss scuttles left then right, like a crab. 'But it was an accident. Why don't we just—'

Voices have started up in the street outside. Figures are moving in my peripheral vision, zombies closing in.

'*Liss.*' Mum's metronome control falters briefly. 'The press will make the connection with '97. They'll be all over Alice, all over the pair of you with their Curse-of-the-Capels poison. It'll be the first thing that comes up if your name is searched. You'll *never* be able to escape it. Nor will Rex. We've all come *so far.*'

It hits me like a boxing glove. Mum *doesn't* think it was an accident. She thinks it was The Surge. She doesn't know I have controlled The Surge. She thinks I killed Gabe on purpose and she is prepared to hide it. Maybe she's right. Maybe I did. I don't know I don't know I don't *know*.

Liss melts into the rear of the house. The path to the back door is clear but does she know about the key? Have I told her, or did Gabe tell her, that we keep it on the lintel above the door in case of emergency? There's a clatter and a fumble that could be anything but it's the rush of air, the through breeze, that lets me know she's out.

A man on the street clears his throat. 'The ambulance is on its way, love.'

It takes me a few beats to place the neighbour with the phone in his hand. He's wearing shorts, a singlet and Nike slides, and there's a comb stuck in his afro. Derrick lives on the other side of Priyanka but I've only ever seen him in formal work clothes. I wait for him to point out the switch, but as far as he knows I'm the same girl who's been outside with Mum the whole time. He jerks his thumb at his wife Donna, whose oversized Harvard T-shirt is falling off one shoulder. 'She's done a first-aid course.'

Mum shakes her head. 'It's too late,' she says, but Donna has pointed her hands like a diver's and pushed her way between us in her eagerness to help.

'You never know,' she says. Her conviction dares me to believe that she might be able to revive him. Her scream hurts my ears; it has lights coming on all down the terrace, brings more people running than the fall itself. Mum wraps me in her arms and I bury my head in her neck. Where is Liss? The garden is piled with rubble and old fridges and there's no security light. If she makes it out without hurting herself, will she find her way back to the hotel? Will she think to go the long way round, so that Mum's plan works?

'That house,' some unseen woman says. 'It's been an accident waiting to happen for years. That cowboy Malcolm's got blood on his hands.'

'You want to restore those stone lintels, you need to reinforce them with steel brackets,' says a man. 'We know a guy who does it. He did ours. Got them to replace the baluster and the ball finial while they were at it.'

Gabe will laugh about this, I think reflexively. He'll find the bourgeoisie discussing home improvement while his dead body is almost within touching distance so awful it's funny. The simultaneous realisation that he will never laugh again bends me in half.

'Is Priyanka here?' I ask, scanning the crowd, then bite my tongue. Why would I want to know that unless I was worried what she might have overheard?

'She's away,' says Derrick. 'Don't worry about her place. She sank *serious* money into her reno.'

He's missed the point, of course. Priyanka might not be here to report the argument she overheard or voice her concerns about Gabe's safety but who's to say she won't go straight to the police when she learns what's happened?

The voices blend, rise to a hum, a swarm of hornets, until Derek's rises above. 'Put your phone down, man,' he snaps at a rubbernecker. 'Have a bit of fucking respect.'

The paramedics arrive and give me one of those silver blankets people wear at the ends of marathons. Mum gently eases me out of their way and on to the steps. I'm gibbering, the words won't come, and Mum fields questions from the paramedics. I curl myself up, draw the silver blanket over my head and catch what voices carry through its gentle rustle.

'I can't certify him dead. We need to take him to hospital. And because it's an unexplained death we need to get the police to visit.'

Time isn't what it was an hour ago, a succession of events and landmarks and people, it's a long empty motorway that stretches forever. It's sweaty and claustrophobic under the blanket but it's safe, and when the blue lights of the cop car slide under the foil and bounce reflections around it's rather beautiful. I could stay here forever in my own personal fairground and never have to face reality.

The blanket muffles the ensuing discussion between unseen police officers and ambulance crew. I try to tune it out but can't help overhearing one of the paramedics say, 'You could smell the booze on him a mile off.'

'It's the heat,' says another man I presume to be a copper. 'People don't realise they can't metabolise alcohol when the weather's like this. Sooner it rains, the better.' He turns to me. 'He your boy?'

Mum shakes her head. 'My son-in-law,' she says.

'We're looking at misadventure, but he'll need a post-mortem.'

I scrabble out of my blanket. 'An operation?' I ask. Gabe hates hospitals. The responders exchange pitying looks, and I get it. It's only an operation if someone's alive.

Mum sits beside me. 'Did you hear that? They've already made their minds up, Alice. It's a drunken fall. They don't suspect any foul play. Not that there was any,' she adds hurriedly.

A horrible thought comes to me. 'They're going to wonder why would a husband go home without his wife on their wedding night?' I whisper. 'It's not like we had kids or pets to hurry back for.'

She frowns. 'We won't tell them it was a wedding.'

'*What?*' This is a step too far.

'If it's just drinks, it's not remotely suspicious that he left you in a bar with your parents, is it?'

'But what if they—'

She places a cool hand on my thigh and presses down. 'Trust me.'

But I am already complicit. I'm hardly going to contradict the account she's just given the authorities, am I? She has given me no choice.

61

Alice

A middle-aged man in a waffle dressing gown, trailed by a sullen teenager in a Nirvana T-shirt who reeks of weed, approaches the police officer.

'We live at number six. My son saw the accident.' He points to a house a few doors along, a top-floor balcony just like mine, with colour-changing lights cycling softly through the rainbow. Like all the houses on Avalon Road, it faces the train tracks. The kid would've been able to see the street but not what happened behind my window. 'Tell them what you saw, Jody.'

The kid looks at his feet.

'You're OK, son,' says the copper. 'I'm not interested in what you've been smoking, just what you saw.'

He points to me, then to Mum. 'These two were walking up the road, and they were, like, there . . .' he points to a spot on the pavement '. . . when the dude just, like, fell out the window?'

Mum nods, a private confirmation that her plan has worked, as the kid's father shakes his head. 'Good God, Jody, you could've phrased it more delicately than that.' He turns to me, tightens his dressing gown. 'I'm terribly sorry. Do let me know if there's anything practical we can do.'

'Very kind of you,' says Mum. She's almost under the foil blanket with me now. When the neighbour goes back into conversation with the police, she whispers, 'He's been more helpful than he'll ever know.'

I look at her, horrified.

'Sorry. You know what I mean. You've got enough to deal with without them grilling you.'

289

While the officer takes notes from a stoned teenager, Mum yawns. I catch it. When I was little she told me there was one yawn, constantly sailing around the world, passing from one human to the next. I was well into my teens before I thought to question it.

'What were you arguing about, anyway?' she asks. 'You looked so happy when we waved you off.'

I'm not *never* going to tell her. I just can't handle it now. I need time to think, to sift through the mess with Liss.

Her eyes search my face. There's never been anywhere to hide from her. Every second I don't respond is a second I get closer to caving. 'Hmm?' she prompts.

'Liss and Stef.' It comes out of nowhere, smooth and easy. 'They don't like each other and we were taking sides. It was nothing. It wasn't worth a *life*.'

She doesn't challenge me. 'Oh, sweetheart.' She strokes my hair. 'It could've been you. It could so easily have been you.'

When the police talk to me it's very informal. They don't even split us up. I recite the story Mum outlined. Gabe went home, followed half an hour or so later by me and Mum. As we turned the corner, we saw him fall. I feel like a beauty-pageant kid, performing not for her own sake but for her mother's.

The police weave blue and white crime scene tape through yellow plastic barriers. The paramedics leave to find a life to save and an undertaker arrives in an unmarked black van. The sound of a long zipper releasing, the body-bag sound effect from a hundred TV crime dramas, has me shrugging off the blanket and leaping to my feet.

'Alice!' Mum reaches for me but she's too slow. I scrabble up the stairs.

'You can't take him away like that,' I tell the man in black. 'He hasn't got anything to wear.' The part of me that knows he doesn't need clothes and never will again is silenced by the part of me that is mentally dressing him in his vintage Ben Sherman shirt with the brown and orange arrow print. He looks so good in that, with the sleeves rolled up and the collar popped. I rest my palms on the front door. 'I won't be a minute.'

The policeman moves fast for a big man. His arm swings down like a car-park barrier. 'Love, no. I can't let you up there, it's not safe.'

'I don't care.' I look up at the house, dare it to do its worst, invite the jagged remains of the window to fall, to hit me between the eyes.

The stretcher glides past me.

How can he be dead when he's *right there*?

Dawn is marbling the sky over the railway by the time they leave us alone, with instructions to go to the station in the next few days and make our statements formally.

I shuffle back to the Travelodge still in Gabe's underwear, the Chloé cape, and a pair of flip-flops retrieved from the hallway. My hair is matted from the shower. There's a patch of shampoo I didn't rinse properly and it's starting to itch. Tonight is an endless wall of moving parts, each one too big and complicated to take in at a single glance. Gabe's betrayal, Gabe's fall, the blind faith and clinical detachment of Mum's cover-up. My heart hurts, my head hurts and every inch of my skin feels tender as a bruise.

London is going about its day as though the world didn't end overnight. A newsagent pulls up his shutters and a man in acid-yellow overalls skirts his street-sweeper along the gutter. These are the early risers, the people who would've gone to bed while we were still in the restaurant last night. Trying to marry the horror of this new day with the bliss of last evening is like trying to make a jigsaw with broken glass from a dozen smashed mirrors. When we cross the road outside the stadium, there's no traffic but Mum takes my hand, the way she did when I was little. I've been holding this hand for twenty-four years. It doesn't fit like it used to.

My question bursts free without my permission. 'Where did you learn to be so cool in an emergency? So *ruthless*?'

Mum looks over my shoulder, as if to some distant horizon. 'When you were little you had a reaction to some plant in a friend's garden,' she says. 'All these little spikes were sticking into your hand and it was swelling up. I sucked them out and spat them on the ground, then I got in the car and drove you to hospital and honestly, when I got you to the children's A & E I couldn't remember having done any of it. They only worked out what I'd done because my own lips had swollen. But I'd saved you. I had known, somewhere so deep I couldn't even tell you where it is—' she waves her hand over her abdomen, as if she's describing some essential but mysterious organ '—I had known what I needed to do to protect my child. Something takes over. When you have kids you'll know what it's like.'

'I didn't mean to kill him.'

'I know,' she says, but her eyes tell me that even if I had, she would've acted the same. Instead of reassuring me this terrifies me: it opens a crack through which I see that motherhood is not a tenderness but a ruthlessness with no ceiling.

The doors part on to a computer-game maze of identical doors.

'This is us.' Mum gestures with her key card to one door, then to an identical one opposite. 'And that's Liss. You can stay with me and Dad. We can get them to put a fold-out bed in our room?'

I sense movement from Liss's room. It's her I want. 'Easier just to bunk in with Liss.'

She *almost* hides her disappointment. She gives me one last bone-crushing hug, and says, 'I'm so sorry, sweetheart. Wake me up any time if you need me.' Then she puts her fingers to her lips and touches her key to the door. I replay her little speech, split-screen it with her actions over the last few hours. What I saw tonight felt more like skill than instinct. She knew how to cover up a crime, she didn't miss a beat, she lied to police with a steady voice. How did she know how to do that? What prior experience could she have had of something so—

Oh.

She can't have been—

Can she?

62

Karen

Alice knocks softly at Liss's door. My poor little girl, her bad blood finally brought to the boil. She will relive tonight for as long as she's alive, remember it as the night innocence zipped up behind her, and I can never tell her that I know how exactly how that feels.

Rex's and my hotel room is dark except for a cord of white light around the blackout blind. Liss hasn't told him, then. When I sit on the edge of the bed, he shifts under the covers and the movement brings his smartwatch to life. 'Six-fifteen,' he mumbles. 'Have you and Liss been up drinking all night?' I hear the sheets crinkle as he pulls the corner back. 'Get into bed, you dirty stop-out. We've got to check out in less than four hours.'

I fumble around unfamiliar switches on the headboard until I hit the one that operates the bedside lamp. I don't know what my face is doing but it's enough to bring him bolt upright.

'What's happened?'

I just come out with it. 'Gabe died.'

A nervous, disbelieving laugh erupts from his lungs. '*What?*'

I tell him what I saw, what Alice said, what I had to do to protect her. Rex listens with his face in his hands. Every time I blink it hurts, as if I have grains of sand lodged under my eyelids. He's out of bed and half dressed before I've finished. 'I'm going to go to her.'

'I know you want to be there for her but she said she wanted to sleep. I think we should let her. She's got a long, shitty day ahead of her tomorrow.'

He sits down, runs his hand through his hair until it forms a stiff peak. 'And Liss knows?' he asks. 'You made her a part of this?'

I'm too tired to tell whether he's trying to get the story straight or whether he's telling me off. Maybe it's a bit of both. I need Rex to understand.

'Look, I know, alright? I did what I could in the moment. I think I scared her.' I can hear a dull, deadpan note in the delivery of my words. Why can't I cry? Why aren't I screaming? 'I scared *myself.* I *terrified* myself, Rex. But I did it for her.'

The things we do for Alice.

'Oh, God. Of course you did,' he says, and something inside me lets go. He forgives me. He gets it. His forgiveness is bigger than he knows. His words give the adrenaline that has carried me through the last few hours permission to recede, replaced by a fatigue that won't take no for an answer. Still in my dress, still in my tummy-flattening knickers, still in my make-up, I lie back on the hotel pillow. I try to say, 'I just need to shut my eyes,' but my tongue is heavy as a stone in the bottom of my mouth. Rex kills the light. I go under within seconds.

'Karen.'

Multiple Gabes leap out of high windows, one after the other, piling up in the street like broken mannequins. A lorry deposits a skip outside Alice's flat, and she and Liss haul the dead Gabes into it.

'*Karen.*'

Alice and Liss fight in a window as the building falls down around them, bricks hitting the ground and exploding into powder. I put my arms out to catch my daughter but there's brick dust in my eyes and I can't tell her apart from Liss.

'Karen!'

The house vanishes, to be replaced by a cup of coffee in front of me, Rex's fingers curled around the handle. The rest of the room comes into focus. Fake, greyish wood furniture. Corporate abstract art, a desk with a padded chair, a TV flush to the wall. Across the hall, Alice's heart will be breaking in an identical space.

'I think you were having a nightmare.' He pushes the cup into my hands.

'I still am,' I say. 'This is the nightmare, and it's never going to end. Have you seen her?'

He shakes his head. 'I listened at Liss's door. I think they're both still asleep. OK, listen. I've booked us and the girls another night here so we don't have to worry about checking out. It doesn't sound as if Alice could go back to her flat even if she wanted to, and we can hardly leave her alone. Mind the coffee, it's quite—'

I've already taken a sip. It's scalding: it flays a layer of skin from the inside of my mouth, but I barely flinch.

'My parents!' I forgot, last night, that they were down the hall.

'It's OK,' says Rex. 'I woke them up to tell them what had happened. The kennels will keep Pegs for as long as we need. And I've moved the car into a long-stay.'

I have never loved him more. If I weren't already in bed I might collapse with gratitude. 'And how did they . . . ?'

'Devastated, obviously.' He puts his hands to his eyes for a moment or two. 'But I persuaded them to go home. I said you'd ring them as soon as you could. And I—' Something catches in his throat. 'I called Jonny and Harriet.' He inhales, holds the breath in his lungs for an unnaturally long time before letting it go. 'They're going to meet us at the mortuary at noon.'

What a kind, thoughtful, loyal, *brave* man I married. He must've been out of this room and on his phone as soon as I fell asleep. He's delivered the worst news of Jonny and Harriet's lives to them, and I know he'll have used the right words, the right tone of voice, even knowing he must withhold parts of the story to protect Alice.

'Once Alice is awake I'll get the number of that crook of a landlord. Um, I've hired someone to brace the front of the house with a scaffold so we can at least get Alice's things. And then we can take the girls home.'

A high-pitched keening breaches the hotel's soundproofing. Alice is awake, but it's Liss who bangs on our door, still in yesterday's dress, her eye make-up incongruously immaculate.

'She needs you.'

She's talking to Rex, not me. She can't meet my eye. She's found out what it means to be folded into this family. What have I done to her? What might she do? The shudder I repress comes out in a desperate flapping of my hands.

Alice is on the rumpled bed, knees drawn up to her chin, wearing a red sundress she must have borrowed from Liss, which she may have lent to Liss in the first place. She shields her eyes with her hands, as if she's seeing the real me for the first time and the glare is blinding her. I remind myself that I have saved them from rumour and attention and accusation. Drawn a clean line between them and tragedy. It's just too soon, too big, for them to understand.

'It's real, isn't it?'

Alice's question snaps my heart in two. I want to fling myself beside her on the bed but know that if she flinches from me I'd never be able to get up again.

'We're here,' I say helplessly. She lets out a long, one-note wail. Her breath is sour. I wonder when she last ate. We'll have to keep an eye on that.

'I know it hurts,' says Rex. 'But you're not going through it alone. You'll never be alone.' He puts out his arm. Alice lets him hold her. I rub my eyes, and when I open them Liss has curled into his other arm. The three of them always look the same, but, I see now, never more so than when they cry. I give it a minute, straighten the little toiletries in the bathroom, align the towels on their rails. When the silences become longer than the sobs, I drop to my knees in front of Alice and take her hands.

'We're going to meet Gabe's parents at the hospital,' I say, in my bedtime story voice. 'Do you think you're up to it?'

She shakes her head violently. 'I can't go,' she says. 'They'll all *know*.'

'There's nothing *to* know.' I stroke her arm. It's important I stick to my cover story even around her. This is the only way to do it: ideally, you don't admit the truth even to yourself. 'It'll do you good. There's nothing worse than losing someone and not getting closure.' My pain at seeing Alice's pain is alleviated, just a little, by her ongoing need for me.

'*They're* going to ask why we didn't come home together, even if the police didn't.'

'We'll handle it,' I assure her.

Liss rolls her neck, shifts in her seat. I've asked too much of her. She's only twenty-three. I point to myself, and then to Rex. '*We'll* handle it.'

Liss needs to know that we are a place of safety for her, as much as we are for Alice. I need to keep her on side the way I once had to keep Gabe. Yesterday she was an ally. Today she is a threat. Last night drove a wedge between me and Alice. I know my girl, I shared a bed with her every night for the first decade of her life, I know when she's pulling away. I wish with all my shattered heart that I could carry it for her. I have space; I can make space. I am a mother, I am infinite, I could hold the grief of a hundred girls.

63

Karen

Mortuary. The word evokes blue-tinged light and a biting cold, the thought of which raises the hairs on my arms.

Twenty-four hours after we gathered on Upper Street to witness Alice and Gabe making their vows, we are reunited with the Villiers family. Having come from home they are already in black. Ursula has her arm around Harriet; Nate has his hand on Jonny's shoulder. In both cases the child appears to be the only thing keeping the parent from falling to the floor.

Alice is tackled rather than hugged by Harriet. 'What are we going to do without him?' she says.

'I'm so sorry.' Rex takes Jonny's hand in both of his. 'I can't imagine the pain of losing a child.' I find that I cannot speak. Jonny – oyster eyes in a ham hock face – tries to reply but it's clearly beyond him.

Our lack of familiarity is stark. We've met once, in a state of forced, wine-slicked jollity. Now we have been thrust into the terrible intimacy of death.

'I just can't get my head around it,' Nate says to Rex. 'He couldn't have been more alive than he was yesterday, y'know?'

'It sinks in in stages,' says Rex and then, when Nate tilts his head in enquiry, 'I lost my sister. It was a long time ago now but I still feel like I'm working my way through it.'

It's not like him to mention Biba, but I suppose everything has been stripped back to nothing now. I'm reminded of the terror I felt on the MDMA night, the danger that presents when the barriers come down. We need the barriers up. We need to stake bars in the ground around our girl.

The viewing room is small. There are only three seats,

old-fashioned dining chairs, a red carpet. It has the look of a hastily cleared provincial restaurant, right down to the tablecloth-white sheet that covers Gabe.

'There's not going to be room for all of you,' says the hospital person. 'Who's his next of kin?'

Alice and Harriet step forward at the same time, bumping shoulders.

'Oh,' says Harriet, and retreats.

'Maybe if Alice goes first?' suggests Liss. 'And then you can have as long as you want with him.'

It's Liss who puts a hand on the small of Alice's back and guides her through the double doors.

'Next of kin,' Harriet mutters to Ursula. 'As of about three hours.' She seems to realise who she's standing next to, and begins to paw desperately at me, uncomfortably close to my breast. 'I didn't mean – I know she loves him – but I carried that boy. He's *mine*. You get it, don't you, Karen? Our babies are our *blood*.' She shoots Jonny a horrible look. 'The men will never, ever know.'

'*Mum*.' Nate shakes his head, murmurs to Jonny, 'She doesn't mean it.'

Blood. Babies. Men who don't know I gag on the irony.

'Harriet, I know.' The lump in my throat is growing: pip, grape, apple. 'I mean I *don't* know – I can't imagine . . .' This is messy, choppy territory. There is a script for this, but it's the same few words repeated until they're almost meaningless.

Ursula – who is not as stoical as I first thought, but who has simply mastered the art of crying silently – hands Harriet a tissue. She dabs her eyes then turns to me.

'You were there, Karen. You saw it happen.' There's hope in her face but accusation in her voice. Or am I paranoid? I *should* be paranoid. No: I should be scared. Paranoia is a baseless fear, and this is not baseless, this is real: I can almost reach out and touch it. I'm used to hiding truths but this is monstrous. The script has run out; the page is blank.

'It looked like it would've been over in a second,' I say, but that's not what she's driving at.

'Why were you there?' asks Harriet, each syllable a sob. 'I mean, I know you were with Alice, but why wasn't she with him? Who goes home on their own on their wedding night?'

Last night's ingenuity makes an encore. 'He was actually being sort of secretive, and smiley? I'm only guessing but I think he was planning something special for Alice back at the flat.'

Harriet's smile looks grotesque, almost fake, in her tear-stained, swollen face. 'That's typical of Gabriel,' she says. I notice the tense but don't correct her. 'He's a romantic at heart.'

I'm happy to inadvertantly comfort her. Let her imagine Gabe strewing rose petals on the bed if that's what she needs.

Jonny asks Rex if he's managed to get hold of the landlord yet.

'I got his number off Alice, but so far no reply,' says Rex.

'Send it to me,' commands Jonny. 'I'm going to get charges pressed against that grabby, negligent bastard if it takes me the rest of my life. I'm gonna see him rot in jail.'

'If I'd had any idea how bad the window was,' mutters Rex. 'Last time I was at the flat I didn't—'

'Woah woah woah *woah*.' Jonny leans forward. 'You'd been up there, Rex? You *knew*?'

Rex turns so white his freckles stand out. 'I knew it wasn't in great nick, but . . .'

Jonny is breathing fire. 'What sort of father are you? To let your daughter live in a place that was falling down?' His eyes travel from Rex's threadbare polo shirt to his well-worn shoes with their trailing laces. He's in his bully-boy element. 'I suppose it was the best you could afford.'

Bullseye. Rex, the failed provider, loses an inch in height, then instantly regains it as Alice pushes her way through the double doors, steps aside to let Harriet and Jonny in. She looks so frail I almost want to ask the hospital staff for a wheelchair.

'Let's go home,' I say. 'You can stay for as long as you want.

Liss, we can pick up anything you need on the drive.' I need the girls to know that I know they come as a pair now.

'We're not going to Suffolk with you.' Without stressing the word, Alice makes it singular. She's not going back with *me*.

'But love, where else are you going to go?' Rex's voice breaks high. 'You can't stay in that flat.'

Liss rakes her fingers through her fringe while she considers, exposing a flawless white forehead. Her bleached eyebrows are shot through with thick black spiderlegs. 'We're going to rent the flat over Hollie's shop,' she says.

'Can you afford that?' asks Rex, but, before either of the girls can answer, an unholy noise starts up, a bass rumble that it takes me a second to understand is Jonny. I didn't know a human voice was capable of that kind of volume. It's an avalanche-triggering, brown-bear roar. In the viewing room, he and Harriet are holding each other, so close in grief for their lost boy, they form a single black column. You cannot tell where the father ends and the mother begins.

64
Alice

who gives a shit
they're only clothes

Mum exits the building with a stack of my *Vogue*s in a cardboard box. 'Here you go, sweetie!'

The calculating Karen of my wedding night is gone, replaced by a tone I'd almost call ingratiating. As though she's scared we could turn on her. I haven't told anyone, not even Liss about the awful thoughts I'm having about her, but Mum knows.

'Thank goodness you don't have to do another night in the Travelodge, eh?' she says, all teeth and bulging eyes.

Malcolm the landlord has gone AWOL, so Dad got someone he knew through work to put up a scaffold, mates' rates. He and the scaffolder are clearing the flat of our stuff now, head torches on as they navigate the stairs in the dark. There is pitifully little of it. It was a small flat and not even the crockery and cutlery was ours. The only exception is the mattress. We shoved it up the stairs ourselves in the dark, christened it on the landing during a break in operations. I've asked them to leave it there, covered in sheets that will still smell of Gabe. Let the building collapse around it.

Stef is here, loading his bike trailer with protest kit. He hasn't spoken apart from a few grunted words to Dad. His eyes are bloodshot and he can't stand up straight. It's like someone is repeatedly punching him in the solar plexus and he can't catch his breath between windings.

Liss and I are locked in a murmured conversation that's been going round in circles for two days and a night. She is the only person who knows what I found on Gabe's phone, and therefore what we were fighting about.

'It *must* be related to the Capels,' she says for the hundredth time. 'What was he, like a secret true crime stan? A *stalker*? I mean, he was well into the investigation side of things.'

'The first he knew of the murders was when we found those photos in Biba's old handbag,' I say.

'So he *said*.' Liss won't let me follow the siren call of denial. Whenever I try to argue in Gabe's defence, she redoubles her case for the prosecution. 'He was never going to be happy with a bunch of dirty dresses. He kept saying, didn't he, that he thought you should approach Jules Capel for more cash? He would've felt absolutely justified in funnelling the Capel money into the movement. I think that's why he didn't like me. He thought I was after it too.'

I don't even bother protesting. She's right. 'But the way he was with me. The way he was in bed. That wasn't fake.'

'I'm not saying it was,' she replies. 'Maybe he really loved you *and* maybe he wanted your family's money.' She does this: switches roles, depending on what she thinks I need to hear.

'It's such a mess,' I tell her. 'I can't untangle it.' I look at my hands, splaying my fingers as though they're bound in a cat's cradle. She mimics the gesture.

'Then give some of it to me,' she says, hooking invisible yarn towards herself. 'We'll untangle it between us.'

Dad huffs his way down the front steps with Gabe's books, blue-spined Pelican classics, lined up in a shallow cardboard box that once contained apples. He holds up *A History of the USSR*. 'What do you want me to do with these?'

Stef holds his arms out for them, but Liss gets to them first. 'Not so fast.' She balances the box on the wall.

'What do *I* want with these?' I say. 'Let Stef have them.'

'In a minute.' She picks up each book, flicks through the pages from first to last and shakes it. She's looking for evidence, some hidden clue as to Gabe's behaviour. Only when she finds nothing does she let Stef take the box. When he puts his hands on it, she pulls. She's not letting him have these without a fight. 'What was Gabe playing at?' she asks, a challenge in her eyes.

Stef's shutters come down. 'Dunno what you mean, babe.'

'Come on,' she wheedles, even as he wrests the box from her hands and slides it into a crumpled Aldi Bag for Life. 'You can break the bro code now.'

Stef suddenly straightens up to his full height. 'My best friend is dead,' he spits through tears. 'Can you stop sticking your pointy little nose in and show a bit of respect?' He secures the box with two more ropes. The trailer wobbles behind his bike.

'I swear to God—' begins Liss, but I step in front of her.

'Please. Stef. I need to hear it from you. I've got nowhere to put my feet until I know what Gabe was doing from the inside.'

Liss silences me with a hand to my knee. 'Karen alert.'

I look up to find Mum holding Gabe's bedside drawer. 'Dad said it was easier just to bring the whole drawers out,' she says.

The tears start up again as I view its contents. A Polaroid Hollie took of us in the pub. Aviator sunglasses with one arm missing. Flyers from marches he's been on. A used Covid mask. The receipt from our first date. Some condoms. It's a Kim's Game of Gabe's belongings, each burning itself into my memory, each making him feel more dead than the last.

Liss fingers the earring on the chain, a habit she formed as soon as she put it on for the first time. Mum's eyes fly wide. 'Where did you get that?'

'I took it from your jewellery box,' I reply. 'I figured since Biba was Liss's birth mother, it was something to . . .'

'No, it's right that Liss should have it. I just wish you'd asked me. Got a bit of a shock there.'

'Karen, can you give me a hand?' Dad calls. Mum joins him at the rear of the Volvo to play a game of Car Boot Tetris with bags of clothes and magazines.

'She knows you're keeping something from her,' says Liss.

'*She's* keeping something from *me*.' She looks a question at me that I can't answer until we're alone. 'I'll tell you later.'

I look up at the building. Memories slide by like stills from a film. Those early weeks when I lived with all my stock, like a documentary about a hoarder, turning myself sideways to fit in between the racks, sleeping with a fire extinguisher at my side. How cold it was before Gabe moved in. How I thought the two of us filled the whole building, even the locked rooms, but it turned out there was space for Liss too.

My phone pings with a text from Nate Villiers. 'Jonny's found Malcolm in a Welsh Airbnb,' I say to Liss.

'Good.'

'I almost feel bad for him.'

'No.' She puts her hands on my shoulders. 'If anyone killed Gabe, it's him, right? That balcony should've taken Gabe's weight. It should've been able to hold *both* of you. This is on him.'

Liss has been repeating variations on this little speech since the morning after. She's sensed that I can't hear it often enough. It shifts the blame away from my palms and on to Malcolm's bricks.

Dad honks the horn and beckons us into the car.

'It's really no bother to go all the way to Suffolk . . .' he says, key in the ignition. I have some sympathy for him, but, if I'm right about Mum, he's in on it too.

'Soon,' I say.

I'm halfway into the car when I catch sight of the postie in the wing mirror. 'Hold on!' I catch up with her as she's about to slide a package through the letterbox. 'Don't post it.'

She's caught a tan since I last saw her, or maybe this is what she looks like when she's not half-dead from heat exhaustion. She gives me a faltering smile.

'I heard about your boyfriend,' she says. 'I was so shocked, it's so awful, I'm so sorry. He always had a smile on his face. You were a lovely couple.' She hands me my post. As well as a bubble-wrap jiffy bag, there are a couple of bank statements I'm scared to open.

'Thank you,' I say. 'I just wanted to let you know, we're moving to Upper Street right now. We've got one of those mail redirection thingies but it might take a few days to kick in, so if you get any post for us can you, I dunno, put it back in the system?'

'Of course,' she says. 'Take care. I really mean that.'

There's an awkward moment of tentative leanings and awkward jerkings where we almost hug. This is how people are going to be around me for a while, I realise. They don't know what to say. They don't know what to do with their bodies.

'Anything important?' asks Liss, when I slide into the back seat beside her.

I study the label for the first time. 'Oh, it's the DNA kit. The replacement for the one that got lost in the post.'

'DNA kit?' Mum twists her head round like an owl. 'Can I see it?'

I show it to her.

'It's addressed to Gabe,' she says, frowning.

'Yeah, I ordered it on his card when I maxxed out mine.'

He always let me use his card; he'd pay for anything. How does that square with the lies he told? I feel the full-face burn that heralds tears.

Mum hands the package back to me. 'I was just surprised, given his resistance to those websites, that's all.'

Her words are evenly weighted in pitch and length. Everything about her says *control*. There's something big trying to get out of her. It feels like something that's been years, not days, in its gestation.

I need to talk this through with Liss.

Maybe she can tell me I'm wrong.

I want so much to be wrong.

65

Alice

The studio above Hollie's shop is smaller than its eye-watering rent would lead you to hope. At just over two grand a month, plus a huge deposit, it's already swallowed a huge chunk of our tea-party bonus. But the walls are a calming shade of lavender and the high ceilings have their original roses and mouldings. I sit in a half-lotus on the sole item of furniture – a lumpy futon that makes me wish we'd taken the mattress from the flat after all – and roll a joint from scrag-ends we found in a Golden Virginia tin in Gabe's bedside drawer. Sash windows with bowed glass give a fish-eye view of Dead Girls' Dresses. There's an inch-wide gap where one of them doesn't close properly.

'This'll be fun in winter,' says Liss, sliding her fingers under the frame.

'As if we'll still be here in winter,' I say, running my tongue along the edge of a Rizla. 'We'll be sleeping on the floor in the bloody shop.'

'Then so be it.' Liss flings the window upwards and rests her elbows on the ledge. An urge to grab her by the waist and yank her from the edge almost overwhelms me. Intuiting my fear, she turns around. 'You can't avoid windows forever.'

I don't so much walk as slither to join her, and then inch my forearms on to the sill. Old stone, older than the masonry on my old flat by a good century, and solid as the pavement. There's barely an inch of this view that isn't soused with memories of Gabe. He chained his bike to those railings, he bought me a matcha latte from that café, he threw me up against the wall of that pub and kissed me as though the world was about to end.

He called me a liar among the rails of dresses. He sat at one of those pavement tables and took notes while I made plans for a night out.

Liss checks in with me. 'You OK?'

'Obviously not.'

'Yeah.'

She strikes a match and sparks the joint, taking one drag before passing it to me. I take it deep into my lungs, letting the smoke spread out to my internal walls and make an Impressionist blur of the jagged images in my mind's eye. Maybe this is the way forward.

'Oi!' Liss shouts to the street below, where the dachshund woman has paused with intent at the doorstep. 'Don't even *think* about it.'

The woman gives us the finger but moves on.

'What you said earlier . . .' Liss's voice, so strident a moment ago, softens as she feels her way into this next conversation. 'About Karen hiding something from you.'

I make a peace sign with my fingers; she rests the joint in the cleft. I don't actually want it any more. I just need a prop. 'That night,' I say. 'Did you not think she was really cold and calculating? The way she straight-up lied?'

Liss considers, her head at an angle. 'You do hear wild things about parents when their kids need protecting. I read about a woman once who lifted a car that was crushing her kid with one hand.'

'She tried to fob me off with that too.'

'Fob you off?'

'It was like she was acting from a fucking manual, you know?' Now I do inhale, and hold the sweet smoke in my lungs for as long as I can. 'I can't shake off the idea that she'd done it – something like it – before.'

Liss's eyes widen. I will her to get it: to say it so I don't have to.

'In '97? You think she was *there*?'

Our weird cousin telepathy only goes so far. She's at the edge of it, but needs a push. 'What if I've been barking up the wrong tree the whole time? What if it's not Biba my dad's been protecting?' The words come out like a breath I've been holding for three days.

Liss's hands fly to her mouth. 'You think *Karen* killed those men?'

Even though I led her to the conclusion, she said it out loud. She said it for me because it was too big and awful for me to manage.

'I think she might have.'

She gives a high, hysterical laugh. 'All this time we spent trying to work out if my mother might be a killer, and it might have been yours all along.'

'It's not funny,' I say, even though I know she can't help her laughter, I know it's shock finding its way out of her any way it can.

'I'm sorry.' Liss regains her focus. 'It would explain some stuff. Like, why she didn't want you to go digging into the past. And I've seen the way your parents are together. Your dad adores her. If there's one person other than Biba he'd do time for, it's her.'

'Mum hated me listening to *Travesties*,' I say. 'She used to say that these were real people and it wasn't OK to treat them as entertainment. Anyone else who said that would mean the victims, but they barely get a mention on that podcast; it's one of the reasons people hate it. I thought at the time Mum meant the killers, the accused, were real people. I thought she meant Dad. Or even Biba. But what if she was talking about herself?'

Liss twirls the pendant around her neck, fingering the green amber. 'Rex is one of the loveliest people I've ever met – I mean that. I don't want to use the word "weak" but he's . . . soft. I can see him panicking, freaked out by a gun, worried about his sister, but I honestly cannot imagine Karen losing it. I've never met anyone with such iron self-control.'

66

Karen

On the way back to Suffolk, I feign sleep, tipping my car seat back and closing my eyes. It doesn't fool Rex.

'Don't read too much into it,' he says. 'She'll come to terms with it in her own way, and right now that means Liss, not us. I don't like it any more than you do. I wish she were in the back seat. But it is what it is.'

It is what it is. What does that mean? It is something different for all of us. To Alice, it's a loss of temper and the loss of her lover. To Rex, it's a tragedy that's brought his old helplessness to the surface. To me, it's . . .

It's not what I thought it was.

Support, support, support. If there's one thing *Liebesbomb* taught me, it's that. Don't express your doubts even when you know that your future son-in-law has ordered a DNA test to fell your family tree at its root. Support, support, support. When he clicks his fingers to summon you, you go. Support, support, support. Don't undermine him even when you're convinced it was he who stole Biba's earring from your jewellery box; don't flinch when he points out your overreaction to the idea of Rex working on the New Houses. Support, support, support. Smile until your cheeks hurt as your only child promises her life to someone you can't stand.

I thought I was doing the right thing. No: I *was* doing the right thing, given what I believed in the moment.

After Alice and Gabe left the Travelodge, Rex had gone to bed and Liss had made us powdery hot chocolate from the machine. The conversation was light, low-stakes, full of relaxed pauses during which we tested for sleepiness and found none. We talked about language a lot, about brain formation and growing up bilingual, and identity. She told me about her family in Bristol, picked up her phone to show me a picture of some new cousin. Eventually we got to boyfriends. Liss has never had a relationship longer than six months, and didn't seem bothered.

'I mean, I've definitely never felt about anyone the way that Alice does about Gabe. Or had anyone feel that way about me.' She paused, blew on her chocolate. 'Thank God.'

I sat on my hand to stop myself punching the air. 'Oh?'

'Oh, you know, he can be a bit . . .'

'Controlling?'

'Maybe?' She drew her weird eyebrows together. 'I was going to say *intense*. Like, he can be funny and stuff but he can also be so self-righteous. Obviously I respect his activism, obviously he's fighting the good fight and all that, but he and Stef think they have *all* the answers about *everything* and he issues these proclamations like he's some sort of guru, and it's not a strength, it's a weakness. I realise all the time that I've been wrong about things. You *have* to be able to change your mind, back down, be open to debate. Is it a man thing?'

I remember being struck by Liss's maturity. Alice was still very much in the entrenchment phase. 'I'd have said it was a young-person thing,' I replied. 'Except you seem to have worked it out about two decades earlier than most people I know.'

Liss's reply was interrupted by a phone – Alice's, we hadn't even noticed it on the table – lighting up with Gabe's name. Liss picked it up, and I could only hear her side of the conversation. 'Me and Karen are still up. Shall I put it through your letterbox? I've got three espresso martinis to burn off. See you in a bit.'

She got to her feet, stretching. She's curvier than Alice but her waist is so small, her belly so flat that I wondered how she had space for all her vital organs. Twenty-three, I thought. Your body knows nothing. The wings of her cape made her look like a nymph, a dragonfly, a rock star. Out of place, too exotic, too beautiful for this horrible bar. Vulnerable, too.

'You're not walking to that flat on your own.'

When *I* stood up to stretch it was with the usual accompaniment of crunching noises.

There were a surprising number of people out strolling, while a couple of women in hi-vis T-shirts had decided to go for a midnight jog. It made the night seem unreal, but this wasn't the magic of the summer nights of my youth. This spell was a dark enchantment; we were in the upside-down of climate change. 'Normally these streets would be deserted,' I told Liss.

She shrugs. 'It's normal to me. We get like one hour of sunshine in winter. You have to do stuff in the dark or you'd never leave the house.'

As we turned on to Avalon Road, music was pounding from at least two sources. In one of the nicer houses, a teenage boy sat on the balcony of his top-floor window, legs dangling over the railings. LED strip lights changed colour in the bedroom behind him; the tip of a joint glowed orange. My eyes went to the equivalent window in Alice's place and everything else fell out of focus. Liss's fingers brushed my forearm, telling me she too was watching the awful shadowplay. I stopped dead, and exhaled rather than spoke the word, 'No.'

Two lean silhouettes wrestled in the proscenium of the window. Gabe had finally got physical with Alice. I am ashamed to say that underneath my fear for her safety was relief, triumph even. I hoped he would leave a bruise, something we could call him out on. That's how I remember feeling now, but I don't think I articulated that in the moment. In the moment, all I could do was pray we got to her before he really hurt her.

'Should we shout?' asked Liss. 'If he knows we're here he might—'

Before I could think of an answer, let alone express one, the window banged inward. Gabe balanced like a dancer on the balcony which, viewed from beneath, was only a ledge with some spindly railings around it. Alice came at him, hands outstretched. For no more than two seconds he was suspended, so still that I could see the outline of his calf muscles, and then the balcony came away from the window and he fell like a toppled statue.

'Was that . . . ?' Liss breathed, before correcting herself. 'She would never.'

Whatever force was gathering in me, telling me what I needed to do, made a note: Liss had never witnessed Alice lose control. Liss didn't know what Alice was capable of.

'She would never,' I agreed as we closed in on the house. That same force reined in my instinct to tell Alice to step away from the window, to make herself safe. It knew what I was doing before I did.

The stoner kid shrank back into his window but further along the terrace a front door swung open, spilling yellow light. A guy in shorts and sliders flapped his way down his stairs.

'Did you hear that?' he asked me.

I pointed up at the window. 'He just fell! Please, can you call an ambulance?' I asked him, even though both Liss and I were holding our phones. The deep, capable part of me that knew what was best for my daughter told me I needed the neighbour gone. I decided to listen to it. Call it maternal instinct, the wisdom of experience, post-traumatic survival response – whatever it was, it was clearly several steps ahead of me. The neighbour didn't question me; just turned on his heel and ran for his phone.

One of the streams of music fell silent. Liss took a baby step towards the place where Gabe had landed, behind a bank of bins.

'Maybe he's OK?' she said, as though he'd jumped from the ground floor on to a mattress. The maturity she'd shown less than half an hour earlier had deserted her. She was a little girl, I realised. She and Alice, they were both *babies*. No one was going to sort this out apart from me.

'Stay there, sweetheart.'

Gabe lay on his back in a rhombus of light. His right leg was crossed over his left in a figure four and his back was crooked at a sickening angle. I saw him with a kind of hyper focus, as though my eyesight had kicked up a gear. I noticed the fraying waistband of his underwear, the beads at his neck and string bracelets on his wrist. His eyes were wide open, misty blue.

I knelt to check for a pulse.

He blinked.

I thought about the gaslighting.

I thought about the DNA test.

I thought about the fact that it could have been Alice lying there.

I thought about everything I'd done to protect her and how no threat had come close to this man.

His pupils dilated; his eyelids stretched wider as though opened out by the force of it. I noticed that the whites of his eyes were immaculate, blank as new paper.

I thought about the podcast I'd overheard in this very flat, two women describing how Edmund Burke knew how to strangle a victim without leaving the telltale red lace on their eyeballs.

I decided to save my daughter's life.

Any mother would have done the same.

I rested a knee on each of Gabe's shoulders to trap the blood and I put my hands around his neck and pressed the life out of him, the departure as unambiguous as though he had walked out of a room. After he was gone, I laid my hands on his chest, as though to heal him, and then I straightened up and returned to Liss, knowing that the next few ticks of the night's clock were crucial. If she suspected I'd done anything other than take his pulse, I was dependent on the force inside me to come up with a Plan B, and I didn't have faith that there was one. Momentarily unable to speak, I shook my head. Liss's hands flew to her mouth.

'Oh, no,' she said. 'Oh, *no*.' Her body swung away from me on the last two words: I followed her gaze to where Alice stood in the doorway. Even in shadow the look on her face was almost enough to bring me to the ground. It all flickered repeatedly across her face, almost too fast for me to read. Shock, fear, grief and yes – blink and you miss it – guilt. That was the one that got to me. You can move through everything but guilt. When she called me

Mummy it was as though she was acknowledging how much she needed me, that only I could protect her. It was as close as she'd ever be able to come to giving me her blessing.

Both girls assumed a kind of complicity, dropping their voices as we waited for the neighbour to come back. When Alice said, 'People are going to think I pushed him!' that was the prompt I needed to act out the script that had been writing itself in my head ever since I saw Gabe fall. Two pairs of identical dolly eyes fixed on me as I gave my instructions. I could tell they found my calm delivery eerie, but screaming and shouting would not have served any of our interests.

I could sense a distance in Alice as I helped her back to the hotel. I knew that in saving her I had lost her when she chose Liss's room over ours, and shut the door in my face.

67

Alice

1989 Jean Paul Gaultier corset dress in rubber and satin
Victorian mourning cape, black lace with jet beading
Black Louboutin heels, A/W 2009

@deadgirlsdresses
#outfitoftheday #ootd #vintagefashion #sustainablestyle

I'm little more than jelly in a bag of skin, so everything I am wearing today is an exoskeleton to hold me upright. My dress is fitted with a built-in torpedo bustier and laces up the back like stays. It's not a dress for a lonely girl. It's a dress a friend should fasten and a lover should loosen.

'I need to change. This is inappropriate.'

'You look perfect,' replies Liss. 'The dress on its own *would* be too slutty for a funeral but the cape makes it work.'

She's in a sixties Jean Patou shift, her fringe slicked back and hair in a ponytail, while mine is down. It's unthinkable that I should go to the funeral without her, but attracting attention by dressing the same is the last thing we want.

'Rex is parked on a double yellow,' she says gently.

I slide my feet into unyielding high heels, enjoying their lack of give after months in sandals. I am building myself from the outside, brick by brick. These shoes are a scaffold.

'We've got this,' says Liss.

At the door to the street, I hesitate.

'Is it your mum?' she asks.

'A bit.'

We've talked about this: the deal is that I'll do my best to

compartmentalise the bin of maggots that is my present relationship with my mother until after the funeral. Gabe's death is
layered enough on its own. Something else is blocking my exit,
sure as the bolts on the door.

'What if she's there?' I ask Liss. 'I can't help *picturing* it. Her
big arrival, like something from a film. Dressed in black, all the
drama. Do you know what I mean?'

I want Liss to reassure me, but she replies, 'I've got to admit,
I've imagined it too.'

I should know by now: Liss doesn't do platitudes. For someone
so spiky, she can be a blunt instrument. That's the problem when
someone is your mirror: you can't depend on them for the things
that are missing in you. It's up to me to push back against my own
theory.

'If she didn't turn up to her own father's funeral, she's got no
reason to come here,' I say. 'She never knew Gabe.'

'As far as we *know*.' Liss straightens the cape on my shoulders.
'And we still don't know who was behind that note. But you're
right. If she's been, like, skulking around for twenty-odd years,
there's no reason for her to turn up today.'

'There's still The Woman unaccounted for,' I remind Liss, and
for once she has no comeback.

A rapping on the door, inches from our noses, makes us flinch
in an identical startle reflex.

'*Girls*,' Mum commands.

The drive to Windsor is strained. Silence rises in the car like heat
to the top of a tall building. It's almost a relief when we arrive at
the funeral parlour to decant our tense bodies into sleek mourn-
ers' cars, low to the ground and with beige leather seats. I let
Harriet and Jonny directly follow the hearse. If I can't be stretched
out next to his coffin, it doesn't matter how far behind I am.

All Saints' is your typical English church: arched stone
entrance, tumbledown graveyard, steeple, double wooden doors
pocked by woodworm. In the churchyard, Stef shuffles index

cards next to a marble tomb. He is a smoking pile of rubble in a high-street suit.

It's only maybe the tenth time I've been in a church. We are definitely a weddings-and-funerals-only kind of family, and because we're so insular we don't attend many of either. As we file in, Harriet nods to a hexagonal bird bath thing and says, 'Gabriel was christened at that font.'

Ursula, standing at the altar with her hands on Grandpa Villiers' wheelchair, sees me hesitating and whispers, 'Just copy me.'

The left-hand front pew is reserved for the Clarkes: Grandad and Nanna, Mum, Dad, me, Liss. I pick up one of those funny little cross-stitched cushions you're supposed to kneel on. It's embroidered with a golden goblet, what I think is supposed to be a bread roll, and fish swimming either side.

Crying had become my default state but these tears hurt on their way out, they make themselves known, shards of glass that scrape their way out of sandpaper eyes.

Stef takes the pulpit to talk about Gabe, his voice a steady, commanding baritone as he outlines his friend's commitment to the cause, his loyalty to his mates, his love for me. I'm impressed by how well he keeps it together, but he stumbles on the return to his seat and spends the rest of the service leaning on Jonny's shaking shoulder. There's some singing, one of those hymns you can somehow guess the melody of even if you've never heard it before. Nanna and Grandad are openly crying. Dad's eyes are roving all over the church interior, the work part of his brain doubtless assessing the weight-bearing capacity of those joists and thinking about how it might be converted into luxury flats. Mum's face is impassive, her eyes fixed on a spot of whitewashed wall. She could be anywhere, I think. Does she know what I've been thinking about her? Can she read me—

No. Compartmentalise. You've got forever to deal with her.

I am no stranger to doublethink. For the first half of my life I happily lived with loving my father and knowing he had killed.

Why can't I do the same with Mum? Mothers are different, I guess. He is my water and sun, but she is the tree I grew around. If she is cut down I'm just a bunch of flailing tendrils.

Gabe's family have their own plot in the graveyard – of course they do – and I spend the burial aware that people I don't recognise are watching me. What should I do with my face? I don't know how to experience this, let alone act it. Even as Harriet drops to her knees and Stef makes animal noises I envy them their uncomplicated grief. Stef is howling for a man he knew, and Harriet for someone she believed she knew. No need for them to reassess and re-examine every word, every touch.

The wake is held at a bowling club. On a distant lawn, septuagenarians in white stoop to the green. Inside, everyone's wearing black. I feel strange, swimmy, as though I could pick my feet off the floor and the air would support my weight as I moved through it in a determined breaststroke. The walls are a collage of Gabe. Pictures I've never seen of him as a schoolboy, on a horse – I had no idea he rode; on an expensive holiday drinking out of a coconut; at protests, arm-in-arm with other mud-streaked activists; as a baby in Harriet's arms. With me, in a photo booth strip from someone's party. There are a handful of pictures from our civil partnership. With each new picture, each unknown aspect of his life, I lose him again. I lose him in ways I never had him.

If Liss leaves my side for a second people come up and commiserate with her, so we stick together and she fields comments about our likeness. Mum keeps making encouraging faces across the room. I try to return them but my mouth won't do what I want it to. Not now, Mum. Not *today*.

Kostas from Global Rising has a plate piled sky-high with vine leaves and mini quiches and tiny sausages glazed with honey and mustard. I hear Gabe's voice saying *I'm starving*. I lose him again.

'I can't work out whether it's a good thing or a bad thing that he was so happy when he died,' says Kostas. 'He was mad about you.'

I lose him again.

An activist called Anne envelops me in a suffocating hug.

And again.

Kevin – fresh out of prison, thanks to Gabe – tells me what a great loss he is to the movement, to the world.

And again.

Amer the lawyer says he'll dedicate the rest of his career to doing the work Gabe will never get to do.

And again and again and again.

I don't notice that Liss has slipped away until I see her snaking back through the crowd towards me.

'There's someone here you need to meet,' she says. 'She thought I was you.'

She motions nervously towards the little terrace where, wearing a black trouser suit and holding a glass of white wine, is The Woman.

68

Alice

Roses, pepper and bright silk shot with gold: The Woman's scent carries on the air. You can tell she's got the bath oil *and* the hand lotion *and* the *eau de cologne*. This time, surrounded by memories of Gabe, it hits differently. This is the fragrance that lingered in his clothes when he moved in; it – *she* – was embedded in everything he carried. I can't believe I didn't make the connection before.

'I'm Delphine.' She extends a slender hand that sparkles with diamond rings. 'Harriet invited me. I hope you don't mind.' I picture Delphine at a long table with the assembled Villiers clan – for some reason they are in Tuscany, in an olive grove – and everyone simply *loves* her. 'I'm so sorry, Alice. Gabriel and I didn't part on good terms but this is just an unthinkable tragedy.'

'I'm so sorry too,' I say, and I mean for her loss, not (only) for stealing him from her. After all, they were together for years and I only knew him for six months. Actually, no. I only *truly* knew Gabe for a couple of minutes, those frenzied seconds between his shower and his fall.

I lose him again. My superstructure of clothes is all that's holding me up.

'Just to confirm,' asks Liss, 'you came to see Alice at work, right?'

Delphine nods.

'You have no idea how I wondered who you were,' I say. 'Even Gabe didn't recognise you on CCTV.'

Delphine gives a head-tilt of pity. Of course he recognised her. That was why he was suddenly so keen to have access to my CCTV. That was why he walked me home. He was keeping an eye on her. Not because he thought The Woman was Biba but because he knew she was Delphine.

I feel naked in front of her: she has made a fool of me. Or rather, he made a fool of me and she can see it.

'I should've told you then,' she says. 'But I saw how young you were, how earnest, and I couldn't do it to you.'

Liss takes over. 'Couldn't do what?'

'I'm very wealthy.' Delphine speaks with understated confidence, not a trace of a brag. 'I married well in my twenties and divorced even more wisely and Gabriel knew it. He hand-delivered me my decree absolute, then "coincidentally" happened to be in the same coffee shop as me a few days later.'

Oh, oh, *oh*. Her voice increasingly seems to be coming from somewhere far away.

'A while after Gabriel moved into my place, this girl sent me a message on Facebook. Cara. She was heiress to a – a . . . shipping fortune or something.' Delphine waves her hands dismissively. I suppose one fortune is much like another, once you reach a certain level. 'Cara warned me that Gabe saw women as – and I'm quoting her here – "piggy banks with tits", and that he was after whatever he could get.'

Me, Delphine, Cara. Each link in the chain diminishes me. I lose him again, and this time it's a loss that would still be true if he were alive.

'She said he thought the "idle rich" were the perfect class to fund his activism.'

'No, but I'm hardly idle, and definitely not rich,' I protest. 'I did have an inheritance, but it was modest.' This thought has been a running stitch through my mind since I learned of Gabe's betrayal. If I *did* overlook a piece of clothing that would've set me up for life, I can't identify it.

'So you chucked him?' asks Liss.

Delphine shakes her head with a rueful smile. 'I didn't want to hear it. I managed to forget what Cara had said until Gabriel suggested . . .' She looks anguished for a second. 'I'm so sorry,

Alice, but until he suggested that we get married. I didn't want him having a claim on my house. And when I didn't jump at it, he changed overnight.'

'When would this have been?' asks Liss.

I know the answer before Delphine gives it. I stare unfocused at the blown-up photos of Gabe on the far wall.

'He proposed on New Year's Eve and he was gone by March.'

'But you didn't come to Dead Girls' Dresses till July,' I say.

'I just wanted to put it all behind me. But the more time passed, the more I thought about Cara. What she tried to do for me. I thought I owed the next woman that chance. I lost my nerve that first time because . . . no offence, but it didn't strike me, from your shop and the way you dressed, that you were rich enough for him to be taking advantage of. And then I thought, not everyone wears their wealth on the outside, so I called you. I heard Gabe's voice in the background, and I thought, well, I can't bloody well say what I need to if he's *there*.'

I flash back to the boys storming the shop with Big Nonna's sequins. If they'd arrived five minutes later, Delphine would have had time to tell me everything. Would I have listened to her? Every rewritten day of my history burns; every recast incident is like having a tattoo lasered off.

'You should've tried harder.' Liss's hands are on her hips. 'Alice deserved to know this shit before she got civil-partnered with him.'

I wonder how tightly you can grip the stem of a glass before it breaks.

'And I would have, but he changed my mind.' Delphine makes flute-player's lips around a long, sad sigh. 'He came to the house. I thought he was coming to threaten me but he ended up persuading me he really did love you. I mean, look at you.' She puts a forefinger under my chin. 'You're like a china doll. And I *did* write to you at the shop.' Delphine pouts. 'I said I hoped that we could meet in person one day soon.'

I recast the note's discovery: Gabe, sliding the single leaf of paper from the pile of junk mail in his hands. It would have taken him a second to tear Delphine's signature from the foot of the note.

It turns out you can grip the stem of a glass so tightly your fingertips go purple and it still won't break, no mutter how much you need a release, even if – no, *because* – it will hurt. For a wild, crazed moment I consider biting into the glass's rim, turning my face into a screaming red fountain. *That* would clear the room.

'But the messages to Stef,' says Liss, and gives Delphine a précis of the conversation I saw.

'Ah, Stef.' All three of us cast our eyes about the room for him and spot him arm-in-arm with Big Nonna at the buffet table. 'If anyone knew the contents of Gabe's heart, it was him.'

'Gabe was his person,' I say, and only then realise, 'And Stef was Gabe's.'

I wait for Delphine to contradict me, but she doesn't.

'I'm going to ask him,' says Liss, an hour later. The crowd is thinning out, the older generation departed, but the GR contingent still going strong.

'You can't,' I protest. 'He's still got Big Nonna.'

'That's what he's banking on,' she says. 'Let's call his bluff.'

'Don't make a scene.'

'You need to know,' she says. 'You deserve to know.'

She takes my hand and marches purposefully towards Stef. He stares her down for a few seconds, then finally emerges from behind Big Nonna's chair. 'Not here,' he says, and puts the huge paddles of his hands on our waists to steer us to a quiet corner. Up close, his olive skin is grey and the cracks in his lips glisten red. Even I don't look this shit. I fight the urge to take him in my arms.

I see Liss spread her shoulders wide as she recalibrates her setting to strident. 'Alice deserves to know—' she begins, but I shush her.

'Stef, I'm going to ask you this once.' The room dissolves and it's just me and him facing each other in our final tug of love. 'Was he planning to ask me to go after my grandfather's money?'

Stef goes pale under his beard.

'I know about Delphine and Cara.'

The air between us seems to crystallise; the wrong word could send splinters flying. Liss interprets his silence as a rebuff, and seizes her chance. 'How would your right-on mates feel if they knew he was using women for money?'

'Stop it, Liss,' I say, partly because I think a lot of the activists would approve of it, but mostly because I can see something she's blind to. Stef wants to talk; he just *can't*. I resent the fact that it's up to me to make this easy for him, but this moment is fleeting as water. I make my tone as gentle as Liss's was harsh. 'If you want to honour Gabe's memory, then you need to let me know who I'm grieving.'

'I mean yeah. He was convinced you *were* getting a big payout. But there was more to it than that.' Stef wields the truth gently and with regret. 'He was used to, like, bored housewife women. You were already on your own journey, living our values, with your work – hang on.' He's so clearly having an idea that I almost expect it to come with an accompanying tone, like a phone notification. 'I can *prove* it was for real.'

With some difficulty – his trousers are straining over his vast quads – he produces his phone from his pocket. He skids through Discord messages until he gets to a selfie that Gabe took of us on Brighton beach in May. I'm wearing a high-cut red swimsuit, a towel over my shoulder and a sunhat with points around the brim. I'm holding up a chocolate ice cream, pretending to be the Statue of Liberty. Gabe's in board shorts, pale chest, bad hair, crumpled old man's face. On the train back to London that night we had said *I love you* for the first time. We'd both admitted that the biggest three little words, eight letters and two spaces, vital for lovers to catch their breath, had been expanding inside us, ready to burst our lungs, for months already.

Stef had responded, *Punching above ur weight there mate.*

Too right. I'm gonna marry this girl.

In a stiff black dress, at the dark heart of Gabe's funeral, I feel the tummy-flip of the proposal he never made.

Thought you thought marriage was bullshit.

OK civil partnership then. Whatever she's a keeper.

Stef had fired back the money-bag emoji.

It's not just about that anymore, wrote Gabe. *Alice is what all the songs are about. She's the one.*

69

Alice

1972 Ossie Clarke wrap dress in red crêpe
2002 Red or Dead black crystal-encrusted platform shoes

@deadgirlsdresses
#outfitoftheday #ootd #vintagefashion #sustainablestyle

Last night was November the fifth. Spent fireworks litter the flag-stones in Camden Passage and the Christmas party orders are coming in fast. I'm in the stock room, checking returns for flaws, and Liss is behind the counter, when the seashell phone rings.

Liss picks up and before she can say 'Dead Girls' Dresses' she's going, 'Rex! Long time no speak!'

After the funeral I retreated into a dark, echoing space where neither of my parents can get to me. The suspicion that while I was on my wild-goose chase for Biba the real killer was under my nose, in my heart, in my veins has been hollowing me out. I'm basically just a nervous breakdown in a fabulous dress. In the three months since Gabe died I haven't ghosted my parents, exactly, but I've flipped into a response-only mode, my texts monosyllabic. I tell myself I don't have time to miss Mum but this morning when I was grocery shopping I found myself buying Bold lavender detergent, just so that my bedsheets will smell of her.

I emerge from the stock room mouthing, 'I'm not here.'

'You can't ignore them forever,' she says, and the next thing you know she's got the receiver pressed to my ear.

'Enough's enough.' The sound of Dad's voice pulls a pin inside me; it makes me want to drop to all fours. 'Your mum's in bits. If this is about what happened the night Gabe died, you know she was protecting you.'

His uncharacteristic directness disarms me; my honesty takes even me by surprise. I find my voice. 'You weren't there. You didn't see what she was like. How cold. It was like she . . .' The words dissolve into a yowl.

'We need to talk this through. Me and you and Mum and Liss. Proper family conference, have it all out.'

'I don't want to have it all out. I don't want to say what I'm thinking about her.'

Dad's silence starts small and stretches to encompass the distance between London and Suffolk. It is his to break. 'OK, we're coming up,' he announces. 'We'll meet you in the Camden Head at six o'clock.'

'Tonight?' I squeak.

'Tonight.'

He hangs up without saying goodbye.

'Well, someone had to force the situation.' Liss is clearly impressed. 'Never thought it'd be him.'

'I can't,' I say.

'We can,' she replies.

For the rest of the day we are muted, uneasy. We both know we're on the edge of something huge and real that we can never come back from.

My parents are tucked in a booth in the corner, surrounded by shop workers, tourists and suits, looking old and tired and emitting such tension that I wonder why the other drinkers can't sense it. Dad's turning his glass round and round on the table, creating a little vortex in his barely touched pint. Mum appears to be wearing Hallowe'en make-up, like she's dipped her fingers in stage paint and drawn crude half-circles under her eyes. My longing for her is bodily, more powerful at touching distance than for the whole three months we've been estranged.

'Thanks for coming.' She's practically vibrating. 'That's a

lovely dress. You do suit red. It is new? Obviously not *new*, I mean is it new to you?'

I planned to work up to it, to ease in, but the words that have been crouching in my belly since Gabe died have only gathered strength. They force themselves up and out of my mouth without warning.

'Mum, did you kill Tom Wheeler and Guy Grainger?'

'*What?*' splutters Dad.

'Oh, my God,' says Mum.

'Fuckin' *hell*,' says Liss.

I almost say 'What?' myself. Where do I go from here?

'Why would you possibly think that?' says Mum. Dad is angry, a vein worming on his temple, but she's not. If anything, her tension of a moment ago has dispersed, as if some internal knot has been unpicked. Is it the relief of an imminent unburdening? I will her to tell me I'm wrong, but no denial is forthcoming.

There's only one way to go, and that's forward. I take such a deep breath I can feel the seams of my bodice straining. 'When Gabe fell, you'd hatched a plan to cover it all up before I even got down to the street,' I say. 'You knew what you were doing. Everything about it was new and confusing to me but you knew what to do, I could feel it in my gut that you were acting on experience. And I asked you and asked you and asked you if Dad's conviction was bullshit and he was covering up for Biba and you both said no and I put two and two together and . . .'

My voice is rising in pitch. Dad's eyes do a sweep of the room, but the booth is high-backed, and red leather traps the sounds inside.

'We have to tell her, Karen.' I've never heard him speak so decisively. 'We can do it in your words or mine.'

Here it comes.

All of us are rigid, leaning forward into the conversation, heads frozen inches away from each other. If anyone were paying us the slightest attention, it would surely look as if we're slowly turning to stone, although inside me dark things are writhing.

Here it comes.

The pathetic thought comes to me that I would like to be ten again, when Mum was unimpeachable, when all I knew was the facts as they'd been presented to me – that Dad was a good man who'd done a bad thing – and I'd never looked up his case online. I wish they'd lied to me my whole life, told me it was tax evasion, changed all our names completely and brought me up in America.

Here it comes.

'I was at the house on The Night Of.' Mum closes her eyes but it doesn't feel avoidant: more like she's watching the movie of that night flicker across the inside of her eyelids. 'Your dad had written this rash, angry letter to Roger and Guy had posted it. Biba was going off him; he was trying to win her back. I really think he thought it would persuade Roger to sign the house over, if he saw how desperate Rex and Biba were to have that security. But it had the opposite effect. Roger turned up on the doorstep and effectively threw them out of the house, said he was going to sell it on, make the kids stand on their own two feet.'

Dad takes his eyes off Mum for just long enough to flick a glance at me. It's too brief, surely, for him to be able to read my face. God knows I can't read his.

'When Roger left, Christ.' Mum's eyelids flicker more quickly now, like she's deep in REM sleep, trapped in a bad, bad dream. 'All hell broke loose. Biba was screaming, throwing things. Dad and Guy were throwing punches.'

Please just confess, I scream internally.

Liss reaches for my hand. She is as invested in this as I am. I take comfort in the thought that the outcome will be good for her. In learning that my mother is a murderer, she will have confirmation at last that hers is not.

'She was like a wild animal,' says Mum. Liss's hand is sweaty in mine but I can't let it go. 'I promise she would have killed Guy with her bare hands. But he carried a gun, so she used that instead.'

Boom.

It is somehow detonation and anti-climax.

'Are you OK?' Dad asks Liss.

She shrugs, shakes her head; she doesn't know yet.

'So not self-defence?' I didn't know, till I asked the question, that a part of me was hoping it was. 'She killed him in a fucking *tantrum?*'

'If you like,' says Mum. She starts to cry: really cry, the kind of tears that pull your face into weird shapes. Liss gets up, elbows her way through a cluster of braying men in suits, and comes back with a wad of napkins from the bar. Mum presses the whole lot to her face.

'And Tom Wheeler?' I look to Dad for my answer now.

He strokes his neck upwards, as if he has to massage out the words. 'That was pretty much as we told it to you. In that it was done in a panic, by someone who didn't know what they were doing. I just put myself in Biba's place.'

'And then *you,*' I turn on my weeping mother, 'left Dad to pick up the shit.'

'No.' Dad is firm. 'I made them leave. I sent them to your mum's old student house, so they could alibi each other. I didn't see the point in ruining three lives when one would do.'

'We left through the woods. There was a hole in the fence . . .' Thin tears escape the corner of Mum's closed eyes. 'I didn't see Dad again until you were a few weeks old.'

I have the feeling that acceptance is going to come slowly, over the next few days, weeks, even years, but I want *all* the information *now*. I want to gorge on it so that I can digest it at my own pace. I never want to sit through a conversation as painful as this one again.

'So the night Gabe died. You were . . . I feel like I want to say using skills you learned back then, on the night of the murder?'

She opens her eyes; they are bottomless wells of sadness. 'If anything, I was acting based on my experience of press attention. I was worried sick about what they'd do to you, if they connected you to the story, if they found out about Liss.' Shadows flit by in the passage outside, dark grey shapes sliding across the frosted glass. 'But maybe on some level you're right, love. Maybe I learned to keep a cool head in a crisis. It was totally different, though, what happened with Gabe, nothing like what we did in '97. I was just making sure a tragic accident didn't get misinterpreted.'

Her saying it out loud, in front of witnesses – even if they are witnesses who are on our side, who would lie for us – makes it official. It was an accident. It was. Wasn't it?

The door opens, letting in cold air and a trace of cigarette smoke. It brings me back into the room. A few tables away, a middle-aged man and woman, both wearing wedding rings, start snogging with an enthusiasm unusual for a married couple. Someone behind the bar smashes a glass and a cheer erupts. For our fellow drinkers, the night is unfolding in real time. Everything is keeping its shape.

'Why didn't you tell her?' Liss asks Dad. 'How fucked up is that, to let your kid think you're a murderer?'

'Liss . . .' I warn her.

'She's right,' says Dad. 'At first, it was because of Biba. Even after we had her declared dead, there was always the chance, wasn't there? I couldn't let her go, girls. I couldn't shake the thought . . . if she comes back, and Alice knows, and there's the tiniest chance she lets it slip, and that person does a Sophie, on a grander scale and posts something online . . .'

'You didn't trust Alice.' I know Liss's accusatory tone comes from loyalty to me but it doesn't feel right.

'I didn't earn it,' I say.

The facts have stopped coming but the relief continues to snowball.

'You can't imagine how sorry I am, for all of it,' says Mum. 'I love you so, so much. Whatever we did wrong, we thought it was for the best.'

She is crying in a way a little child cries: openly, not caring what anyone thinks of them. The four of us join hands across beer mats and tear-soaked napkins and glasses that we must regard as half-full if we are to survive. In this quiet corner of a rowdy pub, I experience the truth I've been chasing for the last year of my life and it's horrible, like having my skin peeled back and doused in salt. Humans cannot be capable of sustaining this intensity of feeling for any length of time without going insane. This is why people live in denial. It's because the alternative is literally unbearable.

Dad is the first to withdraw his hand. 'Look at the state of us,' he says, wiping his eyes on his cuff. 'Thank God we're in a booth.'

Somehow, we all dredge a laugh.

'You can trust me now,' I say. 'I'll take it to the grave. I swear on my 1954 Balenciaga ballgown. I'm never going to mention the name Biba Capel outside this family again.'

'No more playing detective?' asks Mum.

'God, no. It's not as if I got very far anyway. I want nothing to do with crime in any form as long as I live.'

I mean it. No more podcasts, no more investigations. I know death's stain now and am horrified that I ever chased it. If my parents can trust me with their truth, this is the least I can do.

70

Karen

I'm reading my German thriller in front of the wood-burner. It's actually very good, although I've got one eye on the clock. At 4pm I have arranged to video-call Nina on the number she sent me. Alice says the quest is over. She doesn't want to look for Biba. She wants to move on. I believe she means it for now, but I need to take one more step, in case she changes her mind, or Liss decides to poke the ashes. The ingenuity that let me protect Alice the night Gabe died handed me an idea. I'm nervous – if Nina goes along with it, it will all be OK.

It rings out for so long that I think she's not going to pick up. When she does, I catch my breath. Her dark hair is pale grey now, and her voluptuousness has deflated. I'd foolishly pictured her as frozen in time but of course it's been twenty-five years. I wonder what she thinks of me, the eye bags, my gouged smile.

'Karen,' she says wryly. 'Long time no see.' She's blurred out the background so I can't see where she is. Her wild curls keep escaping the filter, making her hair look like a living thing, a gorgon's nest of snakes.

'Thanks so much for picking up.' I start to burn up, as if I'm under hot lights. God, I'm so *tired*. I would like just one conversation that doesn't come with a list of terrifying physical symptoms. 'What did Alice's message say?'

Nina says. 'I left it showing unread. I didn't want anything to do with it. Still don't. I only picked up to tell you to leave me alone. You're toxic, the lot of you.'

Once upon a time it would have gladdened my heart to have Nina include me in the Capel family. Now it lands like the insult it clearly is.

'Look, I *want* to leave you alone. But I need you to do something first.'

Nina scoffs: I am in no position to issue ultimatums and we both know it.

'I want you to write to Alice and tell her that Biba is definitely dead.'

'*Is* she dead?' asks Nina.

I give the only answer I can. 'Legally. A body was never found.'

Nina puts her head to one side, silver earrings listing with the movement. 'I last saw her in '07. I'll level with you, she wasn't the picture of health then. Or sanity.'

'The last confirmed sighting was Denmark, also in 2007.'

Nina nods. 'She went after the kid, then?'

'You know about Liss?'

'Is that what she's calling herself? She was Alice on her birth certificate.' The harsh syllable that follows may or may not be a laugh. 'Yeah, I know about her. I *delivered* her.'

'Wow,' I say, although it shouldn't be a surprise. Earthy, unflappable Nina, three times a mother herself, would have been an instinctive midwife.

'It was fine. But then second births usually are. I'm presuming *your* Alice is Biba's first?'

My throat constricts to the width of a needle, and all I can do is nod.

'Does Rex know she's not his?'

My voice is loud now. 'She *is* his. In every way that matters.'

Nina holds up her hands. 'Like I said. I don't wanna get involved. This is the last contact I ever want with you. So go on, what do you want me to do?'

There's a movement in the unknowable background behind Nina, as if someone's come into the room. One of her children? I yearn to know how those golden toddlers turned out, but have no right to ask.

'In the vanishingly unlikely event that Biba *is* alive, and the even more unlikely event that Alice tracks her down, she could be dangerous. Biba, I mean. There are things from back then that she wouldn't want getting out. I worry what Biba might do to keep her quiet.' This is as much as I can say about The Night Of. I have no idea how much Nina knows. 'You know how volatile Biba could be.'

'Indeed I do,' says Nina, and I can see that she too is recalling something she is in no hurry to put into words.

'So. We have evidence she was using other people's names. Including mine.' I see from Nina's face that this is not news to her. 'So, let me look up foreigners who died in Morocco and no one ever claimed their body or something. We can say it was her, using someone else's ID. I'll do all the research and then I'll send you a message that you can cut and paste and send to Alice that brings the story to a full stop.'

Nina pinches the skin between her eyebrows while she considers. Eventually she nods. 'Right, I'm going now.'

The sun is sinking at last on the mystery of Biba Capel. I try to enjoy the release, not think too hard about what might be rising in the east. Since this is the last time I'll ever talk to Nina, I ask the question that's been burning a hole in me since I found out about Liss.

'Before you go . . . Do you have any idea where she went after Denmark? And where she was in the missing years?'

'No idea on either count,' says Nina. 'But like I said, she was in a bad way. Wherever she was, whatever she was up to, it won't have been pretty.'

71

Dubai is as unlike Ibiza as two places with palm trees and beaches can be.

Ibiza runs on sex and anarchy.

Dubai runs on laws and money.

Luckily for you, the person you've come here to visit has lots of cash.

As Rachael says, Dubai is a place where you can really enjoy your wealth without judgement. She wears rings with stones so big you'd swear she only had one knuckle in each finger. Rachael had her children and snared her man. She's given up her 'career', an abuse of privilege that makes your blood fizz with rage you somehow mask. A maid keeps her house gleaming, a chef keeps the meals coming, and a nanny shields the children from the worst of their mother.

She takes you to the hotel bar where she met her husband. It's thronged with ex-pat men who are supposed to go home at the weekends but when the kids are at boarding school and the weather's bad, what's the point? One of these guys, Mel – something big in construction, talks about a palm tree they are building in the sea, whatever that means – takes a shine to you, and you take a shine to his AmEx. It's just so lovely, after all these years struggling, to be looked after again.

The flat overlooks a building site where new towers seem to arise overnight, like grass after rain. You no longer miss acting because your entire life is a performance. You have gone method. The irony of you being anyone's personal assistant when your own life is such a car crash is not lost on you, but ex-pats can't stay in Dubai without a job and couples can't live together unless they're married. This way, Mel can write you and your apartment off as a business expense.

A day that starts with brunch with Rachael ends with you being arrested for public drunkenness. Mel bails you out, of course, but he's terribly cross. He thinks you might have 'issues'. The good news is, he knows just the man for you to see.

The stuff they've got you on slows you down and makes you docile, which Mel likes. It takes the best part of a year but finally you achieve a state of – what would you call it? It's not the pink cloud you've been chasing but nor is it the stormcloud that doesn't want you to survive. When Rachael's husband is posted to Saudi and she moves away, you dread to think how you would have coped without the meds. The day they pull you out of the pool and pump your stomach, they tell you what a good patient you are. How co-operative, how calm.

Hours turn into days turn into months turn into years. The desert horizon vanishes; the city encroaches.

The internet is a godsend: days spent refreshing gossip sites, a kind of meditation in itself. Jossip, Perez, Dlisted. Paris, Lindsay, Britney. You order in every night. This city is a miracle. You never need leave your apartment. You become more familiar with your reflection in a screen than a mirror. Friends Reunited, MySpace. Neither Karen nor Freddie exist online. YouTube is a revelation. Someone's uploaded your turn as naughty nun Sister Saint-Esprit, inviting Charles II into the convent and showing him what's under your habit. There are three thousand views on that clip. Most of them are you.

You learn via Friends Reunited that an imbecile with biceps from your year at Queen Charlotte's has been mooted as the next James Bond.

In time your research skills improve. The parole board has a website. You pause for a moment to consider the miracle of being able to read up on the English prison system from the UAE, then do some maths for the first time since you were at school: time on remand, length of sentence, behaviour in prison.

Five Christmas trees are installed, shed their needles, and are taken away. You get fat, and Mel dumps you. Rex's release coincides beautifully with the deadline Mel gives you to leave your flat. It's time to bring your family back together.

You take yourself off the meds. It's like surfacing from a warm bath into a night where there are always fireworks, each one a memory. Guy is a sparkler, a short sharp fizz. Rex is a Catherine wheel, tightly wound, nailed in place, not going anywhere. Karen is a Roman candle, stuck in the ground. You are a rocket, a screech and a bang. Your daughters? They are the stars. You can't always see them but they have always been there.

Israel is virtually on the way to Denmark, isn't it? Mel's 'severance package' was generous so you treat yourself to a first-class ticket, travelling under your own name for the first time since the last century.

You're excited to share your plans with Nina. She's going to be so thrilled for Rex! You are giddy when you get to the airport. The first-class lounge has champagne on tap and as for the shopping . . . you plough through eight thousand dirhams in an hour with presents for Nina and the kids. New make-up and perfume. A pair of seventies-style Chloé sunglasses that you buy for the sheer buzz of walking through the airport in them looking like a fucking film star. You are Elizabeth Taylor on her fifth divorce and her third Oscar. When you leave the plane, you press them into the hands of a stewardess who admired them on the way in. What is money? It's only numbers.

'No,' says Nina, when she sees you. She actually keeps the door on the chain. A little girl, brown skin, hair like black smoke, plays in her skirts. You bend down to her.

'Hello,' you say. 'What's your name?' You look up at Nina. 'I don't want to stay. I just want to talk. To catch up.'

Reluctantly, Nina opens the door. 'One hour.' The child regards you solemnly, trustingly, through oily black eyes. She is a sign, this child. A girl. A message. You are doing the right thing.

Christ, that Nina – she knows how to rain on a parade. When you tell her your plans, she lists your failures, as she perceives them. She tells you that you are having a manic episode, that you are not well, that you need a doctor, that you're a danger to yourself, and then, 'You can't do that to children, Biba,' she says. 'You've got a chance to break the chain of . . . whatever it is, that runs through your family. It sounds like those girls are settled. Rex and Karen will be brilliant parents, you know that, and the others . . . well, they've gotta be better than you. You're a fucking grenade. You should go and detonate yourself somewhere safe, like a desert.'

You don't regret giving Nina a piece of your mind, although you're sorry the little girl had to see it. You don't like making children cry.

Denmark does not go well. It turns out that you can't just turn up to a school and pick up your kid, even if you recognise her through the playground railings and she looks so like you that no one could doubt she is yours.

Freddie and Kofi keep pelting you with the word 'safeguarding'. They say that contact isn't out of the question but they are deliberately obstructive, insisting on 'doing things properly', which means lawyers which means paperwork. And of course you can't, because all the official documents that prove you are Karen Clarke, mother of this child, are in an evidence box somewhere on Ibiza.

Well, then. You will come back to Copenhagen with the first Alice. Once they see she has a sister they'll have no choice.

London has shifted somehow. Known but not. Home but strange. You go to buy a ten-pack of Marlboro Gold, nearly faint at the price, and settle for a tin of rolling tobacco and papers. When the salesgirl hands you your change, the coins, cold metal loose in your pocket, are familiar. Seven sides on a twenty-pence piece, same on a fifty, the chunky pound and the tiddlywink five. What will that buy you now?

Rachael is living in one of those garden squares you only get in west London, where the houses have big white pillars with black numbers painted on them. You stand outside and count the windows. There must be half a dozen bedrooms. Surely there will at least be a sofa you can sleep on.

A Filipina maid opens the door and takes you for one of her class, in your cheap emergency winter clothes and the charity-shop scarf, big as a blanket. After some persuasion she leads you to Rachael, who is in bed, surrounded by three yappy chihuahuas. She must weigh about five stone.

The maid brings coffee and biscuits, which you all but swallow whole. Rachael feeds the corner of a biscuit to a chihuahua. Five minutes later the dog shits liquid chocolate all over the cream rug. The maid is at the ready with some kind of sour chemical foam that eradicates all trace of the mess.

Your hopes rise when her husband comes home. Maybe you can sweet-talk him into giving you sanctuary? Unfortunately he remembers you from Dubai. 'You,' he says, 'are the last person Rachael needs right now. If you don't fuck off out of my house right now, I'll pick you up and carry you out myself.'

'Alright, alright, I'm going. Jeez.'

You have Rachael's credit card and two hundred quid cash from a handbag in her walk-in. Enough to get you a taxi to Liverpool Street. Enough to get you on a train to Suffolk.

72

Alice

1970s black deco feather print Bus Stop dress with angel sleeves
Thigh-high tan boots, Topshop, circa 1984

@deadgirlsdresses
#outfitoftheday #ootd #vintagefashion #sustainablestyle

For December, Liss has recreated Miss Havisham's wedding breakfast in the shop window. The unveiling of the new Dead Girls' Dresses display on the first day of every month is becoming a bit of a thing. This one got three thousand likes on Instagram in the first hour. The mannequin wears a high-necked ivory lace and satin Edwardian wedding dress, a 1900s Spanish lace veil and a long pewter wig that tempts me to dye my own hair that fake old-lady grey. The table is set with silver teapots, spilled wineglasses and cobwebs Liss made from cotton wool and hairspray. Her brainwave was to create a 'selfie space' in each installation, so that customers can insert themselves into the tableau. All we need now is for them to start buying the clothes as well as posting their pictures.

This morning I got a voicemail from Maya at Crawford Southern. I got as far as, 'It's about, among other things, the tax situation on your inheritance,' before deleting it. If they come after me for capital gains, I'm fucked. The energy bills are twice what they were last year: I've had to put this month's heating on another exorbitant credit card.

Liss is going through her bank account on her phone. 'I can scratch together about five hundred quid,' she says. 'And my dads can lend us two thousand, although they'll need it back. Will that be enough?'

'I honestly don't know,' I say. 'I know it's part of life and you've got to do it but when I look at a spreadsheet of numbers it's like they literally slide off my eyeballs.'

Liss adds another column of figures to her notepad. 'What's the balance in the business account right now?'

I tell her the figure. She grimaces.

To put off returning Maya's call, I go through my phone, deleting old photos and messages that are cluttering it up. I notice a message in my 'other' folder in Facebook and open it, hoping it isn't a customer I've overlooked. I pride myself on a prompt response.

It isn't from a customer.

'Liss,' I say. 'I've got a message from Nina Vitor.'

All thoughts of tax leave my head. This is bigger than money.

'Nina the jewellery woman?' Her eyes widen. 'What does it say?'

All I can see is the top line.

Dear Alice, I'm sorry it's taken me so long to get back to you.

'I'm scared to look,' I say. 'I meant it when I said no more investigations. I really want to leave the whole Capel shitshow behind me.'

'We could delete it?' she suggests. 'If we really want to put the great big hunt for Biba behind us, we can just wipe it.'

'As if either of us have that kind of willpower,' I say.

'Fair enough.' She drums her fingers on the counter. 'Dutch courage?' she asks, and I nod. She takes two of the coupe glasses from the display cabinet and the bottle of cheap vodka I use to spritz clothes, pours a shot into each glass and we down them. My throat burns, then my cheeks.

'OK,' she says. 'Let's do it.'

'What if she tells us Biba is alive?' I ask her. 'What if she wants to see us? What if she's decided to come over? Do we still want that? Knowing what she did?'

Liss closes her eyes. Biba was, after all, her mother. They shared a body. They shared blood. Who wouldn't want to know their mother, no matter what crimes she had committed?

'Let's just cross that bridge when we come to it. It's probably nothing.' But she pours us both another shot. 'You've got this,' she says, in a voice that doesn't make it clear whether she's talking to me or herself.

I open the message. The hairs on my arms seem to crackle as they rise.

Dear Alice,

I'm sorry it's taken me so long to get back to you and I'm even more sorry to be writing to you with bad news. Biba Capel had a troubled life. She came to see me when I was living in Tel Aviv in 2007, and she was in a bad way then.

You probably know that she used a series of aliases. Not something I encouraged but it wasn't something I was going to go to the authorities about, either. She was living under the name of Iris Olsen when she died in a car crash, and she was buried under that name too. I was the one who identified her body and I'm attaching reports of the death announcement.

I'm glad you wrote actually because I've been meaning to tell Rex for years but I knew he'd had her declared dead and for various reasons I didn't want to go raking up the past again. If you decide to share the news with him, please break it as gently as you can. I was very fond of him once.

Nina xox

I dry-heave. Even though I'd called off my search for Biba, I had expected that proof of life, or death, when it came, would feel like the answer to a question. Relief, maybe, that this maniac isn't coming after me. Instead I am hollowed out by loss. My head feels suddenly leaden, too much for my neck and body to bear. It tips forward into my hands and I catch it like a ball.

When I look up, Liss has her arms wrapped around one of Biba's dresses, the peach chiffon gown. She's holding it tight as a teddy bear, inhaling it as though a trace of her mother might remain. Her mouth is wide and features slide down her face, pulled by the falling weight of her grief.

73

The gins-in-tins you buy at the Liverpool Street branch of Marks and Spencer are underwhelming, little more than fizzy water. You've got used to setting your own measures, that's the problem. There's no trolley, and by the time you get to Ipswich station the bar is closed.

The overhead light stutters and strobes, giving your reflection a flickering, silent-movie quality. You don't flinch from the looking-glass girl with the big black eyes. She's gone by a few names this past decade, but now she's on her way to take ownership of the one that will mean the most. A name billions of women answer to every day, yet is uniquely theirs.

You let your eyelids fold and picture you and Rex, swinging a little kid by the wrists, like parents do in films. You know it's mawkish and strange: the obviousness of your siblinghood, the impossibility of your convincing shared parenthood. Rex will be able to think of a way around that, just like the way he took the gun from your shaking hands, wiped it clean of your fingerprints and pressed his own into the warm steel. He knew what you needed and how to make it happen.

You are the only passenger to disembark at the station in the cold dark middle of nowhere. You feed coins into a slot and punch in Karen's number, then blow on your fingers while you wait for her to come and get you. She picks you up then drives at speed around hairpin bends on a narrow road. It's a clear night. The moon silvers fields of stubble. A white owl hovers over hidden prey, her wings a blur.

She won't let you smoke in the car, and pulls over at a building site, a clapboard show home guarding a few acres of mud and concrete. The stars, last contemplated over Dubai, are all in the wrong place. Karen's breath comes in cold, fast, round little puffs that quicken further when you tell her you have come to relieve her of her burden. Fucking . . . not a word of thanks.

'I'm the only mother Alice has ever known,' she says. 'You told me to look after her. I'm not saying you can't come back, but not like this.' You light your cigarette, wait for her to dial down the drama but she's still bleating on. 'This would destroy Alice and Rex. They've been through so much. I've worked so hard to make them secure. If you care about them at all you won't tell them the truth.'

It's an effort to keep your voice even as you explain the facts to her. You stand facing each other, your long scarf a red flag between you in the breeze, her pupils dilated, her nostrils flared.

'They're not your family.' She's talking like someone in a film, possessed by an alien. 'They're mine.'

Woah. This could get nasty, you think, this could—

There's a beauty in the way she catches both ends of the scarf at once – the grace of a dancer, the precision of a table magician – and that moment of enchantment blinds you to her intention. At first, your hands are slow to your neck. She's just trying to scare you. By the time you understand that she is a machine you will never overpower, it's too late.

'They're mine!' The words and heavy breaths are Karen's, which means the sickening gurgle must be coming from you.

You didn't think she had it in her.

You are resigned to your death in the same moment that you understand it. Yet still you claw and grasp. One more breath. One more word. If it must end like this, let the girls find each other. But the coil around your throat tightens and traps them, even as your mouth forms the word 'sister'.

A black circle narrows around her grunting, contorted face, replaced suddenly by a velvet silence and an image so clear it almost hurts your eyes. Chessboard squares, black and white tiles. They are clean, gleaming, new. The black squares expand and the *white squares shrink until all that remains of them are pinpricks, like stars. You know stars are dead light but you reach for them anyway. Far beyond your grasp, they die one by one by one.*

You push the glass. It turns to gauze and then to mist, and at last you are through to the other side.

74

Karen

It is December again. A year almost to the day since we moved Alice into Dead Girls' Dresses. The field at the back of our house is being ploughed, driving Peggy to distraction. I close down the document I'm working on and move to the window seat in my study, watching the earth turn over and over, letting my thoughts do the same. Since the girls heard from Nina, and Biba's death became official for the second time, it's freed me up to remember her life.

Do I wish I'd never met her? I *still* don't know. Everything in my life, from the bookshelves Rex fitted in the alcove to the dog scrabbling at the back door, to my daughter's widowhood – it all goes back to a chance encounter in a university corridor. Like Biba, I am a killer twice over. All that carnage for two months' hedonism the summer I turned twenty-one. Was I so empty that it was really Biba who created that in me? Would I have found someone else? Would I have had a nervous breakdown in my mid-twenties; would I have had a glittering career?

Would I have carried a child?

I dare, now, to wonder what Biba's trajectory would have been without me. If I am honest with myself – and I can be, I must be, at last – I don't think it would have been that different. I ended her life, but I didn't influence it. She absorbed nothing of me except for a few dozen words of German, and even those she forgot as soon as she didn't need them. If it hadn't been for the events of The Night Of, I wouldn't have impacted her life at all.

Rex took the job at the New Houses. It's not my area of expertise, but even I know that a loft conversion doesn't require digging up a house's foundations. Biba is somewhere under that estate, encased in concrete, far deeper than the regulation six feet. He may be walking over his sister's grave but he will never know. It would take an earthquake to exhume her. It would take the kind of disaster that nothing survives.

I'm pushing a trolley round the big Tesco. Rex is on the other side of the shop, choosing wine for Christmas dinner. We're hosting Freddie and Kofi. I find myself in the books aisle. This time next year *Love Bomb* could be there; maybe the year after that the thriller will be finished.

My phone buzzes: the sight of Alice's caller ID sparks a little dopamine hit. After those months where we didn't speak, I never take contact for granted.

'Hello, sweetie!'

There's blubbering where there should be words. I'm not happy that she's crying but she's done this before, called up just to share her grief with me, and, while I wish she didn't have to, I welcome it, because it's a sign she hasn't completely vanished into Planet Liss.

'Another bad day?' I say in my best mum voice. 'Cry it all out.'

'No, it's . . .' she manages, then breaks down again. '*S'good.*'

I listen carefully. Like birdsong, tears can be translated if you know what to listen for. This is the sound of overwhelm, not grief. I hear Liss in the background saying, 'Put her on speaker!' The connection develops an echo.

'Is Rex with you?' asks Liss breathlessly. 'He's not picking up.'

I picture his phone charging in the car and try not to mind that they called him first. 'Let me find him.' I begin to steer towards the booze aisle. 'What's happening?'

'Karen, it's *insane*.' Liss's voice is climbing in pitch with every word. 'You know how Alice thought her inheritance from Roger Capel was all those clothes? Well, it turned out they were just something Jules *gave* Alice to tide her over while all the paperwork was being sorted out. It turns out Roger Capel left Alice a *house*.'

'Not just a house, Mum.' Alice manages through a rattle of snot. '*The* House.'

I crash the trolley into a shelf of greetings cards. 'Not Queenswood Lane,' I say. 'They sold it to a developer. It was turned into flats.'

My eyes land on a card that says, *To a Wonderful Mother at Christmas Time.*

'No and yes. They had it converted into flats, but they kept them. All the Capel kids have lived there at some point.'

'Rufus only moved out a couple of years ago, and they've been letting it ever since.' It takes me a second to understand that Alice has taken over. The girls' voices, always similar, are becoming indistinguishable, Alice picking up Liss's burr and Liss borrowing Alice's staccato London delivery.

'They couldn't tell me right away because they had to sort out, whatjimacallit, assets and liabilities, share things out among the cousins – who have all got like two houses each, by the way – before they could make it formal.'

The Christmas cards blur in front of my eyes, red and white blending to a rosy pink.

'I thought Jules was a bit of a bitch but she's actually really nice? She just didn't want to say anything in case it all went to shit. This is insane, Mum. I've got a fucking *house* in fucking *London*.'

'Christ, Alice. It must be worth—'

'Three point five.' The laughter that ripples up is nervous and wild. I see Rex at the end of an aisle, squinting at the label on a bottle of red, unaware of the news I bring.

'I know. I *know*,' says Alice. 'I literally can't even, I *cannot*. So listen, Jules has got a couple of bits of furniture to swap around and then she's giving me the keys on Saturday evening. I know it'll be a bit weird for you both, but do you think you could bear to come?'

75

Karen

The outer London suburbs throb with brightly coloured lights, dancing Santas and inflatable reindeers bobbing outside pebble-dashed semis, but, as we close in on Highgate, the front gardens are strung with tasteful white bulbs. Rex – as far as I know – hasn't been back here since the day I collected him from prison in 2007. There's nothing to be gained from telling him about my visits.

'I remember when that was planted.' Rex nods to a towering laurel tree. We make conversation about how quickly trees grow so that we can ignore the fact that we're driving past Tom Wheeler's former home.

We park deep in the woods, where it all began. The wind goads bare branches into sword-fights and the forest floor is already frosted at five o'clock.

'There was a time I would've been able to tell you a story about almost every tree in this wood,' says Rex. 'Now they're all just . . . trees. Another life, wasn't it?'

'A parallel universe,' I say.

'I can't wish any of it away, though,' he says.

I turn my head sharply towards him. 'None of it?'

He stares into the dark heart of the wood. 'Obviously large swaths of my life have been *incredibly shit*, and Christ knows I wouldn't wish Alice's last few months on anyone, but you know what I mean. Everything that's happened has got me here. Today. You know, I'm free, we're all healthy. I've let B go, laid her to rest, whatever you want to call it. We've got the girls, and they've got *money*, Karen. You know me, I've never wanted to be rich, but the security that money can buy? That's what having this house was always about. I never achieved that for Biba, you could reasonably

352

say that I sabotaged her chances of ever having it, but now this place has passed to my kid and . . . it's huge, Karen, it's everything. Alice has got somewhere she can live in, or let out, or sell, and she doesn't need to worry. That's such a rare thing, and she deserves it. I feel like it's my dad's way of saying sorry and forgiving me all at the same time.'

He's slightly out of breath and no wonder. That's the longest speech I've ever heard him give. His eyes shine as he inclines his face to the treetops and for a moment he is himself at twenty-five and he is his sister at twenty-one and our daughter and our niece as they are now but he is also the man I have known for more than half my life, his cheeks pulled tight in a rare smile.

'Rex Clarke,' I tease. 'Are you . . . are you *happy?*'

'Don't tell anyone.' He taps the side of his nose. 'Ah, here comes trouble.'

The twin figures of Alice and Liss, walking from the Tube, appear in a pool of lamplight. They're both wearing platform boots and those hippy Afghan coats with matted fleece frothing out at the collars and cuffs. Their hair is unbrushed, giving them an otherworldly, manic edge. They look like a pair of Manson girls who've staggered out of the sundrenched Californian ranch and into the London winter. They look like their mother has clawed her way out of her unmarked grave.

We come face to face outside the front gate and hug our helloes.

'Jules is waiting inside,' says Liss. 'Are you two sure you'll be alright?'

Rex and I turn in unison to regard it, the much-photographed, much-talked-about Highgate House of Horrors where I saw two people die and he saw three.

'The strange thing is, I think we will,' says Rex.

'Plan is,' says Alice, 'to live in the big flat and let the rest out while we save up enough money to turn it back into a house. We're going to share it. Half each. I'm getting Maya to sign fifty per cent over to Liss. She's just as much Roger's granddaughter as I am.'

'We are *not* going to share it,' says Liss, in a weary, we've-been-over-this tone. 'I don't want anyone accusing me of using you.'

She gently slaps Alice's hand away and effortlessly lifts the latch. The gate glides silently open and we're back on the property. I've boarded rollercoasters with less trepidation than I set foot on the tasteful resin driveway. Motion-sensor spotlights pick out features in the garden. What was a tangle of weeds and discarded bottles is now a manicured front garden with lollipop bay trees in neat little pots and glossy, symmetrical acers. It's like standing in an estate agent's photograph.

Alice points to the Velvet Room window. 'That's going to be our bedroom,' she says.

Our bedroom? I dart a look of concern at Rex but it's gone over his head. They're not toddlers, they're young women. They've been sleeping on a crappy futon in a rented studio for months; you'd think they'd be delighted at the thought of some privacy. They could have a floor each, a *flat* each if they wanted. How long will they keep this up, living in each other's pockets, locked in a world of in-jokes and crossfire conversation that no one else can follow? What about boyfriends? How healthy is this?

'We're already planning the housewarming party,' says Liss.

The girls start discussing at scattergun speed the drinks, the invitations, the dress code, the playlist. I could tell them the best place to put the decks, the most strategic positions for bin bags, which bathrooms get queues and which rooms are best sealed off, but that was for another house in, as Rex says, another lifetime.

At the top of the steps, the front door swings inwards and there is Jules, lit from above by a Tiffany chandelier and from the side by a fire that glows in the grate, underneath an immaculate arched mirror. 'Good to see you.'

She smiles, beckoning us up. Alice and her looking-glass counterpart are first across the threshold, standing side by side on the immaculately restored chessboard floor. The tiles under their feet gleam, as black and white as truth itself.

'Welcome home,' says Jules.

EPILOGUE

To: *number1criminoid@gmail.com*
From: *traceyandfaye@travesties.com*

Dear Alice,

Thanks for reaching out and we're sorry it's taken us so long to reply to your email. We like to keep our powder dry and finally we're ready to share our findings with you. We're pretty sure we're writing to Alice Clarke, daughter of Rex Clarke, the artist formerly known as Rex Capel. We traced your IP to a shop called Dead Girls' Dresses which btw is an ICONIC name. We did call a few months ago but got cut off, and after that you stopped picking up. ANYway. We're absolutely stoked to know that you are a criminoid!

Reading between the lines of your email, you've been wondering if there's more to the Highgate House of Horrors case than meets the eye, and since we looked into it WE. ARE. OBSESSED. Biba Capel died but no body found? We can't let that lie, can we? Well, guess what? We have discovered that she paid a very short visit to an old university friend in London in the winter of 2007 and during that visit she stole her friend's credit card, which was then used to buy a train ticket to Saxmundham in Suffolk, where we think you grew up. And there the trail goes DEAD.

The plot thickens, right???? What happened to Biba? Did she make it to Saxmundham? Where is she now? Where had she been?

Erin Kelly

Why did she fake her own death? It has to be to do with the Queenswood murders, right?

We feel like there is not just a standalone episode but a whole season's worth of material here. Once our army of criminoids get going, who knows what truths will emerge. Exciting times!

Yours in justice,
Tracey and Faye

ACKNOWLEDGEMENTS

Thank you to my three Hodder's Angels, Jo Dickinson, Leni Lawrence and Alice Morley. Thanks also to Sorcha Rose, Kate Keehan, Sarah Clay, Drew Hunt, Will Speed and Dom Gribben. Thank you Andrew Davis for making this book beautiful on the outside. Linda McQueen, you are the absolute don of copy edits. God bless your eagle eyes and your red pen.

I'm grateful every day to be agented by Sarah Ballard, who plucked me from obscurity fifteen (!!!) years ago. Huge love to Eli Keren, Jen Thomas, Jane Willis, Amy Mitchell, Georgina Le Grice, Alex Stephens, Lucy Joyce, Lily Down and all at United Agents.

More thanks are due to Helen Treacy and Michelle Patel for their early feedback, Ana Siso-Chan for research, Lisa Jewell for her wise advice on writing unexpected sequels and Rosie Donnelly, for being my wing-woman / advisor / shopping enabler for all things vintage fashion, Dr Stuart Hamilton for introducing me to the repulsive world of Burkeing, Florence Woods and Alice Vink for the legal advice and Amanda Geard for helping to rescue my manuscript when it slipped into the void between Scrivener and Word.

Friends and family, as ever: thank you, I love you.

Finally, I'd like to thank every reader who has told me – via email or social media or in person – that they still think about that tumbledown house on Queenswood Lane and wonder what its surviving inhabitants are up to now. Thank you for waiting for Alice to grow up so that their story could continue. I wrote this book for you.

A family reunion ends in murder . . .

The *Sunday Times* Top Ten Bestseller

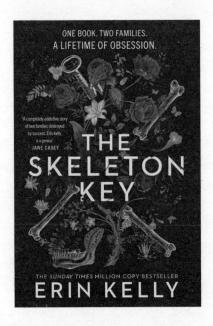

'The ultimate entertaining thriller' *EVENING STANDARD*

'Moody, propulsive, and one of the most intriguing set ups I've read in years' GILLIAN McALLISTER

'With rich characterisation and intricate yet propulsive plotting' *GUARDIAN*

'A gorgeously intricate puzzle of a book' *OBSERVER*

'Pacy, brilliantly plotted, and full of complex characters and relationships' *GOOD HOUSEKEEPING*

'There's layer upon layer of mystery in this frankly brilliant read' *BELFAST TELEGRAPH*

'Twisted family dynamics and toxic, compelling characters' RUTH WARE

'A completely addictive story of two families destroyed by success' JANE CASEY